K.S. King is an award-winning Canadian journalist, reporting and editing publications on crime and courts, education, politics, oil and gas, agriculture, indigenous relations and the environment. Growing up in a rural Newfoundland out-port community, Savage Cove, (pop. 133), King was surrounded by storytellers, fishermen, hunters, tanners, gardeners, and crafters. She is married to an Anglican pastor; has two LGBTQ2S+ sons and routinely volunteers in the LGBTQ2S+ community, Anglican ministries, and facilitating Christian women's retreats.

Today, King shares her journalism and communication knowledge, as well as her love of reading, to students and staff as middle-school librarian in Calgary.

I dedicate this book to my husband Rob and sons, Heath and Ian, who have supported me throughout this venture. You are an amazing family rooted in faith, love, inclusion, empathy, grace, and silliness, and I am so blessed to be in this union with you.

I also want to give credit to my parents, Aubrey and Amy King, and my siblings Dorothy, Gloria, Herman, Sandra, Annette, Allison, Doreen, and sister-niece Tonya, all of whom helped groom my love of books, nature, culture, traditions, and the art of storytelling, especially when humor is involved.

For all those who fight against extremism, in all its polarizing, divisive, and judgmental forms, I applaud you. May love and inclusion; balance and equity replace alt-right and alt-left leanings so that we may live in peace and harmony with each other, the land, and its resources.

K.S. King

THE CURE

Book 1: Contamination

AUSTIN MACAULEY PUBLISHERS®

LONDON * CAMBRIDGE * NEW YORK * SHARJAH

Ordering Information
Quantity sales: Special discounts are available on quantity purchases by corporations, associations, and others. For details, contact the publisher at the address below.

Publisher's Cataloging-in-Publication data
King, K.S.
The CurE

ISBN 9798889103813 (Paperback)
ISBN 9798889103820 (ePub e-book)

Library of Congress Control Number: 2023921650

www.austinmacauley.com/us

First Published 2024
Austin Macauley Publishers LLC
40 Wall Street, 33rd Floor, Suite 3302
New York, NY 10005
USA

mail-usa@austinmacauley.com
+1 (646) 5125767

Chapter 1

I cleared the dust from the plexiglass wall of the bus shelter with my finger, drawing a unicorn standing on its hind legs. Behind me, the traffic became static. Ignoring its chaotic clatter, I focused on angling a Stetson on the mythical creature's head without erasing what made it unique in the first place. This was Calgary, after all, Cowtown with no more cows, and once home to the Greatest Outdoor Show on Earth, the Calgary Stampede, which served its last deep-fried Oreo and mini doughnut nearly 25 years ago.

Opening the top compartment of my backpack, I pulled out a paper-wrapped "I can't believe it's not meat" veggie burger that I picked up from the Patty Melt counter at the school cafeteria. Peeling back the plant-decaled paper, I was greeted with a corn flour, sesame-seed dusted bun sandwiching a few leaves of lettuce, a slice of tomato, and a brown, round patty. Biting into the bun, my taste buds sprung to life with the flavors of beef bouillon, mashed beans, grains, spicy barbecue sauce, mustard, ketchup, and sweet pickle relish.

The best faux burger seventeen dollars could buy.

As I chewed, teenagers worked with municipal crews to clear the sidewalk of weeds across from the shelter. Reflective vests glared in the subdued light as they bent over to pull up dandelions and quack grass from the cracks between squares of cement. Despite the masks covering their noses and mouths, the teens were coughing and heaving.

Dust Bowl Season really was living up to its name.

Leaning my backpack against the side wall of the shelter, I pulled a water bottle out from the side pouch and swallowed mouthfuls of the lukewarm liquid, sputtering drops onto my chin on first contact. As I downed the dredges, throngs of students began to make their way down the adjacent avenue that connected Stampede Heights High to Centre Street. Backpacks, satchels, messenger bags, totes, and the occasional faded plastic grocery bags were hoisted onto shoulders, stretched across chests, and dangled from the crooks of arms as my comrades scurried to the plexiglass box in which I sat roasting to a medium-rare. As they moved, a hot wind churned up debris around their feet, ringing dust devils between legs and causing many to bend forward, hands over mouths, to prevent the particles from flying between lips. A few donned masks like my own to prevent the vacuum, but it was too late. Once it started, the coughing didn't stop until you got a lung of clean air and Proximity Alert: There was none.

Legs galloped across cracked, uneven sidewalks, resting only when they got to the intersection in front of me. Before them, cars squealed by with tires braking on hot asphalt. Horns honked and drivers cursed. Then the light changed and the herd crossed. One pink shirt-wearing dude skipped over the pothole in front of the shelter's concrete base, his white shorts bright against the rosy haze.

They came at me, voices muffled in fog and fabric.

Happy.

I turned away and slunk deeper into my corner. I put my water bottle back into the side pouch and unhooked the mask that was dangling over my right ear, connecting it to my left, wheezing as I did so. I tried to dissolve into the aluminum frame holding up the ground-to-ceiling windows, but I'm not the dissolving type.

Looking down at my now weeping unicorn, I wiped the image away and a trail of sticky dust clung to the palm of my hand, which I rubbed down the front of my thigh. The smudge was laced with mustard and ketchup. Fascinated, I spread the colorful stains into a mishmash of dots and lines; swirls and splatters—my very own Jackson Pollock sticking to my thigh and smelling of burger. I saw a painting of his once at the Glenbow Museum. As I stood staring at the drips and smears on a crimson background, I felt something strange: Understood. Abstract and bleeding, as if even the condiments saw my wounds.

Dumb, I know.

The rumble of the 787-bus churning its wheels up the hill from Chinatown caused many of the newcomers to turn their heads. An Out of Service sign flashed above its windshield. Leaving a trail of black smoke in its wake, the red and gray vehicle came to the intersection and braked. A high-pitched squeal made my teeth ache and my eyes cringe.

I scanned the horizon behind it, taking in the boarded-up businesses, the decrepit storefronts with neon signs missing letters, and beyond, the fuzzy Calgary Tower, barely visible in the layers of rose soup.

The lights changed and the bus sped by the shelter in a puff of smoke and dust.

As I watched, several students entered the shelter, laughing into thin layers of cloth, moving their arms and hands around to animate their tales of cyber war games and virtual-reality shows. They were dusty and smelled of sweat and body spray, not the best mix in 40-degree-celsius heat.

My stomach churned as nausea overcame me in ebbing waves.

Stay down, Patty Melt. Don't want to upchuck in my mask, Mr. Beano Bun, so listen to your Momma and quit complaining.

As I chastised my summersaulting abdomen, someone butted up against my backpack and my cheek connected with the plexiglass.

"Watch it," my low voice grumbled, pulling my arm around my midsection to push Mr. Beano Bun back down since he, obviously, wasn't getting the message.

"Sorry, Jewels," the boy in the fuchsia shirt and white shorts responded.

I looked into the boy's face, confused.

Do I know you?

"The 301's crossing the Chinatown bridge. The Transit app just sent me an alert."

Thanks, mystery dude.

Tilting my gold-tinted aviator sunglasses down over the bridge of my nose, I squinted to see beyond the skyscrapers and dust clouds to find a peak of granite, but they were lost in a pink fog filled with small particles of sand. Cotton candy fingers stretched across the city, tickling the balconies protruding from twenty-story brick towers and intertwining around the red sun.

Were mountains really behind that haze?

I wiped the sweat from my brow with my forearm and left a brown streak along my pale, freckled skin. Despite my mask, the heat was sucking all the moisture out of my throat, leaving a dry, cotton ball lodged between my tonsils.

I coughed.

"Hard to breathe out there today, eh?"

The mystery dude in the fuchsia shirt was talking to me but I wasn't in the mood.

I was tired of getting up at 6 a.m. to get to school in June, when all my other classmates were sleeping in, not to mention all the energy it took trying to breathe in this dirty desert.

Fuchsia Shirt got the hint and left the shelter to stand with a group of teens by the bus sign.

I coughed again.

Dust Bowl Season? If you ask me, it's more like The Hacking Age.

Inhaling fresh air, unfortunately, was the least of my worries these days. Since The Episode three months ago, I had had my brain scanned and seen a psychologist at the teen counseling center, and the consensus was I indeed had post-concussion syndrome, as well as ADHD, anxiety, and depression. Turns out having seven concussions in three years wasn't such a good thing. Who knew?

You did, but you played anyway.

No one stopped me, so I must have been OK, right?

Who could have stopped you? You would have never survived high school without rugby and wrestling, and you know it. Don't you remember why you tried out in the first place? So, you wouldn't feel so weird; disjointed; lost? And let's not forget about all those illegal thoughts buzzing around in your brain that could have made you go nuts!

So, what's a few headaches?

Crystal would say otherwise, genius. In fact, she'll have a lot to say after that move you pulled on her if she ever talked to you again.

She deserved what she got.
Didn't she?

Keep telling yourself that, Fruit Loops!
You went bonkers, anyway, so who is the nutter?

I put my hands in the pockets of my jean vest and found the two bottles of anti-anxiety and depression medications I'd been prescribed since the end of April. My head no longer pounded, my eyes no longer hurt looking into lights but despite all that, I still didn't feel normal, whatever that was.

As the bus shelter began to empty, I glanced up Centre Street to the pot shops, herbal healers, vegan take-outs, and the teen counseling center in an old paint-peeling blue house with a white veranda and trim. A few teenagers were already sitting on the steps, waiting for their turn to enter and spill their guts.

My last session with my psychologist, Ali Cameron, was yesterday.

Was it all working?

Well, that depends on what working looked like.

"Name ten items you can smell; ten items you can touch; ten items you can see; ten items that you hear," Ali's voice had oozed into the dimly lit room. "Now, let's do breathing exercises."

Anti-anxiety exercises were so lame.

Better than flicking that elastic on your wrist, Fruit Loops, and you know it.

I shifted the weight of my backpack so that the textbooks jostled around and stopped cutting into the butt of my shoulder blades. Adjusting my Calgary Flames red baseball cap so it tilted over my eyes, I squinted behind my sunglasses at the rosy, dusty haze, trying to identify the faces of my fellow summer school students, and not recognizing anyone. Ahead of the pack were the grown-up versions of my younger brother, Jake. Their giddy discussions were interrupted with bouts of laughter and agitated revelations. Their obvious excitement over their extra-credit classes annoyed and angered me. Behind them lagged my clones: The crest-fallen shufflers who moved with a mad and moody gait. Dressed in oversized coats, hoodies, and shirts, they were trying desperately not to be noticed, and failing. No doubt, like me, they were just trying to pass a grade so they could enjoy what remained of the summer. Trailing behind the teen parade were the regs: Commuters who were likely regretting their bad departure timing and were now doomed to share a bus with the likes of us.

I sat on the metal bench in the shelter, not wanting to be a part of the swarm, and began drawing a Manga face with large eyes and mouth. I cut out the corners of the pupils and thinned the lips so the mouth was an ellipsis.

While my Grade 12 classmates were busy planning graduation festivities, I had been lying on a CT scan bed, getting my noggin photographed. The concussions had altered my brain, surprise, surprise, so yeah, I had headaches and lights hurt my eyes. All it took was one scan and Mom and Dad went on a rampage: Gone were screens and loud noises. I spent most of the two weeks of my school suspension in my bedroom, lights off, drugged to near unconsciousness by anti-anxiety and depression pills.

I was numb.

Four weeks later, another drug, another kind of numbness.

I slept for hours.

Then, not at all.

I ate lots, then nothing.

Then, school was over and summer school began, and nothing really changed for me.

It took two months before I didn't have a dull throb bouncing around my skull when I woke up, and I no longer had to squint when Dad turned on the living room lamp. Mostly, though, I didn't feel like I was going to explode. On the plus side, my post-concussion syndrome led to an Individualized Program Plan and I was able to get extensions on assignments, all of which were completed before my diplomas began last week. Four cores, four diplomas. The two-week suspension, however, meant no Grade 12 graduation party to wound up my final year of high school. As of today, it was just—over.

Talk about anti-climactic.

You haven't even graduated yet, genius, so what was there to party about, anyway?

I thought of Crystal Hayter. Her soft, caramel skin and ribbons of chocolate hair that smelled of coconut and lime. Brown silk caked in blood from an over-zealous wrestling move gone wrong.

Shaking the image out of my cranium, I tried to focus on something good; something I didn't screw up. Today, I handed in my final diploma exam—English-Language Arts—and closed the book on summer school for good.

Yay, me.

The re-dos had given me a B-grade in all subjects so unless I totally trashed my exams, I graduated.

Now what?

Condensation was causing the Manga mouth to drool.

The light turned green and the 301 grinded gears through the intersection and approached the shelter.

Falling gray flicks descended onto the heads of the students queued to board.

A loud explosion rocked the shelter, causing the plastic walls to wave and bend.

The ground shook and the students waiting to enter the accordion black doors frantically started grabbing at each other for balance. Some fell against the gray wave on the side of the red bus for support. Inside the shelter, my head connected to the aluminum frame and I braced myself as the seat shook and the concrete pad groaned. To the east, a massive dark gray cloud plumed, turning a sickly shade of purple when it connected with the pink fog. Fingers of black smoke spread over the coral sky, mingling with the dust and ash fog. My legs began to tremble. The vibrations sent shocks of electricity from my toes and ankles up my calves and knees.

The cement pad under my bench began to crack.

I leaped up and sidestepped the rectangular piece of metal just as the anchors gave way in the concrete and one end bent down while the other tilted upward. Underneath, the crack widened.

I stepped backward out of the shelter, trying to figure out what was going on, and bumped into the mass of students being slammed up against the side of the bus.

The folding doors opened, and everyone scrambled to get inside, their shoes pounding onto the steps; their shoulders careening into the doorframe as the ground continued to shake.

A pair of white shorts bounded up the steps and as they moved, a shocking glimpse of bright pink fabric caught my eye.

Who the heck wears white in this dust-bowl city?

Someone awfully courageous, I guess, because if I'd had been wearing them, they'd be covered in brown-gray handprints and smudges. Whoever this dude was, at least he wasn't letting the dirt in the air stop him from donning the one color you didn't see much of these days.

As I joined the queue, I frantically looked up Centre Street, trying to see beyond the haze and identify the source of the commotion.

Were we having an earthquake? In Calgary?

My breathing quickened.

Not now, Sir Thumps A Lot, slow down those heartbeats or you'll be hyperventilating.

I flicked my mask off, reached into my vest pocket, popped the lid off a pill bottle, and dry-swallowed one of my Calm Down Capsules.

Mask back on, I boarded the transit vehicle, but things didn't seem much better inside than out.

For starters, the bus driver was frazzled.

"Sit, sit, sit," he gestured to our bodies, trying to close the door when people were still boarding. "Go, go, go."

I climbed aboard, my backpack squeezed between the doors as they were trying to close, and sat on the seat closest to the door to get the best view of the chaos unfolding outside.

I folded my aviators and put them in my breast pocket.

As I did so, the driver's hand flew into the air and began to flick the rest of the students down the aisle. His agitation made me uneasy, but not as much as his ashen face.

His midsection swiveled to the passengers behind him.

"Sit, sit, sit," he repeated in a high-pitched lilt.

The silver name tag on the navy fleece vest caught my eye: Raj.

Under the vest, Raj wore a pale blue short-sleeved dress shirt. The air conditioner on the dash was blowing cold air into his face and his lips looked almost the same shade as the freaky cloud that had suddenly burst onto the skyline. A trickle of sweat slid down from the red turban tied around his head to his jaw. The beads glistened in the overhead lights and dried in the blast of cold air from the vents. Turning his head to the street in front of him, he put the bus in gear and the engine revved into motion.

Dark fingers shook as he gripped the wheel, turning the vehicle into traffic.

I didn't need to be a genius to know Raj was scared.

He wasn't the only one.

Behind me, the clamor of teenage voices was raised in curses and outbursts as they tried to make sense of what was happening outside.

The red vinyl seat beneath me shook as the bus moved. I gripped the nearby pole so hard; I could feel my nails bending from the strain.

Some of the girls were sobbing, hysterically.

I cringed.

Grow a backbone, sissies.

Turning my head away from their tear-streaked faces, I tried to focus on the scene unfolding from the large windshield: vehicles being lifted up and back as they sat like ducks on a river of cracking pavement. Raj maneuvered the wheels over one fissure, tires plummeting down and then rising up as they connected to the uneven surface. I slammed into the pole. My ponytail flipped over my forehead and got caught in between my head and the pole, pulling my hair at the roots. Yelping, I readjusted my position, freeing the mane and tied it into a haphazard bun, securing the auburn rope with the cap's snap strap.

Sobbing Blonde fell off her seat and into the aisle.

Really?

Actually … same.

The bus roared and swerved to avoid a Taxi barreling through a red light. The white car hit the light standard, crumpling the front fender on impact. We drove past as I saw a marshmallow airbag deploy.

"Can someone tell us what the hell is going on?"

The yell from the back of the bus was chanted by others. Voices rose in shouts and guttural groans of complaints. Curses flew through the stale, smoky air of the cavernous vehicle like bats.

We bumped up and down potholes and cracks in the pavement as we headed north on Centre Street, the bus moaned and banged, mimicking the passengers inside. I thumped along with it, nearly banging my head into the metal pole, the window behind me, and the boarding barricade to my right.

I felt like I was in a blender.

Purée, blend, mix.

Pulse.

My body jostled back and forth, side to side, up and down.

So, too, did my not-quite-digested burger.

I rose from my seat and surveyed the mayhem down the back of the bus.

Two ladies with shopping bags full of groceries were sitting on a long bench in the rear, their silver wavy hair shining like halos in the streaks of light that cut through the dust fog and entered the grimy windows. Each old Granny was knitting. The pale gray needles were flying in their laps and every few seconds, one wrinkled, spotted hand would leave the needles and stretch down to their totes to pull at the yarn buried under boxes of food. They looked like reflections of each other, if not for their different floral dresses: One wore blue; the other, yellow. Their pursed lips were moving wordlessly while their beige-nylon legs bounced up and down in agitation.

In the row in front of them sat a businessman in a black suit and tie. His blazer was unbuttoned and I could see sweat stains forming splatter patterns on either side of his chest. His lips were moving as his body rocked back and forth in his seat.

Were they all going insane?

Was it contagious?

Sweat poured off the man's sleek forehead and slowly dripped down his temples and cheeks. Yellow Granny handed him a cloth handkerchief from the inside of the pink and white plaid purse dangling from the crook of her arm. He accepted and dabbed his furrowed brow. Knuckles turning white, he resumed his grip on the man-purse strap that crossed his chest, his copy of How to Make Your Female Boss Like You by Tania Ibbitson, Ph.D., and CEO of Radium Industries, discarded on the adjacent seat. I watched as the vein in his neck began to pulsate as his jaw tightened.

Sobbing Blonde's torso began to shake causing her cropped bob-cut hair to live up to its name, as her chin went up and down in frantic nodding.

"What the hell is going on?" she screamed, tears streaking her black mascara down her face.

She was pounding the tops of her thighs with her fists, causing red blotches on her sunburnt pale skin.

I was suddenly happy I wore jeggings instead of shorts, despite the trickles of perspiration running down my knee pits and into my shoes. At least, my pants had UV protection.

"You know as much as we do." My deep voice roared above the din of terror. "I think the best thing we can do is not panic. Raj, the driver here, needs to be able to focus and we can't be a distraction."

Twenty or so heads nodded in agreement.

Some shook in frustration.

Others bent low, putting their heads between their knees, trying not to hyperventilate.

I sat back down, doing the same, willing my meds to kick in.

"Thank you, Miss," Raj's voice shook over his shoulder. "This is not a good day."

Then mumbling to himself: "Not a good day at all, no, no, no."

No shiitake mushrooms.

We sailed through a playground zone.

Kids played inside these days so why the city felt the need to keep the zone signs up was anyone's guess.

Outside, people were scurrying from buildings, running away from splitting concrete and screaming.

Screaming.

The noise grated down the back of my head and lodged into my aching spine.

"Is your radio working?" I leaned over Raj's shoulder and asked quietly.

"Too much interference," Raj said, not taking his eyes off the road.

"Anyone have service? Anyone? There must be something in the news," a frantic voice said, plopping down beside me.

Cursing, he muttered: "This damn phone is a piece of shit."

My cell was locked away in Dad's study.

See, you're not the only thing in suspension hell.

A window blew out of a grocery store along Centre Street.

Shards of glass rained down upon the throngs of pedestrians trying to escape the quaking earth. More windows followed; bulging and blowing.

The bus shook from the impact.

Raj revved the engine.

The vehicle's windows couldn't dampen the screams outside, and neither could the propelling bus.

A fist punched my shoulder.

I turned and looked into a pair of brown, bulging eyes.

"What the hell was that?" Sam Taylor was looking furiously at me while hanging onto the same pole my fingers were wrapped around, his basketball firmly tucked under his armpit. His sleeveless green and white-trimmed Toronto Raptors basketball jersey was sticking to his brown skin with patches of sweat. His matching knee-length shorts bagged around his skinny, dry, scabbed-over kneecaps.

"Shockwave," I said, rubbing my shoulder. "And … you're welcome."

"From what?" He turned his head to look out the windshield, then whipped around to address the passengers. "Shit's getting real outside, folks."

Like they didn't know.

As if the day wasn't screwy enough, I had to deal with Crystal Hayter's boyfriend, too?

I mean, really? Sam Taylor? Was there no end to the madness?

He pivoted on his heel and saw me.

"Hey, I know you," he shouted into my face. "You're Jewels, right? The dyke that tried to steal my girl?"

I ignored him.

This *dyke* wasn't going to take the bait—this time.

Maybe counseling wasn't a lost cause, after all.

"Cat caught your tongue, Jewels? Must be a first," he swiveled to look at the other passengers and proceeded to bounce his basketball off the shoulder of a student wearing a black tee with retro gaming system controllers outlined in white on his chest. He was holding a cell phone.

"Dork, anything?"

The kid's shoulder buckled on impact from Sam's basketball bounce and he winced.

"No," he groaned. "There's an alert on my phone but it doesn't say what it's for."

Sam grabbed the phone from the student's hands and pushed him back into his seat.

"Idiot, it says, 'State of Emergency: Seek Shelter.'"

He threw the phone back into the red-faced boy's lap and waltzed up to Raj's back.

"Hey, driver, what gives? We need to seek shelter, not cruise in the path of a friggin' earthquake."

"Sit down, young man. I'm trying to get us out of here," Raj's shaky voice commanded over his shoulder.

Sam made a lewd gesture with his finger to the back of Raj's head and then turned back to me.

Find someone else to annoy, Flaky Cake.

But he didn't hear my screaming head any more than my screaming head stopped the rising anxiety that was bubbling in my stomach.

Or, maybe he did.

He bounced his ball on the top of my cranium.

"Ouch!" I spat into my mask.

"Oops, sorry! Don't want to give you another concussion and make you go ballistic," his mouth contorted in a grimace. "Or, give someone else a concussion, now do we?"

"Just sit down, Sam, and leave everyone alone," I said through clenched teeth. "No one knows anything about what's going on outside, so shut your pie hole and let the driver get us to safety."

I reached up to check for a bump and found red twill fabric instead.

"Geeze," I seethed.

Thank goodness for ball-cap padding.

C'mon, Calm-the-Crap-Down meds, get working already.

I began the five senses countdown, starting with the things I can smell, and trying to ignore Sam and steady my electrified nerves:

1. Sam's garlic breath
2. Sam's raunchy BO
3. Smoke
4. Diesel
5. Urine
6. Pizza
7. Coffee
8. Curry
9. Cheap perfume
10. My nacho-smelly sockless feet

I took a deep breath and exhaled into the fabric of my mask. Sam's mask-less face was coated with dust particles that stuck to his sweat in a film of grim.

That's attractive.

"I heard you got some of the good stuff at the counseling center: uppers and downers. I could use something to settle the nerves right about now, so cough up your stash."

"Frig off, Sam."

"Holy moly," Raj breathed, slamming on the brakes.

We lunged forward.

A few of the passengers fell onto the floor.

Sam's head collided with mine.

"What now?" I groaned.

"Traffic lights are down." Raj's voice was strained.

I gingerly rubbed the side of my head and turned to look out the windshield.

Before us, light posts were uprooted and leaning awkwardly over the intersection, forming a triangular peak.

"I don't think I can make it," Raj said, shaking his head, eying the space and the downed wires sending sparks across the pavement.

"What's the alternative," I asked, standing and leaning over the driver's shoulder. "Can we go around?"

"Too many cars on the road, miss, there is no way through."

In fact, the cars were bumper-to-bumper, stalled and staring at the lights, willing them to right themselves.

"Look there," I pointed to a bus pullout beside a transit stop sign. In front of that was a miraculously pristine stretch of sidewalk. "Go there."

Raj nodded.

"Hang on, everybody," he yelled over his shoulder and shifted gears.

The transit vehicle swerved in front of the intersection, curled around the hoods of cars lining the street, entered the pullout, hopped the curb, and slowly drove up the sidewalk past the intersection with sparking downed wires and creaking metal.

I patted Raj's shoulder. "That was amaz, Raj my friend."

My excitement over the driver's maneuvering skills disappeared as we approached the growing black-purple cloud.

It was overtaking the pink fog.

The bus rose and bounced and I lost my balance, stumbled sideways and fell back into my seat, and would have fallen face first into the pole if not for the hand that braced my fall.

"Watch it! You could have broken a finger."

Shaking his hand, Sam took in my Guns 'n' Roses tee topped with a bleached blue-jeans vest and denim-printed leggings that hugged my hips and long legs. I tucked my limbs up under the seat, crossing my blue and white Asics runners at the ankles as I did so.

"How on earth did you ever make it onto a wrestling team with those spaghetti legs?"

Looking down at the thirty-eight inches of stretch-printed blue material, I re-crossed my ankles, tilted my head, and retorted: "Simple. I'm that good."

Sam snorted.

"Yeah, that good at bustin' people up, ya mean."

I swallowed the lump in my throat. In fact, I had picked up the sport in Grade 8. "Julia, if you're going to act out, do it on the mat and not in this house," Mom had said after I had put Jake in a headlock for changing the channel on my favorite TV show.

"Aren't wrestlers short and squat? Maybe if you would have joined the basketball team, you'd have graduated with the rest of us."

Mom had been a wrestler in school, too, and had an Alberta Summer Games gold medal hanging on her belt hook in her closet. At five-foot-nothing, she had the typical physique of a wrestler. I, on the other hand, did not.

"Yes, but then I'd have to carry a ball around everywhere and get my jollies by annoying people on buses with my stank."

"Burn," the kid with the cellphone squeaked and Sam threw him a glare.

Turning back to me, he leaned in so I got a good whiff of his BO.

"You really did a number on her, ya know. When she's done with concussion therapy, they're sending her to GAD camp. They're going to scare the lizbo out of her, so maybe wrestling isn't your thang after all."

I gulped.

Poor Crystal.

No one deserved to be brainwashed by the Gender Appropriation Division police, not even someone who accused me of sexual assault just to hide the fact she hooked up with me on an overnight school trip.

"I hear they were going to pick you up, too, but Mr. B held them off; said your brain was scrambled eggs. That … man … needs to mind his own damn business."

So very open-minded of you, there, Sam. I mean, why on earth would Crys cheat on a great guy like you? You're so *progressive*, after all. Mr. Blackfeather was the Grade 12 social studies teacher and a member of the Blackfoot First Nation. His classes were always the highlight of my week and I owed him big time for sticking up for me. Why was anyone's guess but sometimes he felt like a kindred spirit: Not quite belonging; not quite understood.

I wondered if Sam had ratted on Crystal and me to the division. His parents were strong supporters of the Christian Conservative Party, after all, and their anti-gay propaganda was one of their electoral promises: To Make Alberta Straight Again. Maybe if our hook-up during the provincial wrestling tournament hadn't been broadcasted, The Episode wouldn't have happened, and I wouldn't have spent the past three months in summer school jail.

That's a lot of ifs, Klassen, and besides, you got your grades up and graduated, right?

Fingers crossed.

"I say we get off this death trap," Sam shouted in the direction of terrified passengers. "Who's with me?"

I could see their fear and uncertainty as they considered the proposition. Eyes dashed to the windows; hands to their hearts and mouths, poles and seats. Faces paled and heads shook.

Sobbing Blonde started up again.

Others joined in.

Shaking his head, he rolled his eyes and added, "Figures. Bunch of losers, all of you."

In seats all around me, jaws lifted and eyes bored into Sam.

Lashing out: The coward's way of dealing with fear.

And I should know.

The teen with the retro-gamer T-shirt threw a wadded-up piece of paper at Sam's head, it fell short and landed by his feet.

"Same," I retorted.

"What's that supposed to mean," Sam bounced his orange ball into my shoulder. "Are you saying I'm stupid? I graduated. You on the other hand …"

I gripped the metal rim on either side of my knees, my knuckles going white.

I know. I didn't graduate with the rest of the Grade 12s, hence the summer school.

Hence me being on this stupid bus with a stupid jerk bouncing a stupid ball on me.

My head was beginning to ache as my pulse throbbed in my ears.

Next exercise it is.

Deep breath in through the nose; hold for five; out through the mouth for a count of eight.

Deep breath in through the nose; hold for five; out through the mouth for a count of eight.

When Ali told me that trick to calm down, she obviously hadn't tried it with a focaccia mask on in a dusty, smoky bus while we were bumping up a focaccia sidewalk to avoid earthquake mania.

I spurted a cough into the folds.

What I did inhale, though, was a sniff of Sam's skunky clothes.

I didn't want another altercation.

I wanted to know what the hell was going on outside. Because inside, that was one Pandora Box I wanted chained shut with a 'Do Not Disturb' sign plastered all over it.

My silence, however, was Sam's invitation to lean further over me, until his Raptors jersey swung open at the neck and I could see his shiny, dust-splattered torso.

"When she gets fixed, Crys is going to the University of British Columbia," the orange ball nudged me in the cheek. "Top that."

Crystal didn't need fixing; the world did.

And if she did, what does that say about me?

Don't let him get a rise out of you. Didn't concussion therapy help you get 80s in your courses, even if they were completed in the month everyone else was partying? Didn't your meds help you focus so you could finish your diplomas with the likelihood of meeting university admissions?

I turned my head to the window behind me. It was smeared with a thick layer of air-conditioning condensation and dirt but I could still see the bumper-to-bumper cars on the side streets connecting to the Centre. With a name like

Centre Street, no wonder everyone was hightailing it to the one road that almost divided the city in half.

"Not talking today? That's fine," he punched me in the shoulder. "You did give a good show, I got to hand that to ya. Those three dykes never stood a chance!"

Doughnut hole.

"I guess you saved me," he rose and fell with the bus and careened into the pole, smacking his shoulder into the steel. "Ye-ouch! Easy on the driving, there, Paki."

"Not every East Indian is from Pakistan, Count Chocula," I growled at him. "Raj happens to be from Mumbai … that's in India."

"Ah, it speaks!" he let go of his death grip on the pole and threw his arm up in the air as if he were a ringmaster at a circus. "Even if it's spewing garbage. Brownies are all the same, ya know, so who cares where this one is from?"

The bus moved, and as he lost his footing and returned his vice grip to the metal, I mumbled in reply, "I do, granola brains."

I kicked his high-tops and his arm curled around the pole and his hand instinctively covered his groin. In the process, he knocked his jaw against the metal.

I snickered. I guess he hadn't forgotten how I generally respond to his asinine comments, after all.

He lost his grip on the basketball, and it rolled to the back of the bus as the 301's nose rose to climb a hill.

"I care, and I would hazard a guess that Raj does too." I got up from my seat and stumbled to the back, swaying with the bus, and leaving Sam to scramble to find footing.

"Immies should have been turfed years ago!" Sam bellowed to my back.

The other passengers glared at him.

"You're an immigrant," I spat over my shoulder. "If they were all turfed, you should be the first to go."

"Yeah, but I'm fourth-gen! There's a dif," Sam shouted, causing a barrage of crushed paper balls to be thrown at his head.

I guess the bus patrons weren't impressed with his comment, either.

"The only non-immigrants in Canada are the First Nations people, genius, so your logic is based on stupid entitlement," I countered and more wads of crumpled paper were thrown in Sam's direction.

One landed on his forehead, leaving a clean splatter-shaped circle where there was previously a layer of grime. He lost his balance and started to slide back down to the floor. Gripping the pole with both hands, he hoisted his body up and planted his butt in the same seat I had vacated.

The bus swerved.

Distraction forgotten, the passengers resumed their angst and began sliding down red vinyl seats, slamming into poles and falling over each other.

Sam face-planted on the dirty, corrugated floor.

"Good thing there's nothing between your ears or you would have gotten a concussion of your own." I swayed and plopped down on a vinyl bench two rows up from the grandmas. A metal armrest protruded down the middle of the long red cushion, which I grasped as I ungracefully flopped on the seat.

On the side closest to the window sat Fuchsia Shirt.

The sobs had now turned to snickers.

I turned to the two elderly ladies. Needles clicking, they continued to look at Sam and shake their heads in disgust. Their grocery totes were now planted firmly between their feet and inner calves. As the bus moved, their legs pushed tighter together to prevent the bags from falling over. I waved and they each raised a needle in solidarity.

My backpack nudged me to the edge of my seat. I didn't want to remove it; who knows where it would end up with the bus feeling like a rollercoaster.

I put my runners firmly on the dark gray rippled floor, right foot slightly in front of my left, bracing for the rise and fall. Wrestling poses had their purposes, I guess.

The aisle was sighing.

It moved in waves, rocking back and forth, up and down.

There was a collective intake of breath as the vehicle tilted side to the side. I turned to look over the torso of the boy sitting beside me and then fixed my eyes on the growing indigo cloud to the northeast.

"What do you think that is?" I pointed.

"Something not good," Fuchsia Shirt's dark head turned to look at where I was pointing, "and thanks for sticking up for Raj back there. Although," the boy's lips spread into a thin line. "Raj is from Pakistan."

I felt the tension ease as laughter bubbled out of my mouth and into my mask.

Fuchsia Shirt turned and his lips curled up in the corners, causing dimples to appear on either side of his dark-skinned face. He had a square jaw and cheekbones that seemed chiseled from his skin. Silky black hair was whipped away from his smooth, high forehead and was woven into a braid that rested between his shoulder blades. Wayward strands tickled his ears. One lobe had a large white circular stud with what looked like cobwebs in the center; the other had a long string of white and pink beads that ended in a gold feather.

"No prob. I was just blowin' smoke, anyway. It's A-holes like Sam that give Alberta a bad name."

"Todd," he said as a way of introduction, tilting his head so that his beady earring dangled down onto his pink shoulder.

"Jewels, I mean, *Julia*, but everyone calls me Jewels," I wiped a hand over the window to clear a better view.

"Oh, I know you," Todd said, his lips twisting in a lopsided grin, "you're famous after that showdown by the high school. Saw the vid. Respect."

I could feel the heat rising in my cheeks and turned away from his gaze.

"Apprech," I mumbled.

Squaring off against Crystal Hayter and her two cheerleader peeps was not something I wished to remember, or relive. Relive it I must, though, since it seems everyone recorded the altercation and uploaded it to their social media accounts. Felt more like infamous than famous, as if there was a poster on the school's display board. *Wanted: Psycho Wrestler Known as Jewels. Call 1-800-PSYCHO if found.*

"Earthquake?" he wiped his brown hand over the clearing I had made to make it bigger.

The sky was black and orange.

"Those are flames," I sighed. "And they are awfully big."

Several large fires burned, the smoke from which was bellowing high into the sky, joining with the mushroom cloud a few kilometers away.

"An earthquake doesn't look like that," I moved closer and pointed at the black plume rising from the skyline. "That looks like an explosion. Correction: A lot of explosions."

I pointed to the infernos, "Isn't the airport over there?"

"Holy...." Todd touched the spot on the glass where I pointed. "What would blow up a bunch of planes?"

"Something big, really big," I tapped the window. "That … that looks like that cloud from those photos in Japan during the Second World War. You know, it was in … Hairy-something."

"Hiroshima?"

"That's the one. It looks like the Hiroshima mushroom cloud," I said, my voice rising. "Mr. B mentioned it in his last lecture."

"The cloud in Hiroshima was from a nuclear bomb," Todd's voice was low and shaky.

"Everyone, sit," Raj's thick East Indian accent cut through the dusty, tense air. "And for goody-ness sake, hang on. Things are about to get bumpy."

The engine reeved and the transit bus began to bounce.

Todd stared at me as if to say: *"Now, it's going to get bumpy?"*

I had no time to digest what Todd had said about the explosion; no time to crap my pants. Turning from the window and his now ashen face, I gripped the silver metal pole by my left knee with both hands. Todd's hands found the back of the seats in front of us. He turned to me and mouthed, "Holy shit."

Car alarms blared.

Sirens wailed.

My brain screamed.

Passengers mimicked the sound.

Their wails filled the air around me.

Outside, the air thickened.

The rosy haze became dark gray-brown fog.

The only light making it through was from the orange-red flares near the airport.

My knuckles went white.

My knees shook.

Inside, the sobs had returned.

I mimicked the sound.

Todd's left white-encased thigh moved closer to mine; his hands slid to the back of the seat in front of me. He turned his head, his eyes wide, and hooked the ear straps of his Queen-decaled face mask around his face, being careful not to tangle them in his earrings. The mask puffed and deflated as he breathed. I removed my right hand from the pole, gave his left hand a squeeze of reassurance, and tried to smile but the bus bounced and I bit my tongue. I could taste the metallic blood flowing through my teeth and I swallowed, wincing.

Todd nodded, wordlessly, and I put my hand back on the pole.

His bright pink tee moved up and down in a blur.

I tried to focus on the flashes of fuchsia and not on the grinding, the screaming, the beat of my heart that threatened to explode the organ in my chest.

My vision blurred.

The pavement beneath the wheels moaned and the tires dipped and rose in opened crevasses in the surface of the road.

I saw lights flickering through the soupy air.

We were passing a Tim Horton's coffeehouse.

People were trying to get out of the drive-through and they were driving over the dividers, getting their axles stuck in mid-motion like a teetering see-saw.

We were approaching the intersection of Centre and McKnight and we had our first decent view of the northeast.

The McKnight onramp to Deerfoot Trail was a broken bridge leading nowhere. Blocks of cement lay in boulders on the road, some between cars; others atop them. Tall pieces of rebar protruded from exposed blocks, reminding me of toothpicks in a clubhouse sandwich.

"Oh-my-God-oh-my-God-oh-my-God," someone was saying over and over again, their voice rising in hysterics.

It took me a few seconds to realize it was Sam.

On the jagged overpass, vehicles dangled; noses pointed downward to the congested Deerfoot highway below. Flickering taillights cut through the curtain of fog that had fallen over the city.

Someone was screaming.

Was it me?

We moved forward, through the intersection and up the hill, trying to ignore the destruction to our right.

Almost home.

We're almost home.

If I chanted long enough, would I get there like Dorothy in the Wizard of Oz?

No, genius, you're more like Alice going down the rabbit hole.

We approached the intersection of Centre Street and Beddington Boulevard.

The traffic lights were uprooted from their posts and bent over the four lanes below—tired marionettes with cut strings.

Squealing air brakes sliced through the interior of the bus, followed by a loud crash as the windows across the aisle shattered. Bench seats folded over each other in slow motion; tall metal poles squealed and bent as the left side of the bus started to cave inward—toward me. I pressed my back up against Todd, who pressed his back up against the window. We watched in horror as a semi-trailer grill pushed through the 301's side, T-boning the transit bus and tearing a hole in the red and gray vehicle as if it was opening a can of beans. Glass shards began to fall onto the heads of Granny 1 and Granny 2. They scrambled on their hands and knees toward my side of the bus. The businessman fell onto a bench seat in front of me, his book flying out of his hands and landing against the square window just in front of Todd's head.

More breakage.

More glass.

I tucked my head down between my knees so my backpack would get the brunt of the pieces. Beside me, Todd groaned. I turned my head slightly but all I could see was his hairy calves. His pink-belted white walking shorts sparkled and I watched, transfixed, as an elongated triangle of glass sliced across his thigh, tearing the cotton and leaving a ribbon of blood.

His deep-tanned hand covered the growing patch of red.

The noise was deafening.

The bus scraped.

The passengers screamed.

The semi pushed.

The seats collapsed.

Then I was on the floor, squished between the seat where Todd and I had sat and the one in front of us, where the book-reading dude was lying on his belly, head pressed into the other side.

I couldn't move.

My black, stuffed backpack had wedged me in, tight.

Todd was trying to yank me out by my right forearm.

His hand was covered in blood.

Red fingerprints tattooed on my skin.

I was being jostled.

He was shaking my backpack, and I was shaking with it.

As the bus continued to slide to the right and lift from the left, Todd yanked repeatedly at the straps around my shoulders until I was lifted off the floor between the two seats, only to fall sideways onto the gray ripples in the aisle.

I half crawled; half slid to the accordion doors near the front. I could hear Todd scurrying behind me, mumbling something about corrugated flooring and bare-ass knees.

I careened into Sam's shins, hitting my chin against his left patella. I fell flat on my back with a loud groan. My backpack elevated my torso as my head and legs flopped downwards. I turned to the door and into the lights of oncoming traffic on Beddington.

"Watch it!" Sam was yelling, flipping me over like a turtle.

I reached for the pole at the entrance steps. My fingers curled around the cylinder and then promptly slid off. My palms were too sweaty. I rubbed them against my jean vest and tried again. This time, I got a grip. The bus was scraping toward the headlights of vehicles waiting for the transit bus to come barreling toward them as they sat like sitting ducks.

I was about to descend the steps when the bus's front end rose in the air and I began sliding toward the back. Sam's knees were gone. I had nothing to brace and brake against. A hand reached out to try and grab me as I hurtled backward, smack dab into Todd.

"Arumph," he exhaled, pushing my backpack off him and me forward.

His hands must have found a shoulder strap because I was being swung to the right and before I could stop my momentum, I was flung through a glassless window.

I scrambled away on my hands and knees, skin scraping on pavement, and pebbles cutting into my palms and jeggings.

Behind me, the 301 flipped onto its side, right-side windows smashing as they hit the pavement. Glass shot up into the air from the impact as if they were frozen water droplets, and then hailed down. I tucked my head between my knees in a tight ball, with my backpack exposed like a shell. After the shards fell, I chanced a glance behind me. There was a four-meter sinkhole directly in front of the oncoming Beddington traffic.

The 301's side was wedged inside.

Coughing up dust, I turned my head to look closer at the bus.

It creaked and moaned as it rocked into the jagged giant hole in the pavement.

No screaming from inside; no moaning or groaning.

I carefully stood up and turned to face the transit vehicle.

The artistic dust and mustard smear on my thighs was now caked in dirt and blood, ripped at the knees, which were now red and raw. I brushed my hands down the front of my vest to get rid of as much crud as possible. Streaks of red were left in their wake. I jostled my body out of my backpack and let it thud onto the pavement below. A billow of dust rose up from the speckled asphalt on impact. Putting my runners on the white line that ran the shoulder of Centre Street, I bent down, palms arched in bridges in front of me. Today, the white streak was my starting line. I stretched my legs, groaning as my bruised and scraped shins and knees flexed with the motion, and jeté́d over the sinkhole and to the stretch of pavement on the other side.

Hoisting myself up the side of the bus near the engine, I climbed over the grill and hood and stretched my long limbs over the windshield until I was kneeling on the skyward driver's side.

My mask was no longer covering my mouth and my voice was loud and strong as I yelled at those inside. Where it was, was anyone's guess. I swallowed to lubricate my throat and stifled the cough that threatened to erupt from my body.

Inside, the passengers were stirring.

I could hear the sobs, the cries, the moans.

I blocked them out.

I had to block them out if I wanted to help.

Taking off my vest, I wound the denim around my right forearm. The pill bottles jingled like maracas as I dragged my arm around the window frame on Raj's left, clearing as much of the broken glass as possible.

Raj's seat was ripped up from the bolts in the floor and tilted to the left, leaving the right parallel to the floor. It looked like he was skydiving with his transit seat as a parachute. The shoulder strap was at his throat.

He wasn't moving.

There was a pool of blood by his head as it tilted downward toward the floor. There was no way for me to enter. No way for me to get him out.

My heart pounded in my ears. Move on. If he's alive, you'll get him later. I knew I had to move on and find someone who didn't require much effort to rescue.

I poked my head back out of the window and turned to one in the next row, removing the glass around the frame with my jean-coated arm and shimmied my torso inside.

I could feel my skin peel from the small pieces of glass left in the frame.

I inhaled sharply and grabbed the first pair of wrists I could find: Sam Taylor's.

As I pulled, he climbed up my arms, until his torso was through the window.

Between grunts, he cursed.

Between curses, he spat blood onto my Guns 'n' Roses tee.

Then, he gingerly slid on his belly until he was down over the side, the windshield and hood and onto the pavement below.

Taking a deep breath, I turned to the window again and went in search of another passenger.

One by one, I pulled my summer school classmates out of the 301, along with the other passengers, down the nose of the bus, over the hood, and to safety on the pavement. Some emerged holding arms close to their chests; others nursing cuts. They grunted and cried, cursed and prayed. Their exclamations tried to break through the barrier I had erected around my brain but I nailed that door shut with the clenching of my teeth and the shaking of my head.

As I dropped each one down, drivers from the oncoming cars exited their vehicles and helped the passengers slowly wind around the intersection and onto the median that divided the east and westbound Beddington traffic.

The two elderly ladies emerged, still holding hands in a Granny chain. Their grocery bags tied firmly around their wrists. As I lifted each one, their arms wrapped around my neck as if giving me a hug. Their totes slammed into my back causing me to take a sharp intake of stale, dusty, exhaust-laden air that tasted of metal and smelled of blood. The ladies, on the other hand, had the aroma of lavender, mothballs, and arthritic cream. It was comforting. They smelled like Nan; like family.

I hugged them back.

They slid down the front of the bus, their floral cotton dresses—one sunshine yellow, the other cornflower blue—rose up their legs and I could see their dark beige compression stockings, stained, ripped, dripped with blood. I wondered if it was their blood or that of one of the passengers. When they landed, I followed in pursuit and carried each over to the median, plopping them down on the dry patch and checking their legs for cuts.

"Go on, my dear, that's just a bit of a prick from the needles," one white-heard Granny said.

"Yes, we jabbed each other with our needles when we fell," said the other, softly laughing. "I hope and pray everyone is alright."

"I'm sure they are," I said, patting sunshine-yellow Granny on the shoulder.

"I'm glad you both are OK," I said to blue cornflower Granny, my words coming in bursts. "I have to go back inside."

Yellow Granny nodded and shooed me away with the flick of her arthritic hand: knuckles enlarged; fingers, twisted. I wondered how on earth they could still knit with digits like that but I guess when you're in pain, a little more is nothing.

I turned and went back to the bus.

This time when I ducked my head in, the dark-skinned businessman emerged from the shadows. He was tall and lean and only needed my arm and elbow to get leverage to lift his body out of the motorized coffin. His suit was dusty and ripped on one leg. His black eyes looked into mine and then his lower lids curled in the corners.

He was smiling.

I could see his white teeth spread wide, and a thick scratch down the side of his left cheek. It was red. If he had been home, Mom would have rushed for the Polysporin but he wasn't at my home. He was here, climbing out of a window by scaling red vinyl seats turned on their sides. "Praise be," he said in a thick accent that entered my ears in a rhythmic song, tickling my eardrums. "God is great."

He patted me on the back as he slid down the hood, skirted around the edge of the sinkhole, and joined the other passengers waiting on the median.

Underneath me, the bus groaned.

Sirens were getting louder.

I turned to the window again, and another set of outstretched hands, waiting to be rescued.

I pulled.

The bus creaked and tilted.

I pulled.

Todd's silky black hair emerged from the shadows.

I leaned forward and grabbed him by the upper arms.

He let out a moan and I saw a gash that was oozing blood along his cranium.

Should I move him?

You have to!

All my first-aid training told me he was safer outside the bus than in, but how to pull him to safety without risking further injury?

I was inspecting his injury when a voice croaked from the front of the vehicle, almost inaudible.

"Here, miss," Raj was holding out his unwound turban. "Use this."

He was hanging out of his seat, suspended above the floor by his seatbelt. Even in the shadows, I could see that the shoulder strap had risen and cut across his throat. The wide threads were embedded between the folds of skin across his trachea. I didn't need to see the blood around the belt, I could smell it; I could taste it. It was as if I was sucking on a nail and the air was so infused with the metallic aroma, it was stifling. It wafted up from Raj's seat and into my nostrils, curdling my stomach.

The red Rorschach pattern on his once pristine blue Calgary Transit shirt stretched from the collar to the chest. I stared, transfixed, at the pattern and the wound around the driver's throat. His left arm was swung behind him and up, outstretched and straight. His hand was a deep shade of scarlet. He had freed his hair from the red turban around his head and it now stuck to his shirt, and he was thrusting the fabric at me.

"I need to get you out," I said, pointing to his shirt, "You need a doctor."

Raj shook his head. As his head moved, the shoulder belt fell out from the wound and blood squirted out of his throat. He sputtered and more blood bubbled from his mouth and down his chin.

"No time," he croaked, "Please … brave miss, get everyone out. I'm … not … just get everyone out."

He took a deep breath, his eyes rolled back in his head and then he tried to focus on me again. "I'll wait … you go get help."

Raj shook his turban at me a second time. "Use this … bandage."

I grabbed the red folds, nodded and wrapped Todd's head with the thick cotton.

"Now, get out," Raj took a sharp intake of breath. "I smell … petrol."

Round and around, I wound, until Todd was wearing a shoddy, makeshift turban of his own.

Once bandaged, I began dragging the teen out of the window. He went through as someone began tugging my shoulders to give me leverage. Todd lifted from the interior of the bus, slid through the window, leaving a trail of red fabric behind him.

Focus!
Pull!

I heaved again and felt the pull from behind me, and Todd's white shorts slid over the frame. The once pristine fabric was now a dull gray, with streaks of blood and dirt down the legs. There was a red handprint where he had injured his leg but the blood had clotted and the dirty white cotton was suctioned to the wound on his thigh. I grabbed Todd's belt and yanked, giving the poor guy a massive wedgie as his shoes scraped across the pane and the side of the bus.

Turning around to see who had been pulling me, I came face to face with a bloodied *Santa Claus?* The heavy-set man stood with his arms dangling at his sides. Shocking white hair curled around his ears and a long white beard stretched the length of his neck and ended by his collarbone. His bushy white eyebrows were marred with drops of blood from the cut that spanned the length of his forehead. His rotund belly was contained in a blue and green plaid shirt, buttons strained and sleeves rolled to the elbow. An orange, reflective safety vest glared in bright light. Stamped on the left breast was emblazoned Whitecourt Trucking Ltd. It took me all of five seconds to realize that the bloody Santa Claus was the semi-truck driver. He lifted a large flashlight from his side and pointed it into the interior of the bus.

His meaty hand was shaking as he pointed the lantern into the window that Todd had been birthed just seconds before. "Take him to safety, I'll check the bus for more people."

I nodded and helped Todd half-climb, half-slide down the hood of the bus and to the pavement below. Once he was on solid ground, I lifted his arm over my shoulder and followed the other rescued passengers as they skirted around the sinkhole and to the median. I gently lodged Todd on the dried, scratchy grass and gazed at the faces who stared blankly back up at me in shock.

Like me, Todd's mask had fallen off in the collision and he looked up into my face and I saw the beginnings of a thin mustache growing on his upper lip, now dusted with brown particles. His pink shirt was coated in blood and dirt, as were his white cotton shorts. His ear was bleeding, too, and as I stared at it, his hand reached up and touched the lobe.

"Earring," he breathed, "it's just from an earring. It's fine."

I nodded, then turned to the faces before me.

"Anyone have a knife? Anyone?"

A dozen heads shook in the negative.

Blue Granny handed me a pair of small, sharp scissors from her tote bag.

I turned back to the bus and began walking around the sinkhole to the engine.

Todd was yelling at me about a gas leak but I had to make sure everyone was out, including Raj.

I couldn't just leave him there.

Once by the windows, I joined bloody Santa in scanning the inside of the bus.

"Jewels," I said.

"Hank," he replied, shining his flashlight into the cavernous 301's belly. "I … I was sideswiped by a pickup truck and I … I couldn't brake fast enough."

His breathing was labored and his round belly rose in huffs of air as he tried to control his breathing.

I nodded.

His large, thick fingers were making the flashlight shake.

"All out," he confirmed as he shone the light from seat to seat.

Seats were empty, the floor was littered with books, tablets, papers, backpacks, and a couple of smartphones.

But no more passengers.

"What about Raj? The driver?" I was out of breath and gasping for air, only to get mouthfuls of dusty heat that made me cough. "Maybe you can lower me down and I can shimmy in there and cut the seatbelts and set him free."

Was that my voice?

It sounded high and shaky.

Frazzled; electrified.

There was shuffling and groaning. The semi driver leaned in and checked Raj's pulse by his neck, and shook his head.

"He's gone." His voice was throaty and rough.

I swallowed and licked my lips.

I could taste my salty sweat, dust, and blood.

"Jewels, get back here," Todd was shouting from the median. "I see the leak."

"He's gone. We have to get out of here." The semi driver turned and awkwardly slid down the engine hood, making the metal squeak with his butt as he did so, and once landed, turned and urged me to do the same.

"You can't save him," he was pleading, now. "He's gone. You need to save yourself."

He wiped a big, thick hand over his face, smearing blood, sweat, and tears into his white hair.

Do I?

Was it that simple?

I surveyed the bus, Raj's dead body, the semi-truck grill jammed up to the metal frame, the bumper-to-bumper cars on the other side of the sinkhole, waiting.

I took a deep breath.

My lungs burned.

Well, Jewels, get your rump out of this mess and get the hell home before you get blown to smithereens.

I slid on my side down the hood and landed on my feet.

Joining the semi driver on the ground, we both skirted the hole before getting to safety on the median.

"Thank God you came back. I didn't think you were going to," Todd was leaning on his elbow, holding his head with his other hand, trying to stop the remaining red fabric from unwinding. "And thanks, Hulk, for saving our lives."

The passengers applauded.

Sam leaned over and punched me in the bicep, nodding his approval.

Barf.

"What?" I was breathing heavily.

Sweat was trickling down into my eyes and I lifted the tail of my shirt to wipe it away.

"The Hulk of Honeysuckle Hills. You know, your nickname," he had a feeble grin on his face that was half-grimace and half-smile. "The one you got after you smashed up Hayter and her gal-pals with those wicked wrestling moves."

"I'm not from Honeysuckle Hills," my voice was cracking and my breathing haggard. "I'm from Poplar Hills."

I plopped down on my back as we touched the brown, dried grass.

"Doesn't have the same ring to it," he laughed-coughed.

About twenty passengers lay beside me.

I heard the swoosh of flames before my head touched the scratchy grass surface.

I saw the river of gasoline curling around the back of the bus, trickling down into the sinkhole and around the edge, heading toward the median, the rescued passengers, and the bone-dry grass that was thirstier than I was, which was hard to believe.

Ignoring my shaking limbs, I bounded up and stood unsteady by Todd's reclined body. I turned my head frantically in search of something, anything, to help stop the blaze. Then I saw Blue Granny unscrewing a bottle of orange juice she had retrieved from her bag of groceries. A white box with a blue label had fallen out of the tote and onto the brown grass and beside it, a small square box with a red label. I pointed and got the nod in reply. I grabbed both boxes, ran and leaped another jeté toward the ribbon of blue and green swirls, scaling over the sinkhole and landed mere inches from the edge. Peeling off the sticker that covered the metal spout, I shook the white granules onto the ribbon, emptying the box in the process. Then I grabbed the smaller box, poked my thumb into the perforated opening, and poured the fine powder over the top of the granular mound. As the fire curled around the sinkhole, heading to my powdery hill of white, I leaped back to the median and fell on my hands and knees. As I watched, the curls of orange, blue, and green came to the mound, flickered, and went out.

"What the hell?" Todd was holding his turbaned head with eyebrows raised in wonder. "What did you do, Jewels?"

"Salt and baking soda," I coughed, "natural fire extinguishers."

"Screw The Hulk! Are you sure you're not MacGyver and Black Widow's love child? Cause, that was *amaz* to the third degree," Todd slowly lay back down on his back. The haphazardly wrapped turban splaying out beside him. "And what was that freaky jump you did across the hole?"

"It's a ballet leap," I coughed and spit out blood and brown phlegm onto the brown grass.

Beside me, Todd was shaking his head in astonishment.

I looked away.

I never thought my Girl Guide and Air Cadet first-aid training would ever come in handy, but it was.

I never thought ballet leaps would get me over a sinkhole, yet they did, and back again.

I never thought the useless camping knowledge Mom spewed on our many vacations to British Columbia before the forest fires took hold a year ago would ever be useful, either, yet here I was, watching salt and soda put out a flame.

I plopped on the grass, folded my legs in front of me, and rested my arms on the kneecaps, and my head on my arms.

My breath was ragged, my arms were sore.

"You OK?" Hank asked, giving me a bottle of water.

I drank as if my lips hadn't seen water in days, and nodded.

He returned my nod and hobbled back to his spot on the grassy island in the middle of the street. I put the empty bottle in the sea of brown and cradled my head.

I began to shake.

The convulsions began in my stomach and rose to my shoulders.

I didn't want to see the passengers beside me, the bloodied spiky brown grass, the keeled-over transit bus, or the drivers of the now parked cars get out to help. I wanted to close my eyes to the whole mess. I wanted the images to go away. I wanted my heart to stop thumping erratically in my chest. I wanted my head to stop pounding. I wanted the sirens to stop wailing. I wanted the horns to stop honking.

But, mostly, I wanted Raj to still be alive.

I smelled the smoke, the fuel, the flesh.

He was in there: Inside that burning bus, cooking.

I raised my head to Raj's coffin and realized the gasoline fire was still burning near the exhaust pipe. The salt had only stopped it in its path; it hadn't extinguished the river of fire at its source.

Turning to the motley crew beside me, I yelled, "The bus is going to blow."

As the words trickled from my mouth, Hank began ushering the group to their feet and nudging them further east on the Beddington median. Beside us, doors opened and drivers and passengers exited vehicles and followed in pursuit.

The bus exploded in a burst of light and noise.

It rose out of the sinkhole about five feet, flipped backward, and then fell with a loud crash atop the engine hood of the semi-truck. The impact caused the truck's white engine hood to pop off and take to the wind, landing in the Centre Street northbound lane atop a minivan. The impact caused the vehicle's alarm to sound.

We lurched forward.

I landed on my hands and knees from the blast. I turned and saw the 301 resting atop the semi-trailer's exposed engine.

I was rising from my landing spot just as the ambulances and fire trucks appeared in the bus lane on Centre and behind them, a YYCTV news van, its roof-top satellite dish a lighthouse in the fog. Paramedics moved toward us with stretchers and medical bags.

Firefighters sprayed the gasoline river with foam.

I lay on the brown, itchy grass, spent.

My eyes burned from the smoke and dust but I couldn't stop staring at the 301, roadkill across the caved-in transport truck's engine.

As I stared at the unbelievable scene, Sam's basketball smashed through the shouldering rear emergency exit window of the 301, rolled to the flaming gasoline ring around the sinkhole, and popped.

****

Walking beside her, Dad's arm curled around Mom's shoulder, hugging her head into his armpit as they approached. Then she saw me and, leaving the sanctuary of Dad's embrace, ran to me as I sat on a gurney in the emergency room of Nose Hill Hospital, sucking on a lemon popsicle. Beside me, the other passengers sat on their mobile beds, waiting for someone to take them home. The two elderly ladies, I learned, were Gladys and Grace, 79-year-old twin sisters. Gladys was getting a cast applied to her leg and foot after breaking her ankle in the accident. She was eating a chocolate pudding with a white plastic spoon. Grace had fished out a magazine from her shopping tote and was reading it as a nurse was cleaning a cut on her forearm. Sam was lying on his back, his arm over his eyes to block out the bright lights. He was waiting for a CT scan. Todd was being pushed toward the elevators for his scans when Mom's red hair emerged from the swinging doors into the room. Piled high on her head in a twisted bun, it was a vibrant contrast to her sallow skin.

I was enveloped in a hug so tight my popsicle slipped from my grip and landed on the bed. Dad's arms joined hers and together, they squeezed the breath out of me until I began to protest and draw away.

"You could have been killed," Mom sobbed, wiping the tears from her red eyes with the sleeve of her navy waffle Henley shirt. "We could have lost you."

Dad was nodding in silence.

"I'm so proud of you, Jewels, honey," his voice was rough and deep. "You're amazing, you know that."

"The best daughter in the world," Mom said between sobs, hugging me again; her wet tears sticking to my shirt. I forced the bile that rose to my mouth down my throat and willed myself to smile in appreciation.

"Thanks, guys. It was nothing." I flicked the blue fuzzy hair elastic around my wrist, leaving a red streak on my green-blue veins.

Chapter 2

Three Months Earlier

Sonja Lee was congratulating me on my two gold medals at the Alberta Junior Wrestling Championships. Her short black bob, well, it bobbed—up and down, up and down—as her head moved. The silky strands were whisked up in the breeze with each motion and she looked like a bobblehead on a car dashboard. Sonja's high-pitched voice was buzzing in my ears and I heard tidbits of what she was saying through the strips of navy cotton decaled with bright red poppies.

I nodded as she spoke.

I wasn't paying attention to what she was saying, however. I was too focused on the person behind her, walking towards us from the entrance of our high school.

Crystal Hayter.

My eyes narrowed.

She was flanked by two of the girls on the cheerleading squad: Melissa Simms and Annya Hosseini.

My attention, though, wasn't with Mel or Annya.

It was on Crystal.

Her caramel skin, big brown eyes ringed with long sooty lashes, and ribbons of chocolate hair that flowed in waves behind her as she moved.

She didn't wear a mask and her red lips were pursed to keep out the dusty air.

Her hips swayed in a tight, Prussian blue sundress as she approached in three-inch black strappy sandals that elevated her five-foot-four stature above those who strode beside her. As she moved, the gold locket around her neck swayed between her exposed cleavage. Crystal wasn't drawn to the lineup for the bus or the two who walked beside her, chatting non-stop as they strode.

She only had eyes for me.

And they were throwing darts.

She smirked.

I swallowed.

Despite my fabric mask, I could taste the smoke from nearby grass fires and a smoldering boreal blaze along the Alberta-British Columbia border.

It was less than 24 hours ago when that scowling face was being held between the palms of my hands as she kissed me. The face I had kissed. So, what changed?

I cringed.

Emotional confrontations were not my thang. Physical, sure, but outing your *feelings* in public? Hell, no. That's one dramafest I had no interest in whatsoever.

My stomach started to flutter: that nervous shake your insides do when your body is in panic mode. I knew that feeling all too well. I could feel it convulsing up my abdomen, gripping my lungs so I could barely breathe, clenching my heart so every pound reverberated in my ears, releasing bile in my mouth to sting my lips, and a feverish heat to my face so that my eyes burned in their sockets.

Panic attacks sucked eggs.

Look around; focus on something else.

Particles of ash and dust hurtled through the brisk breeze, whipping up pieces of dehydrated leaves, flaky bits of burnt tree bark, and fine pebbles. They whirled in mini tornadoes at my feet as I stood on the street in front of Stampede Heights High waiting for the 486 to take me home. I was one of a half-dozen standing in line, all of us constantly being sprayed with Mother Nature's dried vomit. Some of my fellow students tried to shield themselves from the brewing dust storm by holding textbooks to one side of their faces. My books were in my backpack, so I bent my head instead, trying to avoid the onslaught of sand and dried leaves.

My own legs were dust-covered, from the scratch-worn thighs of my skinny jeans to the tucked-up legs that fell short of my shins, all a ruse to disguise the three-inch shortfall in fabric. My white canvas runners were filthy. Coated in dry soil and a thick layer of floating earth-skin, they joined twelve feet trying to escape the onslaught of debris being spat in our direction.

As I counted the legs queued with me, taking note of the choices in footwear and exposed socks, a tumbleweed smashed into a pair of legging-clad limbs, bounced, got caught up in the breeze again, and rolled over to the cement steps that led to the school's entrance.

I watched as the curly-sue-looking mangled mess careened into Crystal's bare brown shin, and she kicked it away as if it was something vile. The tumbleweed bounced and continued rolling across the cracked, dry lawn.

To call the brown Chia-Pet grassy earth a lawn was an overstatement of the greatest degree.

Like all the parched topsoil in Calgary, the grounds around Stampede High were a veritable wasteland.

My heart thundered.

"Jewels," she announced, turning to her fan club walking alongside, "there's a rumor going around that you and I hooked up at provincials on the weekend, which is *outrageous*, especially since, unlike you, I have a *boy*friend."

Crystal's boyfriend, Sam Taylor, was on the basketball team and when he tried to get handsy with me a year ago, he got a swift kick in the nads.

She coughed and flicked her hair behind her in a river of silky brown waves.

I watched, knowing it smelled of limes and coconut.

"And you want me to say we didn't, is that right?" My voice grumbled behind my mask. Seeing their confused faces, I removed the mask and tucked the bright pink fabric into the front pocket of my jeans. The heat smacked me in the face as soon as the material was removed. Wearing a sleeveless muscle shirt emblazoned with the Stampede Heights wrestling team's gold and red bullseye, I was sweating bullets, leaving stains under my arms and around my neck, which also meant my sunscreen-coated arms were flypaper to the grimy crap flying around in the dusty wind.

Of course, she wanted me to say we didn't.

If word got out, our parents would be visited by the Gender Appropriation Division and would be instructed to attend a GAD 'camp' to remove all gayness from our minds.

As if it was that simple.

I repeated my question but without the mask to shield me, I breathed in a chokehold.

The air was suffocating.

My nose hairs tingled with heat and smoke.

My throat closed around the dusty intake.

I coughed into my elbow.

The reprieve was glorious, so I went for a second attempt.

I inhaled through my mouth like some inverted vacuum but the ash and dirt stuck to my palate and tonsils.

This time, the cough turned into a hack and I spit gray phlegm onto the pathway.

Crystal and her entourage busted a gut laughing.

And then erupted into a coughing fit of their own.

I smiled.

Crystal's creamy peanut-butter complexion was causing my heart to pound in my ears. I couldn't think without remembering how soft her skin was under my hand, and that it tasted of her cherry-vanilla moisturizer. Sweet. I tilted my own pasty, pale face to the left and studied her high-arched black brows as if they were abstract paintings hanging in the Glenbow Museum. Her half-moon lids were lightly dusted with dark maroon powder that shimmered even in today's hazy light.

Smooth peanut butter and grape jelly.

Jewels, you're obsessed with food, you know that, right.
First swear words, now comparing a girl's complexion to PB&J?
Ya got a prob, dude!

My lips curled and I saw a pink flush appear on Crystal's high cheekbones dusted with mauve blush. Her full, ruby-red lips twitched and a soft pink tongue darted out to lick the plump bottom. She got a tongue-coating of dust particles stuck to her lips and her face squished up as if someone was pinching her lips together, and then began to spit dust out of her mouth in little bursts.

I couldn't stop my belly from shaking, though, which caused Crystal's cheeks to redden and her eyes to narrow in frustration.

Must be hard trying to be all serious when you have to contend with spitting sand off your tongue.

"Well, here's the thing," she was twirling her tongue in her mouth, trying to relieve it of the dirt.

My lips spread wide and I could feel the dehydrated skin of my cheeks go taut as I smiled.

Crystal humphed and continued: "Whatever you thought happened at the championships was all in your head. I mean, I'm not into girls—that's disgusting."

Right.

She raised her voice to make sure everyone was listening to her pronouncement and then turned her eyes back to mine, pleading.

"It's all a misunderstanding," her voice was strained, as if it was made of elastic and being stretched taut. "So, tell them, Jewels, so we can set things straight."

You want to be straight? Too late for that, Princess.

"Please," her eyes were saying and I let out a long sigh.

"Sure, Crys. You're into boys, right, so it must have been." Turning to Annya and Melissa, I said: "That *straight* enough for you?"

Crystal's breathing was labored, and not just because of the dust and smoke.

She was fuming.

Her hands were fists at her side; her face was purple; her jaw was tight, the muscles flexing; and her perfectly tweezed eyebrows squished together to form a unibrow.

"That's not good enough," she said between clenched teeth, "and you know it."

Her voice was low.

She stepped closer to me so her cheerleader peeps couldn't hear and whispered: "What's wrong with you, Jewels? Don't you see how this could play out? Why don't you just admit to being a confused jerk so we can get on with our lives?"

"Jerk? I'm the jerk here? How am I the jerk in this scenario? You're the one making a scene, not me."

Her pursed lips thinned.

"If you don't do this, I'll have to file charges."

The edge was there, threatening me with every syllable.

"For what?"

I shifted my weight, my stomach doing somersaults.

I was starting to feel nauseous.

"For assault," she breathed, "and if you're charged, you'll be thrown off the team."

It dawned on me, then, that she was serious; that she'd rather lie and accuse me of sexually assaulting her than own up to the fact she liked girls and had spent a few hours snogging with one.

Was homosexuality that deranged? Was kissing someone you were attracted to, even if they were the same gender, so mental and wrong that honesty and integrity were thrown out the window?

I took a step back and saw Crystal for the first time: A scared little Barbie doll wanting approval, acceptance.

And would do anything to get it.

Was I really any different?

"Yeah," Mel growled, leaning forward, poking her thick index finger into my chest. "Crys should file charges against you, after you assaulted her like that!"

So, Crystal had already set me up. She had already told her friends what we did was an assault and not mutual.

You sure can pick 'em, Jewels.

The sting grew until my whole chest ached from the stabbing.

Crystal told them it was all me, that I was some kind of perv who couldn't keep my hands to myself, but that's not how it went down.

My hands started to shake as they held tighter to the shoulder straps of my backpack.

I knew what was coming: An outing of the worse kind.

"Listen," I began, holding up my palms as if we were playing a game of cops and robbers, "I never *assaulted* Crys; I would never assault anyone. Tell them." My sapphire eyes pleaded with a pair of brown moons.

Crys was shaking her head. "You had your chance," she mouthed.

I turned frantically to the students in line, to my classmates, pleading.

"C'mon," my raised voice was almost hysterical. This couldn't be happening. "You guys know me, for goodness's sake."

"We thought we did," Mel's almond-shaped purple nail poked into my chest. "But I guess you had a dark side; a perverted side you didn't want anyone to see. Well, she got an up-close-and-personal, in-your-face view of that side and now everyone knows just what kind of sicko you are."

Then came the onslaught of cruel, hurtful, harsh needle-to-the-brain insults that only teenage girls could deliver.

Words that cut you to the bone.

Permanently injected into the brain.

I tried to block them out.

"Thinks she's a bigshot now that she's got a few medals under her belt and can do whatever she wants, to whomever she wants," Annya's loud voice cut through the dusty, clammy air. "Well, you're not going to get away with it."

Vowels and consonants flew in front of my eyes, flashing in speech balloons that floated up over their heads, blew into my face and popped. I tried to imagine the trio as cartoons; caricatures of themselves, with enlarged facial features and tiny bodies. I stood there, watching hands fly around them in angry gestures; fingers being pointed at my chest with long, painted nails—and smile.

It was working.

What I couldn't block out were the agitated legs lined up beside me.

My homeys, now thinking I was some crazy scumbag who sexually assaulted the IT girl of our graduating class. These were my classmates, my neighborhood friends, the kids I played tag with in elementary school and attended wrestling meets with, living houses away from mine, with parents who attended my dad's church and shopped at the stores where my mom got her groceries—and they were all staring at me as if I had grown horns on my head and a forked tail.

Annya punched me in the stomach.

"That's for Crys," she seethed, her words filled with salvia.

I bent over, almost hitting her in the head with my backpack.

While I tried to catch my breath, I realized I had just as much to lose as Crys, maybe more.

After all, wasn't it my dad who was the pastor; my parents who organized youth retreats with me as a counselor?

I could feel the anger rising from my gut, pounding the nerves to a pulp, and beating a rhythm through my veins on its journey to my head. It was getting louder and louder and I could feel my hands clench tighter on the wide black straps that curled around my arms and rested on my chest. The twill cut into my palms as I squeezed. My heart squeezed along with it.

I looked at the three before me and they took a collective step back.

My blue eyes narrowed, scanning their bodies, looking for grip holds. I could feel my meagerly trimmed bushy brows dipped in a furrow above my straight, freckled nose. I could see the hair shadows across my line of sight as I took inventory. My jaw tightened so much, my cheekbones ached and my mouth pulled into a tight, straight line.

As if I was watching myself in a slo-mo action flick, I reached behind me and tied my high ponytail into a messy bun, the fine light-auburn wisps fluttering across my flushed pale cheeks as I did so.

No thick, silky waves for me.

Just fine, straight threads of pale copper.

Sonja was telling Crystal to leave me alone.

Annya pushed her down into the street.

She fell with her hands behind her and I heard her wince from the pain in her wrists. The books she carried splayed beside her, some open, others spilling loose, lined paper onto the pavement and were picked up by the breeze to scatter across the parched grass. Sonja reached to grab some of the sheets but fell back onto the road as soon as she lifted one anchoring hand.

They laughed, and coughed.

A low din in my brain.

I leaned down and grabbed Sonja by the bicep.

"Thanks," she whimpered as I pulled her up. She rushed to pick up the scattered sheets as I turned to the three taunting her.

I had no voice.

I didn't need one.

This was my eye of the storm.

Void of sound, of turmoil.

Focused.

Until it wasn't.

I swallowed.

Dusty saliva slid to the back of my throat.

I spit it onto the path, but it landed on the vibrant blue-painted nail on Crystal's big toe.

Foamy phlegm sliding down over the digit.

Providence, I thought with a smirk.

Very slowly, I removed my backpack and threw it onto the spiky earth.

It landed with a thud.

Crouching low, I flexed the muscles in my arms. Biceps and triceps bulged; tendons stretched across taunt skin.

Annya charged first.

I flipped her Stampede High cheerleader shirt over her head and kicked her white-skirt behind toward the tumbleweed that had hit Crystal in the legs. She fell face-first into the brier sphere. Her skirt flipped up to reveal the hidden underwear, which now had a Size 11 women's Converse print across both butt cheeks.

She screamed as the sharp thorns and twigs cut into her face and tangled into her black hair.

Mel came at me with her arm raised.

Big mistake.

I grabbed her bicep with my left hand, placed my right hand behind her neck and snapped her head down in a quick fluid motion. My right hand then joined my left. Twisting my body, I pulled Mel's torso over my back and yanked, hard.

She landed with a loud thud, white skirt splayed, stirring up a cloud of dust as she fell, hyperventilating, which is not something you want to be doing when the air is a veritable dust soup.

Leaving her to cough and spit, rubbing the dust out of her eyes, I turned my attention to the person I thought I had formed a connection with; who liked me for who I was; what I was.

Man, how could you have been so delusional?

Crystal was backing away from me, high heels clicking on the pathway, hands raised in a plea for me to stop.

I was blind.

I didn't see her as the girl I crushed on and had the courage to kiss not 24 hours before.

I didn't see her as the beauty that caused my heart to ache when she had kissed me back.

I saw the snake that was trying to poison my spot on the team.

I saw the witch that was trying to curse my chances of acceptance in a school of 1,500 students.

I saw the she-devil that could ruin my dad's pastoral career.

I saw my own demise.

The blood pulsing through my veins was a sounding gong, it thundered, vibrating off my muscles and bones, sending shockwaves to my skin, causing the hairs on my arms to rise and my pasty, freckled face to redden. I could feel the heat rising to match the 37-degree-Celsius breeze that circled me.

This was far worse than choking down smoke and dust balls.

My fists tightened at my sides and my black painted nails dug into my palms.

Get your shiitake mushrooms together, Jewels!

Oh, but I am.

My *shiitake* was staring at me with scared, dark brown eyes, willing me to back off.

"Jewels," she said, her chest rising and falling in rapid breaths, "I … I shouldn't have said that. I take it back. You didn't molest me, OK. It was … was … mutual."

"Louder," I growled.

My voice was hoarse and throaty.

"What?" She turned her head side to side, taking in the cell phone cameras pointed at us from the long line of students waiting for the bus, and began shaking her head.

"Louder," I repeated, taking a step toward her.

Behind me, I heard the 486 engine as it approached the school, and behind it, three other Calgary Transit buses to collect the feeder-school's students after another day of classes. The building was emptying.

Crys was shaking her head frantically.

Behind her, students clambered down the cement steps of the school entrance, butting into Crystal's shoulders as she stood, blocking their escape. As I approached, she turned her head side to side, trying to find an escape. Students brushed by, slapped me on the back for my wins, oblivious to the scene unfolding in front of them.

As they noticed the filming smartphones, they joined the throng and whipped out their own devices to record the afternoon entertainment.

"I said," she swallowed, "you didn't assault me."

"You're right, I didn't," I said through gritted teeth.

I could hear bus doors creak open and footfalls as students began to board, but they were few. They all wanted to see what would happen next.

We were invisible to the mayhem.

Yet, there was no escape for me either.

Why is it that obnoxious bullies had names to go along with their screwed-up persona?

Hayter? Crystal might as well have had a Bully First Class stamp on her forehead.

How could I have been attracted to her?

How could I have thought she had been attracted to me?

I stepped forward.

"I admitted it, Jewels, now back off," her head turned to Mel and Annya, still nursing their limbs on the ground. "Stop being so cra."

"You think I'm being crazy? You turd faces just accused me of assault and now you're saying I'm cra for sticking up for myself? Well, if you want to see cra, I'll give you some cra."

She backed away from me toward the entrance steps.

My head pounded.

The hazy sunlight hurt my eyes as I tried to concentrate.

"Look at you, just look at you," she was screaming now, her mass of hair bellowing around her. "You beef up like a dude. Who the hell wants to have pipes like that? I tell you who: messed up girls who want to be guys, that's who."

Now, who was talking crazy? It was illegal to be trans, or any other gender than male or female, thanks to the Bible Belt fanatics that rose to power. To be anything but put a target on your back and one night, when you least expect it, *they* would come, arrest you as a *cultural threat* and you'd be gone.

Until you weren't.

"What did you say," my voice was deeper than the dust, the dirt, the roots of the petrified dandelions poking up from the cracks in the path. "Say that again. I dare you."

There was a hush behind me as I felt the bustle come to a full stop.

Everyone was watching.

Everyone was listening.

I unclenched my hands, letting the dry wind pass through the spaces between my fingers.

Was she right? Was I trying to be a guy?

Screw her. She's trying to get in your head. Kick her out.

I shook the thoughts from my brain and my messy bun flopped behind me, tickling the nape of my neck.

She frantically looked around for backup, but there was none.

Just her and me.

Melissa and Annya had gotten off the ground and were scurrying back into the school like rats abandoning ship. I watched as their dirt-smudged behinds entered the double doors behind Crystal, turning only to flip me the finger before entering.

She was trying to join them.

Her heels clicked as she took another step back.

More students were spilling out of the school behind her, with phones raised, taking up their voyeur spots around us.

I strode toward her, stretching to my full height of six-foot-two, squared my round, muscular shoulders and hunched my neck.

"Look, everyone, Crystal *Hayter* is tired of shoveling shit about me so she's trying to run away, as if she could," I sneered, spreading my arms wide and turned to make sure I had everyone's attention, "You know who's good at shoveling shit, Crys, your screwed up Dad for being part of the Christian Conservative Party. Like father, like daughter. And I'm the one who's cra. Crap, girl, look in a mirror."

Crystal turned her head frantically to the left, then the right, willing someone to come to her aid.

The onlookers looked on.

The phones kept recording.

The school doors remained closed.

"They saw us," her voice hissed. "They know." Head was shaking side to side. "They can't know, Jewels. It'll be the death of me."

She began to pant and cough.

She bent down and picked up a handful of dried dirt and brown grass. Her blue fingernails were now filthy and chipped.

She held the earth as if it was a baseball: off to one side, ready to throw.

Her glistening, plump lips in a thin line.

Her large chocolate eyes narrowed.

Her nostrils flared as her chest rose and fell.

Fear really did make a princess into a frog.

She let go of her handful of dry, flaky soil and charged.

A gust of wind whisked the cloud of dust out of my face.

Crystal was rushing me, nails scratching at my face but missing their mark. Her chocolate dome hit my chest like a battering ram. I stepped backward on the impact but stood my ground. I grabbed her forearms and pulled; her torso tilted downward.

Leaning down, I hoisted her up.

Her legs lifted off the ground, black heels reaching for the sky, her Prussian blue dress flipped over to reveal a black thong, which earned a few whistles from the audience, and then her lower half went behind me, over my left shoulder. I arched my torso backward to follow through.

As I did so, my half-out messy bun got entangled in Crystal's gold necklace.

I tilted further back to dislodge the noose.

The gold links snagged into my hair and pulled.

I could hear her throat gurgle.

I shook my head so the bun was untied, and let go.

I heard the crack as I was straightening up.

I turned and Crystal Hayter was lying beside the front steps leading to the school. Chocolate hair splayed over gray speckled blocks; a filthy peanut-butter cheek resting on one of the rectangular edges.

Concrete steps.

Now covered in blood.

Chapter 3

I touched the three-inch scar that rose from my shaved scalp and felt the stitches. Five ridges—my souvenir from the bus ride from hell. Sitting in our living room, watching the news on the 50-inch flat-screen above the white-painted fireplace, the bus ride home from Stampede Heights all seemed like a dream, now, if not for these stitches. My hand rested on them, confirming their existence.

"Don't pick at it," Mom said from the brown leather couch across from me. She was holding a cup of tea in a mug that had the faded logo of the Calgary Stampede: A sideways C and S intertwined. It bounced on the armrest as she re-positioned herself. "It won't heal if you pick at it."

"Not picking; touching," I continued to rub my index over the scar as Mom shook her head in an *I give up!* look of frustration.

Jake snickered beside her.

I gave him my best impression of *the look* that Dad used when he was mad at us.

Jake burst out laughing.

Needed more work, I guess.

We had arrived home from Nose Hill Hospital an hour ago and promptly cooked a frozen pizza in the oven, which we ravaged in minutes, washing it down with glass after glass of water until my tongue didn't feel like a prickly cactus in my mouth. It was 9:45 p.m. and we were all sitting on the edge of our seats, waiting for the ten o'clock news broadcast to begin.

All except Dad, that is.

He sat in his recliner, legs up, rubbing his scalp as if it was a lamp with a genie trapped inside. On his lap was a ukulele, Ukey to be exact, which he was strumming as a fidget toy. The soft twang of the strings brought happy notes to the somber room. I was on the loveseat adjacent to Mom and Jake. My fuzzy pink bunny slippers crossed at the ankles in front of me, stretched under the glass-topped coffee table and nearly touched Mom's tan beaded moccasins on the other side. I sometimes had to shake my head in wonderment at the length of my legs compared to those of my five-foot-two mother's stubs. While hers were neatly contained in her pale gray capris, mine were encased in soft pink cotton pajama pants printed with pastel unicorns the hem of which ended mid-shin. My bare feet were cocooned in slippers and I turned one to the side and poked at a long, red cut just above the ankle. It was inflamed and coated with a thin layer of Polysporin. A white line was already starting to form in the center.

A scab will be next.

I watched as Jake curled into Mom's side, his knees tucked up under him and his blond mop of hair intertwining with Mom's red waves. He was wearing red Calgary Flames hockey PJs and black slippers that looked like plush skates.

Was this really *my brother?*

He was so … *baby-like.*

So *small.*

For starters, he was a good inch shorter than Mom, and if she was sitting down, Jake was curled into her side. He had just turned fifteen, for goodness' sake. At fifteen, I was refusing to be hugged at bedtime, pushing both parents away in a snide brush-off that caused lips to frown and eyes to water. Yet, here was my brother acting like he was three. Would he ever grow up? Would he ever feel safe outside of Mom's arms?

Would I?

The Calgary YYCTV logo appeared in a red banner across the television screen and in one collective movement, the Klassen family inched forward in their seats, leaning into the news. Dad's fingers stopped strumming *Somewhere Over the Rainbow* just as the logo faded and two anchors appeared at the news desk, separated by stacks of paper and two coffee mugs with the YYCTV logo emblazoned in red. I wondered if they actually contained coffee, or was it water? Maybe even something stronger? The man to the left sported a neatly flipped bang of black hair speckled with gray at the temples.

"Quiet, everyone," Mom turned her head and looked at Dad, who tucked his uke into the space between his left hip and chair, and then fixed her gaze on mine. "It's starting."

Was I really the only one who disrupted things around here?

Her hands folded in her lap as she leaned forward. Jake moved with her; her very own conjoined twin. The only thing missing was a thumb in his mouth to complete the picture.

Dude, grow up!

"Don't look at me," I pointed at Jake, "he's the one you got to watch out for. After all, *big baby* here might want to go down for his nap."

Jake's head shot up from Mom's shoulder and he stuck out his tongue at me.

"See," I shook my head and rolled my eyes, "big-ga bab-by."

"Enough! Leave him alone, Julia, and listen to your mother," Dad piped up, folding the leg rest of his recliner down into the chair with the push of a button and planting his Birkenstock feet on the floor. He mimicked Mom's eager sitting stature: head forward, chin jutting out, hands folded in lap, feet firmly planted on the floor—only he could do the latter without having to have a foot of space between him and the back of the chair. I could see Ukey's neck jutting out by his side, waiting for another one of its strings to be struck.

I flopped back into the brown leather loveseat and moaned, flicking one of the pink bunny slippers so the ears flopped in protest. My strawberry-blonde locks were braided into a long strand behind me, pulling my head back against the backrest.

A black ribbon with the anchorman's name appeared on the screen: Jason Polet, YYCTV news. As the news intro music played, our living room became a tomb of silence.

"Our top story tonight, June 21: A global ecoterrorism attack rocks cities around the globe, leaving thousands dead, tens of thousands injured and the possibility of radiation contamination that could see those numbers skyrocket.

"The terrorism attack on small modular reactors was the action of the environmental group known as Terra Nova, under the direction of its leader, Jon Solberg."

Polet held sheets of white paper in a firm grip. His dark eyes looked intently into the camera and I wondered why he needed the notes if he was using a monitor. I must have unwittingly mumbled because Mom piped up, "Backup," from the couch.

Yes, Miss Know it All.

"Calgary, along with many cities throughout Canada, was among those affected in the coordinated attack that began at the White Sands Energy operations in Tennessee at four o'clock this afternoon," the anchor paused and the camera switched to a wide screen with him on the far right and images of the White Sands facilities on his left.

"Oh, my," Mom's gasp echoed my own, and she kissed the gold cross hanging from around her neck.

She repeated the two-word phrase over and over as the images flashed onto the screen.

"Lord have mercy," Dad's deep growl bounced off the pixels and rumbled into my ears.

Jake started whimpering and squeezed Mom tighter.

"We must warn our viewers, the content you are about to see is disturbing and graphic, and may not be suitable for younger viewers."

Duh!

"That warning should have been *before* you scared your viewers for life," Mom's stern voice rose in a chastising menace and spewed at the news anchor's face.

Looking over at Jake, I had to agree.

The first image was that of the guard kiosk positioned at the entrance of the gated small-modular reactor facility. The windows were blown out. Black burns rose from the cement pad on which it stood, climbing up the walls and curling around the edge where the roof would have been. The drone taking the images panned upward so as to look down into the kiosk. A blackened form was sitting in the chair by what would have been the check-in window.

I gasped and covered my mouth with my hand. I could see the petrified guard's glasses still atop his nose; his blackened hands still poised above a keyboard. I looked over at Jake. He was shaking into Mom's side, hiding his face behind her back.

"The first explosion at the White Sands facility occurred at the security kiosk," Polet glanced down at his notes, swallowed, and then back into the camera lens, "which killed a security guard on duty, and was followed by the systematic rupture of all six SMR tanks buried underground at the facility located some 220 kilometers southwest of Nashville. At the same time, mirrored explosions occurred around the globe, including that of Alberta's small-modular reactor facilities located 35 kilometers northeast of Calgary and 248 kilometers northwest of Edmonton, destroying five SMR tanks in our province alone.

"The SMR explosions at Bow Valley Fuels facility, located 63 kilometers northeast of the Calgary International Airport, killed 22 BVF employees, and subsequently led to the destruction of six 747s being refueled on Runway 168. According to the Calgary Airport Authority, 14 crew and 243 civilians were killed in the tragic event, which also saw 687 people injured."

"Lord have mercy," Mom breathed.

Dad had no words. He just shook his head and joined Mom mumbling under his breath.

Jake squeezed tighter.

I tried to focus on something, anything, to control my breathing, which was ragged and causing my chest to rise and fall as if I was inflating the world's largest balloon.

The newscaster swallowed again, his Adam's apple bobbing in his throat as he did so.

Good, focus on that.

Why did guys have Adam's apples?

Dad would say it was a God thing.

Since my Grade 11 biology teacher, Mrs. Colburn, couldn't come up with an answer, I was loath to agree with The Father.

"In addition, six personnel are presumed dead in the Aurea Energy facility located some 70 kilometers northwest of Athabasca. These fatalities do not include the many subsequent deaths, especially in Calgary, where a 4.2 earthquake wreaked havoc on the city, causing the collapse of several office towers in the north end and numerous motor vehicle accidents, including one involving Calgary Transit driver, Raj Manoor."

Dad looked at me and I nodded.

I grabbed the white fake-fur pillow from the couch and hugged it close to my chest. Looking over at Jake, I suddenly had this urge to tuck myself into Mom's other armpit. An anger was boiling under my skin that only he got to be consoled; only he had the freedom to let loose and bawl his eyes out onto his mommy's shoulder.

Why not me?

Why did I have to behave like an adult?

I wasn't.

Part of me was crying inside; screaming to be let loose.

Mom reached over to hold my hand across the coffee table, but her short limb didn't even reach the center, so I just gave her a reassuring smile and she inched back again, hand back in her lap, squeezing the fingers of her left.

How did she know I needed that?

Because we all do, genius.

I looked at the two of them and realized Jake wasn't the only one being consoled on the loveseat.

"But first, we go to our sister station in NSX Nashville, and news anchor Gabe Bloom, for details into the explosions that started this tragic and devastating global attack."

Polet swiveled in his seat to face the wall that previously held drone images of the kiosk and now showed another anchor. Her long blonde hair curled around her shoulders and hung in front of her pink silk blouse like gold. Her oval face was perfectly dusted with pale makeup to highlight her piercing blue eyes and pouty lips. Fine lines, barely noticeable, creased by her long black lashes and I wondered if they were fake. Did it matter? No, but she was far too perfect; far too put together to be real.

And then she spoke.

"Good afternoon, Jason," a commanding husky voice filled our living room. She didn't have papers in front of her; only a glass of water. "And good afternoon to your viewers at YYCTV."

A white ribbon appeared under Gabe Bloom's pink chest denoting her name and station call letters.

"Gabe, could you please tell our Calgary viewers what NSX has uncovered following the attack?"

"Certainly," she began, and the camera switched to fill our television screen with just that of Gabe Bloom. "The Tennessee Sheriff's Department released a report shortly after six o'clock this evening, stating that at approximately 3 p.m. Central Daylight Time—that's four o'clock in Alberta— White Sands Energy's head of security, Richard Bouchard, entered the White Sands facility, detonated an underground charge that first led to the tragic death of security guard Henry Platt, a 43-year-old employee and five-year veteran with the company."

The American anchor paused to let her listeners absorb the information before turning to another camera in the newsroom. Behind her, images of the White Sands facility flickered on a virtual screen: A collapsed office tower with emergency crews digging through rubble; some carrying stretchers with bodies encased in black bags.

"Shortly after the initial explosion, Bouchard, who is originally from Montréal but moved to Chattanooga with his family as a child, entered the eighteen-story main building … wearing a suicide vest, which he initiated upon reaching the 18th floor, and leading to the collapse of the top four floors of the White Sands headquarters. Among the dead in that blast were White Sands CEO Nigel Featherington and 28 company department heads who had been meeting at the facility for a groundbreaking maintenance and operations merger, the names of which are now appearing on screen."

Business profile photographs appeared on the TV: Men and women smiling in business suits, and now all dead.

Mom covered her mouth with her hand, and using the other, pulled Jake closer to her side. Dad twanged on Ukey, causing a C note to fill the room.

"And what of the reactors," Polet's face filled the screen, now, his forehead creased in a frown, his hands still gripping the paper on his news anchor desk. The sheets were moving in a soft shake. "What led to the reactor explosions? Do we have details about that catastrophe?"

Bloom solemnly nodded, her golden mane shimmering in the studio lights. Taking a deep breath, she turned slightly to her left and images of huge craterous holes appeared, and in the foreground, the still smoldering remnants of the guardhouse.

"Six of White Sands' SMR containments, which were stored underground about 68 kilometers away from the main building, were compromised when the maintenance security codes were hacked by an external source, leading to all six reactors going offline in what appears to be a terrorism infiltration of the maintenance program designed to keep the reactors functioning at optimal levels. However, once hacked, the SMRs overloaded, causing them to explode. At last tally, the death toll was at 113 onsite, with another 25 White Sands emergency personnel seriously injured during the response.

"Globally, the ramifications are far-reaching, as each of the 28 CEOs who were attending White Sands amalgamation meeting had their own SMR facilities in their home countries, all of which were similarly attacked in a synchronized event. We are still gathering intel from the Associated Press, Canadian Press and Reuters, and hope to have an update within the next few hours on those outcomes, but we are talking about hundreds, if not thousands, of casualties worldwide."

"Oh, my; oh, my; oh, my," Mom was chanting. She sounded like my Nan and I had to do a double-take to make sure she wasn't in a rocking chair because I could have sworn my Newfoundland grandmother had suddenly replaced my mom on the leather cushion.

"Lord have mercy," came Dad's voice from the recliner, mimicking Mom's earlier reaction. His long, jean-clad legs were stretched out, the hems frayed from a multitude of wears and washes. His Jes/us: The Rock on Which I Stand T-shirt crinkled around his pecs. The decal was designed like that of an old 80s rock band, AC/DC, with a lightning strike between the 'Jes' and the 'us'.

Our living room was sobbing.

From Jake and Mom, and me.

I wiped my tears away with the pillow. Mom shielded Jake's face with an arm holding his head into her chest.

"There, there, Jakey," she was muttering, rubbing her pale hand across his thick, wavy blonde hair. "Everything is going to be OK. Everything is going to be OK."

I didn't know who she was trying to console: Jake or herself.

Either way, it wasn't over.

"And what of the compromise?" Polet was asking Bloom. "Do we know how the facility was hacked, and why?"

Bloom's professionalism was awe-inspiring.

She didn't shake, or frown, or tear-up. How could she be so strong? How could she be so *detached?* To me, she just looked like a poised talking head— like one of my Barbies before they underwent a Be-*Jewelled* makeover. However, Gabe Bloom was no plastic brainless doll. Her voice was strong, assured, confident and she spoke as if she was reporting on any news story, instead of the chain of events that rocked our own city mere hours ago.

I envied her.

I wanted that detachment; that lack of emotion.

Instead of the seething anger that rose on a regular basis; the out-of-control feelings of panic that made my heart pound in my ears so that I couldn't listen to reason. As my family engrossed themselves in the details of the attack, I focused my attention on Bloom, herself; her mannerisms; her control.

"An hour after the initial SMR explosion, ecoterrorism group Terra Nova took responsibility for the incident, citing the world's reliance on nuclear power and fossil fuels as their driver for the attack. The cyber-hacking was done through the use of a malware computer virus, which Terra Nova referred to as The CurE. This *cur* computer virus was designed by Richard Bouchard's twin brother Michel, who's company, TN Security Solutions, held the maintenance contract for White Sands' SMR units. The brothers' younger sister Marie, who was the White Sands Information Technology Director, apparently launched the computer virus using a remote proxy into CEO Nigel Featherington's account."

"That's one inside job," Dad was standing now, with his large hand firmly planted on Mom's right shoulder. "I mean, three siblings in one company, all terrorists? Man. I wonder how they got to that point. I mean, no one wakes up one day and decides to kill hundreds of people, especially against their fellow Americans."

He shook his head, trying to figure out the logic.

"What does being American have to do with anything?" I was irritated and my voice held an edge. "I mean, terrorists come in all shapes and sizes and some would say the people who made this province into a desert were terrorists first."

Dad was staring at me.

Mom was smiling.

"Good point," he strummed Ukey in the key of G. "Really good point. However, systematically destroying the environment and planning an attack that killed thousands are not the same thing: One is done through inaction and poor decisions and the other, through a hatred so deep, it's an excuse for murder."

"How on earth did a terrorist attack in Tennessee lead to an attack in Calgary, as well as every other city with reactors?" Mom's voice rose from the couch in a puff of airy words.

"Th … th … the wo … wo … worm," Jake stuttered, his head rising like an ostrich from the sand of Mom's chest.

I could see the red eyes and wondered how he could be my brother.

So sensitive.

So *weak.*

You were weak once, too, you know.

That's what rage does: Turn you into a meanie.

I looked at Jake again, this time while trying to see any hint of anger—of course, there was none. What did Jake have to be angry about anyway? I, on the other hand, had more fires in my belly than there were smoking up half the prairies these days.

But why?

When the answer didn't come, I squinted at Jake's red-rimmed pupils.

I saw insecurity, immaturity, sadness.

Maybe he wasn't so far removed from me, after all.

Maybe you should give your bro a break and not be so judgmental.

Yes, but that would require a ton of work and I didn't have the energy.

"Yes, Jakey," Mom encouraged, pushing him upright on the couch so he could explain. Her cardigan had left a pattern imprint along Jake's round cheek. "Take a deep breath and try to use a sing-song voice, OK, that helps you sometimes with your stuttering."

Jake sat up, nodded, and took a deep breath. I watched his face relax, the plural and plain imprints from Mom's sweater moving and dissolving into his skin. He closed his eyes, inhaled through his nose, opened his eyes again and began.

"My … my guess is … is that … that they used a phish … a phish/ing mal/ware pro/gram mas/que/rad/ing/ as an/ e/mail/ or some/thing."

As he continued, Jake's voice grew stronger and the musical lilt decreased until it was hardly even detectable.

"Something like a Trojan that tricks you into giving the program access to your account. Zombies would allow them to control the virus remotely, so they don't even have to be there to initiate it."

I knew my mouth was open because I could taste the potpourri Mom had in a dish on the mantle: dried orange slices, nutmeg and cinnamon.

"Go on, son," Dad urged, his head nodding in approval.

"Well, since this all happened at the same time, they … they probably used a … a worm program, so it self-replicates before sending itself to others on the network."

"That's one smart program," Mom said. leaning forward and tapping Jake's knee in encouragement. "Wouldn't big companies have firewalls, though, to block the program?"

"Yes, but if the hackers used a cur virus, it goes through the backdoor."

"A *what?*" I asked, intrigued and a little confused by all this computer jargon.

"A cur," Jake repeated, sitting upright and fidgeting with a crease in his pajama pants. "A cur virus is a hybrid zombie-worm malware program," he croaked and Mom squeezed his hand in support.

He inhaled, exhaled, as if speaking was exhausting.

I was tired just looking at him, so he must be exhausted trying to get all those words out in one go. I almost felt sorry for him.

"It uses Trojan phishing email or direct code to get access into a main operating system using a backdoor."

"Backdoor?" I asked again, extremely interested in how this cur virus worked. It was so devious. "What kind of backdoor?"

Mom and Dad glanced over at me, both with tilted heads. I could see their curious brain gears grinding, wondering if I was going to make some kind of joke or tease Jake. Mom squeezed Jake's hand again. I could see their eyes connect, waiting for me to pounce. All I wanted right now, though, was answers.

"It's not ac … ac … act … ually a backdo … door," Jake continued, swallowing and reverting to his sing-song voice, and then slowly gaining normal momentum and inflection. "That is what the proxy was for—once you get control over someone's email and accounts, you have access to their protocols and then you can use them to launch a string of code to do whatever you want. In this case, the backdoor was the maintenance program on the reactors. It's there to maintain the operating levels of the reactors but if it gets accessed by a terrorist, they can change the operating levels on the valves so they overload."

"Or blow up?" I was intrigued that a computer virus could be so exact, so devastating. All I knew of hacking was someone trying to steal your identity on social media or get access to credit cards, but not this.

Jake nodded.

"And the firewalls wouldn't stop it?" Mom's high-pitched voice squeaked in the room.

"No, they wouldn't detect it as a virus. It's just signals in an already used program."

"So, is that why no one knew what was happening?" I was impressed my little bro knew so much about viruses—impressed and a tad jealous. Baby or not, he was a genius, no doubt about it.

"Yeah, and once it spread to the other reactor operations, it deleted itself, so it couldn't be traced to the hacker—that's the *cur* part of the virus."

I marveled at how much more confident my little brother became when he was talking about something he knew.

I rose from my seat and pointed at the television screen where Gabe Bloom was showing more footage of the White Sands devastation, and then images of similar facilities and similar explosions throughout the globe, from SMR operations in other parts of the U.S., Canada, the United Kingdom, China, India and South America—all now open pits.

"How could one virus blow up all of that?"

Before he could answer me, Gabe Bloom's mouth opened and Dad shushed us.

"This synchronized attack could not have been possible without the recent contract awarded to White Sands by the International Nuclear Operations Conglomerate," she explained, gesturing to her right with a nod of her head.

A map appeared and on it, red stars.

"These stars denote SMR facilities throughout the globe, owned and operated by a member of the INOC. Yesterday morning, White Sands CEO Nigel Featherington signed a contract that would see his company becoming the hub of each members' maintenance operations through White Sands' remote maintenance hub onsite in Tennessee. This agreement meant once White Sands' operations were compromised, so too were those of the conglomerate."

"Turducken," I breathed into the room, staring at the red markers that dotted Canada's landmass: British Columbia, Alberta, Saskatchewan, Manitoba, Ontario and Quebec. The only places without stars were in Atlantic Canada Nunavut, and the Yukon.

Jake snickered at my PG curse.

"And what of nuclear fallout," the Calgary newscaster asked his model-esque Tennessee counterpart. "Do we know if there will be contamination?"

Gabe Bloom shook her head.

"Not yet, Jason," her pale pink lips thinned. "Members of the U.S. Nuclear Power Agency have requested field studies on the affected areas to determine the fallout, if any. Fortunately, these reactors were underground for a reason—to contain any radiation in the event of a catastrophe such as this. However, when you're talking about groundwater and underground riverbeds, there's always the possibility of contamination."

Mom got up from the couch and went into the kitchen, shaking her red head of hair.

"Anyone want some tea? I could use a cup to calm these nerves," her voice shook, as did her hand as she held onto the black electric kettle and placed it under the kitchen faucet in the island that separated the kitchen from the living room.

"Yes, please," Jake said, his voice cracking.

Puberty had hit none too soon.

Maybe that will toughen him up: hormones raging and teen angst and all that jazz.

I doubt it, though, that'll take a lot of hormones, or a lot of hurt.

Did I really want my little brother to be as angry as me, all so I wouldn't stick out like a sore thumb in this family of do-gooders?

Lame, Jewels, even for you.

"Me, too, please," Dad piped up and slumped back down into his recliner, exhausted.

That's how I felt: worn out; void of energy. As if all the strength had been sucked from my muscles and all that was left was fatigue so strong, my legs felt like rubber.

I plopped back down into the loveseat, causing the leather to make a fart sound.

Jake giggled.

I smiled.

"Yeah, sounds good," I said and stuck out my tongue.

Jake stuck his out, too.

Tension eased.

While Mom was getting the cups down from the cupboard, the image on the television changed. On the screen were Centre Street and Beddington, and the 301 wedged into a sinkhole by a semi-trailer. An ambulance was treating a tall teen with light auburn spikes protruding from the crown. My blue, red-ringed eyes stared back at me and I gasped.

"In local news on the SMR attacks, reporter Doug Faulkner was on the scene of the city's own SMR explosion and filmed this footage of the heroic life-saving actions by local seventeen-year-old, Julia Klassen."

"Jewels," Mom shouted from the kitchen, "I had no idea you were interviewed!"

She hurriedly walked back into the living room and stood in front of the large, rectangular screen on the wall.

I frantically searched for the remote control. It wasn't on the glass-topped coffee table or the side table near where Mom and Jake sat. Dad's side table only had a study Bible with a golden tassel hanging from inside the gilded pages.

Where was that damn remote?

"Me neither," Dad said, rising to stand beside her, ukulele stretched across his torso. It looked so tiny lying there, a miniature guitar across a giant's chest.

I stayed on the loveseat and dug my hand into the cushions, and came up empty.

Dad began to strum *What a Wonderful World*.

Jake sat on his knees on the couch, bouncing up and down in anticipation.

I slid to the other side of the loveseat and dug into the space between the side and the cushion.

Nothing.

On the television, a middle-aged man with curly, light-brown hair was asking me questions while he crouched beside my lap. I was sitting on the back step of the ambulance and an EMT was stitching my head from behind as he did so. The reporter's microphone was stuck into my face and I was wincing from the pain of the sutures.

Remote forgotten, my hand absentmindedly rose to the scar again on my head, feeling the stitches.

I got up to leave and Dad raised his hand in front of me, the uke dangling by his side.

He looked like a crossing guard and I paused mid-step.

"Sit right back down there, young lady," he instructed. "I want to see this, and I think it would do you a world of good to see it, too. You need to know just what you did today. Correction: *We* need to know what you did."

No, Dad, you really didn't.

Covering my right wrist with my left hand, I flicked the blue fuzzy elastic and winced.

Dad's face was solemn. His big, bushy black eyebrows furrowed, almost meeting above his nose; his beady blue eyes squinted behind his rimless glasses; and his nostrils were flaring. Yeah, he was serious, alright. I sighed in frustration and flopped back down on the loveseat, flicking off my pink bunny slippers as I landed. One hit the top of the glass coffee table and the other hit Jake squarely in the back of the head.

He turned on his heel and said, "Hey, watch it!"

I snickered.

"Same," I sneered.

Mom tsked and shook her head at me, her red hair shaking with her.

On the screen, the EMT was putting a piece of gauze over my head. My red Calgary Flames hat was in my hand and my exposed light auburn hair was an electrified mess around my head.

I looked deranged.

And bloodied.

The reporter began talking into his microphone: "Passengers on this 301-bus heading north on Centre Street state if it wasn't for your heroic actions, Miss Klassen, they would not have survived the accident. Can you tell our viewers, and readers, what happened, in your own words?"

As I recalled the day's events, my strawberry mop unfurled from the makeshift bun I had made during the bus ride from hell and strands of light auburn hair flew across my face and over the reporter's microphone. The reporter nodded to keep me talking until I ended my tale and flopped back against the legs of the EMT standing behind me.

"Wow, salt and baking soda! How on earth did you think of that as a fire extinguisher?"

"My mom. She's from Newfoundland."

From the couch, Mom's laughter rang in the room and my heart suddenly felt light; lighter than it had all day.

"Yes, Jewels, that explains *everything,*" Mom snickered.

"Well, it kinda does, honey," Dad said, displaying his pearly whites in the world's cheesiest grins.

I could hear the merriment; the joy.

I turned to look at her smiling face and it was contagious.

I felt the hurt fade into the background of my skull, and the anger be put to bed with a comfy, cozy blanket of happiness covering it up.

Why couldn't I feel this way more often?

Why couldn't I see the joy?

Because you're different, genius.

On the screen, however, the TV me was being chided by the EMT for not keeping still while she tried to apply pressure on my sewn-up wound. I was scrambling, trying to get off the step; trying to get free of the paramedic; trying to keep the bandage from falling off my head as I shimmied away; and more importantly, trying to end the interview.

Faulkner would have none of it though, and neither would the EMT, who raised both hands and pushed down hard on my shoulders to keep me in place.

"Hey, where do you think you're going? Sit your butt back down on that step, there, while I bandage up that hole you have in your head," she said. "Now, let me do my job."

I could see the 'same' in Faulkner's eyes, and the wide grin that spread across his face.

I watched as my head turned and I saw all the sweat and dirt that had coated onto my pale skin as TV me glanced up into the EMT's suntanned face. She had short, dirty-blonde hair that curled around her ears. She wore no makeup and from my vantage point on the loveseat, she only looked a few years older than me but I guess those few years did a lot for a person's confidence because she was giving me the what-for, and her firmly pressed lips was a look I had seen in many when they addressed me—the look of pure frustration.

"Hate to break this to you, but I have several holes in my head. There's my eyes, my nostrils, my mouth ..."

"Oh, I know about your mouth," The navy-uniformed paramedic snickered as she secured another sterile pad to my scalp. "Now, hold still. I don't want these stitches to rip and have your brains spell out onto my nice clean uniform."

Jake snickered from the couch.

Couldn't they have edited that bit out in the studio before airing it?

Mom tilted her head down so that her eyebrows lowered and she was glaring at me from the tops of her eye sockets, as if to say, '*Jewels, what are you saying?*'

Dad's abdomen rose and fell in an inward chuckle.

What a Wonderful World began to play from the recliner.

I folded my arms in front of my chest and stared at the screen.

I had been a captive source, and Doug Faulkner was eager to take advantage. He had shoved the mic into my face again and was waiting for me to respond.

"Ten minutes," the EMT said to the reporter, holding up her two palms and splaying her fingers wide. "Ten minutes, then she needs to rest."

Before leaving, she draped a blanket over my slumped shoulders.

My Guns 'n' Roses black tee was now splattered with blood and dirt. As I tried to identify the sources from our living room, TV me adjusted the fabric to cover the exposed belly and belly ring.

Dad paused in mid-strum, looked at me and raised a bushy eyebrow.

"Got it a month ago," I mumbled, trying to sink further into the loveseat.

Shaking his head, he moved onto *You Are My Sunshine*.

As I watched myself on screen, I remembered the feel of that blanket: scratchy with heat radiating from the fabric. I hadn't even been aware that I was cold but as soon as it was in place, I found myself shaking uncontrollably, and hugged it closer around my chest.

Faulkner was asking about the semi-driver, the passengers, the onlookers.

Did they help?

Did they offer first-aid to the passengers who were rescued?

Why was I on the bus in the first place?

Dad began lightly plucking strings; Mom was wringing her hands. Jake shifted from his knees to his butt on the couch, and I tried to ignore the whole spectacle by looking out the window onto our back deck.

Bad move.

Everything was so *brown*.

The patio table and chairs were covered in flakes of ash and dust, the deck floor had a layer as well, and the glass walls that encircled the deck with black iron spacers had a layer of grim so thick, I couldn't see through to the grass below. I wasn't missing much. Everything was, you guessed it, brown, from the dying trees that ringed the yard to the fading bushes and hostas to the blades of grass trying to grow in the cracked, dry earth.

Brown, dying, or dead, and all illuminated by security lights illuminating the yard.

"Who is Julia Klassen?" the reporter was asking TV me.

"Wha? What kind of a shiitake question is that?" TV me responded.

Dad belly laughed, his booming chuckle low and rumbling in the room.

I turned my head away from the crappy world outside and smiled.

"According to on-the-scene witnesses, you single-handedly pulled every passenger out of the transit bus, while it was over-tuned and lodged into a sinkhole. So I ask, what made you do that? What fueled that desire to help and do you consider yourself a hero, as others obviously do?"

"I'm no hero," I said, my voice low and cracked. TV me looked away from the camera and at the people being treated by other paramedics on the median. Gone was Todd's red turban and replaced by a mummy head wrap. He was drinking a juice box, slurping red liquid through a small bendy straw. Sam was there, too. His green basketball shorts were splattered with droplets of red and his right shin was scraped and blotchy. A paramedic handed him a compression bandage and he was applying it to his skin. He looked up and caught my eye.

He winked.

"Anyone would have done what I did," I was saying, turning back to the reporter. "And I did get help from Bloody Santa."

"Who?" Faulkner was looking at me now as if I had just lost my last marble.

"Sorry, I mean the semi-truck driver that hit us."

I watched as my face tilted upward and to the right, squinted and puzzled.

"I can't remember his name right now—I've had several concussions ya know." TV me was tapping on my head and wincing. "He helped, so I'm not a hero."

"His name is Hank Robertson. I interviewed him a few minutes ago, so given his account of what happened, I'm not so sure about that!" Faulkner responded, gesturing to the bystanders and passengers. "What you did was extraordinary and from someone so young—a teenager no less."

"What's that supposed to mean? That teenagers care less? That we don't have the common sense to think on our feet?" My face contorted.

From the couch, I groaned at the expression.

"Thank whoever called 911, but don't thank me."

"According to dispatch, Raj Manoor called 911," Faulkner said, his head bowing in reverence.

"What?" I could see my own eyes bulge. I inherited my mom's big eyes, and my dad's eye color. From my seat, I steadied them on TV me: Long, sooty lashes, large blue pupils in a sea of white and red.

"You look so tired," Mom moaned. "You poor thing, Jewels. You poor thing."

She looked up from the TV screen and glanced at me, her hazel-green eyes on the verge of tears. She shook her head and touched her hand to her heart.

"I'm OK, Mom," I said from the loveseat. "I'm here, see …"

I flapped my arms like wings, and lips spread wide in a smile.

"I see, my darling girl. I see very clearly," she turned to the TV again, and wiped her hand over her eyes.

Did you?

Did you really see … me?

I stared at Mom's back, then turned to the screen.

"Mr. Manoor radioed Calgary Transit dispatch shortly after impact, asking to be linked to 911, and reported the incident."

"Well, then, *he's* the hero, not me!"

Even through the TV speakers, I could tell TV me was cracking.

"That's very noble of you but it was *you, Julia Klassen*, who rescued the passengers and *you, Julia Klassen*, who stopped a fuel fire from reaching the survivors with salt and soda, of all things, so in my book, and I'm sure the book of all our viewers, *you* are the real hero here, today."

I braced myself for the end of the interview, and fixed my gaze on Mom and Dad, waiting for their reaction. My heart pounded a rhythm that would be a great accompaniment to Dad's strumming. All the saliva in my mouth vanished and my tongue stuck to the roof as my throat closed shut.

Here it comes.

Where was that damn remote?

I watched as I shot up from the step on the ambulance.

The reporter nearly fell over, caught himself and then stood alongside me. He turned so he wasn't blocking the camera's view of my face. Roughly my height, Faulkner's head tilted to the side and I could see a wrinkled, dust-covered white shirt and black tie from my vantage point on the loveseat. I hadn't noticed his disheveled appearance during the interview and I wondered if he had arrived on the scene from the SMR explosion in the northeast.

"So, why did you feel you had to be the one to get these people to safety?"

TV me tried to dodge the microphone, the face that was imploring me to talk, and the camera aimed at my face. Faulkner blocked every attempt. I remember thinking this was the longest ten minutes of my life, and where the hell was that paramedic!

I watched as my head whipped back to stare at the camera, defiant, angry.

Find the remote, Flaky Cake!

"I don't bloody well know! Maybe because I am a *human being* and I was raised to *help people* when they are in trouble? Isn't that what we all should be doing? Helping? Now, get that camera out of my friggin' face, you … you … stupid fart!"

"Whoa, whoa, whoa, Jewels," Mom shouted at the TV.

"Language!" Jake snickered, throwing a cushion at the screen.

Dad's belly rose and fell and his nose air puffed out of his nostrils. I watched as the uke rose and fell with each intake of breath. I could tell he was either trying not to laugh or trying very hard now to blow his lid. His face was going three shades of red before settling on scarlet rage.

"OK, I think we are done here," the paramedic said to Faulkner, as she walked back to where I was standing. "Julia is exhibiting symptoms of shock. This interview is over."

"Good! I wanna go home!" I screamed and walked away from the EMT, the ambulance and the reporter, who was now filming the back of my sweaty, black Guns 'n' Roses T-shirt.

Faulkner turned to the camera, raised a bushy brown eyebrow and stifled a laugh. His mouth moved jerkily as he tried to restrain himself. His square jaw stretched so tightly, it looked ironed, and his brown eyes creased in merriment. Faulkner swallowed, and a veil of seriousness fell over his face.

"There you have it folks: Local hero Julia Klassen on this afternoon's accident involving a bus load of passengers and the tragic death of Raj Manoor, who was pronounced dead on the scene. A memorial service for Mr. Manoor is planned for Friday at 1 p.m. at City Centre Cemetery. A Cash for Causes funding page has been set up to help support his family in their hour of need, the details of which will be displayed on the ticker tape below."

"This is Doug Far … I mean, *Faulkner*, reporting for the Calgary Tribune and YYCTV," he said before the screen went black.

I looked around.

The remote was in Dad's hands and his thumb was on the power button.

He turned to me with a raised bushy black eyebrow.

"Hey, don't look at me," I yelled, rising from my spot on the loveseat. "You weren't there. You weren't trying to haul those people out of the bus. I was!"

"Calm down, Jewels," He said, red shade number four engaged.

"Calm down? How can I calm down?" My head whipped from his angry, contorted jowls to my mom's shaking head. "You two weren't *there*!"

"No, we weren't but that doesn't mean you have to act that way in front of a camera," Mom said curtly, her normally high voice low and controlled.

She was holding a tray of mugs with steaming tea and a plate of chocolate chip cookies.

"Your father is a pastor and head of the largest Anglican parish in the diocese. How do you think *this* will play with his parishioners, with the bishop?"

"His *parishioners*? The *bishop*? Is that all you two care about—*appearances*?"

My hands turned into fists by my side, squeezing my nails into my palms. I rose to my full height, feet now bare, parted on the rug. I looked down at my baggy pullover and skinny jeans.

"And what about *me*? I'm the one that had to watch *that!* Had to see a man get his throat slit with his seatbelt and then watch him die."

I was shouting.

My voice shook with rage.

Thunder roared in my ears, blocking out the soft voices trying to urge me to be calm.

Calm down? Like that ever calmed anyone down in the history of hysterics.

I grabbed the remote from Dad's hand and threw it down onto the glass table top. It cracked open, spilling three triple-A batteries onto the shag rug below.

Mom slammed the tray down on the kitchen island.

Dad stepped forward.

"You two think more about appearances than me," I raged, swiping the two halves of the black remote of the table with my hand. "Don't bother denying it."

"Julia," Dad said softly, "that's a lie."

My head tilted back and I laughed.

"Yeah right!" I spat.

Mom rounded the island and stood in front of me, hands at her hips, tea tray forgotten, chest square, lips in a thin line. I was going to have it, now. I mimicked her stance and stared back, my own lips thinning to match hers.

She puffed out air from her nostrils and her lips curled in the corners.

Mom. Was. Not. Amused.

"You stand there, yelling at us about what we may or may not be thinking as if you are some kind of clairvoyant," she hissed. "You know nothing."

"Shelly, enough," Dad said, reaching out to grab hold of Mom's forearm.

"No, Pete," Mom turned to face Dad, "Julia, here, needs to get a reality check," Mom insisted, staring back at me. "She thinks the world revolves around *her* 24/7, when it doesn't. We've been very accommodating, these past few months, dealing with her suspension, her concussion therapy, getting her to all her appointments … and for what? To have this backlash response? Ungrateful, that's what."

Her chest was heaving as she spoke and as words erupted from her lips, my heart pounded even faster. I tried to focus on her pursed lips and the thin lines that were beginning to form around the coral lipstick but the more I stared, the more my pulse raced.

My breathing intensified until I felt like I was hyperventilating.

"This outburst is one of the side effects of Julia's concussions, remember," Dad was saying behind Mom. "It isn't *really* Julia talking as much as it is her scrambled brain."

"Thanks a lot, *Dad.*"

My sarcastic words cut through the heavy breathing like an ice-water shower.

"Julia, I'm trying to rationalize your behavior, here. The least you can do is know when to button it."

"Harumph!"

"Stop grunting at us, young lady," Mom hissed. "A healing brain can't be blamed on everything, you know, not the least of which is your behavior toward your brother."

"What about Jake? What did I do to him?"

Mom shook her head, glanced at Jake curled up on the couch, turning red from embarrassment and turned back to me, adding: "You treat him like he's an insect, and you know it. He has done nothing to you—ever."

"Well, maybe your *favorite child* should speak up for himself if he feels so put out. Or, is he too *perfect* to want to defend himself?"

"Agh!"

Mom's exasperation caused her cheeks to turn as red as Jake's, only hers were angry blotches.

"Honey, why don't you go and sit down while I handle this," Dad soothed.

Mom's thumping footfalls on the hardwood floor sounded like she was a five-ton elephant. She flopped back down onto the couch beside Jake. "We have no favorites," she sighed. "We love you both, equally. The fact that Jake doesn't light us up means we aren't angry at him as much, that's all."

Now it was my turn to growl.

Dad's hand was now resting on my shoulder.

He squeezed.

"I know it often seems like we are grilling you but we are just correcting your over-the-top reactions," he turned to Mom and Jake. "When Jake hits puberty, mark my words, his attitude will change, too. That's part and parcel of being a teenager. Who knows what he'll do? Maybe he'll grow a biker mustache, with the handles down to his jaw, and get a nose ring."

Jake giggled.

"Not … like … likely, Dad," he chuckled.

Picturing Jake in leather with piercings and body hair was too much and I laughed.

"Or, maybe he'll be slamming bedroom doors in our faces every time we want to talk or spend time with him," Dad added, turning to me. "The point is, who Jake is now will not be who he'll be three years from now, guaranteed. We just pray that he'll remember we are here for him when he needs to talk or get support."

His large hand squeezed my shoulder, and he stared into my eyes.

He added, "We'll always be here."

The rage inside me subsided.

"The doctors said this would be tough, for all of us," Dad continued. "You've had many concussions, Jewels, and with each one of those concussions, your brain was injured. Are you still having headaches?"

"Yes."

"What about feeling confused or unfocused?"

"Of course, why do you think I had to go to summer school?"

Dad scowled.

"Sorry," I grumbled.

"And suffice to say, there is a big yes to mood swings, crankiness, irritability and inability to control your emotions, right?"

Mom covered her mouth with her palm but I could see the wide grin curling upwards between the fingers.

"I guess."

"Well, then, if *you* know all these things and *we* know all these things, don't you think there should be an effort made to correct some of this behavior? Don't you think *you* should *apologize* when you take it too far and you hurt others?"

"I guess."

I stared down at my feet.

He was right, of course, but that just made me feel worse.

"Listen, the sooner you realize *your* role in all of this and the things *you* can do to make things better, the quicker things *will* get better."

I nodded.

"Sorry, Mom," I said to the couch, too upset with myself to even meet her eyes. "Sorry, Jake."

"I forgive you," Jake said softly.

"I forgive you, too," Mom's voice was back to being a soft, high lilt.

The demon had cowered down to hell in her, too, I guess.

She rose from the couch and walked over to me and wrapped her arms around me.

I stood there, stoic, waiting for her to finish.

She stepped back, her eyes sad and her arms at her side.

"I know all this is hard on you, Jewels, but it is hard on us, too. Your concussion isn't just affecting you," she made a circle with her index finger over my body, "it affects all of us, as a family. So, yes, there needs to be give-and-take and allowances for your recovery."

There's a *but* there, I know it.

Wait for it …

"But …"

Aha!

"… You need to take ownership for your actions. You need to have more *respect*; more consideration of others."

I grabbed hold of her finger and twisted it away.

Mom winced and flinched.

What are you doing, Nuts for Brains?
You just hurt your mom!

Dad reached out to grab my hand but I had already released Mom's index.

"That's rich," I scoffed, breathing heavily. "If it wasn't for me, those people," I turned to the TV set and pointed, "those people would be dead."

"We know that, Jewels. That's not what we are saying," Dad's calm voice sounded but it did nothing to relax my muscles. "What we are saying is that you need to express yourself better—not like some roid-raging testosterone head."

"Well, maybe we need more roid heads in this world to do the right thing, cause if we did, we wouldn't be in this mess, and environmentalists wouldn't have to resort to blowing shit up to get our attention on climate change," I fumed, I turned to walk past them but Dad grabbed my arm, swinging me around to face him. "And yes, I said *shit*, because that's what this is—crap."

"Those *terrorists* killed hundreds of people today, and almost killed *you*," he said through clenched teeth. "And you'd best remember that."

"Oh, I remember," I pulled my arm out of his grasp, "Raj was one of them and I couldn't save him."

I stomped across the hardwood floor, and began walking up the carpeted stairs.

"This is getting out of hand," Mom was saying in the kitchen. "She needs counseling."

"She's going to counseling," Dad reminded her. "Maybe this is more than just the concussions and puberty."

Mom looked up into Dad's eyes and nodded.

"I have the same feeling," Mom was tired and her voice faded into walls.

I tried to ignore the concern, the sadness as I climbed step after step to my room.

But how could I?

I felt the same way.

There was more going on inside me than a scrambled brain and hormones. I couldn't put my finger on it; I couldn't even explain it. I just felt … different; *abnormal.* Where did I fit in? Where did I belong? And if not here, then where?

Didn't you join all those clubs to fit in, and it didn't work?

Didn't you join wrestling and rugby to deal with all those raging emotions bubbling over from NOT fitting in?

What did you have now?

Nothing.

Absolutely nothing.

I slammed the door to my room and belly-flopped on the brown and turquoise striped duvet. A narrow ray of moonlight peeked through my large window and landed on my cheek, warming the tears now cooling on my skin. I closed my eyes and squeezed the lids.

You want to be oblivious in your own little perfect world with your own little perfect son and your own little perfect Christian friends. You don't want to know your daughter is struggling with belonging in her own skin. No, that would be too real.

As my thoughts screamed, my head pounded.

My jean vest with my meds was still sitting on the side of Centre Street and Beddington Boulevard and I wouldn't get backups until tomorrow. I involuntarily curled my body into the fetal position, with my wet lips touching my knees. I pulled my legs closer to my chest, hugging my thighs, willing my heart to resume its normal pace.

I was sobbing now, uncontrollably.

My newly washed and still damp fine, pale copper hair was sticking to my forehead and face, clinging to my cheeks and ears as if they were statically charged.

"You OK?" Dad was outside my door.

He sounded tired, or was that scared?

I ignored him.

Fear was already ripping through my soul; I didn't need him to add to the tears.

I could hear a deep intake of breath from the other side of the door.

"Your mother and I are well aware you've been through a lot these past few months, Jewels, and we just want you to know we are here for you but you need to make an effort, too, you know. It can't be just us."

I could hear his exasperated heavy breathing on the other side.

Then he was gone.

His footsteps pounded across the carpet and down the stairs.

A beam of light from the streetlamp outside my bedroom window cut through my darkened room and caused the hair on my arms to sparkle.

Minutes ticked by.

Cars honked.

Tires screeched.

Sirens wailed.

There was a light rap on my door.

"Je … Je … Jew … JewELS, I brought you some … some tea and … and cookIES," Jake's low, stammering voice said.

I sighed.

I wasn't hungry.

I just wanted to evaporate.

No amount of wishing it would make it happen, though.

It's not like I was some wand-welding magician.

Uncoiling, a foot cramp curled my bare feet into arches and I stretched the soles until the pain dissipated.

Things you can't do when you're a beanpole: Be a baby again.

I lifted my body off the wet cotton and glared at the door through red, filmy eyes.

I blinked away the layer of tears and tried to focus.

The beam of light shone on the white polyester kerchief tied to my bedpost. Green maple leaves and navy sash covered with sewn crests—souvenirs of my days as a Girl Guide Pathfinder—dangled from the dark wood. There was the Think Green circle crest I had earned by forcing our family to adopt a waste-free kitchen for three months straight, and then kept it going. From my sitting spot on the bed, the Summer Camping crest looked like a piece of pepperoni pizza, and my mind drifted back to the jamboree, where I was responsible for constructing my own tent out of a sheet of canvas, build my own fire, and cook my own food. Other badges were sewn in colorful threads: row upon row, down the length of the front of the sash; each with its own memory to taunt.

On the other post was another piece of unrequited love: My Royal Canadian Air Cadet wedge, a blue rectangular paper-boat looking hat that folded up at the sides, one of which was sewn the crest of the 918 Griffin Squadron. The uniform itself was hanging in my closet, still pressed, still adorned with my medals and covered with a plastic garment bag, except the boots, which I wore on a daily basis until I outgrew them.

Just how many failures did you have in your life?

Ballet.
Gymnastics.
Guides.
Cadets.
"You can't decide whether you like something or not at the first go-round," Dad's voice had rumbled across the kitchen table as he stuffed a hard-shell taco into his mouth, eating half in one bite. "Three bites of food; three months of a club."

In fact, I had lasted several years in each activity. I just quit before I graduated to the final levels. Who wanted to spend their entire teenage years going to drill practice, events, performances, camping trips, and jamborees where you got to be the awkward beanpole no one wanted in a canoe or in front of them in a tutu?

Not me, that was for sure. So, one by one, they dropped off, until all that were left were school-based clubs: wrestling, rugby and track and field—all high-energy sports that gave me extra credits in school and an outlet for the anger that kept creeping into my brain.

Despite this, I couldn't remove the fear that deep down, I was a quitter.
Like school.
Like dating.
Like myself.

At the time, Dad had said the sports clubs made me more aggressive; Mom had countered with: *"girls are constantly at risk for being overpowered by boys and you should know a few skills to keep you safe."*

Maybe if I had stuck with ballet, I wouldn't be suspended; Crystal and I would have had to have had it out with a cheesy dance off, or some cra steppin'-out contest only found in teen musical movies.

Barf.

The idea of wearing all that exhibition makeup and rhinestone, sequined pageantry made me physically ill. Guides? Same. Cadets? Well, I actually liked all the army stuff in cadets, especially not having to wear skirts and sashes. What got me with cadets was just the *strictness* of the whole thing.

I mean, the idea of me standing at attention and saluting a superior was *not* something I could wrap my head around.

Should I have stuck it out?

Who the hell knows? I did last until the Christmas wind-up party, though, so that should count for something. It's too late now, anyway, so why add all these failures to the heaping pile I'm already sitting on?

Opening the door, I picked up the tray Jake had left and brought it back to my room and placed it on my bed.

He really was a rather sweet brother, and I really should treat him better.

Turning on the bedside lamp, I watched as the yellow light bathed the room and stripped the darkness away.

Ever since *The Episode*, I've felt like I've been on pins and needles in this house. Neither Mom nor Dad had talked about the videos that were posted.

Ignorance is bliss, I guess.

Yet another thing to discuss with my therapist, Ali.

At this rate, I'll be going to therapy until I drop dead.

I sipped the milky, sweet tea and took a bite of the large cookie with dark semi-sweet chocolate chips protruding from the grainy biscuit. Underneath it was a yellow sticky note with Mom's scrawl: "Julia, we love you. We're sorry for overreacting about the interview. We just wish we could understand what you're going through. Love, Mom."

Same.

****

An hour later, I emerged from my espresso-stained double bed, still agitated; still pissed. I cast aside the goose-down duvet, causing it to puff fine feathers around my head. Barbie dolls fell on top of me. I picked each one up and placed the crowd of onlookers back in their resting spot: sitting in a row along my headboard. Their plastic eyes stared at me, willing me to join them. I stared back, taking in the dolls' cropped spiked hair, dipped in blue, green, red and yellow food coloring; their perfectly symmetrical oval faces were devoid of makeup, thanks to nail-polish remover and cotton balls. I had placed duct tape over their genitals and torsos so now they stood, arms raised on some, pointing downward on others, looking like an army of cyborgs, waiting for their commands.

"What are you guys looking at," I barked at them, and picked up a pink bunny slipper from the cream shag rug under my bed and threw it at their faces.

They toppled like bowling pins and scattered to the floor, their heads landing in cream rug loops, legs splayed.

Once upright, I flew open my closet door and started grabbing clothes and stuffing them into the wastebasket beside my bed. Dresses, skirts, blouses, tights spewed from the black mesh wastebasket to overflowing. Next came the makeup. With one swift move of my arm, the glass bottles, jars, and powders careened off my built-in desktop and into the wastebasket on top of the garments.

Next, I turned to the army of Barbies in the creamy graveyard at my feet.

I grabbed one with blonde hair and orange tips and threw it against the espresso-framed mirror above my desk. It landed on the glass, then on the art supplies on the cabinet's surface. A paint-splattered mason jar of brushes tipped over, knocking a palette of dried watercolors onto the chair. The white, paint-stained plastic suitcase of colorful squares was immediately joined by a one-inch flat brush, shifting it to the back of the brown-black stained piece of furniture, lodging between two wooden rungs.

The Barbie's head popped off on impact and rolled onto the sheet of plastic pressed into the cream shag rug under my desk and chair. The plastic overlay was held in place with small triangular plastic spikes—an accessory demanded by Mom if I wanted to paint in my room.

I stared at the head, then at my reflection in the mirror.

My bedhead was impressive.

I looked like a fiery Medusa, if Medusa had slept in a vice so all her hair was spiked in a disheveled mohawk.

In one swift movement, I walked to the desk and picked up the scissors protruding from the pencil mug with Art Attack emblazoned in white on the black ceramic.

My blue eyes stared back at me, daring me to do it; daring me to push it.

"They want to *understand?*" I seethed at my reflection, contorting my face so my brows formed a V above my nose and my mouth curled up in a scowl. I lifted the scissors and scraped the blade across my forearm, leaving a trail of red on the white. Another flaming line in the rows on my skin. "Then they need to face *reality.*"

You needed to face reality.

There was no turning back. If they wanted to know the *real* me; to *see* the real me, this is where it starts.

This is the beginning.

I pulled the pale red strands atop my head to the ceiling and squeezed the scissors over the knotted mess, and cut.

Long tendrils of soft auburn floated to the transparent plastic below.

Belonging was for fools.

I snipped again.

You may not be the sharpest tool in the shed but at least you knew that.

And again.

I glanced in the mirror and my butchered hair.

"Well, hello, there. Nice to finally meet you."

Chapter 4

As I brushed my teeth, I could hear Mom and Dad arguing downstairs.

At least Jake was in bed. He'd be a slobbering mess, otherwise.

I gripped the orange and white handle and brushed harder.

Mom's mouse voice rose to the roof and Dad's low rumble sunk to the floor.

Spitting into the bathroom sink, I rinsed and went back into my room.

It was a mess.

A pile of hair lay on the plastic at the foot of my bed. Strawberry blonde strands scattered by the foot, under my chair, under the desk, on top of my knocked over art supplies, resting on the silver lamp clipped to the frame of the mirror.

I connected my cellphone to the speaker on my nightstand and found a 90s playlist and plugged cordless earbuds into my ears.

The argument downstairs was suddenly replaced with the low buildup of music.

My body was beginning to dissolve into Jell-O; the muscles losing their taunt pulls to my bones and joints and forming a pool of goo inside my body. It had been a long day; a tiring day; a day I wanted to put in the rearview, if I ever got to bed.

The voices below faded into the background as Nirvana bellowed Smells Like Teen Spirit into the room.

Turning to the wastebasket, I carried it over to my discarded mane and began to stuff handfuls of strawberry strands atop the jars and compacts, the camisoles and skirts. Hair fluffed around me as the mounds heightened in the basket. As I bent below the desk to get a piece of cardstock from the box of art paper tucked into the shadowed corner, I chanced a glance into the mirror. My cropped, wiry hair stood on end, only a few inches above my scalp, creating a forest to hide my stitches.

What had I done?

What was necessary.

I used the one-inch flat brush to brush more hair onto the edge of the cardstock, which was now a makeshift dustbin.

My door knocked.

I jumped.

The knock pounded louder.

Dad's knock.

I paused the music, took a deep breath and walked to the door.

Opening it up, the hinges creaked.

Dad stared into my face, aghast. Both bushy eyebrows were raised, I could see the whites of his beady blue eyes, which were now enlarged to almost Mom-size, and his mouth was open, jaw dropped. His bumpy tongue resting against the inside of his bottom lip. He didn't move; didn't say a word. Behind him, Mom nudged him aside like a pit bull only to let out a sad squeak and then fall silent. Her expression reflected Dad's. Her hand rose slowly to reach out to touch my hair and she emitted a sob that sounded part-cry; part-hiccup.

"Oh … my … Jewels," she breathed. "What have you done?"

"I had to," I said through clenched teeth. "I had to."

Mom's small arms surrounded me.

"I'm sorry," she whispered into my chest, her wet cheek pressed against my hair-covered unicorn PJs. "I'm so very sorry if we drove you to this. You've been through so much."

Dad pushed the door wider and scanned the room, shaking his head at the clothes strewn over the floor and bed, the headless Barbies scattered in the carnage, the wastebasket full of girly attire and hair, and the jars of foundation, crème blush, powder compacts and eyeshadow palettes now hewn into the basket.

I watched as his face relaxed: his eyes softened and glance at my desk, and the spilled splatters of colorful makeup and the strands of auburn hair; his jaw closed as he picked up a long strand of braid.

Turning to me, he sighed.

"Did we make you do this?" he asked, his low voice cracking.

I saw the guilt on his face, the concern.

"No," I said softly over the top of Mom's head. "I did."

"Oh, Jewels," Mom sobbed, squeezing me tight enough to cause me to take a sharp breath in, "we never said how proud we were of you, and we should have. That should have been the first thing out of our mouths, and not the disappointment."

Dad was nodding.

Mom stepped away from me and gazed into my face, black mascara running down her wet, puffy cheeks. "We're so glad you're alright, Jewels. You are so *brave*! I don't know if I could *ever* have done what you did."

The tension in my shoulders relaxed.

Mom was proud of me.

Mom thought I was *brave*.

Mom—the rock, the spunky, in-your-face, hard-ass who almost made Principal Durrie piss his pants when she threatened a lawsuit if the school didn't accommodate my concussion recovery—didn't think she could have done what I did.

My resolve buckled and the cement that had seeped into the tendons to hold me upright over the past ten hours gave way.

I crumpled into her arms.

I let her soft, warm hands caress my cropped hair, the nape of my neck. I dissolved into her chest as she held me tighter, smoothing away the granite exterior I had built to keep everyone out. My body shook as I let the sobs bubble to the surface and ooze out of trembling lips, but Mom didn't let go. She held me tighter and whispered softly into my ear, "You're OK, Jewels, I've got you; I've got you, my lovey, and I'll always be here for you, my Julia Jewels; my baby girl. You're OK; you're OK. It's over, my darling girl, it's over."

Her voice was barely audible but I heard every word.

Dad's arms joined hers and I was held in the warmest, most comforting bear hug I could ever imagine.

I let go.

The sobs racked my body.

Dad held my head in the palm of his big bear hands. I was against his chest, now—a wall I melted into. Mom's hand caressed my back as I shook.

"It's going to be alright," Dad's voice croaked. "It's all going to be alright. We'll make it alright, with God's help."

But would it?

Was I brave enough to let go of the rest?
It was time I found out.

Chapter 5

Panic has a weird sound.
Car doors opening.
Trunks slamming.
Children crying.
Parents scolding.
Shuffle, shuffle; creak, creak; bang, bang.
Our neighbors were getting out.

Inside the house, headlights were beaming through the slits around my gray window blind, making it glow around the edges. My cellphone was blaring some god-awful sound and I couldn't make it stop, so I flung the device into the open clothes closet, where it continued to sound. I punched my pillow down the center, folded it in half and covered my ear with a side to block out the noise. It trickled in any way. I turned onto my side, putting the window and its distractions at my back. Inside our house, the furnace came alive, blowing cool air up through the vent near the closet. I watched as my newly purchased gray binder swayed in the exhale. The tight spandex fabric lifted and fell; lifted and fell until the air stopped flowing. On the stairs outside my room, floorboards creaked. Someone was up. I removed the pillow from around my head and listened to heavy footsteps on the carpeted steps. With footfalls like that, it could only be Dad. I heard the deadbolt click and slide as he unlocked the front door.

The panic outside filled the house.

I took the pair of clean underwear off my alarm clock to reveal the face: 2:03. Since the concussion therapy sessions, all lights had to be dimmed. What do you do with the bright blue numbers of your alarm clock? Well, pull out a pair of your vintage-inspired Pippi Longstocking panties from your dresser and cover those annoyingly bright lights, of course. Small long, crooked red and white stockings glowed a pale blue on the folded garment, sending a periwinkle haze into the room. Once the undies were removed, the clock face was exposed, the blue numbers blared through the darkness. I never realized how bright the clock was until I started covering up the face as part of my concussion treatment and now, they lit up the room, casting a blue glow over the night table, my cellphone charger and the stack of drawing sheets with sketches of Shade.

Downstairs, the front door slammed shut.

More thundering footsteps on the staircase, then the creak of my parents' bedroom door opening, then muffled conversation: Dad's low growl; Mom's high-pitch squeak.

I waited.

The blue lights flashed 2:11.

I turned away from the light, as blue fuzzy dots flashed in front of my eyes. Blinking them away, I turned to the door and the sounds on the other side.

A loud knock and Dad's gruff voice interrupted my focus.

"Jewels," knock, knock, "Up … downstairs in five."

He paused.

"Jewels?"

"I'm up," I shouted groggily at the door and the impatient bear on the other side.

His footsteps moved on to Jake's room.

I flung my gray and turquoise striped duvet off my body and rose, stepping into my fuzzy pink bunny slippers as I did so. My exposed legs immediately broke out in goosebumps. It was so hard to dress for bed these days. During the day, it was so hot that we had to turn on the air conditioner to cool down the house. At night, the temperature outside dropped so dramatically, the furnace kicked in to heat it back up again.

Calgary had turned into a desert.

I grabbed the unicorn onesie hanging in the closet and slipped my legs inside, sighing as the warmth of the fleece touched my skin. I went to bed wearing red and green plaid boxer shorts and a faded, white T-shirt. Pulling the rainbow fleece over my arms, I zipped up the full-piece suit and pulled the hood over my cranium. The unicorn head flopped forward over my forehead and I pushed it back to its rightful spot.

Was this day ever going to end?

When I got downstairs, Dad was busy pouring freshly brewed coffee into three thermoses, his shoulders slumped forward as if he didn't have the energy to pull them back; Mom was packing a jar of peanut butter, a large bag of oranges, several cans of beans, a bunch of celery and corn tortillas into a tote bag. Jake was sitting at the kitchen island eating a bowl of Cinnamon Toast Crunch, scooping up the small squares in his oat milk with his spoon and making sound effects as he did so. I had entered the space, apprehensive, staring at my family as if they were a jury that could condemn me to life in prison.

"We have to evacuate," Dad said, turning from the coffee maker and screwing lids onto thermoses. He handed one to Mom, who took a long swig, and continued with her snack packing. The other, he handed to me and smiled, his bloodshot eyes barely open. "We are now in a radiation zone."

"What does that mean?" I accepted the coffee and followed Mom's example and took a long swallow.

The hot brew burned the tip of my tongue as it slid down the back of my throat, leaving a trail of dark-roast Columbian with hints of vanilla. As I turned to my parents, the caffeine already waking me up and spreading a warm glow inside my belly, I suddenly realized my parents were already operating in survival mode: Dad filling bottles of water and lining them up by the stainless-steel sink; Mom gathering nonperishable food for the road ahead.

Four backpacks were sitting by the front door, their zippered mouths agape, waiting to be fed.

"We have to leave," Mom's voice was hoarse. "Pack up and go."

"I need you two to go grab one of those backpacks over there," Dad pointed to the hungry zippered beasts by the coat closet, "and fill it with jeans, underwear, socks, T-shirts and one hoodie, your toothbrush and toothpaste. Nothing more."

Turning back to look at me and Jake, he added: "That's all you get so all your stuff has to fit in one bag." He tapped his wristwatch. "We don't have a lot of time."

Jake turned. His Mario Brothers flannel PJs wrinkled and constricted his arms and chest. The sleeves stopped short of his wrists, the elastic ankles, in mid-shin position. The blue and yellow pajamas were a Christmas gift from Nan and now, nine months later, they were too small. Last night's news coverage must have led to a *nighttime booboo*, as Mom called it.

"Yes, but first I want to talk about something important," I stuttered, sounding an awfully lot like my little brother, whose eyes widened as if Bowser had just walked into the room.

Dad turned around, his He > Me yellow T-shirt splattered with water, a small splash of black coffee and a few dark granules sticking to the wet stains.

"Jewels, *we don't have time*. Get your bag full and maybe then we can talk on the road."

"No," I said, standing my ground.

Not sure how menacing I was presenting myself, or how serious. After all, I was wearing a pastel rainbow unicorn onesie, with the head pulled up so the horn was pointing at my parents, and my hands on my hips, with a plush fleece tail swung over one wrist.

Not the most serious outfit for what was to come next, that's for sure.

Dad slammed his hand down onto the cream granite countertop with brown marble swirls, the sound slapping in the air and startling Jake so much, he nearly choked on the bowl of cereal milk he was slurping and spurted it through his nose and onto Mom's bagged peanut butter and jam cornbread sandwiches.

"Jake," Mom yelled at the same time Dad yelled, "Jewels."

"This is not the time," Dad growled. "Grab a bag and get packing."

I was breathing heavily, my insides screaming for him to listen.

"Fine," I yelled, instead, and marched toward the second-floor stairs and the waiting bags near the front entrance. Grabbing one, I stomped up the stairs.

I slammed my bedroom door, swearing.

From downstairs: "Language!"

Enter Mom's Devil Voice.

I coined the description after watching a B movie in Grade 6 about Lucifer and realizing that the deep-throated, shrill, send-shivers-down-the-spine tone was almost identical to Mom's angry voice. From that point, it was her *devil voice* and it was being used right now and the effect was the same.

How could such a scary-as-shiitake noise come from such a shrimp, high-talking mom?

I'll tell you how: Anger, that's how.

Redhead genes, Dad called it.

No focaccia wonder I was mental; I had them, too.

As I stuffed my black backpack with jeans, tees, underwear, socks, flannel shirts and a hoodie, I mumbled under my breath, seething.

How am I supposed to be honest and tell them when they won't even give me a chance to talk?

Stupid.

I'm so stupid to think I could have this conversation with them; that they would give me the chance to explain *me*.

Screw them, Jewels. Screw them all.

"Yes," a voice whispered from the back of my brain, *"but they are packing because we are being evacuated, so what you have to say comes second, get it? They need everyone to be safe first."*

I hardly recognized the voice; I hadn't heard it in months.

Maybe my concussion knocked all sense out of me after all, just like everyone keeps telling me, because it sounded an awful lot like my conscience.

"Hello, old friend," I muttered to the room, "haven't heard from you in eons."

I took off my onesie, pulled a pair of jeans from my dresser drawer and grabbed a red flannel shirt from the closet, underneath which was a hidden undergarment—something I had purchased online months ago but was never brave enough to wear.

The gray spandex taunted me.

"Screw it," I said to the room and pulled it on over my head and then donned the flannel shirt and buttoned the front. "If we are escaping into the unknown, I want to do it on *my* terms, with my true self intact. Don't have time to talk? Well, this might get the conversation going, providing they even notice."

"Are you sure you want to wear that tight thing for the first time on a long ride to God knows where?" the soft voice piped up, again.

"Shut up, you," I muttered back. "I don't hear from you for months, so zip it. I don't want to hear what *logic* you have to spew into my calculated plan to force a conversation with my parents."

Even if I'm right?

"Especially, if you're right."

The voice retreated, rejected.

I pulled on my jeans, jumping up and down to tug them up over my hips and let the red and white checks fall over top of them, concealing the gray spandex underneath. Glancing into the mirror.

My hair, chopped; my chest, suddenly flat.

Better.

I took a deep breath, realizing the spandex did more than just squish my boobs; it constricted my breathing, as well.

I stuck out my tongue, scowled, silently screamed and went to the bathroom to fetch my toiletries. Fully packed, I ran down the stairs and threw my bag against the front door. It landed with a loud thud.

The kitchen was now empty and the rest of the bags were gone.

"Figures."

I was tying my runners when Jake bounded down the stairs in jeans and a hoodie, dragging his navy backpack down the steps. The bag thumped as he descended.

Thump. Thump. Thump. Thump. Thump. Thump. Thump.

"Geeze, Jake, if I didn't have a headache before, I'd have one now," I yelled at him. "Can't you pick that bag up? It's a backpack, dude, not a thump-bag."

He stopped before reaching the last step, turned his bed head toward me and scrunched up his nose.

"It … it … it's … ta … ta … too … hev … hev … heavy."

"Moron," I mumbled, not really sure who I was talking to, him or myself.

Jake was anything but a *moron*. He knew it and he knew I knew it, too, but I wanted to lash out; I wanted to hurt someone.

It could have been anyone but Jake was there.

And perfect.

He didn't have to disguise his identity.

He didn't have to go to counseling and listen all day to Ali Cameron tell you a bunch of exercises you had to do in order to feel like your world wasn't falling apart.

And *he* wasn't constantly exhausted and angry for the crappy hand fate dealt him.

No, Jake just had to be, and everyone was cool with that.

Must be nice.

Jake bent his head down as he pulled the bag to the front door.

"Not nice, Jewels," he said, his anger making his stutter disappear.

I smiled: "You need to be pissed more often, dude. You speak better."

"No. I don't like being angry—unlike *you*."

He opened the door and went outside.

The light was on and he sat under the warm yellow glow on the concrete steps, his face resting in the palms of his hands.

Why did you do that?

I don't focaccia know.

"Because you're mental," the voice whispered. *"You're a mental case, and you know it. Why else would you be in counseling?"*

Mom came up the basement stairs with a brown kennel in her hand and inside, Shade was yowling, his green eyes piercing through the shadows of the interior. I reached in and petted his black hair and he instantly began to purr as if he had swallowed a motorboat.

"Set?"

"Yeah."

"Good. Take Shade and go to the car. Your Dad's packing the dry cat food into the car in the driveway. Take your bag with you, too," Mom turned to put her shoes on and grabbed a drawstring nylon coat. "Did you see if Jake took a coat?"

"No, he didn't," I said over my shoulder as I struggled to open the door while holding my backpack by the shoulder straps in one hand and the kennel in the other. Mom reached over and opened the door for me, hopping on one foot. "Thanks."

"I'll grab one. You got one?" She was pulling a quilted nylon jacket from the closet with a Calgary Hitmen logo emblazoned on the back.

"No," I sighed, turning back to the closet.

"Go, go, I'll grab one for you."

"I want the leather one."

I went out the door. Jake was no longer on the step.

I walked to the hybrid beige station wagon in the driveway. Mom had said she hated the color but at least the dust was camouflaged. Unlike Dad's Kia Soul, this car was bigger, built for longer trips and could run on gasoline and electricity. It was Mom's car and right now, it was our getaway mobile.

Someone had written, "wash me" on the back window in the layer of grime.

I opened the back door, wondering how long ago the unwitty scribe had fingered the tag on the window, and tossed my backpack inside.

It smacked into Jake's shoulder.

"Ouch!" he groaned.

"Baby."

"Jewels," Dad barked from the driver's seat. "Apologize and get in. I swear, by the end of this road trip, you will either have an attitude check or you'll be strapped to the roof."

"Sorry," I mumbled to Jake.

"I for … for … forGIVE you," he mumbled back. "Jus … jus … jusT be NICE, Jewels. I … I … I … IT ain't that hard."

"Easy for you to say," I said, turning to the window, sighing.

I'm still here, ya know. Maybe if you let me speak, you wouldn't be so angry.

Yes, but if I wasn't angry, I'd have to *feel* what was really inside. That's way scarier.

Is it really? How do you know until you give me a voice and find out?

I rolled down the pane of glass, just as Mom was locking the house. In front of us, yellow and blue lights were driving around the crescent and exiting. We were among the last to leave. She stood on the top step, staring at the red door with her keys in her hand. Her shoulders rose and fell and it took me a while to realize she was sobbing. Beside her was a black Rubbermaid bin with a white lid, and on top of that was a bunch of jackets.

She stood still, keys dangling in her hand, staring at the door.

Dad took a deep breath and let it out.

Mom's shoulders shook for a few more seconds and then squared. She blew her nose into a tissue, which she tucked into the pocket of her jeans, picked up the bin, then turned to the car and the three of us waiting inside.

Dad got out and took the bin from her, gave her a kiss on the lips as he did so, and touched her forehead with his own before turning toward the trunk of the car.

As I watched the scene, my stomach curled.

Why was I behaving like an obnoxious teenager?

Why was I being such a shiitake-head to my brother?

Honestly, I didn't really know but I did know, looking at Mom and Dad exchanging care for one another, that *they* didn't deserve what I'd been dishing out lately.

And neither did Jake.

"You don't deserve it either, Jewels," the voice screamed, but I told it to shut up and leave me alone.

What did it know, anyway?

It was just some stupid voice inside my stupid head.

Was it really that stupid? Or, was it just being honest?

Mom pushed a button on her keys and the trunk hood rose.

As Dad packed the bin inside, Mom smiled and opened her door and sat down in front of me.

I turned my head to look out my door window.

I now saw the urgency.

"What on earth do you have in that thing," he said from the back of the car.

"A life," Mom muttered.

When Dad resumed his seat in front of the steering wheel, he turned to Mom.

"There's more to life than the things we accumulate," he said softly. "It's who we have in it, not what."

He squeezed her hand.

"I love you," she said softly.

"I love you, too," he replied, smiling. "We'll be OK as long as we have each other."

"I know," Mom turned to her door window, "I just hate leaving our home."

"Our home," Dad began, caressing her hair, "is where we are."

I felt my throat close.

"Don't you say another word," I threatened, while rolling up the window to block out the noise.

"What?"

"Not you."

"Then who," Jake said, scrunching his eyebrows downward. "Who else is back here?"

"Just me and my shadow," I replied. "Make that, *Shade.*"

"Well, Shade isn't talking or meowing."

"Look out the window and leave me to my muttering," I sighed, suddenly so tired, my head just fell against the cold glass.

Outside, two police cars were parked across from our home. Two officers in black were directing traffic, while two others were escorting people refusing to leave their houses. Some were shouting, others pushing. All were demanding their freedom to stay.

Freedom.

What did that look like, anyway?

Not this.

Idiots.

They're just scared of losing everything. So are you.

Dad pushed a button near the steering wheel and the engine softly came to life. He squirted the windshield with washer fluid and turned on the wipers to wash the grime off the glass.

As we left our suburb neighborhood and followed the throng of vehicles slowly making their way onto the main thoroughfare, Dad left the bumper-to-bumper parade and turned right. We curled around a roundabout, then exited on the other side of Poplar Hills and took the less congested exit onto Stoney Trail South, the ring road that wound around the city.

"You are so right," Mom patted Dad's knee. Dad put his hand over hers and squeezed her small fingers. "It's going to be fine. God is with us."

"Let's hope he's with them, too," Dad sighed, tilting his head to the onslaught of cars following his lead.

Once on the highway, Jake pulled a small bag out of his hoodie pocket and began munching on dry Cinnamon Toast Crunch.

After about ten minutes, and we were traveling at a reasonable speed, Dad looked up into the rearview. "You wanted to talk, Jewels? You have my full attention—or as much of it as I can give while driving, at least."

Now, you want me to talk?

Fudgsicles.

How do I say it? What's the first word? The second?

"Go on, Jewels," Mom urged, turning her head back over the console that divided the driver seat from the passenger. Her red mane wound up in a clip at the back of her head. "We're listening."

Jake kept munching.

I could hear his teeth chomp down on the sugary squares.

Well, here goes nothing.

"I'm…" I began. "I'm … not a *girl.*"

The car hit the rumble strips on the shoulder. Dad turned the wheel to bring it back within the driving lane.

Mom's head whipped around, her clip banging against the headrest and skewing her twisted hair off-center.

"What?" they said in unison.

"I … ah … I'm … a … both," My words stumbled, tripped and landed in the car interior with the welcome of a pimple.

"You're a girl *and* a boy?" Jake questioned, his head tilted, a sparkling square between his thumb and forefinger inches away from his mouth.

Now, I've done it. I've shocked Jake into losing his stutter.

Well, don't say telling the truth doesn't have an upside.

"Yes," I swallowed. "I'm trans … fluid."

Mom's face went blank.

It looked ironed, stretched.

I looked at Dad.

He was staring at the car ahead of him.

I willed him to turn around; to look into the rearview; to make a sound.

Instead, he pushed his glasses up the bridge of his nose and then clenched the steering wheel. Even from the backseat, I could see his tanned brown knuckles going white.

"I don't get it," Dad said. "How can you be *both.*"

I felt like they weren't listening.

How do I explain?

How do I make them understand?

How do I make them accept me?

"Because I am," I said, my voice echoing in a dull tone. "I just am."

Mom sat there, looking at me in the dark car, as street lights sped by, illuminating my face as she stared. Her head was tilted as if she was studying me, trying to figure out a puzzle, then her mouth moved in a soft smile. I watched as her face softened and the smile grew.

"Simple," she said, turning her head back to look at Dad, "Our *daughter* is neither male nor female. They are both."

"You mean like bi-sexual?" Dad finally looked at me in the rearview. "You're attracted to boys and girls?"

I turned away from his piercing gaze and tried to see through the murky window beside me.

"Well, yes, but not really. I'm male *and* female," I corrected. "I'm a boy and a girl. My gender is determined by how I feel, and how I feel changes from day to day, and who I'm attracted to depends on the person—*who* they are; not *what* they are."

Dad rubbed his left hand over his scalp as if he was buffing the surface, while his right tightened around the black bumpy wheel. I saw a vein go purple around the side of his throat.

Mom stretched her arm back, hand welcoming. I reached for it and she held it tightly.

I could feel the heat from her palm, the sweat, the tremor.

"Now that you've said it, I think we've always known," he sighed, smiling into the rearview. "That took a lot of courage, Jewels."

His eyes were glistening behind his glasses and for once, it wasn't because of the smoke and the lack of sleep.

It was because of me.

Did I just make my dad cry?

I found it hard to swallow, to breathe.

Tears were threatening to fall and I didn't stop them from trickling down my cheeks.

I was so tired of being strong; being tough.

"Really?" I asked, my voice rising an octave to sound strangely like Mom's.

Dad's blue-green eyes creased.

He was smiling.

He was nodding.

"It kind of all makes sense, now, especially the Barbies," Mom said, giving my hand another squeeze. "That and the new haircut."

"And the rough-housing," Dad chirped in.

"And baggy-clothes days," Mom continued.

"And the video," Jake chirped in.

My head shot to the side to look at my brother.

I could feel all the blood drain from my face.

Mom and Dad laughed: "Yes," they said in unison.

"That was kinda a dead giveaway, wasn't it, Jakey?" Dad said, chuckling.

"You *saw* that?" I was incredulous and my voice rose in a high-pitched croak.

"Of course," Mom said. "Principal Durrie sent us the link after he suspended you."

"What about … *church*," I croaked. "Won't they be upset? You were all on my case last night about *appearances* and how what I said would affect Dad's congregation—this is much worse than a few curse words."

"What congregation? We are fleeing a radiation leak in our city, so who's going to give me a hard time here? Besides, the *church* is wherever God's people are, even in this old station wagon or out there," his head tilted to the road outside. "*God's People* do the will of God, and Jesus was first and foremost about love, acceptance, inclusion. Given that, I think we'll leave the judging to God, don't you, and let the *church* be the church."

Tears were flowing down my cheeks like waterfalls.

"What about the gender police?" I sobbed, wiping the snot from my nose with a tissue Mom was holding out for me.

My voice was barely audible.

Dad's jaw tightened.

The purple jugular vein pulsed.

Mom turned back to the windshield and sighed deeply.

"The Gender Appropriation Division can kiss my hairy pastor's butt," he said to the windshield, his loud deep voice echoing off the walls.

"Language," Jake hollered, spitting out bits of dry cereal into the back of Dad's seat.

"Right-O, Jakey! Correction: My hairy *Dad's* butt."

I laughed.

"Same," I shouted joyfully, feeling light. So, weightless in fact, that my spine rose up and straightened as if grounding my body from floating away.

Our family may be nuts, but they are my kind of nuts.

"What about you, turducken? What do you have to say about all this?"

Jake swallowed, took a swig of oat milk from a bottle between his knees and looked down into his bowl of squares. "I like oatmeal, but it's overrated and boring. I like Cinnamon Toast Crunch a lot better, don't you?"

Where was his stutter?

"Yes," I said, confused and marveling at his confident voice.

"Well, Cinnamon Toast Crunch wasn't made to be boring or bland," he lifted a square up to the light streaking into the car from the passing lamps, paused and then looked at me, smiling. "It was made to be exactly the way it was meant to be—different: Sweet, spicy and ..."

"Soggy?" I said, hiccupping.

My baby bro was trying to understand me.

Even in the dark car, I could see his white little tombstone teeth.

"That's not what I meant," his body was shaking with giggles and his blond mop was bobbing in the motion as if on springs. "Cinnamon Toast Crunch is not boring or bland but it also isn't strange because you've tasted the flavors before. You know the taste before you even take a spoonful—it's familiar yet unexpected, like you."

"Huh?"

Mom reached between the front bucket seats to nudge Jake's knee in encouragement.

"Well, you being a guy *and* a girl makes sense: Sometimes you act and dress like a dude, like now, and other times you're all painted and stuff. So, you're a two-sided piece of Cinnamon Toast Crunch. Both sides make up the whole, and you can't have one side without the other.

"You're still *square*, though, like the rest of us," he was licking the cinnamon sugar off one side of the square pinched between his fingers with his pink tongue.

"Groan," Dad said from the front.

"And you say *we* make bad puns," Mom said, chuckling and shaking her head.

Dad's shoulders suddenly started moving up and down. His seat started to shake and I could see his belly rippling under his seatbelt. His whole torso was vibrating, and so was his seat. The low rumble reverberated in the car's interior, bouncing off the filthy windows and dusty leather seats and beige plastic.

It wasn't long before we were all giggling.

And it felt good.

So much tension released into the compact station wagon; so much joy with it.

"I'm proud of my *squareness*." I reached over and rubbed my knuckles into his bouncy blond curls. "I think it's a prerequisite to being a Klassen. At least I've got *sparkle*."

Jake was grinning at his own wit.

Easy, there, Jakey. You just might get me to like you, if you keep this up.

My head tilted as I studied his shaggy mop of blond bedhead, the still-flushed-from-sleep round cheeks and the milk moustache above his grinning lips. My little bro had transformed from the whiny baby into this awesome little dude.

"So, are you still our Julia," Mom asked from the front.

She didn't turn around this time. I think she was afraid to look at me; to see my answer. I had always been Julia or Jewels. Named as a baby and baptized with it as a toddler, Julia and my nickname had become synonymous to who I was from the time I could walk.

I could sense her fear and apprehension.

The whole car could.

All we could hear was the low hum of the hybrid engine and our breathing.

My chest rose and fell in ragged breaths.

Dad's large hand left the wheel and found Mom's in her lap.

"Actually," I began, "I was hoping for more of a unisex name. One that is—how did you put it Jake—*familiar* but different."

Was that my voice?

It sounded unsure, shaken.

I could hear Mom take a deep intake of breath, siphoning the stale air in the car into her lungs and leaving me without any.

I was finding it hard to breathe, and it wasn't because of the binder squeezing my chest. This was real now; not a conversation happening in my head. I suddenly felt as if I was letting them both down and Mom's reaction to a name change just proved I was right.

"Like what?" Dad's gaze caught mine again in the rearview.

My tongue became too big for my mouth and stuck to my teeth. All the saliva in my throat evaporated and felt like the air outside: dry and full of grains of sand.

"We named you Julia Louise for a reason," I could hear Mom's voice fade into her seat.

I was killing her.

Well, her heart, anyway.

The pit in my throat moved down to my stomach.

After all, I was named after my great-Nan, her grandmother, Julia Noseworthy, and Dad's great-grandmother, Louise.

I had been baptized with those names.

The pewter birth plate on Mom's wall had it engraved atop an embossed cradle.

The diplomas and certificates in Mom's accordion file labelled *Julia's K-12 Years* had it typed in bold letters.

Everyone knew me by this name and that is how I knew myself.

But not anymore.

How could I change now?

How could I explain to make them understand this was something I needed to do?

Would they change with me?

My voice erupted from my mouth in a parched pronouncement, grated across sand knives on the roof of my mouth: "I was thinking, maybe … Jules Louie Klassen? Jules, as in J-u-l-e-s, not J-e-w-e-l-s."

The car's engine revved.

Mom sniffled.

Dad breathed heavily into the steering wheel.

Jake chewed on dry cereal squares.

"I wanted to keep Great-Nan and Great-Grandma's names," I spat out of my mouth in rapid succession. "I know they are important to you both, but I wanted them to be like me, too."

My heart thundered into my chest and ears, throbbing and pounding so loud, I couldn't hear anything else.

I could see the black clip move up and down in front of the headrest.

"Sounds like you really thought this through, Jewels, I mean, Jules with a U."

Dad was using his sermon voice: loud and articulate.

It sounded like a slow river meandering down to the rapids.

I waited, panting heavily in the back seat.

Was he trying to convince Mom, me or himself that all would be fine?

"I like it." He took a deep breath: "Welcome to the family, Jules Louie Klassen."

"Yes, nice to finally meet you, Jules with a U," Mom's voice was shaky, sad.

I saw Dad's arm flex across the console as he tightened his grip on Mom's hands.

"It's pronounced the same," I stammered. "You guys don't need to say, 'Jules with a U.' It's just *Jules*."

"Right you are," Mom gave a genuine chuckle.

"Like Jules Verne," Dad said, smiling at Mom, "He was this famous sci-fi author from France who wrote *Voyages Extraordinaires* in the early 1800s."

Mom's burst of laughter erupted into the car.

It untied the knot in my stomach.

"That's a little before her time," she said.

Dad chuckled, now: "You and me both."

"You mean, you guys weren't around in the 1800s?" I piped up.

"Now, now," Dad shook his head. I heard relief in his voice and his shoulders lost their tension. The rapids were avoided, after all. "Let's not be mean to your old Ma and Pa. I may be bald but I was born bald, so it's not a good indication of age."

I laughed, relieved that the tension had eased.

"And pronouns? Are we to guess when you are a male and female and use his and her based on how you are dressed? Cause if so, I'm doomed." Mom's uncertainty put an edge to her voice.

"Why don't everyone just use plural pronouns," I suggested, "you know, like *their* and *they*."

"That simplifies things, at least," Dad patted Mom's thigh. "Doesn't it, hon?"

Mom nodded, wordlessly.

"You know…" Jake began, brushing sugar granules off his PJ pants, "it's only a *plural* pronoun when it's introduced by a binary person. We've been using *they* and *their* for one person for years, when we didn't know the gender of a person, so what really has changed?"

I was grinning.

I could feel my lips curl as I stared at the boy who was quickly becoming my advocate: The boy who understood; the boy who was trying to support— my *brother*. My brother, whom I had insulted, shot down, demeaned, ignored, ridiculed … My brother who was *gender-splaining* to my Christian parents, and they were getting it.

I took a deep breath and tried to calm my thundering heart.

I suddenly wanted to hug Jake.

Instead, I reached over and lightly punched his shoulder.

He grinned and feigned injury by rubbing the spot where my fist connected.

Yes, bro, I finally see YOU, now.

I had been wrong about him all along.

I really had been an asterisk to the dude.

You can always change.

Change was scary.

Wasn't the hard part over, though?

No, it was just beginning.

As the voices in my head faced off, the darkness outside loomed.

"You do know what the title of his book was in English, right," Dad's voice had a ring of a magical revelation. "Extraordinary Journeys. I think it's quite fitting, really, don't you?"

I let the words sink in.

He was giving me a lifeline.

I grasped his words with both hands, knowing full well I was lucky to be in this family.

Blessed, really.

Crystal hadn't been so fortunate.

She was in some assimilation camp because her folks couldn't handle gender diversity.

I sighed and caught Dad's glinting blue-green pupils in the mirror.

He got it.

My Anglican priest Dad got me, and reeled me in.

I could feel the warmth rise from my chest to my cheeks. My chin began to quiver; my eyes glistened.

I let the tears fall.

This time, they were happy tears.

Tears of release and I welcomed them.

See, was that so bad? I knew they wouldn't judge. You should have listened to me all along.

Right you are, voice in my head. You just need to speak up more.

No, you just need to acknowledge me more.

"So, does that mean you're my *big brother*, now?" Jake was holding out his small, soft plump fist for a bump.

"If I am, then you're my *cereal killer!*" I bumped his folded digits.

"Jules," Mom groaned.

"Or maybe a big *piece of toast,*" I reached over and grabbed a sugary cinnamon square.

"Bad pun alert," from the front seat. Dad was wagging his finger into the rearview. "Watch it or I'll be forced to give you a ticket for not being punny."

"Mom, make them stop," Jake hollered.

"I would if I could, Jakey. There's no putting *that* genie back in the bottle. Lard have mercy on us all."

I could feel the smile stretch across my face. I sniffled and grabbed the tissue in Mom's extended hand. She was crying and smiling, too. We were fleeing the city I had known all my life and leaving my friends behind, yet I was happy.

How strange.

"Get with the program, Count *Chuckula*, being a *cereal killer* is a profession that's outside of the *box*."

"*Mom*," Jake whined, "Jules won't stop!"

"That's because she's a *real gem,*" Mom retorted, eyes like saucers. "Get it, real *gem*, 'cause her name is *Jules.*"

"You mean *they* are a real gem because *their* name is Jules," Dad corrected.

"Sorry, yes, that's what I meant," Mom said, smiling at me. "That's going to take some time, I'm sorry. Pronouns are ingrained in me, I'm afraid."

"Yes, we are old school," Dad agreed, "and yes, we get it, hon, now stop before you hurt someone."

Mom punched Dad in the shoulder.

We were all snorting, now.

"We either have to join them or leave them, and I'm never going to leave them." Mom looked into Dad's eyes.

"Me neither," he replied, his voice hoarse with emotion. "So, I guess I'd better *milk it* for all it's worth."

"Groan City," I said, realizing Shade had been licking my right hand with his sandpaper tongue this whole time as he lay, contentedly, in his kennel on my lap. "More like Corn *Flakes.*"

"God, I love this family," Dad turned on the signal light and changed lanes.

You and me both. See, that wasn't so bad, was it?

No, voice, it wasn't.

Somehow, I felt … more at peace, now.

Less on edge.

Less confrontational.

Less angry.

It felt good.

Chapter 6

"Heavenly Father, Almighty Creator grant us wisdom for the days ahead; grace in our hearts for each other; and your abundant love as we seek to serve you on our journey. Just as you accept us, may we accept those different from us. Just as you welcomed us into your inheritance, so may we welcome others. For you are a gracious God; a loving God; a God of acceptance; a God of truth; a God of hope and what you have made, let no one devalue or put asunder. You are the almighty, all-powerful, all-knowing God. You know our hearts, our fears, our self-doubt, and may you give us strength to endure the challenges and obstacles before us. May we focus on what is good, what is right, what is gracious, what is just and pleasing in your sight and above all, love one another just as you have loved us. Amen."

Dad's soft, deep voice cut through my sleepy brain.

My eyes flickered open and I saw him gripping the silver crucifix around his neck as he prayed. The car wasn't moving, but Dad was. While his left hand gripped the cross, his right was raised high in front of the windshield and the red taillights of the truck parked on the highway in front of us. I could see the pickup driver's hand out the driver's side window—a closed fist pumping at the long train of vehicles filling the growing light of dawn with anger.

As Dad ended his prayer, Mom leaned over and kissed his cheek.

"Thank you, hon, I was beginning to feel anxious and afraid. I needed that."

She wasn't the only one.

Dad closed his eyes and took a deep breath in through his nose. Through my half-closed eyes, I saw his chest rise and fall. His shoulders dropped slightly as his body relaxed.

"She … they'll be OK," Mom was consoling, caressing the once raised hand as it returned to the steering wheel. "We all will be."

"I know. That's what the prayer was for—to remind me of the grace of God and that there's plenty to go around, even to this … sad soul … in front of us."

Mom snickered.

In front of us, the red truck's wheels began to roll forward a few feet. Dad waited until the space between us measured a car's length before nudging a little forward, and just before the honk that blared behind us. Jake stirred beside me, rolled to one side, pressing his forehead into the window of the door.

"You know what?" Mom turned to Dad and waited for him to glance in her direction before continuing. "I do believe our Jules with a U is nicer."

She yawned.

Dad smiled and then opened his mouth until his top lip touched his nose and his bottom, his chin, as he emitted a long, drawn-out noise that turned Mom's yawn into a squeak.

"I do believe you are right," he breathed out.

Mom nodded and rubbed her eyes with her index fingers.

"How much further?"

"In distance or hours? Another hundred kilometers but at this rate, that could take until lunchtime."

"Give some grace to yourself, hon. We will arrive when our journey is done and not before."

Dad chuckled, "On that, you are correct."

As we rolled forward again, my eyelids began to droop.

Was I nicer?

Well, I did feel more … *content.*

Maybe that's all it took: To be accepted for who I was.

If only I could exist within this car, this family forever.

We all know that ain't gonna happen.

The car was warm, despite the air conditioning, and Dad began to sing in his rumbling baritone one of his favorite old church songs. I listened to the deep sound as if it was a Gregorian chant. Sighing deeply, I let dreamland take me in its pillowy embrace, where monsters no longer dwelled, roaring lies into my head. Instead, my brain was filling up with lyrics of *All Things Bright and Beautiful.*

The car rocked back and forth in the wind as it moved.

"All things bright and beautiful, all creatures great and small. All things wise and wonderful, the Lord God made them all," he sang, his voice lulling me deeper and deeper into dreamland. "Each little flower that opens, each little bird that sings. He made their glowing colors, he made their tiny wings."

He began to mumble and Mom turned, smiled and continued, "The purple-headed mountains, the river running by, the sunset, and the morning that brightens up the sky."

"All things bright and beautiful," they sang together, "all creatures great and small. All things wise and wonderful, the Lord God made them all."

Jake snored beside me.

The engine purred with Shade, and I let the sounds carry me to the other side, where streams sparkled like diamonds and mountains rose against the backdrop of vibrant, colorful sunsets.

Chapter 7

"Treaty 7 is the last of the numbered treaties made between the Government of Canada and the Plains First Nations peoples."

I could barely hear Dad's low rumble from the front of the car as he took the exit onto Highway 22 South. My head pounded and my eyelids refused to drop to block out the congested highway, the irate drivers, and Mom and Dad in the front seats trying to get us to focus on something other than the mayhem happening around our dust-covered station wagon. My neurologist told me I would continue to have headaches for a while but this was a new level; this was Jake pounding on his djembe, kind of throbbing, complete with a cymbal clang every few minutes.

"It was signed on September 22nd, 1877, and includes the five First Nations of the Siksika, or Blackfoot; Kainai, also known as the Blood Nation; Piikani, or Peigan; Stoney-Nakoda; and the Tsuut'ina, or Sarcee. If you remember your Grade 6 Social Studies ..."

Who remembers their Grade 6 Social Studies, Dad?

No one in this car, at least.

As Dad's low rumbling voice harmonized with Jake's djembe between my ears, Mom glanced over her shoulder, nodded, fished out a couple of ibuprofens from her purse and handed them back to me, with a rose-colored aluminum water bottle.

Chugging the headache pills with a gulp of warm tin-tasting water, I turned and saw Jake snoring into his balled-up Hitmen jacket, which was crumpled under his head by the window. He would remember his Grade 6 humanities classes on indigenous history in Alberta. I, on the other hand, had no clue.

Of course.

He was literally Dad's miniature replica with a stutter.

Then, again, you could have paid more attention in class.

Enough logic from you, brain! I'm not in the mood.

Dad paused, took a swig of his coffee thermos and gulped.

"Several years ago, the Anglican Diocese of Calgary approved of a church plant just outside Pincher Creek, under the direction of a Blackfoot female priest, which may not seem a big deal to you tadpoles, but to us ol' warty toads, it was momentous."

Mom punched his shoulder, "speak for yourself!"

Dad chuckled.

"I may be old but I definitely don't have warts."

"Anyhoo, Erin Stillwater has done remarkable things for the parish and I'm looking forward to seeing her again."

"Erin is one of my favorite people," Mom's smile touched her eyes and brought sparkle to the red-veined whites. "She's so *genuine*, not that other priests aren't, of course," her awkward wink at Dad making her look like a one-eyed pirate with a hook in his upper lip. "It's just that—oh, I don't know how to explain it."

"It's alright, hon," Dad chuckled, "it's hard to put someone's personality, their essence into words. Erin just meets people where they are and sees them for *who* they are. That's not an easy task in any profession but it is essential for a servant of God."

"How is the Anglican Church of the Holy Creator doing these days?"

"Quite well, I hear. She's a great one for community and for a church to grow, it needs community. I believe their congregation is about one to two hundred, which is remarkable given the apathy in society these days, and the retreat center is the jewel of the whole diocese."

"Yes, so many people have used the center, including Blackfoot elders. I hear they have language and cultural camps at the retreat almost every summer. Then, there are the diocese-led events. It was so lovely when we held women's and men's faith-building weekends there last year: The place is just so ..."

"Peaceful."

"Yes, peaceful. You can *feel* God's presence, which is what we really need right about now."

"You're not wrong there."

His words drifted through the car with the red rays from the rising Martian sun. As they continued their conversation about retreat weekends, parish councils, and outreach, my headache began to fade, leaving only extreme exhaustion and a burning desire for sleep. My eyelids drifted downward and then up in an elevator movement that blurred the red and orange hues floating through the car. They turned to flickering balls of light, lingering even behind my lids, as I slowly drifted into the void. I let sleep take me away from the lulling voices and the low hum of the engine; back to our house in Poplar Hills and my soft, welcoming bed.

Until a car horn honked and I was jolted awake, and back to reality.

Our house in the Calgary suburb was long behind us and despite moving at a snail's pace, we had moved. We were now near Bragg Creek on the highway known as Cowboy Trail. The nearby provincial park was ringed with motorhomes and vehicles pulling trailers—motorists who had pulled over to stretch legs and walk their dogs on the maze of trails peeking out from the evergreens growing around the perimeter. The dark green branches stretched wide in all directions, some twisted, others defeated. It was the first real glimpse of natural life I had had in years. Yes, there were sparse brown grasses everywhere but there was also green spruce needles resting atop the beige. Roots protruded from the cracked soil, bent and long, but clinging to soil. As we passed, I watched people sitting at picnic tables, drinking bottles of water and eating Proplant Bars, confections of pressed pea powder artificially flavored into a protein bar. Families with young children running around the peeling red table legs; seniors with tufts of white hair leaning over faded roadmaps spread out over the tops.

The children waved as we drove past.

I waved back.

And then, they too, were behind us.

Flanking the road were ranchlands, or what was left of them. More brown; more dust; more falling down fences; more empty fields.

Until we skirted the southern part of the Tsuut'ina Nation borderlands.

Despite the smoky haze, the rolling foothills erupted on our right from behind the vast, black, cracked fields as we drove. Broken down fences limped, disjointed rib cages cracked and hanging by wires stretched and spiked. Winds whisked dirt devils onto the parched topsoil, their spirals churning in mini-tornado formations across the abandoned farmland. The Rockies rose on our right in chiseled granite pyramids, their jagged peaks cupped the rising sun, holding it close before reluctantly releasing the orb into the red streaked sky. The gray peaks turned to silhouettes as the sun rose and with each bend, they brightened and emerged from the darkness, revealing their beauty. Void of snow caps and diminished glaciers, their stark edges cut through the sunrise as if slicing a fuzzy peach.

As Highway 22 curved southeast, dipping down on our way to Priddis, the Tsuut'ina lands changed. The parched earth was replaced with soft mounds of black topsoil from which tall grasses sprouted. I watched the stalks sway, mesmerized by the feather-like motion in the wind. The further we went the thicker the grasses until we were suddenly driving by fields of grain stretching to the now-blue sky, devoid of red haze and gray smoke.

We had left the bumper-to-bumper car line on Stoney Trail about an hour earlier, taking the Highway 16 exit and then Highway 22 South.

Stoney Trail had been gridlocked with cars, trucks, SUVs, motorhomes and semi-trailers—all escaping the rising radiation levels in the north. Cowboy Trail, however, was crowded but at least allowed us to move at a sick-dog's pace rather than a snail's. While Dad maneuvered patiently through the maze of taillights and honking horns, Jake and I spent the time in fits of sporadic sleep, while our protesting caged cat clawed on his prison door.

My neck was stiff, my legs stiffer and electrified with pins and needles.

And why on earth did I wear this Godforsaken binder?

I shifted, tugged at the gray fabric, sighed, tugged, shifted.

Repeat.

If sports bras were uncomfortable, binders were torture.

Dad, on the other hand, drove without fidgeting. There was no clicking of his thumb against the cruise control stick; nor tapping his fingers on the top of the steering wheel.

It felt … odd, as if he was a shadow: Still the same shape, the same presence, yet darker.

Mom sat in front of me in the front passenger seat, head pressed to the window as we rounded the bend.

I could hear her soft snoring whistles.

I shifted in my seat, trying to flow blood into my limbs.

Good thing we didn't take Dad's car. That would have been murder.

Jake stirred and pulled a fleece teddy bear blanket over his head.

"You awake?" Dad turned his head slightly to my seat, capturing mine in a two-second eye-lock.

"Yes, barely," I groaned, wishing I was snoozing like Jake and Mom.

"What's going on?" Mom stirred and directed her foggy tone to Dad. "Where are we?"

"Just going to turn on the radio, hon, and we are just passing Diamond Valley. We'll be in Longview in a half-hour, I think. We should get to the Highway 3 turnoff by about seven."

"I'm awake," she snorted in reply.

Dad smiled.

"Why not sleep?" he insisted, softly. "Sleep, hon. Being awake isn't all it's cracked up to be."

"Want me to drive?"

"No, that's OK. We should be there in a few hours."

Dad's mouth opened so wide that his upper lip almost touched the tip of his nose and his lower, his chest.

"You're spent," Mom breathed into his shoulder. "Pull over. I'll drive the rest of the way and you can nap."

"Alright, if you insist."

"I insist, and so does your poor, beady eyes."

Dad shook his head at the teasing, put on his signal light and slowed onto the shoulder.

A slow stream of vehicles passed us as he got out.

I watched him stretch his long arms to the sky, bend backward, pop a few backbones, twist, bend over and walk around the back of the car as Mom mimicked his actions on the other side.

Jealous, I stretched as much as possible under the seat in front of me— while I still could. The muscles in my calves and feet tightened from not being able to be extended in front of me, and the strangle-hold strip of fabric across my chest was making me agitated. My nerves were on fire, and I needed to move, to get out, to … be free of this torture. Could it get any worse?

As soon as Dad sat down in the passenger seat, he pushed it all the way back to make room for his legs and mine crumpled in front of me—knees bent up against the leather pouch that squeezed an empty box of orange-banana juice—that wasn't so empty after all and droplets of the orange liquid squirted from the white paper straw protruding from the pinprick hole at the top of the rectangular box.

It dribbled down the pouch and onto the knee of my jeans.

Mom sat in the driver's seat and pushed the button on the side to move it forward.

And just like that, Jake suddenly had all the legroom in the world, while I was a folded-up piece of fruit leather.

After adjusting the mirrors, Mom turned on the stereo, chose her Fantastic Fogies Folk playlist and merged back onto the highway, while the mumbling, throaty voice erupted from the speakers, singing about working on Maggie's Farm.

"Bob Dylan, really?" Dad groaned. "I didn't realize I married my grandmother."

"Now, now, Preacher Boy, enough of your sass!"

The bickering, like the snickering, was joyful, easy.

"Fine, Canadiana it is then! If your Nan listened to this stuff, she obviously had great taste—just like me."

"You got that right!"

More chuckling from the front.

How could they do it?

How could they compartmentalize what was going on and still enjoy this trip?

Sometimes, my parents annoyed the hell out of me.

While they chatted and chuckled, I had pins and needles in my calves.

Sighing, I scooched down as far as I could in my seat so that my butt was halfway to the edge, just so that my legs were as flat as possible to sneak under Dad's.

As Dad settled into his chair, leaning it back so it almost fell into my lap, soft, angelic sounds crooned from the stereo.

"Much better," he yawned. "Joni Mitchell. N-i-c-e."

Before Mom could retort, he let out a deep breath and fell asleep.

Must be nice to be so calm inside that sleep comes so quickly, so deep.

I agonized over it: willing myself to rest, to calm, to fade into dreamland.

In the end, it was usually out of pure exhaustion that my brain shut off.

But maybe Dad was keyed into something.

As Mom drove, I closed my eyes, again, and tried to focus on the piano, the voice, the lyrics.

I'm so hard to handle.
I'm selfish and I'm sad
Now, I've gone and lost the best baby
That I ever had
Oh, I wish I had a river I could skate away on
I wish I had a river so long
I would teach my feet to fly
I wish I had a river
I could skate away on
I made my baby say goodbye

Yeah, sounds about right.

As Joni sang, I skated.

My skates glided across the frosted-glass river, churning crystals up into the air around my blades. Snowflakes kissed the evergreens lining the banks and I stuck my tongue out to taste. They melted on impact, making my mouth cold. As my feet moved, frozen ripples moved under me. In the distance, I could hear a car engine moaning, thumping with the silver blades, and Dad softly snoring in front of me but for now …

For now, I let the river take me.

****

Mom's body was being wracked with sobs.

Her back shook as the heaving of her chest sent painful moans and cries into the steering wheel in front of her. Gone were the chuckles of the easy-going conversation with Dad; gone was the confidence, the calm. Instead, my mother crumpled and in my half-asleep state, fear gripped me in a vice.

Thank goodness, the car was stopped in traffic.

We were going nowhere, and that realization raised the hairs on my arms because we were stuck; wedged in between vehicles fleeing a catastrophe that kept on getting worse, no matter how much we prayed.

Dad's body contorted over the gearshift and console and his arms wrapped around Mom's chest, blanketing her in a comforting embrace I could almost feel.

Mom dissolved.

I sat behind Dad's seat, lightly scratching the knees of my denim pants, trying not to watch and finding it impossible to look away. The purple and orange hair elastic around my left wrist taunted me to lift and flick, to let me experience some of the pain seeping through my mother's body; to release it onto my skin instead of turning into a puddle myself. My fingers itched to pull and my nails itched to dig past the fibers of my pants and find the soft skin beneath.

"It'll be alright, Shel. We'll get there."

"And what will we find when we get there?"

Her voice cracked and heaved.

Dad leaned back and took a tissue to my mother's face, gently wiping away the tears.

"We'll find hope."

"I don't know, Pete," her head was turning side to side, red wisps flying around the headrest. "*Everything* is falling apart."

"Not everything." He smiled into my mother's face and tilted his head to the backseat where Jake and I sat. "We have each other."

"For how long? When we get on that train—*if* we get on that train, that'll be it. Jake and … Jules will be on their own. We won't even be seated with them. We won't even be in the same car."

Mom's voice rose as she spoke and the sobs came again.

Then what she said dawned on me.

Why wouldn't we be together?

Did they know something Jake and I didn't?

Obviously!

For starters, what's all this about a *train?*

"I'm sure they have their reasons to split us up."

"Well, I don't care. They are not good enough. They are taking families who have gone through hell to escape the aftermath of those terrorist attacks and now they want to break them apart? That's a sure-fire way of making them crack."

Dad was nodding.

"It's only rumors, hon," Dad's consoling voice levelled Mom's breathing. "What *exactly* did Eliza say when you spoke to her?"

"Mom said there was a caucus meeting yesterday in St. John's to discuss an evacuation train."

"So, where did she get all this about splitting families up?"

"Uncle Vernon."

"Just because your uncle is your parents' MLA, doesn't mean he's got the last word, you know. Only the premier can decide something like that."

"I know but Ma said Uncle Vernon said there's *a plan*. What kind of plan would do that, I ask ya? Not a good one, that's for sure, cause I'm not leaving my kids to fend for themselves—not now, not ever."

Hearing more anger than anguish in her voice, he sat back down into the passenger seat and rubbed the top of his bald head with his palm, a move he often resorted to when trying to make sense out of something.

Mom and I waited, our breath going in and out in a synchronized rhythm.

"Uncle Vernon said it was to prepare them for life at a resettlement base. I can't let that happen, Pete, I just can't."

"I know, love, but I'm sure if they do split us up, it's only temporary."

"You can't be sure of that. This may be the beginning. Who knows what they have planned for them, and where we'd fit in."

"Nothing is written in stone, yet, remember that. And … at least we'll be with your parents. That should occupy us."

Dad's mouth curled in a sardonic smile.

A small chuckle escaped Mom's lips.

"Yes, there's that," her breathing slowed to near normal. The car in front began to move and our station wagon rolled its tires a few meters before stopping again. Mom put the car in park and sighed. "I just wish Jules had chosen a better time to lay yet more things on our shoulders, you know? I'm so stressed about this whole evacuation thing and now, I'm walking on eggshells over our daughter's gender dysphoria."

I gulped.

She wasn't wrong.

I had chosen the worst possible time to come out to my parents; to myself. Could I have waited? Should I have just kept my big mouth shut and climbed into the car and slept the whole way like Jake, ignoring everything else, even the screaming voice in my head telling me that if I didn't announce who I really was, then it wasn't just a global radiation fallout that I was running away from, it was the contamination of my soul?

My finger found my kneecap and the nail peeled back the flesh.

"Love, I'm sure Jules would have liked to have sat us down and had a heart-to-heart over a cup of tea and a plate of chocolate chip cookies, but when would that have been possible? When would we have had their undivided attention? When would we have had the privacy for them to be honest, to find their courage?

"We are all freaking out, here, and trying to keep a calming presence for our kids' sake, and this was one more boulder on the pile of rocks on our chest, but when you finally realize who you are, it's hard to keep it bottled up for that *perfect* time, because that *perfect time* is never going to happen."

My left hand found my right and removed it from my scratched skin.

It squeezed the fingers tight, as my heart ached over what I was hearing from the front seat.

"You're right, of course."

Blowing her nose from tissues she pulled from the compartment in the console, she pushed the wad into the plastic bag hung on the gear shift and took a deep breath.

"It actually reminds me of when you announced you wanted to be a priest."

She was smiling, now, remembering something I wish I had been there to witness.

"Jules was clinging to the leg of my pants, her little toddler shoes on top of my feet, and she was swinging with my leg with each step as I carried Jakey on my hip to the changing table in the nursery."

Dad snickered. "I remember. You looked like you were a jungle gym."

"I sure felt like one."

The joy was back in her voice and for some reason, just hearing her ease into her normal state of control and peace made me feel more in control and at peace, too.

"You came home from your job at the university, barged through the front door and said, 'Shel, drop everything, I've made a decision.' Remember?"

"Yeah, and you looked at me as if I had grown three heads and said, 'Can this wait? I'm a little busy at the moment.'"

Dad's laughter filled the car and Mom tried to shush him.

It percolated inside me, pushing aside my anxious thoughts as I visualized the scene being described, and felt the humor and similarities.

"And then I said, emphatically ..."

"You mean, loudly."

"Yes, smarty-pants, *loudly,* that I wanted to be a priest."

"And I said, 'God help us'."

"Well, let's apply that same response to Jules's big announcement and see where it takes us."

Dad's head was tilted to the side, silently urging Mom to agree.

I gripped the elastic around my wrist, fingering the fuzzy material, stroking the band and trying to will myself to let go or flick. My chosen action all depended on the rounded shoulders of my mother, who was currently staring into the brake lights of a yellow Volvo. As I struggled to slow down my rapidly beating heart, I watched for any change in the woman who had given me the confidence to speak up, to assert myself even if my views were not mainstream—wasn't that who *she* was, deep down? Wasn't that how she came to be such a powerhouse in the financial world before giving it all up to be a stay-at-home Mom and church ministry head?

C'mon, Mom!

And just like that, her neck bent in a nod, her shoulder muscles relaxed and drooped and a long sigh escaped her pursed lips.

"I think they already are." Her voice, barely above a whisper, oozed out of her body with the sigh in one long breath. "I mean, I'd be blind to not see how much more relaxed they are around us, and it's only been a few hours."

"You're not wrong there."

"So, maybe this is a good thing?"

"Hon, I think anytime a teenager is *honest* with their parents and admits to them, and themselves, their deepest, darkest secret, it's a good thing, don't you?"

My heart slowed, but my chin began to tremble.

"A lot happens when your worst fears of rejection are instead met with acceptance, not the least of which is the confidence to break down a few walls built to protect you from the hurt you expected."

"So, you don't think this is a phase?"

The Volvo pulled out of the lane and passed a red pickup truck in front of it, leaving our station wagon to idle behind yet another set of taillights. Mom glanced over at Dad. I could almost see her desire for him to admit my trans-fluidness was just a blip but instead, he was shaking his head.

"Honestly, Shel, does it matter? If you stopped and thought about it, you'd have to admit to yourself that Julia has been Jules for years, and in my book, that's no phase; that's life."

It was Mom's turn to nod her head and while I watched, my gaze transfixed on the profile of her face, tears began to slide down her flushed cheeks. I could feel them; taste their salt on my own lips. I could see the hurt, the realization of the truth behind Dad's words, and the disappointment. It was all there.

Then, they were gone. While I was sliding my hand over my own cheek, Mom was mirroring my actions, wiping away the pain and revealing a face of…

"I know. I guess I'll just have to dream some new dreams for them, that's all."

I heard the catch, the ache in her throat, the uncertainty, the fear.

Same, Mom, same.

As Mom drove and Dad held her hand, talking reassuringly into the dimly lit car, my firing nerves doused. What dreams do I have for myself?

I didn't have a clue.

Mom's fear over my future was echoed in my own head and I wanted to reassure her, and me, but with what? I *hoped* I had passed my finals and graduated but what exactly did that change? Did I want to go to college, university? And what the heck did it matter when the world was in chaos? Were schools even open? Did any of that stuff even matter anymore?

You could make toys. Remember those Barbies?

How could I forget? One was poking its chopped off head of hair up from the mesh water-bottle pouch on the side of my backpack, staring me down with blue eyes faded from too much nail-polish remover. Slipping it out of the black netted sleeve, I admired my handiwork—the lack of makeup, the gray tape that stuck to the chest, the tan cargo pants topped with a tan twill skirt cinched at the waist, slit in the front, exposing the pants.

Was this me?

Ambiguous?

Undefined?

Holding Androgynous Alex in the palm of my hand, I turned my head to the window and rested my hot, now wet cheek against the cool glass, and let my mind wander and slip—away from the questions that plagued me.

"Jules, you awake?"

"I am now."

The sun left its peek-a-boo spot behind the mountains and began to climb and all around me, a yellow-pink glow was rising over the tops of fields of grain and filling the inside of the station wagon with rainbow light.

I felt as if I had sunk into a cotton candy cloud.

"Shoot, sorry!"

"No prob. I was just catnapping, and I would have woken up soon anyway."

Sleep and I had a rocky relationship, even before the car ride from hell.

Between the anti-anxiety and depression meds, I often only slept in spurts, waking with every movement or sound. "We'll find the right balance," Ali Cameron had said after I spent a month of conking out for twelve straight hours, so dead Mom and Dad had to shake me to get the cobwebs out of my head.

And that was before laying a ten-ton gender brick onto the rubble.

Balance was as elusive for me in Dreamland as it was in Awakeland, I guess.

I stretched my arms above my head, wincing as the binder clung to the skin around my armpits as if it was a piece of duct tape.

"OK, I'm going to turn on the radio to get a news report," Dad tapped on a few buttons on the stereo display screen until Mom's folk playlist was turned off and the radio stations were displayed. "I don't want Jake to hear the news and get upset. Not after last night. Understand?"

I nodded.

As I watched both of them move—Mom weaving in and out of traffic and Dad fidgeting with the stereo—I marveled at their ability to break down and then move on as if nothing had happened. Were they still upset over my trans-fluidness? Were they still freaking out over the What If's of my life? Did they still think their daughter was dead?

If they were, there was no indication.

They carried on as if their conversation had been locked up in a parent vault.

Safe.

Never to be opened again.

Dad finally found a station in the queue and tapped.

An ad proclaiming Charcoal Best was the No. 1 toothpaste for tartar control and whitening was playing, with a *dentist* talking to a woman with cotton balls in her mouth. The ad ended with a jingle: "Charcoal Best, the best toothpaste any mouth can attest."

"And now for the 7 a.m. news update: Thousands of Calgarians are fleeing the city after yesterday's small-modular reactor explosions caused several fires to erupt at the nearby Calgary International Airport and surrounding dry grasslands. The closed airport is under armed security as personnel try to assess the damage caused by the destruction of several of its planes on the northeast tarmac and runways. According to the Calgary and Rocky View County Fire Departments, there is now a 100-hectare grassfire burning between Calgary, Balzac and Kathryn. Residents in those rural towns joined their Calgarian neighbors in fleeing their homes in the early morning hours, as the fire gained ground and news of radiation leaks at the SMR facility surfaced."

"Shiit … take mushrooms."

Dad swiveled in my direction, sighed, shook his bald, shining head, too exhausted to say 'language.'

My mind said it anyway. Funny how you decide one morning to fall into line with the 'no cursing' rule by creating new ones with funny food names and then they become curses, too.

"Sorry," I grumbled and yawned.

"The mass exodus from the affected areas has caused traffic jams all over the city, especially routes leading south."

No kidding.

Mom was currently parked behind a white pickup truck with the license plate, *oil spoiled*, going nowhere.

"Radiation alerts from other urban centers are coming fast and furious this morning, following the rupture of the SMR containment backups. In Northern Alberta, Fort McMurray, Fort Chipewyan, Anzac and parts of Athabasca have also been issued evacuation orders."

"Shiitake mushrooms."

"Jules," Dad sighed. "Enough with the shrooms. Just listen."

The radio announcer continued: "Christian Conservative Party Leader and Premier Darrell Kelly made this statement during a live news conference an hour ago.…"

The newscaster paused. There was the squeal of feedback, followed by static and then a shuffling noise around a microphone filled the station wagon.

"My fellow Albertans, your political leaders mourn your loss and share your trepidations. This attack on Canadian soil—on Alberta soil—came without warning and without prejudice."

Ah, I don't really know about that. I mean, how much more prejudiced can you be than to blow up nuclear reactors throughout the globe in the name of environmental protection?

"We join our countrymen in responding to this act of terror; this show of cowardice, destruction and hate. We join our global neighbors in containing the effects of those attacks and protecting its citizens. And we join other nations in fighting back and reclaiming and protecting our resources, and our lands from these … terrorists, that I vow, as your chosen representative of this great province."

After his speech, there followed a round of questions from reporters but very few answers. Premier Kelly dodged, speculated, promised retaliation, rebuilding, and protection without any real plans as to how he was going to accomplish those goals.

Typical.

"In national news, Prime Minister Jacqueline LeBlanc has scheduled a news conference for 9 a.m. this morning with the Minister of Defense and Security, Hon. Mohammad Sawhney, and International Affairs Minister, Hon. Mark Chong, so stay tuned."

"I wonder what they are going to say," Mom's voice rose from behind the steering wheel being grasped by her tight, white knuckles.

"Not much they can say. You can't go to war against an environmental group, even if they are terrorists. They could have members anywhere, in any city, in any town."

"You're right, of course, but these are politicians we are talking about. People will want to see action," Mom pulled the car into the passing lane, accelerating past the semi-truck and took the exit for Highway 3, the Crowsnest Highway.

"And that's what I'm afraid of."

Dad's face looked grim.

"In international news, at 5 a.m. Pacific Standard Time, California was placed on high alert. Senator Alex Ryan announced that following the blasts that destroyed the state's 22 small modular reactors yesterday, scientists at the University of California have declared the already unstable San Andreas Fault was further compromised," a voice said to the car, breaking the manufactured tranquility. "Correspondent Gabe Bloom has that report."

I sat up straight and rubbed any residual sleep from my eyes, as if it would open my ears better.

"The SMR explosions mirror those that happened in neighboring states all up along the eastern seaboard—Tennessee, Oregon and Washington—and on the west coast—from Louisiana and Florida to the Carolinas," the husky voice explained. "All the way to Maine.

"To recap, the June twenty-first ecoterrorism attack at the hands of the group known only as Terra Nova, targeted the state's small modular reactor facilities in a mammoth-scale terrorist attack that can only be described as catastrophic. In Oregon, two SMR facilities were likewise destroyed, and Washington's Cedar Sky SMR facility in Olympia is now buried 158 feet below sea level.

"In California, the initial blasts caused medium-sized earthquakes in the 4.9- to 5.6-magnitude range. However, the U.S. Geological Department has placed the state on high alert, as tremors continue to shake cities and towns that lie in the path of the California fault system. If these quakes continue, and their intensity increases, department officials warn the result could permanently change the U.S. coastline."

The truck in front of us shot out black smoke from the exhaust pipe, and its double wheels began to roll forward. Mom followed. We were moving slowly, but moving still the same.

"Let's hope we get there soon," Mom turned to Dad. "When is Erin expecting us?"

"Anytime. I didn't give her a specific timeframe and she didn't ask. I think we both knew our journey was in God's hands and we will get there when we get there, and not before."

Wise words, *Father.*

Gabe Bloom continued her report on the radio: "Joining me now, in the NSX studio, is Dr. Sarah O'Hearn, science adviser for the U.S. Geological

Survey Department in Pasadena, on what that would mean for the state and its 40 million residents.

"Welcome, Dr. O'Hearn."

"Thank you, Gabe," replied a breathless voice from the stereo.

Mom's grip on the steering wheel tightened, something I didn't think was possible. Dad began flicking his nail against the air vent on the dashboard.

I stole a glance at Jake, who was beginning to stir. His sockless foot was protruding from the fleece blanket and touching my thigh.

I reached out and tickled the sole with my finger, smiling as I did so.

His foot shot back under the blanket, he groaned and turned so that his warm cheek was squished up against the glass of his door.

"Jules," he moaned, "stop. Mom … tell them to stop."

Even in his half-asleep state, Jake remembered the correct pronoun.

Got to give him credit for that, I guess.

"Jules, stop bothering your brother."

From the speakers: "Can you tell our viewers and listeners at our sister radio stations, Ms. O'Hearn, the ramifications of high-intensity earthquakes will have on the State of California and what precautions residents should take to be prepared for the worst."

"Shhhhhhh!" Mom hissed over her shoulder at, well, at me, since Jake had fallen back to sleep.

Lucky duck.

So oblivious to what was going on around him; so at peace with himself that sleeping came naturally.

I was jealous of Jake for a lot of things, I realize now, but his general ability to float when all I felt like doing was sink was the greatest. Maybe, he could teach me some day to go with the tide, rather than fight it, but for that to happen, I actually needed to let him in, to be friends, instead of always feeling like he was the Golden Child—the one with the least amount of problems so got the most amount of love from my parents.

They do love you. Look how accepting they are!

Wouldn't it be ironic if by coming out as transfluid, I had actually *lived up to my parents' expectations and made them proud?*

"Primarily, we at the U.S. Geological Survey Department, would like to advise people living along the fault line to prepare for evacuation. At this stage, these are precautionary measures. We, of course, don't want undue panic to ensue but it is better to be safe than sorry."

The woman's voice was getting stronger.

"Can you tell us how we got to this stage of monitoring and worst-case-scenario precaution planning?"

"Well, Ms. Bloom, as many of your viewers—and listeners—may be aware, the San Andreas is classified as a transform fault, whereby it is the sliding boundary between the Pacific and the North American Plate. It essentially slices California in two, from Cape Mendocino to the Mexican border," she said. "San Diego, Los Angeles and the Big Sur are on the Pacific Plate and San Francisco, Sacramento and the Sierra Nevada are on the North American Plate."

"And what effect has the recent small nuclear reactor explosions had on the fault?"

"They crack me up," I piped in.

"Jules…" Mom and Dad hissed in unison.

"Sorry," I mumbled, "just trying to ease tension, here."

"I know, honey, but humor has its place, and this isn't it," Dad replied, reaching back and tapping my knee with his hand. "Great pun, though."

I snickered, leaning forward to listen better and nearly colliding with Dad's head.

He turned around to face the windshield.

"The explosions are causing fissures in the plates along the San Andreas."

"How big are these fissures?"

"Currently, they are still relatively small but, in our monitoring, we have recorded movements; shifts, if you will, that threaten to create much larger fissures if these quakes intensify."

"But California has a history of its fair share of quakes. How is this any different?"

"You are correct, the plates are slowly moving past one another at a couple of inches each year," she said, "at about the same rate that your fingernails grow. This movement has been happening for years. The problem is when something interferes with the movement."

"Such as the cracks caused by the nuclear explosions?"

Dad turned and gave me a lopsided grin that obviously said, *'insert crack jokes here.'*

And mentally, I complied.

"Yes, precisely, Ms. Bloom. Some years, the plates don't move at all, and when the strain builds to the breaking point, the rock along the fault line breaks and the plates can shift a few feet, causing massive waves in the earth, which we feel as earthquakes."

"How often has this happened in California's history?"

"The most detrimental example of this is during the legendary 1906 earthquake in San Francisco, which happened on April 18, and killed approximately 3,000 people and destroyed more than 80 percent of the city."

"And what magnitude was that quake?"

"It was a 7.8. California often gets earthquakes in the high sixes, but when you venture into the sevens and eights, you are getting into the high-intensity quakes that cause exponential damage to cities and residential safety, putting lives at risk."

"So, what kind of magnitude quakes are your department anticipating: 7.5, 7.8, 8?"

There was a pause on the radio and static crept into the interview.

Dad's flicking intensified.

Mom put her hand over his to still his nails from connecting with the plastic, protruding blades.

He stopped, and covered her hand with his other.

As I watched, they began holding hands across the console between them.

Tears were streaming down Mom's red cheeks and Dad lifted his hand and brushed them away.

No words. No sounds.

I could feel their nervousness enter my own body.

Mom's breath sucked into her chest, and I leaned forward between the two front seats to catch the doctor's response, which was taking what seemed like an eternity.

Dr. O'Hearn cleared her throat.

"We, at the department of geological survey for the United States of America, project that California will be hit with multiple quakes in the coming weeks, all in the 9.2- to 9.8-magnitude range."

Dust mites floated up from the dash, only to be blown by the air-conditioning vents to the driver's side window where Mom's head once rested.

Inside the car, it felt like time stood still.

Jake shifted and coughed.

"Ah, Dad, aren't there fault lines in Canada?"

"Yes, Jules, there are—in British Columbia, known as the Pacific Ring of Fire."

"Do you think Uncle Tim and them will be OK?"

Silence.

"I'm sure your brother and his family will be just fine, Pete."

She had traded her Mom in Shock hat for a Mom in Support one, and having something to do seemed to have changed her focus enough to stop the floodgates. "Knowing Sydney, she and the kids are putting their earthquake drills to good use. I never knew of anyone who took emergencies as seriously as Syd."

Dad turned to her and I watched his Adam's apple slide up and down as he swallowed.

"God be with them."

"Amen to that," Mom breathed.

Holy crap.

Dad's fingers found the air vents and began flicking his nails against the slanted pieces of plastic.

On the radio, the news report continued, as Dad's flicking intensified.

"An earthquake in the nine-magnitude range would, therefore, be classified as a maximum Mercalli intensity of XI, or extreme," O'Hearn continued. "The result of which would be fissures like we've never seen before, causing sections of the land to separate and fires where there were utilities and gas lines line the earth above and below ground. Given the dryness of California at this time of year, we will see wildfires take hold and the destruction to the land and all who live on it will be unlike any we have ever witnessed in any age.

"In short, Ms. Bloom, if we at the department are correct, we are NOT talking about quakes that topple cities. We are talking about the fall of California itself."

"Shit," Mom hissed and then just as quickly, "sorry."

Dad reached over and held her hand in a vice.

I stared at the interaction.

Mom shook his hand off hers and turned off the radio.

She reached over the console, grabbed the plastic grocery bag wrapped around the gearshift and fished out an old Tim Horton's coffee cup, and promptly threw up.

Same.

Chapter 8

As we drove, the news anchors injected the station wagon with truths that made us all cringe. We sat in silence, listening to the voices emitted from the speakers, to Shade purring in his crate, to Jake snoring in the backseat.

Nothing seemed real.

In fact, if it wasn't for the snorts and vocal vibrations, I would have thought I was dreaming and that I would soon wake from this nightmare, but having those grounding noises mingle with the shocking reports made them all the more real.

As I listened, my own fears about what people would think about my trans-fluid identity faded behind a wall of apprehension over how we could ever believe we could escape this devastation.

We couldn't.

The news anchors knew that.

Now, the Klassens did, too.

There must be more out there; more encouraging news to cling to amid all this blah, blah, blah, mass destruction, blah, blah, blah, the world is going to end crap.

I turned to my phone, opened a browser app and began searching to try and figure out how the heck we got in this mess in the first place, and immediately regretted it.

Sometimes, it is what it is.

Plain and simple.

****

(SPECIAL REPORT) June 22nd, 2042—As millions evacuate cities across North America in the wake of the June 21st worldwide terrorist attack on small modular reactor facilities by the extremist environmental group, Terra

Nova, many are wondering how such an attack could happen in the age of cyber security.

The answer to that quandary begins with understanding why nations chose to turn to nuclear power to begin with: necessity.

As oil and gas reserves around the globe failed to attract investment from either shareholders or government coffers, the need to find an alternative fuel source was dire. Fossil-fuel projects were being turned down by energy boards due to their unsustainable and greenhouse-gas emission limitations and renewables such as wind, solar and hydro were being bombarded with the effects of climate change.

U.S. National Weather Centre meteorologist Sanal Kumar explains: "The rising temperatures around the globe brought heat wave after heat wave; wildfire after wildfire; melting glaciers and icecaps. This created smoke, which blocked evaporation and precipitation. You know what happens when it doesn't rain? You got it, we have droughts."

The lack of moisture dried up farmers' fields, even those growing biofuels, she added while being interviewed by NSX News anchor Gabe Bloom during a televised interview that aired April 10.

"These droughts lowered water levels in rivers and lakes, so gone, too were the hydro energy facilities because now the Great Lakes were needed for people more than power generation.

"Worldwide droughts also meant the erosion of topsoil and dust particles entered the atmosphere, which in turn blocked the sun, even to the solar plants and panels on peoples' homes. The only areas not affected by the climate change now known globally as The Climate Crisis of 2030 or the Dirty '30s, were those that had managed to shield themselves from these effects."

Kumar said the *Dirty '30s* moniker gives homage to the original Dust Bowl of the 1930s, which swept across the Midwest and Southern Great Plains and lasted a decade, bringing dust storms much like the ones now experienced in North America.

During the interview, Kumar told Bloom that unlike The Dust Bowl of the 1930s, the more recent Dirty '30s wasn't as widespread because many municipalities had previously instituted recovery measures to sustain their livelihoods, such as high-intensity magnetic fields around their lands to repel the smoke and dust particles, in addition to not relying on fossil fuels within their environments for power and energy and instead choosing non-emission alternatives.

"In the end, only those areas were spared. The rest of us, we were—pardon my French—screwed."

As a result, nations turned to their respective energy think tanks and the experts that have been promoting nuclear energy as the only non-emission alternative to address the demands of large populations.

"According to the forecasts from the International Energy Agency, global demand for electricity was expected to grow 70 per cent from 2012 to 2035, with most of the predominant users hailing from China and India, which is why those countries followed the U.S.'s lead to approve SMR licenses," said Dr. Philip Morton, chairman of the U.S. Nuclear Regulatory Committee, in a May 17th interview with Calgary Tribune journalist, Doug Faulkner from the Canadian daily newspaper located in Calgary, Alberta.

When asked about the decision to turn to nuclear power amid depleting oil reserves, he said the move to SMR power was not one that was made lightly.

"Ideally, alternative energies would be enough, but they are not. If we were to build enough wind turbines for our electricity needs, for example, we would do away with much-needed farmland for crops and cattle production," he explained. "As the world grows, its mouths grow with it. Consumption, whether it is fuel or food, has skyrocketed in the past decade. Due to the carbon dioxide emissions from fossil fuels, the NRC met in January 2012 to discuss solutions. Although uranium was taken off the table after Three Mile Island, there are still proponents in the industry that tout its benefits, the top reason for uranium was that it was, and still is, the cleanest and most environmentally sound fuel source—and it can be made, not mined."

The U.S. Nuclear Regulatory Committee approved the first two modular reactors in February of 2012.

"The first two SMRs were built right here in Georgia: one in Augusta and the other, a twin-unit plant, in South Carolina," Morton added. "These mini nuclear plants were built in tandem with other SMRs throughout the U.S., as part of Congress's commitment to energy production. Others followed, of course, but, yes, these two were the first."

When asked if the storage facilities were safe, Morton said safety has always been the committee's top priority, "which is why it took so long to act upon the initial recommendations."

"What Americans need to know is that these explosions were not caused by any faults in the reactors. It wasn't a production or human error. They were caused by acts of terrorism."

The small modular reactors, each with a capacity of reaching up to 300 megawatts, can supply power to 45,000 homes.

"If you build two or three in tandem, on site, then you have enough power to supply an entire city, which is why they were located on the outskirts of urban areas," he explained. "As for the location near waterways, the reactors are buried deep within the ground, which would lessen the chance of tampering."

In order to place them in the ground, however, the soil needed to be pliable and not in areas where there is a high concentration of bedrock, which rules out mountainous or rocky terrain.

"In our estimation, these were the most secure production facilities on the planet," Morton stressed. "The reactors were standardized builds, meaning they were all fabricated in an undisclosed facility to set plans to reduce tampering. They could be taken offline for maintenance, repairs and replacement without the service being interrupted, and they didn't need all the traditional operations personnel on hand at large-scale nuclear reactors, which limited the clearances required."

In May, the United States Energy Federation gave regulatory approval for White Sands Nuclear Energy to, in effect, be the sole security and maintenance operator for several SMR facilities in North America, Europe and Asia. This led to the outsourcing of security and maintenance operations management to White Sands.

Asked if this made White Sands a target for terrorism, Morton declined to comment, saying only that the facility had extensive firewalls in place to prevent such an attack should one occur.

Forty-six cities were destroyed by these so-called safe, mini nuclear reactors and thousands of acres have become uninhabitable. This is in addition to the increasing radiation radius on the outskirts of these cities, which can no longer sustain life, and in fact, will be quarantined in the coming days. To date, there are 6.8 million dead, not to mention the millions more suffering from radiation exposure in medical facilities, and scores more that will fall to contaminated water supplies.

"We are living in an evolving world in transition," Kumar said. "From land masses to air quality, to changing global climates, we are in a state of flux. When ocean temperatures began rising in the 2020s, we knew what to expect because we have historic data to apply so we can generate speculative outcomes. But there are no studies, no past records, or historical events that can help us predict the total global ramifications of the SMR fallout. We must deal with each resulting catastrophe as it happens, rather than plan for outcomes and implement preventative actions."

The Unknown Factor has plagued governments and think tanks for the past 24 hours, and it will continue to upset the prediction apple cart in the days ahead, the NWC's meteorologist acknowledged.

"What we do know, however, is that change is upon us and what that change looks like could reshape not only our domestic realities but the planet itself, and we, as a species, can either adapt or we expire."

Chapter 9

Chief Mountain had grown.

It rose from the range in a tall, rectangular jagged-topped peak streaked with white striations that wound around the midsection of the mountain like a belt. Around the base were green foothills.

Green foothills.

I blinked to see if I was seeing things; had imagined the lush ground but I had not.

As the car tilted with each bend, the wind farms came into view: row upon row of white turbines that dotted the rolling hills like grave markers in a cemetery. The long blades slowly moved in circles as the wind picked up, making whistling sounds in the interior of the vehicle.

The air wasn't as pink here, or as hazy hot.

Was it my imagination, but was the sun more yellow, too?

I rolled down the window just as Jake was moaning himself awake.

The breeze whisked up more dust inside than out.

"Where are we?" Jake moaned.

"Who the h-e-double-hockey-sticks knows," I muttered, groggy from a lack of sleep. "We're definitely not in Kansas anymore."

"We were in Kansas?" Jake was incredulous.

I shook my head and snickered: "No, *genius*, we didn't drive to the U.S., although we could have, considering how long it took us to get here, wherever *here* is."

"About 20 kilometers west of Pincher Creek," Mom's head lifted up and stared at us through the rearview mirror. "Almost there, kiddos."

Dad was strumming on the console, a tune I vaguely remembered.

Bum.

Bum, bum, bum.

Bum, bum, bum.

Really, Dad?

I turned away and stuck my head out the window, letting the breeze whisk up my spiked locks and caress my shaven nape.

It did feel good, though.

It felt *clean.*

"I've been inclined," Dad sang, tapping in rhythm. "To believe they never would. But now, I look at the night and it doesn't seem so lonely."

"We filled it up with only two," Mom's whisper interjected. "And when I hurt, hurting runs off my shoulders. How can I hurt when holding you?"

Dad turned to her and smiled.

Was that what love looked like in the face of uncertainty?

It was sweet, and comforting.

"One, touching one," he continued and winked at Mom. "Reaching out; touching me, touching you."

Ewooooo.

"Gross, Dad."

He poked his head between the seats and grinned.

Jake giggled.

And then we all chimed in, because we needed to be a part of it, too.

"Sweet Caroline," we hollered into the cabin. "Bum, bum, ba!"

"Good times never seemed so good. I've been inclined. Bum, bum, ba! To believe they never would."

Our voices lifted and the joy spread from lips to lips, smile to smile, thump to thump until we had forgotten we were sad, afraid, full of anguish.

Only Neil Diamond could do that.

And Dad.

"Brocket is that way."

"But we aren't going to Brocket, are we?" Mom asked.

"Nope! We are headed to the Church of the Holy Creator's Retreat Centre just outside of Pincher Creek, so watch for a small little range road sign up ahead."

Dad had interrupted his drum solo on the dashboard to announce to the car, and caused me to jump, knocking my head into the handle near the ceiling.

"Pastor Stillwater's church is adjacent to the center, but it's off the beaten path a bit."

On either side of the road, tall green stalks grew about three feet high, with bushy tails that wagged golden in the sunlight. Long, narrow leaves protruded from the stalks, tinged with brown, burnt and dry at the ends. They stood in fields of cracked, dusty earth, with pole markers on the row ends and above, twine stretching from one end of the row to the other, secured to another pole. Blue and red streamers were pinned to the twine with clothespins.

"Sorghum," Dad said, noticing Jake and me staring out the window. "It's an ancient grass that grows well in drought conditions."

As we drove, the fields of grass grew.

"Beautiful, isn't it?" looking out the window in astonishment, Dad exclaimed, "I never thought I'd see such a sight ever again."

"How are they able to grow fields of it here?"

Turning to Mom, he smiled: "Well, believe it or not, it started in California years ago, when the state began having the same agricultural changes as we are having now. The bread we eat, this is where it comes from."

Curiosity had taken hold.

I was leaning between the front seats, again, trying to figure out what the rows upon rows of tall, drooping stalks were growing on the adjacent fields. The broad, narrow pale green leaves protruding from the thick stalks were tinged with brown. The tips of the stalks were narrow and bushy, as if they were the tails of a Golden Retriever.

Crystal had a Golden Retriever.

His name was Maxwell House.

Funny how I hadn't really thought about Crystal in months. She was once all I could think about but now, her warm creamy complexion rarely crossed my mind. Before the wrestling tournament that lit a fire to everything in my life, I was obsessed. I dreamed about her big brown eyes with their sooty lashes, her bare, soft shoulders as they rose to cheer our team on, and the rivers of flowing brown hair that were so thick and soft, if I closed my eyes, I could drown in their currents. The showdown in front of Stampede High messed that up, however. The scent of lime and coconut no longer brought me back to her arms, and to our first kiss.

It was all gone, somehow. Like the school, like my friends, like my life.

Hidden away in a vault much like the one my parents kept for serious conversations.

Locked up so tight, yet all it took was a turn of a key, and the demons would be free.

Was that what the Gender Appropriation Division Camp was like?

One big vault to lock away all the feelings and desires you had to be something other than binary? Did they teach her how to deny her thoughts, her feelings so that she could forget who she was so she didn't go ape-shit crazy trying to fit in?

No, smarty-pants, they probably used electric shocks to do that.

Don't kid yourself, Jules. This was nothing like what Crystal was going through.

I had my family supporting me.

Crystal had no one.

Was she still there, or did she get evacuated?

Hmm. Let's see. What's more important: conversion therapy treatments to get rid of the gay in someone OR save their life? Decisions, decisions.

Turning to my parents, who sat chatting about how there was no such thing as good '42 folk tunes, that "all the best music was produced in the 1960s, '70s, and '80s."

They didn't seem hung up on the items shoved into their parent vault; far from it, really.

They seemed like themselves: Teasing and joyfully bickering about trivial things—the same as they have always done.

So, did that mean they *really* accepted me?

Did it matter?

Did any of it matter, anymore?

My eyes squinted at the golden tails swaying in the hot wind.

Crystal mattered.
She mattered a lot.

"Broomcorn, that's what many people call sorghum," Dad was saying. "Believe it or not, it was used to make brooms and brushes and now? Now, *this* is where we get our grain for flour and those buns on the fake burgers you eat, Jules."

"Those veggie burgers aren't half bad, actually," I countered from between the seats, pulling on Dad's sleeve, "and you seem to like them enough come barbecue season."

"That I do! Barbecue sauce can make any patty palatable, especially when the main ingredient is habanero peppers."

"You and your hot peppers," Mom's head was shaking as she chuckled. "You'll get an ulcer one of these days."

"Well, if that's the only thing I have to worry about when all *this*," he waved to the windows of the car, "is going on, I think I'm good."

The car ventured off onto the road, the wheels rising on its axles as it went over an uneven patch of asphalt.

"Before the droughts, sorghum was just used to feed cattle and livestock but in India, Africa and China, it was a main part of peoples' diets because it's resistant to drought and heat. In Canada, we use it for porridge, flatbreads and cakes. It's actually quite nutritious."

I could feel Mom roll her eyes—her head often rolled, too, which was a dead giveaway—and I snickered to myself knowing the expression she was giving Dad, without actually seeing it.

"You can take the professor out of the university but you can't take the university out of the professor," Mom groaned, and received a wink and a large grin in reply.

"Those degrees should come in handy once and a while, and not just when I'm writing sermons."

As we bumped over a mishmash of broken asphalt and gravel, the crops grew closer to the road, as the shoulders dropped off into the fields.

Mom looked at me through the rearview mirror and smiled, as if to say, *'I know, I know. He's a know-it-all but I love him anyway.'*

Dad, on the other hand, was oblivious.

"Grandpa Ron tried growing sorghum about 30 years ago on the family farm outside of Strathmore but by then, the lack of rainfalls had made the fields too dry for the crop to take."

"Is that when he sold the farm?"

Mom's query was met with a nod from dad: "Not long after. He tried planting summer fallow to keep the topsoil intact but when we started getting 80- to 100-kilometre winds on a regular basis, the crops didn't stand a chance.

"A farm isn't a farm if you can't grow crops. By then, it was just a field of dust and dirt."

Beside me, Jake dug his naked toes into my thigh and I pushed his foot away.

He stirred, sat upright—eyes still closed—and began snoring again.

Jeez Louise.

"Erin has family in Brocket. That's where her dad's family lived before he moved to Pincher Creek. She still has cousins there, I believe, so maybe we'll meet some of them. I'm actually looking forward to meeting her famous sister, Irene."

"Famous?" Mom quickly glanced at Dad and then maneuvered the car around a pothole.

"Well, she's the chief of the Piikani Nation and has been pretty outspoken about what the province has been doing with its natural resources. Seeing this here … I don't blame her."

We drove, the broomcorn swayed.

I was mesmerized by their movement in the breeze, how the sun's yellow-pink light reflected on the stalks, made the white, waxy leaves glow and reflect the rays.

Here, the red hue wasn't as dark, the heat wasn't as hot.

As we headed south onto Highway 6, the Pincher Creek Station emerged from the grassy field on the left and more sorghum fields on the right. The elongated, single-story building was framed in black and painted a scarlet red. It was at least the length of Stampede High, maybe even longer, and on its roof were shiny rectangular square panels capturing the sunlight. Beside it was the track, which stretched west to east. A train was sitting on the tracks, snaking around the tall, pale green grain elevator with faded white peaked roof and washed-out Pincher Creek lettering on the front. Beside the elevator were tall aluminum cylindrical silos, one of which had a long silver arm stretching across the track and tilted downward over a hole in the roof of the first car in a long line of railcars waiting to be filled with broomcorn kernels. As the grain shot down the aluminum slide and into the car, men with safety vests checked the underbellies of the cars behind it, waiting to be filled. Painted black with red and white upside-down triangles, the railcars were emblazoned with an Alberta Grown label in white along the side. Crammed graphic letters outlined with yellow, white and red were graffitied along several of the cars, spray-painted over the logos—some tags, others slogans. The one that caught my eye was just four letters: black and outlined with white. 'LIVE'

"I wonder where it is all going."

My face was pressed to the window, and my brain was trying to count all the cars but was too sleep-deprived to keep track of where I left off, so had to keep recounting from the beginning.

"Everywhere," Mom's voice sounded tired, as if it took every ounce of strength in her body to form the words and give them sound. "Farmers in these parts feed the nation, Jules, even if we don't see much of it ourselves."

"Why is that?"

"Because we're not millionaires," Dad coughed and took a swig from one of the water bottles Mom had packed. "Where crops are shipped depends on a lot of things, not the least of which is where the politicians who give you grant and start-up money live. There is a lot that stays in Alberta but for the most part, the cash is coming from the federal government, which is why a lot of those cars are destined for Ontario."

"Alberta is the Breadbasket of Canada."

"That would be Saskatchewan," Dad corrected Mom. "This here is more like … the Bread Bowl. Saskatchewan still produces a lot of grain; they just can't feed all the provinces all by their lonesome, what with Alberta and British Columbia's fields being nothing but clay and dirt, and they also ship a lot overseas because that's where they get the majority of their sales, from developed countries with money but no agricultural food chain."

As we passed the operation, Dad broke through the sounds of squealing wheels and machinery with a loud, full-bodied yawn.

His mouth opened so wide that his chin dipped down his neck, nearly touching his chest.

"Not far now," he groaned loudly.

"Good thing you had that nap," Mom turned to grin at his sleepy expression.

"Yes, I know. I can sleep anywhere at any time," he tapped on her knee with his pointer finger, "but that's not my fault. That's just the way I was made."

"Yeah, unlike the rest of us," Mom responded, tapping Dad's knee.

"Well, at least Jake inherited my napping qualities," he consoled.

You're not kidding.

As if on cue, Jake snorted, yawned, moaned, sighed and continued sleeping.

It wasn't until we began bumping up and down the dusty sideroad, that Jake was shaken awake, and only then because he bounced his head into the glass of the car window, causing him to emit a loud whine. As the car churned up plumes of gravel dust behind us, the fields ended and ranchlands loomed, peppered with tuffs of wild grasses and beyond, a tall white steeple peaked through a thicket of evergreens at the edge of the field. A small green, faded sign leaned tiredly over the gravel shoulder. On it was stenciled: Church and Retreat Centre, 5 KM.

"The church is up ahead, and the retreat center is just in the back," Dad was saying when a loud rumble thundered through the car, shaking the dangling cross hanging from the rearview mirror, knocking the magnetic phone holder out of the vent in the dashboard, and causing Jake to rouse awake with a squeaky scream, which was echoed by a now much-awake Shade.

Then, I saw them.

Their long, muscular legs flexed as their bodies galloped through the foliage whitecaps, churning up plumes of dust in their wake. Their elongated heads rose up and down as they moved, their flowing manes catching the breeze in what I could only surmise as the most beautiful exhibit of wild abandonment that an animal could have. Gracefully, they moved closer to the sun-bleached wood posts that lined the side of the highway.

"Wow," Jake breathed into my ear as he leaned across the kennel on my lap, causing Shade to yowl and hiss. "They are beautiful."

"I couldn't agree more." Mom craned her neck, sliding her seatbelt out of the way so she had a better view of the beasts. "They are glorious."

Numbering at least twenty, the horses frolicked in the ocean of green grass tufts, front legs raised, then back; heads tilting side to side, manes flicking.

I was in awe.

Then I saw what they were galloping away from: dark brown-black shapes appeared in the distance.

Hundreds of them.

Broad-shouldered, hairy beasts emerged from the thicket of trees at the edge of the field and as they grew closer, their size filled my vision. Their heads were covered in curly hair out of which protruded short white horns that turned inward. The curls extended to their backs, stopping short of their midsections as if a trigger-happy barber had given their behinds a poodle cut. The hairless hides were bulging with muscle as they moved closer, grazing, as they went. Long tails flicked at the gathering blackflies and the tufts at the end of the appendage reminded me of videos of lions from nature videos in school.

"Well, will you look at that," Dad said. "I knew the farmers and ranchers around here had somehow sheltered themselves from the drought but I had no idea they were able to reintroduce bison into their stock."

"*Bison?*"

Jake's incredulous tone breathed life into my own wonder.

"Yes, aren't they marvelous," Mom sighed.

The car revved and we turned the corner.

The gravel driveway crunched under the rubber tires of our car. Mom parked the station wagon at the end of the path flanked by two plastic topiary trees protruding from brightly painted plant pots. The pale rubber roots intertwined like rope from the plastic moss at their base and rose several feet in the air, ending under a ball of green, plastic leaves. Near the double-sided wooden doors sat picnic tables embedded into small pea gravel, which was scattered all over the front lawn. A winding stone path began at the driveway where we had parked, curved around the picnic tables and joined the sidewalk that encircled the white-stucco building. Trimmed with dark stained oak, the church gleamed in the morning light; the stained-glass windows, shaped like elongated arrowheads, stretched from the foundation to the black-shingled roof. Bordered by oak, the glass panes reflected in the sun like blazing rainbows set afire. The steeple was even more foreboding up close than from our roadside vantage point: The white-painted wooden column rose from the double-oak entrance doors, shooting up past the black roof and towering over the structure as if it was a stairway to heaven itself. At the top, a pewter bell hung in a framed window and above that, a tall, wooden white cross. On the side of the tower was a silver plate and etched into the shiny surface was *Church of the Holy Creator* in black type.

Beside the steeple were five boulders, each bearing a silver plaque bolted into a flat part of the rocks' surfaces. They gleamed in the rising sun. I vowed to check them out later but for now, there was so much else to take in. Not the least of which was the two-story house built into the end of the church as if it was a bookend. There was a white picket sign wedged into the pea gravel beside the steps leading to the front door, *Rectory*. The rectangular building had four small windows that lined the top floor, facing the path, and two more on the main floor, beside a large window with drawn curtains dotted with yellow and white daisies. Steps leading to the front door had colorfully painted pots filled with plants and flowers. They ringed the small deck, following the white railing that encircled the porch, setting it ablaze in morning solar splendor. Leaning my head out the window, I could smell the earthy crops in the fields, freshly baked bread, brewing coffee and something completely foreign. The strong, mouthwatering odor was coming from the opened front door and it made drool form in the corners of my lips.

Behind the building was a rolling field of brown grass and the evergreen trees we had spied from the highway. The stone path that encircled the church divided at the corner of the rectory and meandered over the hills, through the grasses and disappeared into the thicket of trees.

My eyes scanned the path, following the stones to the hidden structures that peaked out between dark green branches. There were three of them, and they were large; at least four stories each, and their footprints were almost double that of the rectory and church combined.

I glanced down at my smartphone charging in the sunlight streaming through my window. Large pale blue numbers stared back at me: Ten minutes to eight.

Looking back out the window, I stared at the church, the rectory, the structures in the distance, and the woman approaching. Dad opened the car door and began brushing off his navy cargo shorts. His head was still bent when the short indigenous woman appeared in front of him, long black hair highlighted with strands of silver weaved into a thick braid that rested between her shoulder blades. Her dark-skinned face was creased in the most welcoming smile I had ever seen. Her eyes sparkled; her cheeks plumped, with bursts of sunlight reflected on the curves; her mouth turned upward, creasing her cheeks and causing the lines around her eyes to deepen and her white teeth to sparkle. Black, white and red dangling earrings flowed like waterfalls from the lobes of her ears in an intricate beaded pattern that reminded me of feathers.

If not for her skirt, I don't think I could have looked away.

Below her black clergy shirt and white collar, a burst of red flowed from her waist and upon it, alternating zig-zag ribbon tape of white and yellow. Below the last red stripe was row upon row of wide white and black ribbons, with little tails protruding from her left hip and thigh, dangling on the side and cut in a V at the ends. The white and black rows ended near her shins to a hem of red, with more white and yellow zig-zag ribbons stitched across the vibrant fabric.

As I unfolded myself from the car, moaning and groaning away the aches and pains—my body was not meant to be folded in half so for so long—my eyes could not move from the ribbon skirt. Sensing my gaze, Rev. Erin Stillwater turned her head and her grin grew even wider, and then her arms followed suit. Before I could protest, I was being embraced, with silky black hair streaked with white pressed into my chest in the tightest squeeze that seemed to drain all anxiety from my bones.

"Welcome, welcome," she said, releasing me to feel somehow naked without her touch. "Pete and Shelly, you did not tell me you birthed a giant."

Her laughter rang into the air like music, dancing on the tips of the corn stalks and swirling with the wind into the swaying tall grasses. No wonder the horses danced.

"Erin, this is Jules."

I felt her warm hand circle around mine and pulled me to her side.

Mom came around the hood of the car as Dad exited the passenger side.

All the drive here, I hadn't seen their faces, only the backs of their heads and the occasional cheek. Oh, I had caught the scatter glimpse of strain, dried tears, and tired eyes but as they stood there on the gravel drive, I saw more. I saw the puffy folds under their lids, the dark crescent under the lashes and the new lines of ageing that had sprung up on their skin in a matter of hours.

Now, released; softened in Rev. Stillwater's presence.

Mom was pulled into an embrace with one arm, while the priest held firm to my hand. Then, it was Jake's turn and he timidly approached the circle only to have his whole body suctioned into her middle, with the hands holding Mom and me encircling my brother's back.

"Now, he's someone more my size," Rev. Stillwater said, her throaty, sing-song voice rising and falling in ebbs.

Jake giggled and blushed.

We were crushed together in a bear hug by a tiny woman who had immediately felt like family.

Dad stood back, hands on his hips, chuckling at the sight.

"Erin, you'd better let go of them before they are fused with your skin."

"They are already fused with my heart, so what's a little skin?"

The priest's voice warmed me, soothed me and I found myself smiling for the first time in days. Looking down into her eyes, I felt something I hadn't felt in a very long time.

I felt … like I belonged.

****

Inside the rectory kitchen, eggs, fresh-from-the-oven clouds of bread and bison bacon—the mouthwatering aroma I had sensed in the car—awaited.

The smells made my stomach rumble and my mouth water. When was the last time we had eaten meat? Or eggs for that matter? Yes, our family was fortunate, financially, but Mom opted for the meatless dinners whenever she could because real protein was a celebration food only brought out during Easter, Christmas and Thanksgiving. "It is a treat, like chocolate and candy, only better."

Translation: My parents couldn't afford real meat to be a part of our regular diet.

We were not alone.

So, the smell of sizzling fried, salted strips of red meat streaked with fat was perfume to our souls. Saliva was already dripping down Jake's chin and if I stared at Dad's chin whiskers, the short hairs along his jawline glistened with it.

We sat patiently at the long, rectangular wooden table in the adjacent room, as Pastor Stillwater said a blessing over the meal, welcoming us to her table and thanking the Creator for our safe journey, then poured cups of tea from a brown earthenware kettle and spoke in a soft, musical voice. The yellow and white curtains were flapping in and out of the opened dining room window, sending a hot breeze of dust, grain and the sweet smell of grass into the room to mingle with the heavenly aromas of the food.

The large room had the kitchen on one end and the dining room on the other. White laminate cupboards gleamed along the wall and under the yellow and white marble countertops. A white enamel farmhouse sink cut into the middle of the countertop and above it, a small kitchen window that overlooked the pea-gravel path leading to the buildings in the trees. Stainless-steel appliances rested on the countertop, and a cherry-red kettle steamed on the white enamel stovetop. At the other end of the room, the large wall was papered with yellow and white stripes, their pattern broken only by the dark-oak stained door that led to the church. To the left of the door, was a raised stone hearth in which housed a metal cradle full of blackened, burnt wood. Beside the fireplace, four long-handled metal fire-tending tools hung on a wrought-iron frame: a brush and trowel on one side and a hook and poker on the other and in between, a rack on which several logs of wood lay waiting. A layer of dust floated on the pale wood and bark. Surrounding the stone fireplace was a plush couch and loveseat. Yellow and white checked pillows filled their corners, holding a spot for someone to lean on. In front of them was a pine, fire-scorched coffee table laden with books and an open notepad with scribbled writing.

"Erin, this has got to be the happiest kitchen I've ever been in," Mom exclaimed, pivoting on her heels to take in all the bright colors that were now glowing in the morning sun. "It *radiates*."

The priest blushed and gave Mom a blast of white teeth that could have easily blinded her. "That's the point, Shelly my dear."

We sat in the middle of the room on faded yellow furniture that divided the living room and the kitchen.

"The farmers, ranchers and my First Nations' brothers and sisters in these parts are blessed beyond measure with our resources, so we want to share them with you," she opened her arms like wings and spread them on either side of her to encompass the spread of mouth-watering food on the table. "They have been selling them to food producers and retailers in the city for years, but they rarely get visitors to taste it the way it was intended—fresh."

I mimicked her expression as I put the first fork of scrambled eggs in my mouth. The fluffy texture made me groan as I tasted the buttery cloud.

"The moment I sent word through the church's directory, the baskets started arriving," shaking her head in pride, she stretched out her arms to indicate all the food on the table and continued, "and they delivered, abundantly. Thanks be to God."

Dad nodded, turned to me, raised a bushy black eyebrow at my eating euphoria and laughed.

"Someone is enjoying themselves," he snickered while biting down on a strip of bacon, which caused his eyes to bulge. "And now I know why. God be praised, Erin, you have blessed us with a feast like no other."

The reverend blushed and put the tea cups in front of our plates.

"Pete, my boy, you ain't seen nothin' yet."

Her throaty laughter rumbled through the room.

I looked around at my family, shoveling food in their mouths, savoring every morsel, and couldn't help but smile. Jake had finally put his cereal away and was scooping up eggs and bacon as if he was finally in a growth spurt. Mom was buttering a piece of toast and topping it with red berry jam.

"Decades ago, the people here in Southern Alberta took it upon ourselves to make some drastic changes in how our land was treated, and many tapped into underground wells and riverbeds to water their crops," the pastor explained. "They even changed what they were growing, and when. Everyone works together, here, for the greater good—everyone, no matter their background or beliefs, and it paid off."

Putting brown-swirled ceramic milk and sugar dishes on the table, she turned to the large dining room window that overlooked the gravel lawn and fields beyond and added, "The bison were introduced about ten years ago. In Northern Alberta, they had raised bison and beefalo—a crossbreed of buffalo and beef cattle—for years but with the changing climate, even they couldn't withstand the droughts. So, down here, they decided to just bite the bullet and go full-on bison."

Her throat erupted in laughter bubbles and they spilled over the table and popped into our plates, making us smile.

"Most ranchers started with just ten cows and a couple of bulls they got from herds up north that were dying of starvation. The next spring the herds had doubled, and they have pretty much done that every year since. Right now, some ranchers have up to 1,800 head."

"Are many sold?" Dad stirred sugar into his tea and tapped his spoon along the rim of the brown swirl ceramic mug.

Rev. Stillwater nodded, rose from her chair, turned on her heel and grabbed a loaf of bread, sliced pieces off and placed them into the toaster on the counter.

"Yes, as soon as word got out how well the herd was doing, food orders started pouring in from all over the country," she pushed down the toaster plunger and winked, "they paid a hefty price, though."

Her merry chuckle made her shoulders rise and fall as her body shook in laughter.

"Which is why Holy Creator is doing so well. Many saw God at work here, and gave back, and that's how we came to build the church, the rectory and the retreat."

"I have a feeling it wasn't just about the blessings of good crops and healthy cattle," Mom's mouth turned up in a sardonic smile. She tilted her disheveled red head to the side, "I have a feeling you've got a thing or two to do with the congregation's growth."

"Now, now, Shelly, don't make me blush—I can do all things through Christ, remember, who strengthens me. So, the glory is HIS, not mine."

The three of them nodded, and mumbled, "Thanks be to God. Amen," in unison.

"Tell me about the retreat," Mom piped up, slurping her tea, and chewing. "I've heard of all the events but that's just items on a calendar and lines in a profit-and-loss spreadsheet."

Rev. Erin beamed at Mom, and nodded with pleasure at my mother's keen interest in understanding the impacts; not just the financial gains.

"You would not believe the support and the ministry being felt here, Shelly. When we opened it up to anyone to book, it took some time for locals to come forth but slowly, and surely, they did. We've had family retreats here where divorced couples have come to realize the importance of communication, empathy and consideration for one another, despite their family dynamics, and because of that, their children have thrived. We've had teenagers hold wilderness survival camps here and our Blackfoot elders have helped teach the forgotten ways of living off the land. It's … spirit-led, and it shows."

Now it was Dad's turn to beam. Hand over heart, he patted his chest, raised his silver crucifix from around his neck and kissed it. Rev. Erin and Mom did the same.

"In honor of the Highway of Tears, we have named all our dormitory buildings after courageous women in the Bible."

"What's the Highway of Tears?" Jake and I said together.

The adults sighed.

Dad took a deep breath, turned to Rev. Stillwater who nodded for him to respond, and he began, "It's a 700-kilometre stretch of highway along Highway 16, between Prince George and Prince Rupert in British Columbia, where there were hundreds of missing and murdered indigenous women in the 1970s. It is one of the blackest marks on Canadian history—that and residential schools."

"Because we are an *Anglican* congregation, with a strong First Nations' influence, we wanted to honor them in a Christian way so we also have the names in Blackfoot underneath, along with a red plaque imprinted with eagle wings."

There was so much history I didn't know. It made me embarrassed and ashamed at the same time.

"Don't worry, Jules and Jake, reconciliation begins with acknowledgement and ends with repentance, just as our Savior taught us."

"You are definitely right there," Dad put his hand on Rev. Erin's exposed arm. "Thank you."

"For what?"

She seemed confused; shocked even.

"For walking in the path of Jesus. That's why Holy Creator is so strong."

The reverend patted Dad's hand resting on her arm and then turned her hand into a fist and held it close to her heart. "God be praised."

"But Shelly, here, wants to know about the center; not little ol' me!" Turning to Mom, again, she continued. "The dormitory buildings have a main floor for offices, counseling rooms, a small kitchen and a chapel. Esther House has a dining hall, where all the meals are taken, and a conference room for special events. Ruth House has a women's prayer and praise room, with handmade musical instruments and a private healing station for the laying of hands and oil. Martha House has a woodshop and worship room where the handy folks can learn beadwork and tufting, while they seek guidance through song and testimonies. Then there is Mary Pentecost Place, where we try and understand one another by learning new languages and cultures, while also learning how to communicate as ministers. It is all very intentional but fluid, much like a lot of things.”

Rev. Erin glanced my way and winked.

“Outstanding.” Mom said in admiration.

“Yes, it truly is. The Spirit moves in this neck of the woods. I have seen it firsthand.”

“I have no doubt.”

The pastor grabbed the pieces of bread as they popped and quickly spread dark yellow butter on them. Seeing our eyes pop, she raised an eyebrow and her lips curled upward: “Goat butter. Ranchers use them to get rid of the noxious weeds and they produce far better milk than oats and nuts.”

“Remarkable,” Dad said.

I took a piece of the toast off the brown ceramic plate and bit down.

“Delish,” I mumbled, spitting toast crumbs onto the table.

Mom’s eyebrows lowered.

“Sorry,” I said, spitting even more brown flakes onto the table.

Rev. Stillwater chuckled again, sat down, and began stirring milk into her tea. “Besides the milk and butter, we also get … cheese.”

Reaching over the table, she lifted a white ceramic dome from a dish and revealed a block of white, crumbly cheese, which she sliced. Jake’s hand shot out and grabbed a piece while her knife was still raised, causing her to rumble with girlish giggles and Mom and Dad to frown in embarrassment.

“Then, there are the chicken and turkey coops, the elk and deer farms, and the traplines, of course,” she added, placing her spoon onto the table. “Many in the Nations have their own kilns to make ceramics and stoneware, as well.” Her head nodded to the dishes on the table and suddenly, the brown earthenware teacup handle felt even warmer in my hand.

“God has blessed us abundantly, so eat up!”

I looked over at Jake, who was still chewing his stolen piece of goat cheese, while putting berry jam on his toast and dipping a corner into his cup of tea.

Dude.

Why?

Shaking my head at the sight, I watched as Dad folded his napkin and turned to the Anglican priest.

"Thank you, Erin, for granting us a share in your bounty. Our family," he swallowed and looked at our faces, "our family is honored by the grace you have shown us, today, and we will be forever in your debt."

"Now, now, Pete, we are all one family in Christ. Feed the hungry, clothe the poor, shelter the homeless, these are the commands we were given and it just so happens Holy Creator's congregation can do that for you in your time of need. I am sure you would do likewise."

"Definitely."

Jake leaned into me, red jam smeared all over his mouth and cheeks, and whispered, "we don't have any of those things," he pointed to the dishes laden with food.

"What would we feed them?"

"Celery," I said, knowing that was the only thing we hadn't eaten on the journey, and pushed him away from me, "celery and your Cinnamon Toast Crunch."

"No!"

"Jules, don't tease your brother," Mom chastised, shaking her head with her lips pursed. "You know as well as I do we don't have any more Cinnamon Toast Crunch."

"No!"

"Dude, it's cereal," I poked him in the shoulder with my butter knife, leaving a yellow stain on his PJ shirt. "It isn't … *bison bacon*."

"That it ain't," Dad said dryly and grabbed another piece. "This is like eating candy."

Jake leaned over and gingerly picked up a strip and placed it in his mouth.

His eyes widened.

His lips curled upward.

His teeth began to chew and his mouth began to moan.

"Bison bacon, where have you been all my life?"

We all burst out laughing.

No. 1, this was coming from Jake, the baby who hardly spoke a word and when he did it was in disjointed sentences. No. 2, it was an easy joke from a guy who seemed to be as at ease here as I was.

Maybe he felt like he belonged, too.

Funny, it never once occurred to me that he may need to be accepted, just as I did, but now, looking at him stuff his mouth with strips of meat candy, I realized that he wasn't that different from me, after all. In fact, the longer I stared at his normally jittery, cowering frame, which was now at ease, upright and relaxed, the more I was faced with the realization that *he* needed this, too. Almost as much as I did.

Actually, now that I thought about it, maybe even more.

****

Alberta Premier Darrell Kelly's announcement aired while we sat on the couch in the rectory's living room. Painted in hues of soft yellow and white, the room made me think of sunshine and clouds. Two overstuffed couches were positioned in the shape of an L, facing the hearth of a stone fireplace, while a couple of reclining chairs pointed their footrests to the couch resting against the side wall. Papered in yellow and white stripes, the surfaces were adorned with Biblical paintings of Moses at the parting of the Red Sea, staff in hand and leading a group of Israelites to freedom; Jacob with a raised hand holding a knife above the torso of his son, Isaac, who lay atop a flat, raised rock; and the crucifixion of Jesus, with Mary and his disciple John kneeling at his feet. Thick, fluid brush strokes mingled with dots and curls of paint. In the corners of the canvasses were artist signatures: Simon Many Guns; Jerome Eagle Feather; Sybil Medicine Bull; Doris Red Antler.

Also scattered around the room were indigenous prints of people dancing, singing, playing drums, riding horses while chasing a herd of buffalo and surrounding a fire, telling stories. One such print drew my eye and captured my attention like none of the others. It depicted a group of dancers in full indigenous dress, their hide-covered feet raised, beads and fringes trying to take flight from calves and arms as colorful blankets swirled behind their shoulders, held tightly by the corners.

They were oblivious to the crowds around them; they were too focused on the drums being pounded and the vocals being sung. Eyes were clenched tight as their bodies twisted and contorted to the music, the song.

Full surrender.

I closed my own eyes, the image still stamped on my inner lids, and inhaled deeply.

Was that what giving up full control looked like?

Release.

Joy.

Darkness and the fading spots of floating, colorful beads flitted across the lids, until only darkness remained. Opening my eyes, a warm breeze from an open window brushed across the hot, sweaty skin on my face.

Dad often talked about lifting things up and letting go, but I never really understood, until now. The dancers got it. They felt it. They lived it.

Could I?

White sheer curtains flapped from the opened windows in the room, sending the aroma of hay, grass and fields into my nostrils.

We sat together on the couch directly in front of the fireplace, trying not to fall asleep in the fresh air and calm that permeated the room.

Pastor Erin sat on the sofa to our right, holding a remote control she had picked up from the wooden, rectangular coffee table moments before, and flicked a button. The TV above the hearth blinked and came to life. The room flooded with the harsh light from the screen. The calm and peace emitted from the sunshine glow retreated into the dark corners of the room to make space for the stark reality of the images flashing across the fifty-inch surface.

The premier said the province was in a State of Emergency; people were fleeing cities in contamination zones in search of sanctuary and the Canadian Armed Forces officers were arriving later in the morning to control the crowds and maintain the peace.

We watched the drone-captured images of clogged roadways, burning fires, emptied cities and towns, and frustrated, scared Albertans hysterically talking to news crews.

After Kelly's address, Pastor Erin flicked off the TV and turned to our family: "Thank the Lord of Great Mercies that our Klassen brothers and sisters made it here safely."

"On that, I couldn't agree more," Dad leaned over and covered Pastor Erin's clasped hands. "You have blessed us beyond measure, Erin, and as I said upon our arrival, we are indebted to you."

"Favor; not debt. Favor is something that has grace; debt is a transaction."

"You are certainly right about that."

He turned to me, Jake and Mom. His wide shoulders crumpled as if the air pumped into them before we left Calgary was deflating with the relaxation and peace we had found in this place. Creases stretched from the corner of his eyes and puffy folds ballooned under his lids, creating shadows.

I had never seen my dad so exhausted.

He leaned back and as my mom caressed his hand, his eyelids closed and he drifted off into deep sleep. Pastor Stillwater rose, touched Dad's forehead and said something in an unknown language before doing the same to each of us.

"Rest now," she breathed over us. "There will be time for strength and wide eyes but not this moment. This moment is for you to rest in his presence and just *be*."

She left us lounging on a couch adorned with stampeding black stallions, as she hummed a song that vibrated behind my eyes and ears until all that was left was the low drone of my deep breathing.

****

As I showered several hours later, washing away the filth of dusty, grimy air off my skin, it occurred to me that all the people who farmed and ranched in the area were sitting ducks. They had no weapons, no walls to keep the flood of people out—just wooden fences that divide one field from the next. All that they had built was now being threatened, and just as our family had found belonging amid the sorghum fields and bison herds, so too would others.

Was there enough for the hordes that will follow?

I dried my body, picked up the piece of spandex that lay on the toilet seat and began pulling the fabric down over my chest, only it wouldn't budge past my armpits. Suctioned to the still damp skin, the binder clung to every pore and squeezed. The bottom third of my breasts were still exposed, as was my lower half. Breathing into the gray fabric across my face, I began to hyperventilate.

Why, oh why, didn't you put on your underwear first?
What if someone walks in?
What if you are stuck like this forever?
What if you have to call for help?

Fighting my raging pulse, I began to twist and pull; shimmy and shake in an attempt to dislodge the tight weave from its strangulation hold on my upper body. Only problem? I couldn't see a damn thing and crashed my hip into the pedestal sink, which launched a series of shrieks and curses from my muffled mouth.

"You alright in there?"

Jake's unsure tone interrupted my mumbling and wincing.

"Fine."

I didn't sound *fine*. I sounded like a deranged lunatic who was about to open a door, half-naked, so their teenage brother could take a jumbo duct-tape bandage off my chest.

"Go away."

"Ju … ju … juST trying to … to … hel … help."

Then he was gone.

"Get off me, you flingin' flangin' piece of bison turd … DUCKIN," I yelled into the gray abyss.

Bending over, I shimmied and squirmed until the binder had risen up to my chin, free of my elbows and shoulders. A few minutes later, I was huffing and puffing while sitting on the floor, shooting darts with my eyes at a damp, gray ball peeking out from the trash by the toilet.

"Good riddance, you piece of sadistic shiitake 'shrooms."

I wiped my hand over the steamed-up mirror, still out of breath. My reflection stared back at me. Despite my flushed pink, chafed skin and exasperation over the binder, I was glad to be here and not out there, still on the road, wondering where to spend the night.

You are safe, remember that.

Was I, really?

I knew the sense of sanctuary I felt within these walls, on this land would be short lived. I had seen the mayhem firsthand: The crazed looks people got when they thought they were going to die, and they were out there, waiting, lining the highway, looking for an escape and here we were, ripe for the picking. As I toweled myself off, completely this time, and donned a tee, jean shorts and flannel shirt, I pondered how long this would last. How long we would be safe. How long we would be sheltered from the chaos—out there. I could feel my anxiety rising and the jittery feeling of an over-pumping heart. I stared into my now wild eyes in the mirror, blinking away unshed tears of frustration, trying to calm down.

"Nothing lasts forever, Jules, not even peace."

My voice was shaky, unsure, scared.

Just like the rest of me.

Chapter 10

The long farmhouse table was overflowing with bounty.

We sat facing bowls of steaming, fragrant rabbit stew, already drooling over the prospect of consuming something other than pea-powder protein bars that had become a staple in our Calgary diet.

Then they poured in: Rev. Erin's family had come to say hello, having braved the backroads from Brocket to greet us. As they stepped over the threshold of the rectory, my family took a collective sigh of appreciation. The elders wore brightly woven blankets over their shoulders, bearing dishes of aromatic cuts of bison in thick gravy; soft, chewy fry bread; steaming, freshly baked rolls, and berry desserts topped with whipped cream. Behind them walked their children, and their children's children.

They deposited their dishes on the knotty table's surface and stood against the wall, smiling. Some were older than my parents, while others were older than Rev. Stillwater. They were elders of distinction in the Piikani Nation, the priest explained upon introductions, and I couldn't peel my gaze away from their beaming faces in the fading light of day. Children beelined for an intricately carved wooden chest tucked into the side of the hearth. Lifting the hinged lid, brightly painted wooden toys were met with tiny shouts of joy and eagerness. As they played with red chunky fire trucks and tractors, handheld scoops tied to a small rubber-band-wound ball with a string, and an assortment of broomcorn dolls dressed in long skirts and floral shirts on the floor, several teenagers shuffled into the room, their gazes shifting from the playing children, to their parents standing against the wall, and, at last, to the food—never quite rising to stare into the faces of the strangers around Rev. Erin's table.

I knew how they must have felt: on display, out of their element, awkward. Yet, even they had curled lips, even if a bit unsure. They had come to welcome us with food and their presence, and I sat at the table wondering why.

"At Holy Creator, community is everything," the priest began, standing so she could see over the heads of those seated at the table. "The same can be said with family. That's what a true community and a faithful church is, you know—family.

"And while we may butt heads from time to time," her hearty laugh elicited giggles from the tiny faces zooming trucks and dancing dolls on the hardwood floor, "we are still a family."

Her face filled with pride as she turned to each relative, adult and child.

"Tomorrow, the ranchers and farmers will grace us with harvests of their own but tonight, my Piikani family wanted to be the first to extend a welcome to your heroic family."

Rev. Erin turned her head to me and smirked. Her mischievous grin was made even more so by the wink and raised black eyebrow.

"Bravery and honor are qualities all peoples value," she added, "but among the Blackfoot, they are the cornerstones of our culture."

Dad got up from his chair and Rev. Stillwater introduced him to the elders. The first was a white-haired woman who couldn't stop smiling, the lines around her eyes and lips forever creased in deep canyons.

"This is my sister, Chief Irene Beaver." The pastor barely had the words out of her mouth before the short woman wrapped her arms around Dad's middle. "Sister, don't crush Pastor Pete."

She let go of Dad and winked, "What's the point of giving a hug if you don't feel the other person's spirit?"

Rev. Stillwater shook her head from side to side and rolled her eyes skyward. "Irene, you are impossible."

"I think what you're feeling right now is a belly full of bison bacon, so don't squeeze too tight." Dad's chuckle was only surpassed by Chief Irene's.

A roar of laughter erupted from her delighted mouth, silver strands flying backward from her head. The Piikani chief raised her hands from around Dad's back to rest on his cheeks. Enclosed in her weathered, tanned palms, his face looked almost pale and his flushed skin, youthful.

"The Holy Creator has given you a sense of humor. Good." Her dark eyes squinted joyously and with intention into Dad's face. "It will serve you well in the days ahead."

Once she had released him, the two clasped hands before Dad turned to Mom and introduced her to the First Nation leader. The two women held each other tightly. Being roughly the same height, their heads rested on each other's shoulders. I could see the tension in Mom's back dissolve as her muscles relaxed in the embrace. Wrinkled hands caressed blazing red hair and rubbed between Mom's shoulders, calming and supporting her.

When they let go, tears streamed down Mom's flushed cheeks as she smiled into Chief Irene's face.

"The mothers take everything into their hearts," the chief breathed. "Even others' fears and tribulations. That's why we were made strong, resilient, fierce."

Mom's back straightened as if she had received an injection of energy, and nodded.

Then it was our turn.

Jake shyly stepped forward and received his bear hug from Chief Irene Beaver.

I was last to go through the reception line.

I stood and watched as dark eyes scaled my slender, muscular legs exposed ankle-to-thigh by denim shorts. They rose to my oversized red flannel shirt and under-tee, and finally up to my cropped, spiked auburn hair, which added yet another inch to my frame. The children stopped playing to stare. The teenagers shifted from one jeaned leg to the other, heads tilted, taking me in. I felt suddenly self-conscious. Instead of the suffocating binder, I had worn a sports bra under my T-shirt. While it was much more comfortable, it didn't flatten my chest to my ribcage the way the binder did. Could they see the curves? Were they disgusted by my boy-girl appearance?

Without thinking, I reached for my wrist and flicked the elastic at the pulse. A wrinkled, calloused hand covered mine and I stood still, as a scratchy thumb softly caressed the now red vein. The old woman's long silver hair glistened as she tilted her head. Unfettered, the long strands floated around her shoulders like tinsel. Then, the chief looked up and spread her arms wide. Without thinking, I stepped inside and felt the embrace of a stranger who, in one glance, knew more about me than the friends I had left behind.

Than my parents even.

They had never noticed the elastic, the white scar lines underneath.

As I left her embrace, I fell into the awaiting blanket wings of the others, each taking me into their folds.

I was still hugging one of the women, getting chafed by the itchy wool on my cheek, when the rectory door opened and a tall man with silky black hair bent his head to walk through the frame and into the room. Slender, fit, and in his early thirties, he wore a navy long-sleeved dress shirt, unbuttoned at the neck, and a pair of dark blue jeans that looked nearly black. Beside him was a woman with a long plait of black hair that fell over her left shoulder and onto the bodice of the most beautiful and colorful blouse I had ever seen. It was like staring at a painting, with swirls of golds, blues, oranges and reds on a canvas of white. Upon looking closer, each flip of a fabric-paint brush formed a spirit animal, and they were all dancing above a range of gray-black mountains. The blouse seemed to almost float with the prints, so light and airy was the fabric. Unbuttoned at the throat, the garment revealed a wide choker, embellished with colorful beads of various hues, tied around a long swan-like neck. Below the shirt, she wore a white skirt that was quite plain in contrast, until your eyes wandered to the hem, where stampeding bison galloped. A wide leather belt was cinched around her waist, with dangling fringes flowing from the knotted, weaved tan hide. On her feet were matching brown pumps with red-painted heels. Beaded, red wild roses were stitched upon each toe. I was still staring at her feet when the man began to talk.

"Nice to see you in one piece, Julia."

"Jules," Rev. Erin corrected. "*Their* name is Jules."

"Pardon me. Jules," Mr. B was smiling in acknowledgement. "You've created a pretty big fan following on the reserve, you know."

My Grade 12 Social Studies teacher vigorously shook my hand and patted my back.

"Not just on the reserve," Rev. Erin piped up. "Oh, what wondrous deeds one can do when they walk with the Creator."

"Indeed," Chief Irene, Mom and Dad said in unison.

I could feel the heat rise in my face as all eyes in the room starred in my direction, and was relieved when Mr. B let go his grasp of my slender fingers, which were so sweaty, he had to wipe his palm down the thigh of his blue jeans, smirking all the while as he did so.

Turning to the woman beside him, he placed a large hand gently on her spine and smiled. Her face lit up. Large, dark eyes creased as they stared up into the face of the man hovering around her. "This is my wife, Savannah."

"Oki."

Her voice was soft and husky, and I wondered why I had never thought that Mr. B was married, and married to someone so intriguingly stunning.

"Savannah is a budding fashion designer," Mr. B beamed.

Savannah chuckled, the sound rumbling low in her throat as if she was about to break out in song. "If you mean, I've got an online store where all our friends and family buy clothes, then sure, I'm *budding*."

I had never seen Mr. B laugh so wholeheartedly, or with such obvious joy.

"Hey, I love my one-of-a-kind ribbon skirt," Rev. Erin pushed her head between Mr. B and his wife, "so don't dis the kin card."

"All right, all right," Savannah kissed the top of the priest's black and silver head and pushed it back behind them, causing Rev. Erin to giggle like one of the toddlers on the floor. Turning to me, she was still smiling and shaking her head, as if to say, *'Aunties, you can't take them anywhere, even if they are ordained!'*

She held out her delicate hand and I took it in my own slender grasp. "Nice to meet you, Jules, and if the world doesn't end, check out my site. I've got lots of designs for tall, young people who like a bit of color in their life, unlike my hubby here, who refuses to wear anything that isn't bland."

"I'm not bland," Mr. B pointed to his belt, which was a navy, red and white weave adorned with a silver rectangular buckle emblazoned with a bison head. "I'm wearing this, aren't I?"

"Barely."

Shaking his head at his teasing wife, Mr. B turned to me, winked and said, "Some of us are just too darn colorful in our personalities, without having to add some to our clothes."

"*That* right there—that's how you get called *bland.* Jules here knows that sometimes, who you are needs to be expressed with what you wear, am I right?"

Without waiting for a response, she tapped her husband on the shoulder in reprimand, kissed her finger and placed it over his lips. "Leave the fashion advice to the experts."

"Shall we eat?" Rev. Erin said at the head of the table, breaking up the good-natured bickering. "This food isn't getting any hotter."

Everyone who had emerged sat with us.

Several adults scooped up their wayward tots from the floor and planted them on their laps and quietly waited for the priest to begin the festivities.

Rev. Stillwater gave a blessing over the food and the company, and Dad said a prayer. As they spoke words of grace and acceptance, blessings and bounty, the food sat still, the children quieted their play, the adults bowed their heads until the words were said in English and Blackfoot.

I listened intently to the sounds rising in song from the throats around the long table, mesmerized, my trance broken only when the speaking ceased.

The aromas coming off the wooden surface didn't do the food justice.

My first bite of the stew sent my taste buds on a journey of discovery. The tender, dark meat floated in thick, brown, rich gravy seasoned with wild herbs, chunks of wild turnip and onions. The aroma, while strong and gamey, was nothing like the sensation inside my mouth. As I chewed, I tasted rosemary, thyme and an earthiness that was both comforting and nourishing, and I slurped every spoonful out of my bowl. I thought I had gone to foodie heaven, until I jabbed a cube of bison meat in a platter of wild onions and mushrooms. Was this really what real meat tasted like? Yes, we had bison bacon earlier in the day, but this was different. This was fresh, this was juicy, this was succulent. The tender meat melted in my mouth, collapsing against my molars with one bite. Again, I asked myself: Was this really what beef tasted like; fresh, *real* meat?

Rabbit and bison, anyway.

I chewed each chunk for minutes, letting the savory juices dissolve the cubes in my mouth before swallowing. Then came the meat pies, smoked trout; crispy mounds of puffed-up bread fried in oil; baskets of warm bannock; something called pemmican, which I later learned was dried bison ground with dried Saskatoon berries; dandelion salad and a curled plant called fiddleheads sautéed in butter; jars of blackberry marmalade—all washed down with elderflower lemonade. And for dessert, berry pies and whipped cream, the latter thanks to nearby ranchers' goats.

As my parents talked, Jake and I sat and ate.

The table was abuzz with activity. While the older people spoke and laughed, the children and teens teased and giggled. Everyone wanted to know about our journey south, the road conditions, the motorists who fled just as we did, only to move at a snail's pace. They asked about the airport and the explosions; the casualties and the conditions, and through it all, they sat, listened, nodded and touched every one of us with their empathy and understanding.

I was lifting a fork of pie to my drooling lips when the door to the rectory opened and a teenage boy walked in. He wore a yellow plaid shirt with black flowers embroidered around the collar, dipping into an intricate display of swirling vines, leaves and blossoms on the front shoulders, and tucked into a long, wrapped jean skirt. As he moved forward, his red cowboy boots clicked on the hardwood planks stretching across the rectory floor. Glancing back up to his dark-skinned face, I saw a white gauze corner peeking out from under his Stetson and the world's smallest band-aid on his earlobe. Walking toward me, his chicklet smile widened and his arms went around my back and squeezed.

"Hulk, my man," he proclaimed to the room, "I thought I'd never see you again."

****

The corrugated truck bed felt like ice against my naked skin and I tugged on the thick, wool blanket padding my butt downward so the itchy fabric created a barrier between skin and metal. Beside me, Todd lay outstretched, his yellow-plaid arms tucked behind his head, cushioning the silky black hair that reflected the moonlight. Turning my cheek toward him, I took in his relaxed face, closed eyelids and cheesy smirk upon his lips.

"I knew we'd meet again," he said, feeling my gaze and opening one eyelid. The dark pupil huge amid the brown iris, a black hole swallowing the chocolate button. "Amaz that it was here, though."

"You and me both," I turned away from his gaze to lift my eyes to the night sky speckled with stars. "You know, it's almost as if we are in our own little bubble."

As tires crunched upon gravel in the distance and horns honked into the black night void of streetlamps and illuminating high-rises, I squinted at the beams of light projected from the cars lined up on the highway in the distance and sighed, "I just hope it doesn't burst."

Twangy country music was playing from his stereo and a warm, earthy breeze whipped up dried grain as it brushed against my face. Todd reached over and gripped my hand in his, squeezing tightly. The delicate fingers soft against my chilled palm.

"It'll be fine," he reassured. "You'll be fine. You're here, with us, remember."

We were parked in the field adjacent to the retreat property. Todd's lime-green Ford faced the highway, while the truck bed faced Holy Creator and the retreat center. The high beams of the vehicles in front us shone through the windshield and the sliding glass window behind our heads, landing on the green rippled metal between our bodies. So bright, so intrusive was the beam, I shimmied the blanket down lower to cover the reality. All around us, voices rose in the still, darkened air, as people were ushered into the church and the awaiting welcome party of parishioners, elders, and my mom and dad. We could hear horns honking, doors slamming, dogs barking, children crying, parents loudly talking about their journeys, and a rush of welcoming voices guiding the guests inside the sanctuary of the church. Jake was there, sitting diligently beside our parents, handing out care packages of food and water to the arriving crowds, waiting for his hand to be shaken and head to be petted like a good little boy.

I was not.

We hadn't even finished our meal when the other travelers began arriving: Families crammed into minivans and cars, squished even more than we had been between keepsakes and salvaged possessions.

"They will have everyone settled into rooms lickety-split," Todd said, pointing to the retreat center's dormitory buildings and to the groups making their way into the dimly lit doorways with awaiting bedrooms. "Thank God for that."

I was contemplating how on earth they could accommodate the growing convoy of cars lining the drive when Mom emerged from the oak door that led from the church building into the rectory. Her disheveled red mane was tied in a ponytail and an apron adorned in a bright red rooster with a yellow comb was cinched around her waist. Even from a distance, she looked in control, in charge. As she directed people this way and that, I realized how comfortable she was in giving orders, how unlike me she was in her confidence. For starters, I had none. Whatever bravado I had was all a lie; a ruse so people wouldn't dig deeper, see me.

"She's a natural at this, your kikâwiy."

Seeing my confusion, he added, "Mother."

"I know," I mumbled. "It's in her blood."

"Her blood runs through you, too."

"Yeah, but it's watered down."

"I don't believe that for a minute."

He rose onto his elbow and leaned over me.

"Dude, don't kid yourself. You're a leader through and through."

He plopped back down onto the scratchy blanket. "And I've got the scar to prove it."

As if he summoned proof, I turned my head to see a group of teenagers walking through the field and toward Todd's Ford. As they approached, they raised their voices and began chanting: "Hulk, Hulk, Hulk."

"What the ..."

"It's my posse, and your fan club," Todd rose, chirping in a high-pitched excited voice.

"Fan club?"

Incredulous, I sat up just as they began hoisting themselves into the truck bed, high-fiving and fist-bumping Todd, then turning shyly to me to do the same. I sat there, in shock, as the half-dozen teens tapped my knuckles in *respect*?

"Peeps, Jules; Jules, peeps."

As they sat down, I sat up, curling my legs under me so they wouldn't get trampled on.

"I bet I know what you all want," Todd began, winking in my direction, "a first-hand account, right?"

"You better believe it," said a tall boy with a blue-paisley bandanna tied around his forehead, who I would later discover was Charmaine. "We live a pretty sheltered life so this is like getting front-row seats to a blockbuster action flick."

Nervously chuckling, I turned to the eyes focused on me and swallowed the uncertainty.

"What do you want to know?"

My throat was suddenly very dry and my words croaked softly into the cool night.

"What's that?" Charmaine cupped a hand to his ear. One bushy black eyebrow was arched over his squinting eye.

I repeated the question more loudly and got the unified response of: "EVERYTHING!"

Todd leaned his back against the sliding windows of his truck cab, crossing his arms in front of him, and turned to me, "See, Jules, you're famous."

Infamous, more like it.

Remember Crystal; never forget Crystal and what you did to her.

And that, my friends, is why I'll never be my mother.

I hurt people.

****

We stayed out until well past midnight, talking about the terrorist attack, as cars continued their march into the Holy Creator driveway. The pebbled road was now a parking lot, as was the adjacent field in which Todd's truck had been hiding. As my fan club faded back into the dark to homes with beds and belongings, Todd and I remained until the temperature dropped and giggles turned to shivers. The rooms kept filling, the people kept coming, and the night wore on, unrelenting.

It was nearly one in the morning when we saw the flickering lights zooming through stalks of sorghum in the field south of the church. They looked like gigantic fireflies fluttering in and out of the two-meter-high stalks, before moving onto the adjacent bison ranch. Todd was leaning over the frosty green cab hood, while standing in the pan of the pickup, his right hand to his forehead, trying to figure out what was going on. The moon's round orb was covered in cloud and the stars gave little illumination on the commotion in the fields. I stood up beside him, rubbing my hand down the length of my legs to get the tingles out of the muscles and to warm my palms. Not having any luck, I grabbed the scratchy wool blanket on which I had been reclining and tied it around my waist in a blanket sarong.

"What's going on over there?"

"Haven't got a clue, but it doesn't look good, whatever they are doing."

"Flashlights?"

"Flashlights."

"For what?"

Why would anyone be scurrying around a field of broomcorn and a bison ranch in the middle of the night?

Before Todd could answer my question, a gunshot rang through the dark, making both of us jump backward, stumble and nearly land on our butts. Two more shots quickly followed. We dropped to the floor of the pan near the wheel wells, gripping the pan's edges with white-knuckled fingers. Our breathing came out in spurts onto the green truck bed: Quick puffs of air that sounded labored and out of control. In the fields, engines came to life. Todd and I turned toward the noise.

The clouds overhead had moved, and moon and starlight rained down upon the tops of the bushy crop and into the bison field. Several minutes went by. I tried to leave but Todd pulled me down by the bicep.

"Not yet," he whispered. "Just wait."

As I knelt onto the hard metal, engines began to rev in the distance. Todd and I lifted our heads over the truck rail just as dust clouds exploded into the air. Tires were spinning and squealing and then the trucks sped off down through the fields and onto a backroad, leaving a wake of dust behind them.

"What the … friggity frack?" I said with a voice out of breath and shocked.

"C'mon, we gotta go."

Todd was pulling me out of the pan of the truck and before I knew what was happening, we were running toward the rectory entrance, hand in hand.

Storming into the house, Todd picked up the receiver from Rev. Erin's phone in the living room and began dialing. The coiled cord connecting the receiver to the beige cradle hung at his side and his slender fingers twisted and twirled around several coils, agitated.

"What's going on?"

"Keep your voice down," Todd hissed, "You don't want to wake up your parents. I have to let Uncle know what's going on—he's the prez of the Pincher Creek Rural Crime Watch."

"And what *is* going on?"

"Poaching, Jules," Todd's eyebrows slanted in a V above his straight nose. Gone was the twinkle in his eyes, constant smirk waiting to break out.

Todd was angry.

No.

He was furious.

Thin purple veins popped at his temples, lines cut down on either side of his mouth as he frowned, and his grip on the receiver was more like a strangle hold.

This Todd was foreign to me.

This Todd was scary.

As he relayed the location of the lights to the person on the other end of the phone, his back straightened and his shoulders squared. His words burst forth in disjointed syllables and vowels.

Replacing the receiver in the cradle, he turned to me, took a deep breath in through the nose and exhaled, deflating his body from all anger.

"So?"

My tentative query was met with a sigh.

"So … Uncle Sam will call the authorities and they will take it from there."

"And the bison?"

"Probably being butchered as we speak. Nothing else for us to do."

Turning to the fridge, he opened the white door, grabbed a cola and tossed it to me.

I caught the cold aluminum can with my raised hand, "So what do we do now?"

"Wait for Fish and Wildlife to do their jobs and if they don't …."

"And if they don't?"

"We do it for them."

He grabbed a cola for himself, flipped the tab and walked to the living room. Turning his head slightly to look in my direction, he added, "And by *we,* I mean crime watch."

"Does that mean you're part of the group?"

"Dude! I'm the tracker!"

"The tracker?"

"Tracker Todd at your service."

"*Tracker Todd?* Coming up with your own nicknames, now, are we?"

Despite the seriousness of the situation, I couldn't help myself from snickering.

"Of course," he grinned and winked, "especially when I have my own business cards."

My mouth was still agape when he flopped down on the couch, his skirt flying up around his legs like a parachute inflating as he landed on the plump cushions.

We were reclining in the rectory living room, warming our bones by the now-lit fireplace. Cocooned on the plush, stallion-stampede printed couches and wrapped in quilted blankets, we spoke, dozed, spoke, repeat, as the flankers flew off the burning logs and flicked into the room.

It was nearly three in the morning, yet I couldn't let myself go. So, we talked instead—about everything and nothing, and catnapping in the silences between topics.

"So, give me the dets, *Tracker Todd*," I crooned, trying to get warm with an orange and black crocheted Afghan but the holes made it difficult, so I played with them instead, sticking my fingers through the loops and wagging them at the boy who was quickly becoming my best friend.

Todd chuckled and blushed.

"Well, you know I teach Blackfoot at summer camps, right?" Seeing me nod, he went on. "Grandfather Alex taught me as a boy—Auntie Irene and Auntie Erin's dad. He would take me out on the trapline and then on hunting trips. When he passed a few years ago, I decided to teach it at the camps."

"And the business cards?"

Grinning from ear to ear, Todd tilted his head and looked at me in a mischievous way, "I had those made-up last year, when the ranchers started getting coyotes and bobcats snatch calves out of the herd. They needed someone to track them to the dens so they could report it to Fish and Wildlife.

"Why? Did you want one?"

"Of course, *Tracker Todd*," I tried not to burst out laughing but my chest was heaving in an effort to contain the mirth. "You never know when I'll need to track Shade."

At the mention of his name, Shade lifted his fluffy black head and turned sparkling green eyes at us on the couch, then meowed.

Todd turned his head to the black cat curled up by the hearth. "With bobcats and coyotes around, I wouldn't count that out."

"Come here, Shade, we don't want to lose you, now do we?"

The cat rose, stretched its black legs, licked itself, then slowly walked to the couch, stretching its hind legs as it did so, and pounced onto my lap, putting a little black, furry paw into one of the Afghan holes.

"I do get the occasional request from hunting parties to help find elk and deer, but that pretty much dried up when vegetation kinda dried up and there was nothing for the animals to eat."

"Still, it's a great skill to have," I said, releasing Shade's paw from the crocheted loop. "Will you show me?"

"If it comes to it, sure, but let's see if Fish and Wildlife can do their jobs first, shall we?"

"I wouldn't think they would be that busy."

"No, but who knows if that department of government is even functioning anymore. Shoot, who knows if *any* level of government is functioning?"

As we lay, Todd on one end of the couch and I on the other, toe-to-toe, with the afghan covering our legs and torsos, he revealed his Uncle Samuel Blackfeather—aka Mr. B.—had invited him to Stampede High to record his university applications. It turned out, Todd was an honor student from the Piikani Nation High School and while he had been accepted in multiple post-secondary schools in Canada, what he really wanted was to go to the University of North Dakota and earn a doctorate in Blackfoot Studies. His application would include a video of him dancing, telling the stories of the Piikani People, and singing rap and pop hits in the Blackfoot language.

The guy had game.

That's why he was at my school yesterday.

Was it really only yesterday?

Two days from there to here.

Damn.

"You know, the Piikani are very studious," he explained, putting his cowboy hat on the pine frame of the couch he was sitting on. "It's tough competition, here, to get into good schools. Yet, we have the highest rate of students ever to go onto post-secondary on all the reserves in the country. So, I had to do something different, you know, to stand out. That's where Uncle came in."

"So, Mr. B is your *Uncle Sam* to go to *Uncle Sam*?"

"Jules, you are a riot," Todd slapped me on the back, laughing so hard he nearly popped a silver snap on his shirt wide open.

"Wait, how did you know the bus driver, Raj, was from Pakistan, if you were only at Stampede High for one day?"

Todd rolled his dark eyes to the exposed timbers above us, tilted his head and said in a voice dripping with condescension: "I asked, dumbass."

I whacked him on the shoulder with the yellow floral throw pillow under my elbow. "Jerk."

"Oooh, Hulk *smash*," Todd chuckled, smacking my shoulder with his own throw pillow.

"Watch it, dude."

"Or what? You going to MacGyver a stick out of that pillow and poke me with it?"

He hit me again. This time, it connected with my cheek and caused me to make a deflated balloon sound.

"No, I'll just Black Widow your ass, doofus," returning a blow to his cheek in retaliation.

Across from us, Jake snorted, snored and rolled over.

We stopped our pillow fight to look at his sleeping form, cushions raised above our heads.

The warm light from the fire flickered across his peaceful face and blond curls.

He looked like a snoozing cherub.

Man, he slept a lot.

Careful, Jules, when you start getting jealous over your bro's slumber habits, things are getting a little out of hand.

Todd let his pillow drop onto his lap and he hugged it close, following my gaze as he did so. "I remember those days. Dude must be hitting puberty, or as my Auntie calls it *Dawn of the Living Dead.*"

"What?"

"Yeah, dudettes slowly grow into adults. Us dudes, not so much: We sleep our way into adulthood."

He howled with laughter, then caught himself by covering his mouth with his hand and snickered as Jake rolled over, moaning.

"I'm normally here," he gestured to the walls.

"At the rectory?"

"No, funny pants, at the retreat center. A bunch of us organize weekend getaways for youth and teach them traditional ways of life—you know, hunting, gathering, trapping, fishing, that kind of thing. In fact, you met a few of them tonight. Charmaine, he's a great archer, even competes across the border, and Robbie, Charmaine's brother, is an awesome tracker. Man, he can track prairie chickens on a rockface. Mmmm. Prairie chickens."

He was almost drooling as he closed his eyes. "Ever have any? Delish. Takes just like chicken."

I howled with laughter, covered my mouth to not wake Jake, as my body shook.

"You're joking, really?"

My sarcasm was met with a chuckle and a wink.

"I bet they'll be on the menu tonight. In these parts, they are fair game for the locals."

"Can't wait."

And I couldn't. Even after the huge dinner, my stomach had already begun to rumble with the thought.

"They aren't as meaty as the chickens they raise in the coop but they are tasty as heck."

It was now Todd's turn to have a vocal middle and he grinned tiredly, yet sheepishly, in my direction, patting his covered midsection.

"What are some of the other workshops the center puts on?"

My attempt to try and change the subject away from food was met with a nod of agreement.

"I have language workshops, and anyone can come join in. You'd be surprised how many farmers, ranchers, and their kidlets come, too."

Seeing my expression, he lifted an eyebrow, "don't look so amaz. I'm good, real good."

I laughed, "I bet you are."

Ignoring my jibe, Todd pulled up the wool to his chin and glared at me in feigned anger, then couldn't hold in the bubbling chuckle that rose in his throat.

"Rev. Erin is very chill. She doesn't get all religious on us; she just offers up the space and we use it. Don't get me wrong, some of my relatives come to Holy Creator to attend services but even those that don't, contribute."

Todd's life sounded like a fantasy: *Everyone* coming together to grow food and raise cattle, share in the duties, and pray to a mysterious God who was probably damning me to hell, despite the acceptance from my dad. In Calgary, there were no fresh fruits and vegetables, no cattle, no grains other than the broomcorn bought from around here. Here, though, it's like time had stood still: creeks were clean, ponds weren't polluted, fields grew sorghum and bison roamed. There were even chicken coops and rows of beehive towers near the paddock fences.

"Hey, Todd," I began.

"Yes, Hulk?"

Sighing, I threw another yellow pillow at him, which landed lightly on his shoulder and he howled like Shade, who was currently curled up by Jake's head after a feed of cooked bison liver. Todd rubbed the spot and scowled for all of five seconds before busting a gut. "Get real. I just wanted to let you know I've … changed my name. It's Jules, now, not Julia, and it's Jules with a U, not like the gems. I … ah … I'm fluid, you know, with … eh … gender."

Todd was nodding.

"And the diff is …?"

"Well, you can still call me *Jules* but when you spell it, it's the male version: J-u-l-e-s."

"Oh, the French name?"

"Yeah."

"Cool."

"So, nothing really changes, other than you not calling me *Hulk*."

"Double cool. But I'm not going to stop calling you Hulk."

"Why the heck not?"

"Because, *Jules,* you are what you are, and you'll always be *Hulk* to me. Unless, of course, *MacGyver-Black Widow* suddenly catches on, and it won't, because it's lame and you are *definitely* not lame."

He tilted his head to one side, squinted so his bushy black eyebrows formed a serious V and turned to me.

"You being transfluid, though, it figures," he paused, rubbing his square jaw with his slender hand. "Hey, you ever hear about people with two spirits?"

"Huh?"

He lifted the blanket and swiveled so that he was facing the fire. Rising, he walked toward the hearth, picked up a long, black iron poker with a hook at the end and began poking at the logs, unsettling them so sparks flew up into the rock-faced chimney. His back was to me, his shoulders squared.

"Two spirits. It doesn't really have anything to do with sexual orientation as much as it does with gender identity. Two-spirit people have a long history in first-nation tribes. They were the holy people, the matchmakers and peacekeepers of the tribe; the people who predicted the future and brought good luck."

Todd turned, placed the iron stick back into the resting horseshoe-shaped latch, and touched the gauze on his head. "Lots of good luck."

Taking a deep breath, he added, "I'm one, you know—two-spirit."

My smile reflected his. Unsure what to say, I said the only thing I could think of: words my parents had said to me when I revealed my secret identity, "That explains a lot."

Grinning shyly, he strolled back to the couch, sat facing the logs and leaned back against the worn, soft cushions. Crossing his ankles on the pine, fire-scorched coffee table, his denim-wrap skirt opened and fell on either side of his hairless calves. All the furniture in the room looked handmade, as if someone had chopped down the trees, tied pieces together with rope and scorched them with a blowtorch before staining and adding cushions. No wonder I felt comfortable here.

Nothing was fake.

His boots discarded, I smiled at Todd's exposed socks: bright pink with yellow polka dots.

"I would say, you, for example, are what we would call Saahkómaapi'aakíikoan—a boy-girl. Me, on the other hand, I'm Aakíí'skassi, hands down."

Pointing to his socks, smiling, he nodded, returning the grin.

"And that means …?"

"Acts like a girl, of course. I just think I've got more flair than others."

He spread his arms wide and bowed, which was difficult to accomplish with his ankles still crossed over the coffee table. He nearly fell onto the wood-planked floor in the process.

"Tell me more," I urged, lifting my legs and tucking them under my butt. "This is fascinating."

"Well," he slid his legs from the coffee table and crossed them on the cushions, tucked his skirt him under his limbs and turned his face to mine, "to begin with, we're talking two-spirited from the beginning, long before the explorers arrived and long after the land was settled. The two-spirited men wore dresses, jewelry and hair decorations. Some even lived with same-sex partners."

"In fact," he leaned forward, jutted out his chin and glared at me, "it wasn't until the Europeans came that they were discriminated against."

"Whoa, whoa there partner. My ancestry isn't my fault."

He chuckled and slapped my knee.

"Lighten up, Jules with a U, just kidding."

"So, what happened when the Europeans arrived?"

"The same thing that always happens when people want to conquer and show their dominance over another: They enforce their values and beliefs. The two-spirited people were fed to dogs, and those that weren't were forced to wear gender-specific clothes. The men had their hair cut and forced to wear men's clothes, while the women were forced to wear dresses. As you can tell, there was a lot of *forcing* involved."

He looked at me.

"Sound familiar?"

"Yeah, why is it that people want others to give up who they are to be who they want us to be? You'd think a democratic country would be more, ya know, democratic, and not totalitarianism."

"I know, right? But ya know, ya ain't got nothin' on how we were treated—residential schools, the Sixty's Scoop, the Highway of Tears, and it all began with the treatment of the two-spirits."

My heart ached for Todd, and all who had lived through such times. Being ripped from your family, having your identity stripped away and then to grow up being known as *drunk Indians* was by far worse than the gender police.

Sensing my thought, Todd placed a hand on my shoulder and added: "All assimilation is wrong, you know, no matter what race you are, the same as all discrimination is wrong. What's going on here, in Alberta, that's just the beginning.

"Those of two-spirit were told to hide their true identities."

He winked.

I was nodding and he squeezed my shoulder. "And we did it for years to avoid prosecution, but you can't hide forever."

"No, you cannot."

"There are now two-spirit societies all over North America. There's even one in Edmonton."

"How did I not know about this?"

"Because they don't want you to know. We are reserve citizens, so not part of the provincial government's constituencies. We have total autonomy. We are our own leaders, our own peoples, living on our own lands, with our own laws, and we can finally live our own truths."

"So, that's why."

"Why what?"

"Why Pastor Erin didn't bat an eye when she saw me." I leaned back onto the pine armrest. "She just smiled."

Now, Todd was grinning, his white teeth beamed in the soft yellow light coming from the pale-yellow lamp shades adorned with bison silhouettes on the end tables flanking the couches.

"Auntie Savannah has a whole line of clothes for two-spirit people. That's where I buy all my diva duds," he flicked up a leg to show off his skirt and socks. "Right down to the socks and shoes. You really should check out her site when all this is over."

"Wouldn't it be … inappropriate," I stammered. "I mean, it's *your* culture, not mine."

"Well, Auntie has this fashion declaration on her site, which basically says that if you wear her clothing with pride and respect, then the color of your skin doesn't matter. She calls it cultural appreciation, as opposed to cultural appropriation, which is when other cultures take ours and make it part of their own."

Pleased, I nodded, already imagining wearing Todd-ish clothing.

Would wearing different clothes change how I feel inside, though? Or, would they just be a disguise; a costume to present to the world when my true self didn't feel enough.

As if sensing my thoughts, Todd turned and gave me an eerily spooky and jovial grin. His lips were curled, giving his cheeks round, red apples that shone in the light of the lit lamps. His dark, black eyeliner-rimmed eyes creased downward, as his whole face moved upward.

"And believe me, if anyone needs a fashion makeover, it's *you*, honey," he drew a circle in the air in front of my body, "cause whatever ya got goin' on here, it's doin' nothin' for ya. Ya need a makeover, STAT."

"Screw you."

He burst out laughing at my indignation and shoved his shoulder into mine.

"Kidding, not kidding," he said, shoving my shoulder again.

His bubbling personality was contagious.

Now that I thought about it, Todd was *constantly smiling*.

Wasn't everybody here?

Was that what 'living your own truth' looked like?

Is that how happy you were inside when you didn't have to pretend?

If it was, no wonder I felt like I belonged here.

Because I did.

As we sat looking into each other's eyes, realizing our truths were on full display, Rev. Stillwater emerged from the shadows with a tray of hot cocoa and caraway biscuits.

"Nice to see you've met someone to talk to," she said, placing the tray on the tabletop. "Nephew, Jules will need to sleep, eventually, and so will you."

"Yes, Auntie."

Todd's face flushed. Rev. Erin wore a long white nightgown and a faded blue robe loosely tied around her middle. On her feet were buttery suede moccasin slippers with pale pink beaded roses stitched over the toes. Her gray-black hair hung loose around her shoulders, falling in ribbons of wavy rivers. Sleepy eyes gazed from Todd to me, and I wondered if she had been awake all this time, tossing and turning. And praying.

"It is through sleep that our minds rest and heal; where our guards are down and the Creator can fill us with his spirit so we can be renewed," she continued, "and that is something Jules needs more than ever, I believe, especially after rescuing you from evil."

"Yes, Auntie."

She smiled, leaned over and her soft lips kissed Todd's forehead, then mine.

"Be at peace, Niece, for the Creator—our Lord and Savior—brought you here for a reason."

Then she was gone, her body dissolving into the dark shadows of the room like smoke.

I turned and looked into the fire, reflecting on what she said.

The day had passed in bursts of activity.

After breakfast, my family had attended Morning Prayer in the church, talked, napped, toured the church and rectory, eaten again, hung out by the bison paddock, watching the beasts lick salt blocks and meander around the grassy fields, and then to the horse stables, where Jake was put on the back of a rotund, pregnant mare and led around the yard. After a lunch of more scrumptious food, including Mom's packed snacks, which made their way onto the table with much flourish by Pastor Erin. While Jake and I had spent much of the day getting to know our surroundings and catching up on our sleep,

Mom, Dad and Rev. Erin had spent much of their time in a closed-door parish council meeting in the church.

While they talked until they were blue in the face, Jake and I watched how goats were milked—I even tried my hand at it, and got squirted in the face, much to the delighted giggles of my little bro. So, of course, I had to squirt him in retaliation. I got a small container to take back to the rectory for Shade, as a little treat, not that he needed it since he loved living the life of a country mouser. Once the meeting let out, we were all taken to homesteads to introduce us to the families who ran the fields and ranches and they welcomed us with tea and honey cake; paper bags to pick crabapples from the trees growing in the thickets and a promise of a larger welcome tomorrow night at dinner. All knew Rev. Erin, and most came to Sunday services each week. We visited the Holy Creator Retreat Centre's health center clinic, where many of the local nurses and doctors were treating the first wave of fleeing Calgarians and sending them off, bandaged and with bagged lunches. The room was small but expertly organized with a few examination rooms, a nurses' station, a doctor's office and a pharmacy. Many who came did so for first aid and were soon continuing their travels south, trying to get across the border to unaffected radiation areas or detouring around the farmlands on their way east.

"Does the church employ health-care workers?"

"No, they are all volunteers, but we give them an honorarium," Rev. Erin opened the center's door to let us walk outside. "Whether they are locals or from the reserves, all who donate their time are treated like royalty here. We may not be able to pay them but we are able to give a percentage of the harvests, which is way more valuable."

As we walked to the boulders in front of the church, she pointed to the silver plaques bolted to the stone surfaces that I had noticed upon our arrival. Etched into the metal were the names of the five tribes that made up Treaty 7: Siksika/Blackfoot; Kainai/Blood Tribe; Piikani/Peigan; Stoney-Nakoda; and Tsuut'ina/Sarcee. "It's an acknowledgement of the land and where we have been planted."

Another, smaller boulder was erected near the front entrance of the health center. On them, a series of names, male and female. "The many doctors and nurses who have helped us get the center clinic up and running."

"We are always hopeful more will come and serve," Rev. Erin smiled, brushing her hand over the shiny surface of the rectangles. "We trust that the

Holy Creator is working in the hearts of others just as he did with those who have already given of their time. Whether we see the plan in action or not, isn't the point. The point…" she turned to Todd and me, "the point is trusting there is one."

After a long nap, we sat down to the meal to end all meals with Rev. Erin's family, and where I came face-to-face with the realization that I was respected, honored despite the dark feelings inside that I didn't deserve it. Then there was the fan-club meeting in the truck with Todd and his friends and now, reclining on this couch, exhausted but too wired to sleep.

So much had happened since the explosion in Calgary.

Despite the less than forty-eight hours since the attack, I felt changed and the boy sitting beside me played a large part in that transformation.

As the night slowly gave way to day, I let my mind wander, reliving the full day spent and the coming dawn.

Would I even recognize myself after all of this, if one day of *community* made such an impact on my life?

Wasn't that the point?

Shade's black form leaped onto my lap as I sunk into the cushions. Curling his body up my chest as if giving me a big cat hug, his black hair tickling my nose, he began to purr. The treble rumbling vibrated into my chest and room, lulling me to sleep. Todd leaned against my shoulder, breathing heavily as he, too, felt Shade's purring pull. I thought of the flocks of people converging on the church, seeking the comfort my own family had found here. I thought of their fear, their worry over what next, and the realization that we were all in the same boat, really—without a home.

I didn't need to see them to know they were sitting, gorging themselves with foods that would sustain as much as they would delight. Meals that they had never eaten; dishes they had instantly longed for the moment they were consumed. Was this aid sustainable, though?

Was anything?

Now, with the dawn of Day 3 approaching, I realized I was not *odd* or *deprived* or, worse, needing to be *fixed.* In fact, Pastor Erin's words of peace and belonging felt true, as if *my truth* was being told.

"Hey, Todd."

"Yeah," he had nodded off and his head jerked awake at my voice, "Jules with a U."

"You're very fortunate to live here, you know. Maybe you should stay. Outside this place, it's not the same."

"Don't I know it," he yawned, tapping his open mouth with his hand as if it were a drum. "Given what's going on out there," his head tilted to the door, "I don't know if I'll ever leave again."

I looked at his reclined body, his long skirt tucked around his calves and the colorful vibrant socks. I absorbed the image like a sponge: His *spirit* was resting, at peace. As I stared, my throat closed and I found it hard to swallow. Emotions washed over me in waves, lapping at my lips to make them tremble; flowing over my tired eyes, causing them to sting and give up the tears they had longed to shed for the past forty-eight hours. Letting the droplets fall, I turned to the one person who finally got it; got me and said the only thing I could convince my clenched esophagus to give up.

"Same."

Chapter 11

Bright yellow light streamed in through the stained-glass windows that spanned the height of the church, leaving rainbow prisms to dance upon Dad's hairless dome. We had risen at dawn and joined the parade of parishioners walking to the chapel for Sunday morning Holy Communion. The iron bell was ringing in the steeple, soft-hided and cowboy-booted feet shuffled and clicked along the pebbled path. All were adorned in bright, colorful fabrics, from cowboy shirts to ribbon skirts. Beaded earrings dangled down napes, swaying in and out of curtains of black. There were even those who had donned more traditional attire, and I watched the dresses and high heels stroll into the building, accompanied by suits and oxfords. It was a mishmash of culture and class that made my mom and dad grin like kids in a candy shop. In our Calgary church, the parishioners were carbon copies of each other, as if there was an agreed upon uniform for worship. That was definitely not the case here, and I saw the advantage of attending, just as you are, who you are. Looking over at Todd, I was glad.

"God wants you to bring your true self, your whole self to him," Dad had said once, when Mom was trying to convince me to forego my jeggings for a skirt. "So, if your true self is more comfortable in stretchy fake jeans, then who am I to say otherwise?" I guess this was Rev. Erin's take on respectable church clothes as well because all around me, people came wearing their personalities with honor. I strolled beside Todd, who wore a relatively toned-down version of Rev. Stillwater's skirt, since it only had ribbons near the waist and hem. A crimson snap-front shirt with white embroidery completed the ensemble. The deep red and white colors matched the ribbons on the black skirt that swayed around his cowboy boots.

I was underdressed in comparison.

Another flannel shirt; another pair of faded blue jeans, and these had ripped, frayed holes in the knees.

Why hadn't I brought more girly clothes?

Because you can't be comfortable fleeing from the apocalypse when you're in heels and a tight mini-skirt, dumbass.

No one cared, however.

Mom, Dad and Jake were walking in front of me. Both parents held onto Jake's small hands as if he was going to run away.

As we neared the arched, dark-stained wooden doors, I heard the singing.

Waves of high notes in the Blackfoot language rushed to my face, lifting my spirit and bringing it back down into my body.

"Beautiful, isn't it," Todd held the door while I walked in. "It always makes me feel like I'm flying on a raven's wings."

"Yes, that's exactly how I feel," I turned to him and squeezed one of his red shoulders. "Soaring."

His face beamed.

After the service, Rev. Stillwater stood at the lectern, her white clergy robe glowing from the bright light of day. Her hand was raised and her wrinkled, pale palm blessed the crowd for the days ahead.

"Go in peace, to love and serve the Lord."

"Hallelujah," the congregation replied.

Everyone sat.

"And now for announcements," the priest began, walking down from the altar and making her way toward the side lectern. "First, I wish to thank all of you—the church family of Holy Creator—for stepping up when the need arose to feed the hungry, just as our Lord and Savior taught us. Thank you."

There was a round of applause from the congregation.

"The Holy Creator Retreat Centre is now housing all those who we received last night, and we are preparing to welcome others who need our help but the need for food and clothing will be constant. So, I appeal to all of you here today to spread the word that the center is open for donations of supplies."

Rev. Erin rambled off a list of nonperishable items, including those for seniors and babies. "I know you have all given from your heart but I am asking you to give, again, because we are all these people have."

Murmurings rose among the congregation as those sitting in the pews turned to each other to discuss the call.

"As you will be feeding their bodies, Parish Council has also decided to try and feed their souls. We will be organizing small-group healing sessions for all who need them. These are trying times we are facing, and while the Lord our God has a plan for each and every one of us, we cannot ignore the possibility that that plan is serving our neighbors, attending to their spiritual and emotional, just as much as their physical needs."

"Amen to that," Dad mumbled.

"There are many in our midst who have witnessed horrific things in the three days since the terrorist attacks—on the news and in their journeys here," she turned to our family sitting two rows in front of her and smiled. "The courage and faith that was needed to get here should not be taken as acceptance and peace. Peace comes from lifting our worries up to the Creator, but first we have to let go, and that is what these sessions will do."

Then, her gaze caught mine, "Anyone who would like to attend need only show up tomorrow at 9 a.m. in the Fireside Prayer Room downstairs. Breakfast will be provided."

Rev. Erin stepped down from the lectern steps. The priest's white robe swayed around the hem of her ribbon skirt; today, the ribbon was a bright blue, the same color of the beads that dangled from her ears. Around her neck, she wore a woven green stole about twelve centimeters wide. It draped down her front, dangling on either side of her neck, ending just below the hem of the robe Dad had once told me was called an alb. Toward the bottom were stripes of white, yellow, black, and red.

"They are the colors of the Blackfoot Confederacy," Dad explained, pointing to similarly hued beads threaded through strands of leather at the bottom.

I wondered if Mr. B's wife, Savannah, had made the priest's garments, for they looked original and personal; much more personal, at least, than the mass-produced versions my dad wore when he led services. I turned to my parents, taking in their peaceful faces, and wondered if their outward calm was just a façade like mine, or were they truly at ease with the situation we had found ourselves in—domestic refugees with nowhere to go, relying on the generosity of strangers for the most basic of needs, even our own sanity.

"I thought this might happen," Dad whispered to Mom. "What the locals have built here is remarkable, but it makes them the envy of the province, maybe even the country, and jealousy begets violence."

I turned to follow his gaze to the faces filling the church. I saw families that toiled together; grew together. I knew there were wolves out there. I had heard their loud howls on the drive here and they would come with honking car horns; cursing, hungry mouths; and guns raised to seek what lies inside the sun-bleached wooden fences. I could feel the anger and anguish rising in my chest, tightening my lungs so that I could not breathe; sending shock waves to the muscles in my stomach so it flipped and my legs so they cramped.

"Jules, I think it's time."

Todd's warm hand covered my vibrating knee.

"Time for what?"

Even I could hear the tremor in my voice, so I knew he heard it, too. It felt like it was running through my whole body.

"Time for healing."

****

Rev. Erin Stillwater had not been wrong. Once we returned to the rectory, we spent the afternoon unpacking and settling into our rooms. Just before five o'clock, we sat down for another dinner buffet. The farmers and ranchers came much like the Blackfoot elders, bearing dishes of scrumptious food and sitting at the long table to regale us with their families' histories in the area, while we sat, ate and got our fill of food and new-found friendship. The food, while different, was just jaw-droppingly delicious: Shepherd's pie with chunks of lamb and vegetables in gravy; roast chicken with broomcorn stuffing; a bowl of savory succotash; platters of buttery green beans; homemade chicken-stuffed ravioli in a cheese and onion sauce; and, my favorite, crabapple pies topped with homemade ice cream.

I was stuffed ten ways to Sunday, as my Nan would say.

And it felt wonderful.

Talk eventually came around to the commotion in the fields in the early morning hours, and some ranchers were threatening their own poacher hunt if Fish and Wildlife didn't bring the culprits to justice. I sat quietly at the table, squishing greenhouse peas with my fork and making their innards pop out from the bright green skins.

"We can't let these people deprive us of our livelihood," a tall, lanky man in a puffer red vest was saying, pointing his butter knife at everyone at the table. "I'm all for giving to the needy, but if we ignore this blatant theft, where will it stop? The next thing ya know, they'll be grabbing the chickens in the coop, the goats in the barn, and the very plates off our tables."

Many of the heads around the large wooden rectangle nodded in agreement.

Dad's brows furrowed.

Mom gripped his hand, which was pressed palm-down onto the oak surface of the table. I could see his fingers relax as she squeezed.

Rev. Erin's lips grew thin.

"I will not have any talk about violence and retribution at my table," she said firmly. "We are here to welcome the Klassen family. We are servants of the Lord, and we are here to not only aid them in their distress but others, as well.

"Now, what they did wasn't right, I know, but desperate times often lead to desperate actions and we have to remember forgiveness and grace; mercy and love are needed now more than ever."

Dad's chin pressed down in a nod.

Several grunts came from the people around the table.

"Now, now, Mr. Gareau," the priest continued, "put away your malice and reach for your mercy."

The tall rancher reluctantly acquiesced.

"I hear ya, reverend, but there's only so much a man can take."

"That's why we lean on our God," Rev. Erin countered.

Seeing tense faces around the dinner table, Mom picked up a buttered roll and inspected the pale yellow-white spread, marveling its appearance, then took a bite.

"Can someone please tell me how you get those stalks of dog tails out there to become these mouthwatering confections of pure bliss?"

Dad burst out laughing.

"What?" Mom was still chewing, but her wide eyes stared into Dad's grinning face. "You know, I suppose?"

"Yes, Shel, I do."

He was trying unsuccessfully to contain his snickering at her question.

"Well, I don't."

"I gathered."

"Well?"

"Why don't you come to the broomcorn demonstration in Mary Pentecost Place tomorrow," Rev. Erin interjected. "In fact, why don't your whole family come? Nephew is leading it and I'm sure he can fit in a few more people."

Conversation successfully changed, the rest of the meal continued with facts about sorghum, the milling process and the railcars that take the grain to various destinations all over the country.

As Jake and I tried to dissolve into the background to avoid the tugging of children's hands to play games, Mom gave us a *'be kind and play, you ingrates'* look, while smiling and nudging her shoulder into Dad's.

Had she feigned ignorance to change the mood?

Mom The Peacemaker.

Sounds about right.

Now, that was a skill I could not master, even among the littles tugging on my arm to play. A swift kick in my shin by a pair of size 7 shoes under the table gave me a nudge, though, and while Mom looked on, Jake and I gathered up the kids and went outside to play tag in the field while the adults continued their discussion on grain and transportation; bison and the cost of beef.

Once it was over, Dad and Mom said their farewells and Jake and I grudgingly hugged sticky bodies before they departed with their families. Rev. Erin *suggested* Jake and I clean up from dinner, so she and the folks could relax on the horse couches in the living room. Despite my belly sighs, no one listened, so we grumbled and did what was *suggested*.

Well, I grumbled.

Jake filled the sink with soapy water and began washing the many towers of dishes on the counter. So, I picked up a tea towel to dry.

"Want to listen to music?" his soft voice interrupted my inner fuming. "It helps me do something I don't want to do."

Without waiting for me to reply, he removed his phone from his pocket, turned on the amplified speakers, and selected a song list.

A drum beat thundered through the kitchen, followed by sticks on cymbals and an electric guitar. Then, the vocalist began to sing:

It might take some time
But I'll do it on my own
You act as if it's a crime
Like I'm bad down to my bones
But I sleep at night time
And I can't understand how you ever did
Sounds cliché I can't live a lie
I was feeling old and tired
Now I feel like a little kid
I think you're suddenly blind
Only see what you want to do
Good God man where's your mind
You don't see me but you're so easy to see through
Now I'm slipping through the corn rows
Now I'm slipping through the corn rows
You can't see me any more
Now you're slipping through the corn rows
Slipping through the back rows
Can't see me anymore, can't see me anymore

"Wide Mouth Mason," he said, blushing in embarrassment. "Like?"

"Like," I said, smiling. "Got another?"

Beaming, he shoved his small hand holding a washcloth into a glass and proceeded to twist. "Loads! Dad helped me create a playlist of ol' timey Canadian rock tunes. Cool, eh?"

"Real cool, dude," I said, nodding. "This ol' timey stuff ain't half bad."

Grinning, Jake put his now gleaming, sudsy glass into the rack, and I promptly picked it up and began drying it. Reaching for a dinner plate, he began to scrub away bits of food.

"See, makes doing the dishes better, right?"

"So right."

With that, I scooped up a bunch of bubbles with my hand and blew them into Jake's face. His head whipped around to face me, bubbles already popping on his chin, his eyes wide.

Had I gone too far?

Then his lips parted and his chicklet teeth gleamed wickedly at me. As I watched his expression, astounded, he reached behind him and did the same to me.

"Hey, hey, hey," Dad barked from the living room, "don't make a bigger mess than what you're cleaning up out there."

Turning to the trio in the living room, Jake and I faced them covered in suds from forehead to chin, grinning.

"Never!" We shouted, spurting more bubbles onto the floor as we did so, and then erupted in chuckles of laughter.

"Jinx!" We said in unison.

"Agh," Dad groaned from the couch.

"Leave them alone, hon, they are getting *along.* "

I watched as Dad's head turned to Mom in slo-mo, "You're … right."

Rev. Erin shook her head, "Family, community, grace and love, that's all anyone needs to be at ease, don't you think?"

"You hit the nail on the head there."

With Dad's affirmation still ringing in my ears, I turned back to the drying rack and picked up another soapy plate.

So, this is how it starts.

Having a friendship with my brother.

Cool.

****

As we all lounged on the plush stallion-stamped cushions in the living room, Dad strode over to the large television screen mounted above the fireplace and pushed a small button above several USB and HDMI inputs, and it instantly turned green. The remote control went missing during tonight's dinner with the local farming families and I had a sneaky suspicion that the visiting children had hid it as part of a game. We had searched for it in between cushions and under furniture with no luck. As Dad slumped heavily onto the couch, a CBC news anchor emerged from the black curtain to give the evening report. Terra Nova leader Jon Solberg had released his manifesto to the press, and they were playing his pre-recorded video on the air. My head turned when the voice changed and the distinctively Scandinavian accent captured my attention.

He stood in front of ever-changing images of earth, talking about how humans had destroyed the planet; harvesting all its riches with little regard to future generations or the planet itself. I gazed at his sea-blue eyes and thought how attractive this man was; how vanilla.

How *average.*

I was half expecting to see a formidable, angry ruler and instead, an average-height, average-built blond man waltzed back and forth in front of the changing video feed behind him and spoke as if he were a politician. Maybe he was, I thought. Maybe this doughnut hole, who thought destruction was the solution to global warming, was some nut job the we had created.

After the Americans had built the walls keeping Canadians and Mexicans out, and ensuring the 'native Americans' remained pure, other countries began to enact similar inane measures. France put walls up around its borders, citing it wanted to keep its French culture from being diluted. Not long afterwards, Quebec began discussing a similar response and within a couple of years, it had become a French-only province in the middle of Canada, with a zero-immigration and zero anglophone inter-provincial migration policy. I wasn't naive enough to believe the rationale for any of the measures: It was just racism in a suit. Politicians used fear all the time to force people to act, or not, and Solberg was just another wolf in sheep's clothing. Keeping eye contact, his passion-filled plea to change or be changed, even his mannerisms, were that of privileged uppity snake-oil salesman, as my Nan would say. But I couldn't look away, and I couldn't ignore his passionate plea and rationale.

That's the point, Jules!

Was this man insane, or were we?

I looked over at Dad, always the reasonable one, to get insight.

He was sitting beside Mom, holding her hand, shaking his head. His jaw was clenched and I could see that his beady eyes were squinting at the image of the man on the TV.

Did Solberg's message resonate with him?

I doubt it.

Dad was too logical.

Maybe his ancestors were from *Vulcan.*

I wouldn't be surprised.

Vulcan, *Alberta*, anyway.

He was probably trying to make sense of it all, rationalizing where this Solberg was coming from, and where he was going with his message of punishment and renewal.

Dad pushed his black-framed glasses up his bulbous German nose and exhaled through his nostrils. I could feel the air flutter the hair on my arms. He was struggling. We all were.

When Solberg spoke of Terra Nova, the group behind the attacks, Mom erupted in hysterical laughter.

Had she gone mental?

Did Solberg break Mom?

We all stared at her as if she had experienced a nervous breakdown—with Mom, it wasn't a far stretch.

"Terra Nova!" she proclaimed.

"Yes, that's what he said. Are you OK?"

"Yes, Pete, I'm just fine. It's Newfoundland."

"Huh?"

"Newfoundland. You know, when the Europeans first arrived, they called it Terra Nova: New Found Land."

Dad put his arm around her shoulders and squeezed.

Probably trying to juice some life out of her, I thought with a smile.

"Really, hon? That's interesting."

"No, really! Coincidence, don't you think, considering Newfoundland was one of the few provinces not to be targeted in the strikes?"

Dad rubbed his chin.

"Well, now that you mention it ..."

Mom smiled and looked at me.

I reached over to the brown paper bag on the coffee table and grabbed a cinnamon-sugar-dusted piece of fry bread left there by the Piikani elves, who had also brewed a pot of rich, black coffee upon our arrival back to the church's living quarters. I munched and sipped my coffee. Jake was doing likewise, only with a tall glass of milk. He already had a mustache that spanned across his top lip and nearly all of his cheeks.

A blonde woman with a short bob haircut appeared on the TV screen.

"Shush!" mom yelled to the silent room, before taking a sip of her black brew.

The woman looked down at her notes and turned her red-rimmed eyes to the camera in front of her. Her chest rose and fell. I knew that look; those actions. It was my survival technique. It was what I did before engaging in a wrestling match. It was what I did before running for dear life up Centre Street only a week ago. It was what I did when I was afraid the fear inside me would overflow and I would be frozen into place.

I had a newfound respect for our prime minister, then.

While Gabe Bloom had shown restraint and poise, Jacqueline LeBlanc was the complete opposite.

She didn't pretend.

She didn't cover up her emotions.

If anything, the red-rimmed eyes screamed them loud and clear.

"Good evening, my fellow Canadians," her soft voice trembled, and the room around her was hushed into dead silence. Even Shade stopped his purring by my feet, lifted his black head and turned to the image cube.

"Tonight, we mourn those whose lives have been lost in recent devastating events around Canada and, indeed, the globe. We mourn those who fell in British Columbia, after tsunamis and earthquakes rippled through that province, pushing most of the shoreline underwater. We remember the dead in all the cities and sites where terrorist attacks lead to unspeakable destruction by extremists wanting to tell the world their skewed view was more important than the sanctity of life, and the lives of mankind itself."

I looked over at Dad.

He was still.

I wondered if he had been praying for Uncle Tim, Aunt Sydney, Callum and twins Jimmi and Hendrix. He had been phoning since we arrived at Anglican Church of the Holy Creator but the landlines and cell phone towers were down in B.C. Uncle Tim lived in Vancouver's West End. Once upon a time, we would meet in Kelowna and camp in a park by Lake Okanagan, but we hadn't in years. I couldn't even remember what my cousins looked like anymore. Blond and short, that's what I got when I tried to recall their faces. My cousins were a lot younger than me and Jake. In fact, they were toddlers when we last saw them.

Now, we may never see them again.

"From small towns to large cities; from factories and plants to office towers and gardens, we mourn. Your loss will not be forgotten," Prime Minister LeBlanc's voice continued from the television.

She paused, looked down at the lectern. I could see her chest rise and fall beneath the white shirt and navy blazer. There was a red poppy pinned to her lapel, a remnant from a Remembrance Day ceremony, I imagined, and I wondered if she'd ever talk again.

As the pause in her address lingered, I watched the fine lines around her mouth deepen, then taking a deep breath, she continued.

"We will overcome this adversity and attack on our democratic, beautiful and highly sought-after way of life just as we have always done: with fortitude, with convection, and with foresight.

"While we reel from recent events that have impacted our nation, we also turn our gaze to the south, and mourn alongside our neighbors in the United States, whose lands were even more targeted by the terrorists known as Terra Nova."

She paused, swallowed and raised her voice.

"The American Border Barrier, or ABB, erected some nine years ago will remain intact, as we put our plan of attack into action. We have already deployed Canadian Forces personnel to patrol the barrier to ensure it is not tampered with, and the safety of our fellow Canadians living in border towns.

"The Canadian Disaster Relief Plan will call upon experts in soil and water management, urbanization and city planning, air quality and food production. It will harness all this information and put the survival of our Canadian way of life at the top of the agenda."

"Well, if we've been evacuated due to radiation poisoning, I'd say we're screwed," I mumbled to the room.

"Jules, c'mon, think of Jake," Mom hissed.

Yeah, think of Jakey, Jules.

"We are Canadians and we are survivors. Despite the cruelty inflicted upon our cities, we will endure. We will come together, as only Canadians can, to ensure our survival is a certainty and done with compassion and empathy.

"Some parts of Western and Central Canada were unscathed; our East Coast and Far North saw no attacks whatsoever. So, we will begin our plans in those locations and decide next steps, which will include a committee of societal, legislative, environmental and disaster preparedness and relief experts. The committee will determine how these recent attacks will affect every aspect of life in our nation—on the soil, the water, the air, the sources of food—the report for which will be presented in the House of Commons thirty days from today's date. This will be a special seating of the House. Upon its presentation, member representatives will vote on the measures brought forth by the committee. Those that receive unanimous votes will be implemented immediately, while those that do not receive unanimous votes will be sent back for further discussion and amendments.

"We … are … Canadians.

"And we will get through this tumultuous time with our identity, our integrity, and our love of country and land intact." She paused and then began speaking in French.

When she finished translating, LeBlanc lifted her hand to the seated reporters in the press room and added: "There will be no questions at this time," and walked off the stage.

"Well, that was depressing," Mom got up and walked into the kitchen and turned on the kettle. "I could really go for a glass of wine, right now, even if it is communal."

Dad walked up to her and hugged her from behind.

"I know," she sighed, leaning her head back against his chest. "Tea will have to do."

Dad kissed the top of Mom's red head and held her closer.

"One day, when all this is over, we'll go out, enjoy a lovely dinner and celebrate with a tall glass of Okanagan red, OK?"

"Promise?"

"I'll even stomp on the grapes myself."

Looking down at his dusty, scraped sandaled feet, Mom twisted back and looked up into Dad's face, "Ah, hard pass."

Dad's chest rose in a hearty chuckle.

I turned to Jake, who was smiling at our parents.

"Gross," I breathed, suddenly feeling alone.

Before I could move away, Jake wrapped his stringy arms around me and squeezed.

"Don't worry, Jules, you got me."

This time, instead of going with my first instinct to punch my little bro in the bicep, I leaned into him and he tightened his grip.

It lasted three seconds.

Then I punched him.

Jake fell back onto the cushions, gripping his arm as if I had hit him with a mallet.

White teeth gleamed in the yellow light coming from the lamps in the room.

I had let my guard down, and he knew it.

The damage had already been done.

My brother knew I liked him.

Jeez Louise, I have done it now.

****

Morning sunshine flooded through the kitchen windows. The yellow curtains clapped the encore and I watched from the living room as Mom walked to the table, a rooster apron secured around her waist and covering a brown corduroy skirt.

A bowl of white and brown eggs resting on the surface of the table, along with loaves of round bread, slices of cured meat and red, juicy tomatoes. She clanged around cupboards until she found a frying pan and began to fry eggs and slice the bread for the toaster. Dad got up and helped, setting the table with plates and cutlery.

Jake rose from the footstool and walked over to the kettle, filled it and put it on the stove before turning it on.

No one spoke.

As the eggs sizzled, Mom ground pepper atop them; Dad scratched butter onto the toasted bread; and Jake put bags of orange pekoe into a teapot.

In the living room, the TV burst through the silence.

"In the news today: A 7.5-magnitude earthquake has rattled eastern United States. Residents in New York, Washington, D.C., and Charleston, South Carolina awoke this morning to at least five minutes of ground shaking, depending on their locations. Nashville, Tennessee and Louisville, Kentucky were among the cities most affected by the quake. Earth convulsions knocked down buildings, reduced homes and roadways to rubble and uprooted trees. In

Louisville, fire department personnel have been working tirelessly since 3 a.m. this morning to rescue 945 children buried during the collapse of the St. Peter's Elementary School. St. Peter's is one of many schools that crumbled in the early-hours' earthquake. Thousands are homeless as municipal governments assess the damage while emergency services still respond to reports of hundreds buried beneath the rubble. The United States Army brought in helicopters to airlift supplies and to carry the injured to unaffected hospitals. However, aftershocks continue to wreak havoc on rescue attempts and aid relief. Air quality remains low and those living in and around the affected cities are urged to stay indoors."

The kettle steamed.

Jake poured the boiling water into the teapot, covered it with a knitted cozy and placed it on a wood-weaved trivet on the table.

"In related news, residents from San Bernardino, Parkland, San Juan Bautista and Point Delgarda—and many points in between—were hit with 5.4 to 6.1 magnitude earthquakes at seven this morning, and while there were no reported damages to buildings and infrastructures, the state department has asked residents to make the necessary arrangements in the event larger quakes are forthcoming."

Dad put the buttered toast on a plate and put more slices into the two-slot toaster before pushing the plunger down.

"In national news, Vancouverites awoke in the wee hours of the morning with shaking floorboards and rattling light fixtures, as a 5.8-magnitude quake hit the province's western coastline, causing Victoria, off Vancouver Island, to announce a state of emergency as the city dealt with a 6.3-magnitude quake. Tremors were felt in Prince George, Fort Nelson and even parts of the Alberta border."

Dad paused by the toaster, held his crucifix in his hand and began muttering.

Mom scrambled the eggs into fluffy yellow clouds and discarded the brown shells into a compost pail under the sink.

"Forest fires in Kelowna, Revelstoke and Cranbrook are being blamed on aftershocks that have erupted gas lines in the areas. The dense smoke is being spread by eastern winds to neighboring Alberta and Washington to the south. Poor air quality was reported in many neighboring states and provinces experiencing a rise in asthma-related breathing problems. Seniors, children and the infirmed are asked to stay inside; all others are advised to use caution when venturing outdoors."

Dad buttered more toast and plopped them onto the tower. Mom scooped up the eggs with a black, slotted spatula and placed a pile onto each of the plates dotting the table.

"In local news, the evacuation of northern and south-central Albertans, which began three days ago, continues to clog urban and rural roadways as reports of more radiation leaks surface at the Bow Valley SMR Facility near Calgary and at the Northern Lights SMR Facility on the outskirts of Edmonton. Initial estimates suggest nearly half a million people have fled to the southern parts of the province, while thousands more are seeking aid from neighboring Saskatchewan."

Images of convoys consisting of RVs, cars, trucks towing trailers, and hundreds of motorcycles and BMX bikes weaving in and out of traffic flashed across the screen. Mom stopped in mid-plate-placement on the table to stare blankly at the video feeds. As if in a trance, her hand slowly placed the brown handcrafted ceramic dish onto the brightly weaved placemat without even breaking her gaze.

"Now for the weather."

Mom's face was ashen.

Dad's expression matched hers from his stance against the counter, a plate of toast in one hand and a butter knife in the other.

I got up from the couch, walked over to the television and pushed the power button.

Trance broken, both parents blinked and placed their dishes onto the table and gestured for us to join them.

"What shall we pray for when there is so much to pray about?" Mom asked, her eyes glistening with unshed tears.

"What we always pray for in times of uncertainty," Dad folded his hands and closed his eyes. "We pray for guidance; we pray for peace; we pray for protection; and, above all, for God's will and grace be done. We pray … the way our Lord taught us to pray: Our Father, who art in heaven. Hallowed be thy name. Thy kingdom come …"

For the first time in a long time, I heard my voice join those sitting around the table, meaning every word.

Chapter 12

The newspapers thumped down onto the torched-wood coffee table.

Dad picked each one up, unfolded it and placed the front pages in a collage against the surface. I wondered what it was like to be a journalist when the world was in chaos. Were you detached? Were you excited for the hot-off-the-press headlines that seemed to come fast and furious every hour? Or were you overwhelmed and still had to hold it together and write, report, speak on camera? Were they all like Gabe Bloom, or were they more like Prime Minister LeBlanc?

As Todd joined me on the couch, his purple and green striped socks crossed at the ankles, Jake scooched over to cuddle into my side as he joined all of us to peer at the pages. Mom was leaning over Dad's shoulder, her cellphone in one hand with the thumb still tapping on the keyboard. I recognized the recipient: Sydney Klassen.

Turning away from my mom's message to my aunt in Vancouver, I glanced at the headlines in big, bold black letters, my heart pounding in agitation as I let the words seep into my brain, carrying with them every emotion, every thought. It was overwhelming. Fear, shock, horror, sadness, hope, excitement—all flashes that stirred my insides into a nervous frenzy and caused my heart to pound in my ears. Like the dust devils that circled the desert drain around Stampede High or the tornadoes that whipped across the prairies, my stomach churned clockwise in a vigorous power-blender twist.

"Any response?"

Dad's voice was hopeful.

"No."

Mom's voice was full of grief.

Jake, Todd and I stayed focused on the newsprint, trying to ignore the truth in the room—that my uncle and his family were missing, and most likely dead.

Beside me, Jake's shoulders began to shake and I reached over and pulled him close to my side in a warm embrace.

Todd reached over and gripped my other hand in his lap, caressing the soft skin atop his orange capris, which had purple daisies on green vines embroidered down the whole length of the outside leg seam. Despite my rapidly beating heart, I couldn't look away from the text. I needed to know. We all did. Yet, we were terrified of the answers.

As we read, our minds annunciating every syllable, every vowel, we tried to control our reactions but shaking shoulders, legs, voices said that was a lost cause.

This day would be one of many in the week ahead.

Each morning, another batch of papers. Until we didn't look. Until we couldn't look, without breaking down. The fate of Dad's brother and his family was still a mystery and I watched him grow more haggard, more resigned with each rising sun, until he no longer joked with mom, or ribbed Jake and me with bad dad jokes.

He, like the rest of us, was changing and as he did so, a part of me was slowly retreating because the day Dad stopped finding hope was the day there was none.

That scared me far more than the headlines.

****

Alberta in a State of Emergency

Premier Darrell Kelly pleads for intervention

By Doug Faulkner
Calgary Tribune
Special Report

June 25, 2042—Alberta's Christian Conservative Government issued a decree during an emergency sitting of the Legislature today, stating that the province was in a state of emergency, and ordered the immediate mass exodus of its 4.4 million citizens to locations yet unknown.

"We are in survival mode," Premier Darrell Kelly announced during a televised address at 6 p.m. this evening. "We have been viciously targeted by an anti-industry terrorism group in the systematic destruction of our SMR facilities, and we must take action to secure the safety of our residents. We are calling on all towns, cities, provinces outside the contamination zone to respond with open minds and homes, as we try and evaluate next steps in recovery."

Premier Kelly stated that due to the province's investment in nuclear power, it's two major cities have been evacuated, following the June 21 terror attack by the environmental group known as Terra Nova, which caused two major small-modular reactor facilities to be destroyed during the global synchronized act of terror. In the aftermath, the explosions leaked radiation into Edmonton and Calgary groundwater and underground riverbeds, contaminating the water supply.

"We are dealing with radiation poisoning in our watershed, which is not good," said Kelly. "We have Environment Canada out here, conducting water and groundwater studies, but it doesn't look good. We are also dealing with 22 wildfires in the province, the majority of which were caused by the explosions at the SMR facilities.

"Things are looking dire and we need help. We are calling on the federal government and my fellow premiers to respond with aid and resources, and that response needs to happen now—not six months from now. Now."

Kelly has requested an immediate, emergency session of Parliament. Prime Minister Jacqueline LeBlanc was unavailable for comment on his request.

While many Albertans fled to areas outside the contamination zones, these remote locations—many of which were First Nation's reserve lands—were not equipped to handle the flood of fleeing Albertans to their communities and conflicts ensued.

In Southern Alberta, an influx of sanctuary-seekers were met with food, water and shelter at Holy Creator Retreat Centre near Pincher Creek. However, unsanctioned hunting and theft of the local bison herds and food stores caused many ranchers and First Nation's leaders to seek the help of local and tribal police to enforce the peace. The presence of law enforcement along reserves and homesteads have caused many to erect blockades in protest along Highway 3 between Pincher Creek and Brocket.

"We understand the frustrations of those seeking help," Piikani Chief Irene Beaver explained. "However, the tribal council's first responsibility is to the Piikani people. We must protect their livelihood and their futures. This is not the Wild West. You can't just come here and shoot bison and rip up our crops. We will protect our inheritance by any means necessary."

The president of the Southern Alberta Ranchers' and Farmers' Association (SARFA) released a similar statement to the press, stating that while they are willing to donate food to the retreat center's new inhabitants, their members are not willing "to sit idly by while their lands are robbed."

"We have given generously from our harvests and our food stores," said Ben Ingreveld, whose sorghum farm had its silos drained in a middle-of-the-night raid on June 23. "So, it is extremely discouraging and disappointing to have our supplies stolen. Quite frankly, it's a slap in the face."

SARFA—along with the Holy Creator Retreat Centre, Treaty 7 First Nation council members, and local constituents—held a closed-door vote following the June 23 raid that no further assistance would be given to sanctuary seekers to the area.

"Those we have received with open arms will continue to be cared for but we can no longer accept others due to the escalating violence along the SARFA and First Nations' borderlands," Rev. Erin Stillwater of the Anglican Church of the Holy Creator and chairperson of the Holy Creator Retreat Centre. "While it pains me to say this, we have no more room to house any others. We have maxed out our capacity, so we ask that people seek aid elsewhere, as it has now become too dangerous and too volatile to admit more newcomers."

However, the locals' announcement fell on deaf ears, and by 7 p.m. that evening, a standoff between local law enforcement and the displaced Albertans was well underway, with police responding with shields and tear gas on those demanding permanent housing and food stores. As of press time at 9 p.m., no injuries have been reported in the altercation.

Outside the province's major urban cores, highways and secondary roads remain bumper-to-bumper. Air travel has been grounded by the Department of Transportation, as the ministry conducts assessments on the likelihood of further terror attacks and airport damage is ascertained. Calgary International Airport Fire Chief Ron Ashcroft told The Tribune that crews continue to address the damage caused by the aircraft fires resulting in the SMR facility explosion June 21.

"We are working tirelessly to get the situation under control but suffice to say, air travel is put on hold. Even without the transportation department's decision, we are in no state to operate safely," Ashcroft said in a telephone interview.

The Calgary to Edmonton Prairie Bullet train, however, was given the green light to resume operations as of noon today but given the fact that both cities remain contamination zones, very few planned to make the journey.

****

(ASSOCIATED PRESS) LOS ANGELES, CA, June 23, 2042—A 7.3-magnitude earthquake hit San Francisco at 3 a.m. this morning, displacing 17 feet of right-lateral strike-slip of the San Andreas Fault system, causing aftershocks along the Hayward and Maacama fault lines, as well, leading to medium-sized quakes, in the 5.1- to 5.4-range, in Richmond, El Cerrito, Oakland, Hayward, San Jose and in Sonoma County in northwestern California in the north.

****

(REUTERS) WASHINGTON, DC, June 24, 2042—Quakes, shocks and rubble: Seismologists along the western seaboard warn California is one major earthquake away from total destruction. As millions flee smoldering, crumbling cities, state officials are being relocated to Washington, D.C. in the aftermath of the most recent tremors. To the south, Mexican officials have stated they are preparing first-aid stations and camps for fleeing Americans but the U.S.-Mexico wall erected to discourage cross-border migration is sidelining any and all efforts for that country's aid. Instead, Californians are being pushed north into Washington and east into Nevada and Arizona, only to be confronted by quakes in those states, as well. As the death toll approaches 2.4 million, Congress has convened an emergency sitting to discuss evacuation measures and the aftermaths of these devastating quakes.

****

(CANADIAN PRESS) OTTAWA, June 25, 2042—The United Atlantic Nation of North America (UANN) announced during a press conference at 8 a.m. EST that it has instituted a resettlement lottery for current residents and expats and their families for their respective provinces.

Comprising Newfoundland, Nova Scotia, New Brunswick and Prince Edward Island, the UANN's resettlement lottery will take entries from June 25–30, with draws taking place on July 1. Drawn names will receive digital tickets to board the Exodus Train bound for UANN provinces, beginning July 4, and will disembark upon their arrival at their affiliated provinces.

Lottery tickets are limited to 80,000 total, with Newfoundland opening its borders to half that amount, while Nova Scotia, New Brunswick and Prince Edward Island each accepting 25,000, 10,000 and 5,000 people, respectively.

"We want to stress that all measures will be taken to ensure those entering the lottery have the lawful right to do so," said Newfoundland Premier Ed Gaulton in an interview with the St. John's Gazette upon UANN's announcement. "You have to show proof of association; your lineage. This isn't for every Tom, Dick and Harry. It is only for those with close ties to our provinces and let me be clear, they will need to prove it to enter the lottery. We are small provinces and we cannot handle an influx of displaced Canadians — we don't have the support structure to accommodate them."

When asked what UANN intends to do with those who are not deemed to have the official documentation to prove their status, Gaulton emphatically said: "Newfoundland has a long history of helping stranded foreigners on our piece of paradise and, yes, we want to do all that again, but our daughters and sons and their families have to come first and mark my words, that's what this government is going to do, by Jove.

"It may taste like vinegar in my mouth but those that don't fit the bill will have to go back, no ifs, ands, or buts about it. There will be no exceptions. Don't get me wrong, now, we'd love to have all yous back here. I dare say there's nar one here who wouldn't take y'as all in but we'd all be drove, now wouldn't we? There's thousands coming, b'y, and we're an island of small facilities and small cities. We just don't have the rooms, the food, the resources to outfit yas. We'll be scrimpin' every penny, as it is, to do what we can, with what we have."

Gaulton, who was overcome with emotion during the interview, added that even if someone wanted to buy their way on the train, money isn't going to change things.

"This is the one time that having a big bank account isn't going to put you ahead of the pack. Everyone will be treated equally, otherwise this isn't going to work," explained the premier, dabbing his forehead with a kerchief, "we can't just buy more food and houses from across the mainland because the mainland is where everyone and their dog is running away from.

"I know I speak for every Newfoundlander here when I say how much this breaks my heart. We are a giving people; a help-out-at-any-cost people and this is the one time we can't do what is in our nature to do, and I know our East Coast neighbors feel the same. We are all givers, ya know: Nova Scotia, P.E.I., New Brunswick … every single province out here is in the same boat. There will be those who will starve to help those needing it, and that's not right. Nothing about this is right."

It is anticipated that the first contingent of Exodus passengers will reach their destinations no later than July 10.

"We want this journey to be a smooth one," added Premier Christie Gillis of New Brunswick, "and for that to happen, there will be personnel checking travel papers and tickets. No one will come in that isn't authorized to come in. That's our plan, anyways."

Once they have gone through security checkpoints to verify their credentials, the new arrivals will be resettled on bases, Gaulton noted.

"These bases are essentially communities living a commune lifestyle, designed to climatize, educate, and train the newcomers in the Progressive Regression Program with the help of our elders. By the end, they, too, will be able to live off the land like the rest of us, and not rely on sectors and industries that led to this hell we are all living in today."

UANN has stated the second wave of Exodus passengers will commence its departure July 17, to give the train enough time to return and pick up the last shipment of passengers bound for the East Coast.

****

June 25, 2042

Editorial by Doug Faulkner
Senior Editor
Calgary Tribune

THE EAST COAST CONNECTION

With the East Coast and Canada's Far North the only areas not affected by the Terra Nova attacks, many provinces are turning their gaze east, as talks of repopulation surface nationwide, much to the chagrin of East Coast premiers, many of whom are shutting their borders to the anticipated influx of interprovincial migration.

Many political pundits have speculated that Newfoundland Premier Ed Gaulton's adamant denial of visitors from mainland Canada is rooted in the federal government's decision to cut all transfer payments to the province 15 years ago, and the blatant non-inclusion of Newfoundland in SMR plant-construction funding.

So, you know what this reporter says about that?

No kidding, Einstein.

If big brother spent his whole life not sharing his toys, and telling me to buy my own or do without, I'd be holding onto the G.I. Joe I saved for years to buy as if it was made of gold. In reality, that is what the Atlantic provinces have here—treasure. Oh, we can call it a resettlement base but it's really Treasure Island; a sanctuary away from the chaos and destruction helping elsewhere just so we can give mankind a second chance.

It's an X on a map and like all treasures, it will attract diggers and panhandlers from all over the planet. So, how can these small, ill-defended provinces stand guard against such an onslaught? Where will they find the resources and finances to keep the hordes away? Your guess is as good as mine.

So, while Premier Gaulton keeps denying politics had anything to do with the UANN's decision to only welcome expats back to their shores, he couldn't hide the fact that he was a tad resentful over his province's shut-out from federal SMR development.

"We put in our application for a SMR facility like everybody else but the National Energy Board turned us down flat," the 53-year-old premier said of the 2025 decision. "We've got more than a half million people here, with no fishery to speak of, no forestry and no mining. So, what were we supposed to do? Crawl under a rock and die? Not bloody likely."

Not only did Newfoundland, Nova Scotia, New Brunswick and Prince Edward Island get cut out of the SMR energy sector, then Prime Minister Paul Renaud signed a bill to dam the flow of all federal funding to the member provinces, citing they needed to be self-sustaining to qualify for monies from the federal coffers. In response, Labradorians went to the polls and voted to leave Newfoundland and become a part of Quebec, where SMRs were not only approved, but received massive federal payouts from the Montreal-based Prime Minister Renaud.

In 2027, with Labrador no longer part of the province, newly elected Premier Jody Moore implemented a regressive economic development plan that capitalized on Newfoundland's former glories: hunting, fishing, gathering, farming and sheep herding.

Not only that but by ridding the province of fossil-fuel production, it created a prime eco-tourism haven in a world of growing pollution and industrial land acquisitions.

"We got grants from bigwigs in the go-green movement worldwide," Moore explained during a phone interview from her home on Bell Isle.

Shunned Newfoundland obtained cultural grants and donations from philanthropists all over the globe to kick start its homegrown green economy. Seven years later, when Newfoundland Green Party leader Ed Gaulton was elected, the regression mandate was kicked into high gear. Under Gaulton's leadership, a state-of-the-art armed coast guard patrolled the waters and the 500-mile limit, ready to engage any and all who fished off its shoreline.

The long disputed 500-mile limit has been the thorn in Newfoundland's hide for decades, with locals blaming the depletion of their fisheries on massive fishing trawlers from Portugal and Japan being permitted to drag the ocean floor and clean it of all stocks before they got to the island's shoreline, and its fishers.

How did the newly elected premier respond? Out of spite, some would argue, and they may not be wrong. During the press conference announcing the new coast guard's jurisdiction, which included the limit, Gaulton was quoted as saying, "So, when they cut the umbilical cord, we said well, that cutting can go both ways."

Now, I ask you: Is he taking the same stance during this SMR crisis?

We may never know, since Gaulton has refused to answer questions from the media on the topic, but one thing is for certain, Newfoundland's focus on traditional lifestyles has earned it prominence in the financial investment and economic sectors and created its own pilot project that was later mimicked by neighboring Atlantic provinces.

So, what's so magical about the UANN's economic recovery direction? Well, for starters, it uses its ageing population to train and educate younger generations. In other words, there's cross-generational job creation and the end result is thriving communities that are self-sustaining, off the government teat and, dare I say, happy.

It wasn't long before Nova Scotia, Prince Edward Island and New Brunswick implemented similar regression and job-creation programs, using Newfoundland's network as a template for economic recovery.

By the time Gaulton was re-elected premier three years ago, the province was well on its way to reversing its environmental footprint on climate change.

Many claim that redirection was the saving grace for the UANN-member provinces, which by no stroke of luck found themselves among the very few places on earth not part of Terra Nova's plans for mass destruction.

"We were so good at it, we weren't on Terra Nova's radar," he said. "They didn't have to blow anything up to force us to turn back the clock on climate change because we are already doing it."

When dealing with terrorists, however, it doesn't matter whether they find enlightenment from enviro green or army green, the fallout is still the same— catastrophic devastation. So, while Gaulton can don his *Stay Calm & Rock On* T-shirt, those doors he has closed will open, eventually, and who's to say Terra Nova won't be among those lining up to enter?

Treasure islands have a way of attracting all kinds of gold diggers, after all, even those that use explosives.

****

LOS ANGELES, CALIFORNIA, June 25—The State of California is in ruins this morning, after a series of high-intensity earthquakes measuring 9.6–

10.2 on the Richter Scale started a chain reaction along the San Andreas Fault at about eight minutes past midnight.

The quakes split the land mass in deep, cavernous fissures that connected along the Andreas path, breaking the landmass in two. As the broken off pieces fell off into the Pacific Ocean, the remaining segments were awash in flames as power lines and electrical stations collapsed atop exposed and broken oil and gas pipelines.

Cities east of the fault line were the first to fall. San Diego, Los Angeles, Santa Barbara, San Luis Obispo, Monterey, Santa Cruz and Daly City have fallen into the Pacific Ocean. While the primary seismic waves moved the land fissures from side to side and up and down, disjointing the land and causing building collapse, it was the subsequent shear waves that caused the most damage.

The 40 million inhabitants in California had been on high alert for the past two days, with state department officials organizing a massive evacuation of residents to Nevada via air, train and automobile; initial reports suggest as many as 10 million had stayed behind. Emergency services and army personnel have been deployed to assist with rescue efforts but due to calamity and risk of future quakes, tremors and the growing concerns over sinkholes and landslides.

"It's total mass destruction. The remaining cities look like war zones," Dr. Nancy O'Hearn with the U.S. Geological Survey Department told NSX News, while surveying the destruction from a helicopter above the earthquake zone. "Those that didn't fall into the fissures or the Pacific Ocean are rubble and glass."

An evacuation alert has been issued for the entire state of California and surviving governmental officials are making their way to Washington, DC to await an Executive Order by President Maximilian Wagner.

White House sources say POTUS plans to address the nation later today.

Among the politicians making the journey is California Governor Justin Sanchez, who is attending an emergency sitting of Congress.

"Congress has been in a closed meeting since the Terra Nova terrorist attacks on the SMR facilities four days ago," Sanchez told NSX's anchorwoman Gabe Bloom. "Yesterday, we received intel that Terra Nova leader, Jon Solberg, was spotted going through Canada Customs at a border crossing in Winnipeg. We spoke to CSIS (Canadian Security Intelligence

Service) and they advised our neighboring authorities of the situation. We were in the middle of dealing with locating Mr. Solberg when all hell broke loose in San Jose."

San Jose was one of many SMR facilities to explode in the worldwide attacks on June 21, Sanchez explained. The San Jose Fault, which is part of the San Andreas Fault, was already under strain from other similar explosions before the June 21 nuclear plant explosions, "and it just cracked wide open, separating the land as it spread."

The San Jose area is crisscrossed by a series of major faults that together relieve the motion and grinding between the huge Pacific and North American plates, O'Hearn explained.

"The San Andreas Fault, and other Bay Area fault zones, are on both sides of the bay: The San Jose Fault, Berrocal Fault zone, Hayward Fault zone, Chabot Fault, and the San Gregorio Fault, to name a few," she said.

When the San Jose reactor explosion occurred, the blast caused a fracture that spread to the neighboring faults. The earthquake in San Jose met up with other earthquakes in its path.

"The National Oceanic and Atmospheric Administration anticipates what's left of California will be hit with 100-plus foot tsunami waves within the next two to four hours," O'Hearn said.

Representatives from the United States, Canada, the United Kingdom, China and India are currently meeting in a global summit in The Hague, Netherlands, located on the North Sea coast, and home to the United Nation's International Court of Justice. On the agenda will be the recent explosions involving their respective countries' small modular reactors, which levelled 32 cities in their wake and killing 6.8 million people. While another 14 SMRs in Russia and Japan also exploded, destroying their urban centers and leading to the deaths of a further 1.8 million people, Japan and Russia have declined to attend the summit, stating strained relations have caused their two countries to act unilaterally.

Military personnel—those in active duty and on reserve—have been called up to help clean up the destruction zones.

****

BANGOR, MAINE, June 25, 2042—News of an express train ferrying passengers to safety to Canada's East Coast has many Americans struggling to seek sanctuary elsewhere, as Mexico closes its borders to undocumented refugees. On the eastern seaboard, patrol boats sit idling along the Canadian border limits, threatening military action if crossed.

Riots have broken out in many U.S. coastal cities along the eastern seaboard, including Bangor, Augusta, Brunswick, Portland and Boston, as many demand inclusion in the Canadian resettlement initiative.

Chapter 13

"So, what am I supposed to do?"

I was sitting in a circle with Todd to my right and some old dude cleaning his nails with a pocketknife on my left. The Prayer Room in Holy Creator's basement was furnished with plump three-seater pastel-swoosh couches positioned in a boxy 'U' formation facing a stone fireplace. I wondered how often that beast got lit, considering the pillar and taper candles adorning the end and coffee tables were already melting in the heat of the un-airconditioned room. Behind the overstuffed seating were white-painted bookshelves almost as explosive as the overstuffed cushions on which I sat. Study plans on the various books of the Bible, faded and torn boxes of board games, an array of various coloring books, Christian romance novels, Greek and Latin dictionaries, art supplies, and umpteen translations of the holy book, some in other languages, others in graphic-novel and children's storybook format.

The room was lit by the morning's blazing light streaming through the gauzy curtains that flapped in the breeze. The opened window overlooked the pea-gravel path leading to the church's front steps. As the curtains lifted like a sail at sea, the near-white pebbles outside sparkled like diamonds. The air rushing into the room was stifling—a mixture of heat and dust, with the faint smell of broomcorn kernels. In the far corner of the room whirled an oscillating, black floor fan, and above our heads, long white blades of a ceiling fan joined in the chorus; and still, I sweated.

I had it on good authority, however, that the drops sliding down my temples had nothing to do with the heat of the room and all to do with my churning stomach at the thought of being in group *healing* therapy. I mean, it's one thing to go one-on-one with a psychologist who can look down at her notes when things get a bit uncomfortable, but here? Here, there are eyes *everywhere*, noticing every twitch, every trembling hand, every quivering lip.

"There is no right or wrong way to be in this circle."

Rev. Erin's sing-song voice welcomed the group. She was sitting in an oak-stained rocking chair in front of the stone hearth, palms face down on the wide armrests and moving back and forth, gliding along the hardwood floor and causing it to creak. Shifting the rungs, she repositioned the chair so that the rockers were resting on the large area rug adorned with pale white and pink wild roses. Satisfied with her muffled motion, she turned to the group facing her and smiled, causing creases to form in the corners of her mouth and around her eyes, which twinkled in the sunshine flirting through the windows.

"You just need to *be.*"

Todd squeezed my hand in assurance that all would be right.

There were ten of us in all in the Prayer Room, ranging from teens to middle-age to seniors. Nail-cleaner dude brushed a large, callused hand through his white, thinning hair and sighed, his short-sleeved cotton brown plaid shirt heaving around his rotund middle.

The room was designed to be cozy, safe. Soft baby-blue walls were adorned in paintings of seascapes, prairie fields and grazing horses. Larger throw cushions of various textures and colors were piled in one corner—casual seating for those wishing to be close to the floor. *Sit-upons,* as Girl Guides called them, only they were cushions rather than bundles of newspaper encased in garbage bags and wrapped with duct tape. I remembered sitting on makeshift cushions when I was a Guide, as we took turns telling scary stories around a campfire during Jubilee camp near Cochrane. The rushing of the creek and rivers, the cool night air as we lay bundled in our sleeping bags in canvas tents, the taco salads in a bag and eggs in a hole.

Then, it all changed. I changed. I no longer wanted to make bath bombs and candles, do sewing and baking projects, or huddle in sleeping bags and talk about boyfriends or play Truth or Dare.

The more my fellow Guiders became hormonal teenage girls, the more I retreated into myself.

The less I belonged.

Now, here I am experiencing it all over again.

You are a sucker for punishment, Jules, there's no doubt about that!

How on earth could I have anything in common with nail-cleaning dude, or the granny crocheting to Rev. Erin's right?

What about Todd?

He's one person.

I shifted on my pastel pillow, raised my legs off the floor and tucked them under my butt.

It was five minutes past nine in the morning, and the once-cool basement room was heating up, fast, as rays of bright yellow turned to gold and then flitted in and out of corners. Despite the bright light flooding into the room, lit candles rose from the coffee table, two side tables, shelves above the fireplace and in the sconces close to the door, removing the last remnants of shadow from the pale robin-egg walls. As I stared at my hands, the room fell into twenty shades of white, kissed by blazing gold.

There was nowhere for me to hide and I curled inward, trying to make myself as small as possible.

If they can't see you; they can't notice you.

"Is someone going to close those curtains?" The granny lifted her head from her purple crochet hook and addressed the priest leading the session. "That blasted sun is blinding me."

"I like the breeze," nail-cleaning dude replied, dabbing his sweat-streaked forehead with a damp tissue pulled from the box on the coffee table. "It's a sauna in here."

"Why don't we compromise, Mrs. Dyke," Rev. Erin gestured to Todd and he got up, walked to the opened window and closed it enough so that the curtains flapped but didn't float. After he sat back down beside me, the priest addressed the elderly lady, "Better?"

The woman grunted and bent her head to the purple hook and the colorful rainbow yarn that curled around and around, forming a square.

"Good. Thank you all for joining this small-group healing session," Rev. Erin began. "There is no right or wrong way to be here. This is an invitation; an invitation to unload our deepest fears and barriers to Christ's love and grace so that we can truly become a servant of the Creator.

"Think of this space as if it was Las Vegas: What happens in Vegas; stays in Vegas."

Then the priest stopped rocking to chuckle at her own joke, her black and gray-streaked hair bobbing in her merriment, creating smooth, rippling rivers down her back.

Her joy was contagious. All around me, shoulders relaxed and lips parted in grins and smiles.

Except me.

I was not going to let my guard down for one second; that's when they get ya.

"We are all here because sometimes, we need to block out the world and all its distractions to focus on ourselves and the things coming between us…" she placed a hand over her heart, "and our Creator." She lifted the same hand to the white ceiling and continued: "You will often hear me call Almighty God the Creator, and I do this not just because it is a term I grew up with among my Piikani community. I find it comforting to know that we were *created* to be something specific. Now, *who* we were created to be is something that is constantly evolving. You were *created* as naive children but that isn't who you *are*, now is it?"

"Is this going to be all religious?" My whisper sounded like a shout and both the priest and Todd turned to me with creased, smiling eyes.

"If you are asking if this will be about faith, then yes, it is religious because we cannot possibly have the courage to be ourselves, to heal from past hurts and to *evolve* into the selves we were meant to be without faith.

"Faith gives us hope that things will get better; it also takes the control in making sure they get better out of *our* hands and into those of our Lord Jesus Christ."

Rev. Erin leaned forward in her rocking chair, elbows on the wooden arms, eyes intently focused on our faces. "We all want to believe we have a destiny; a purpose but what if that purpose has a path and you need to take that path to make your purpose a reality?

"And what if that path is full of roadblocks? What then? Do we give up? Do we turn around? Do we take a detour? Or do we seek help in removing the barriers?"

I thought about all the things that were littering my road.

Big, frickin' mountains that scaled to the sky.

"This is a safe place to seek healing but for you to heal, you first must open up your wounds and treat the infection. To do that, you have to look back on your journey and how you came to be here—this place in time, this moment in your life—and dig deep into the *whys* before we can move onto the *why nots*. We did not get here by accident; we made decisions, choices that either put a rock in the path or cleared the way. We may have had things happen to us that we need to acknowledge as things that were done out of our control. These hurts often derailed our lives and sent us spiraling on detours, away from our paths the Creator laid for us. So, now, this morning—this is the first step in correcting our internal compass so that it is pointing in the right direction because it is only when it is, that we feel we are one with God and one with ourselves."

Rev. Erin's words cut through the brightly lit room and pierced my chest.

Who was I kidding?

I wasn't invisible.

Not here.

Not from *her*.

And certainly not from *HIM*, if he even existed.

Honestly, I didn't know anymore. Were my beliefs my own, or were they my parents? I grew up going to Sunday school, church, and youth groups, but did I actually *believe*? And if I didn't, would this even work? What was the point of being in this room if I thought it was all a load of Fruit Loops?

Because, Jules, you don't know everything.

"In this space, I ask for honesty, integrity, grace, understanding, empathy—all qualities demanded by our Savior Jesus Christ, but which put us on the right path, regardless of our beliefs," the priest's soft voice rose from the rocking chair and floated around my head. "Out there…" she pointed to the opened window, "the world asks us to conform, to change, to adapt, to settle, to be ashamed, to hide from our true selves so that others feel more comfortable but here, here, we welcome our inner spirits to shine instead of hide in the shadows."

She then began speaking in French and then, Blackfoot, and I turned to Todd, who whispered, "everyone in this neck of the woods makes every effort to include our indigenous history as much as possible, and Rev. Erin is all about inclusion."

Soft yellow beams of morning sun shone over the pastor's face as she spoke, and it dawned on me that I wasn't the only one who worried about losing themselves in the pit of normalcy. People have been losing and hiding their true selves for generations to conform, fit in, belong. From the indigenous peoples to the immigrants who landed here for a new life—all leaving their cultures and identities behind, just so they could fit in.

Maybe I wasn't an abnormality, after all.

As if to confirm my point, Todd crossed his legs, pulling his pink and gray striped skirt with a ruffled hem over his knee and exposing his dangling navy socks decorated with gold stars.

Rev. Erin finished speaking and began fanning her face with a church bulletin she had picked up from the coffee table. I watched as her wrinkled features slowly fell into shadow with the rocking motion of her chair. Each glide forward put her face into the path of the sunbeams, while each glide backward sent her into the room's shadows. As she see-sawed between the two, a low, soft hum vibrated from her throat. The sound was a mixture of chant and vibration and it reminded me of the background noise Mom used to lull herself to sleep, when Dad's snoring and her insomnia kept her up at night.

As the sound resonated, seeping into the cells of the people in the prayer room, arms flopped, heads began to hang and bodies slouched as muscles relaxed. Even time itself came to a standstill amid the drone. Eyelids drifted downward, heads began to bow, breathing deepened and beads of sweat began to trickle down my forehead and into the eyes, causing them to sting.

No wonder Todd told me to wear something light.

There was no rush of cool air from an air conditioner to moderate the temperature of the room, only the two churning fans that stirred up the heat.

It was like sitting in a microwave on high.

While he lounged in his skirt and a pink silk scarf patterned with flying navy birds that dangled down his bare, glistening torso, I sat beside him in a pair of borrowed red Adidas shorts trimmed with white and a purple sports bra. Right now, my bare calves were suctioned to my sticky thighs and sweat was starting to slide down my collarbone and into the strip of purple spandex covering my breasts.

Oh, yeah, and I was panting like a mangy mutt.

The red nylon of my shorts felt as if they were fused to my thighs and the more I tried to adjust my sitting position, the more they pulled the skin on my legs.

"It's the only thing I use these for," he had said, throwing them in my face. "So, don't shred them, Hulk-myster. These are vintage."

Vintage: Another word for non-breathable fabric.

My midsection heaved and glistened as I sucked more hot air into my lungs. All around me, people sat in similar attire: tank tops and shorts; short-sleeved shirts and cargo shorts (like nail-cleaning dude); or sundresses (like the crocheting granny). Todd was the only bare-chested person in the ring and I envied him. Seeing how the other men in the tent stared at his tan, muscular chest, I had the distinct impression, they did too.

"Let us begin," Rev. Erin's soft voice cut through the now tranquil room. Looking at her moving back and forth, she, herself, seemed to be part of the beam of the light floating around the room, giving it a yellow-white haze. For starters, today the priest wore a bright yellow clergy shirt and a pair of white capris adorned with embroidered sunflowers along the front pockets, and around the hems that ended at her shins.

Wiping the sweat from her brow with a white cloth kerchief, she lifted her head to the ceiling and said a prayer: "Send your spirit, Holy One, to guide our discussion; to heal our hurts; to put us on the right path to your glory. We welcome you into this discussion and we pray you are present in our thoughts and our words, our listening and our receiving. All these things I pray in the precious name of Jesus Christ, our Lord and Savior. Amen."

After she had repeated it in French and Blackfoot, I turned to Todd, impatient.

"What are we supposed to do?"

My voice was trembling so much I hardly recognized it. Hoarse from an early rise and the moisture-less heat that was filling the room, as well as the uncertainty before me, it sounded like I had a throat full of rocks and sand.

"Just sit and when it comes time to share your story and why you are here, be honest."

Todd's breath was warm against my ear, and reassuring.

That is a lot harder than it sounds.

I felt like a rock amid a pile of potatoes, as my mom often said. It was a weird saying that never really meant anything to me, until now.

Now, I feel like a boulder.

More like a three-headed dragon in a field of sheep.

When her prayer ended, Rev. Erin turned to each one in the circle and asked that they tell their life story and what they wanted from the healing circle.

Their voices floated up to the churning ceiling fan on raven wings, hovering over our heads, waiting to land.

I listened, mesmerized.

Nail-cleaner dude was Rakesh, a 68-year-old man from Okotoks who had arrived at the retreat center early this morning, along with his wife, son and daughter-in-law, and their two small children. He didn't know where to go from here. He was stuck.

"The drive here was the scariest of my life. So many angry motorists; so impatient," he told the group, running his hand through his silver strands in nervousness. "A very, very large truck pushed our automobile to go past us and I went into the ditch. I thought I would never get out. My son and I began digging around the tires with our bare hands. The babies were crying and all I could think of was dying in the sand dunes with all the cars driving past our dead bodies. Then as I was thinking those horrible things, someone hooked a tow chain into the front of my automobile and we were on the road again."

As he spoke, I felt ashamed.

I had judged him harshly, just because he was cleaning the dirt out of his nails.

How was I better than all those girls at Stampede High who judged me?

Maybe that was the point, I wasn't and I needed to be.

Rivers of sweat poured down my temples.

My lips tasted salty and my arms stuck to the skin on my thighs.

But my focus was no longer on my discomfort, it was on the stories being told of the hardships getting here; of frightened, anxious, lost, uncertain voices sitting in a boxy U in front of Rev. Erin.

I heard my own voice in theirs, whispering to me that I was not alone.

When it came to my turn to speak, I froze.

Todd squeezed my knee and the ice inside me melted.

"I guess my story starts a couple of years ago."

My voice sounded distant, as if my voice-box battery had run down and I needed a good charge. I cleared my throat, licked my dry lips and hoped the saliva would find its way down my esophagus, and spoke louder.

"I don't know when it started. I just woke up one day pissed off, and it never really went away."

Many of the heads around me began to nod. Some even murmured agreement.

I swallowed and continued.

"For some reason, *everything* annoyed me and when I say *everything,* I mean *everything:* My clothes, my hair, my makeup, my teachers, my seat in the classroom, my seat on the bus, my body, even my family."

More grunting in agreement.

Todd squeezed my hand and I stared at his fingers circling my slender hand, dark skin over pale, feeling the heat, the sticky sweat on the palm as he held my hand, and I had the courage, the charge to continue.

"It was all good, as long as it meant I was on the rugby field or wrestling mat, but then I caught myself picking on my little brother and … I couldn't seem to stop."

"Hormones," Mrs. Dyke whispered and was immediately shushed by the priest who had stilled her chair, the rocking rungs raised high in the back as she leaned forward.

"That's what everyone kept telling me. 'Oh, she's going through puberty', 'Oh, it's her time of the month', which made it WORSE.

"I got kicked out of a lot of stuff. I told my parents I quit my clubs because I was bored but really, no one wanted me there anymore. I got into trouble for lipping off and the leaders asked me to leave, so I left.

"After a few repeats of that, it became pretty clear: *No one* wanted me."

The room inhaled a collective breath as I struggled to find the words that wanted to escape my lips; sentences that I had struggled to form and release into the world for fear of judgement.

"I don't know—I just felt *batshit crazy*, all the time."

Realizing what I had said, I quickly covered my mouth with my hand and mumbled, "Sorry."

My voice was shaking, and cracking.

Todd lifted my hand into both of his—a Todd sandwich that stilled the tremors that threatened to take over my entire body.

"I was angry with my parents for being all goody-goody," I glanced over at Rev. Erin, "especially since I felt like a bad person. I felt … *abnormal*."

And then …

I didn't want to get into it. I wanted to forget it; put it on the backburner, never to be talked about again, but it just wouldn't go away. It hovered around every thought, every emotion.

This guilt.

"Go on, Jules, you are doing great," the priest's soft words entered my brain and forced my head up to look into her calming eyes. "There is no judgement here."

I swallowed the understanding in her eyes, the compassion, which I didn't deserve.

"And then … I hurt someone, someone I cared about, because they betrayed me."

It felt good to say it out loud.

Admitting my role in the Stamped High Incident was always defended by my parents, but was it defendable? Was I?

"At first, I kept telling myself *she* deserved what she got because I was defending myself. I was right; she was wrong."

"And did she deserve to get hurt?" Rev. Erin stopped her rocking and folded her hands in prayer formation in front of her chest.

I shook my head, which suddenly felt as if it weighed a ton.

"No." My voice was barely above a whisper. "No one deserved to get hurt that way. Not even Crystal."

As the realization sunk in, my bottom lip began to quiver. I could no longer hold back how the whole episode made me feel. I could no longer lie to myself that it meant nothing; that I was right, she was wrong.

"I lied."

"To whom?"

"To everyone … but, mostly, myself."

Rev. Erin unfolded her hands and placed one over mine.

It was warm and the palm stopped my trembling fingers and ran a thumb over the red welts caused by the elastic around my wrist.

"That's a start; a very good start," she said.

Lifting my chin with her index finger, she gazed into my eyes.

"Why do you think you couldn't control your anger?"

"I don't know."

My words came out in gasps.

My quivering bottom lip was in a full-on shake as the tears trickled down my hot cheeks.

"Mom and Dad say it's from all my concussions."

I hiccupped.

"That's what the doctors said, too, but I'm not so sure."

Unable to stare into the dark, compassionate orbs in Rev. Erin's face any longer, I bent my head again and covered my face with my hands.

"There's something wrong with me."

"Like what?"

It was Todd's turn to question me and I just shook my head side to side, as if trying to shake an answer between my ears like a bingo-ball cage.

"I'm just not *right*."

Rev. Erin stood up, grabbed a black book from one of the bookshelves, flipped the pages, and began to read: "For you created my inmost being; you knit me together in my mother's womb. I praise you because I am fearfully and wonderfully made; your works are wonderful. I know that full well."

I sniffed.

Todd handed me a tissue and I blew my nose: a loud fog-horn blow that lightened the tension in the room and caused many to snicker at the sound.

"My frame was not hidden from you when I was made in the secret place, when I was woven together in the depths of the earth. Your eyes saw my unformed body; all the days ordained for me were written in your book before one of them came to be.

"Does that give you comfort, Jules, knowing Our Lord knew who you would be today before you were even a thought in your parents' eyes?"

"I don't know. I guess."

"Think on that a bit: You said you were not *right* and that there was something wrong with you but as it says in Psalm 139, '*you were wonderfully made.*' God knows who you are and who you are destined to be; there is no mystery, no secret. Jules?"

"Yes?"

"You can't lie to God. You can only lie to yourself and others. So, if anyone knows the *real you,* it's him."

"Amen," Todd muttered.

"But what do I do with all this … *hate* … inside me?"

Rev. Erin walked back to where I sat, handed me the book in her hand and said, "Give it over to Jesus: Jesus, the counselor; Jesus, the peacemaker; Jesus, the healer. It is only when we *let go* that he can guide our actions and direct our thoughts."

Todd's bare, hot arm wrapped around my shoulders, instantly sticking to my sweaty skin. He didn't mind. He held me closer, caressed my shoulder with his warm hand as I struggled to control my breathing, and trembling muscles.

Everyone around me disappeared into the burning yellow-white flame of the pillar candle on the coffee table. Outside, the sun rose higher, moving across the vast pale blue sky in an arc above the church, leaving the basement into more subdued light. Nail-cleaning dude and Todd were gone, and so was everyone else in the room—all blanketed in the dulling light. Sparks flew from the burning wick in front of me and I cinched my eyes shut to completely block out my surroundings.

Until I was alone.

My mind drifted back to altercations, cruel words I had said to others, and to myself. They floated in balloons around my head and as I tried to de-fuzz the letters, the balloons popped and the letters fluttered away on white feather wings.

Now it was my turn to drift on updrafts.

I felt myself floating upward, as my body relaxed. My heartbeat slowed and with each steamy inhale through my nose, my anxious nerves stilled.

"Being here…" I opened my eyes, turned to Todd and gazed into the face of a boy I met on a transit bus so long ago by chance, and now by circumstance, he had become my best friend. "I think I finally know why I felt that way.

"I hated myself. I was angry at … *me* … for being *different*, and I took it out on everyone." I hardly recognize my own voice.

I took a deep breath and turned to the group.

Faces were blurred as my eyes clouded over with unshed tears. As I tried to focus, their eyes slowly closed.

Were they asleep?

Why was I still talking?

To heal.

"Do you still hate yourself?" Todd asked, his voice low and sad, with a hint of hope.

"Not as much, I don't think."

Turning to look into my friend's face, I knew a lot of that had to do with him, and being in this place.

"And why is that?" Rev. Erin sat back down in her rocking chair, smiling. "Has something changed?"

"I just feel *accepted* here."

"You are."

"But … what I mean is … *who I really am* is accepted here."

"And that has changed you?"

"Yes."

"How so?"

"I don't feel so out of place, on the defensive." I turned to everyone in the group, seeing their understanding in their expressions. "I can just be *me.*"

When the final words left my body, I felt drained.

The admission had wrung me in a twisted knot and then just as quickly, I was released.

My bones felt as if they were breaking down in my body, leaving me in a puddle of flimsy muscle and tissue. I had no energy to move, so I sat, perspiring on the couch and panting into the mist.

"That's all any of us wants, Jules, to be ourselves and be accepted for who we are." Rev. Erin glanced into each face in front of her and placed a hand over her yellow-covered heart. "To feel true belonging, we need to open ourselves up to allow others to accept us and that takes a bucket load of courage."

She turned to me. "But you don't do it alone."

Standing, she reached out to each of the people around the circle and grasped their hands in hers.

"We do it as a community; we do it as beloved children of God, *perfectly knit in our mother's wombs*. Take comfort in that: Someone out there knows *you*, all of you—every hair on your head, every wrinkle on your body, every pain in your soul—and he is waiting for you to seek his healing so you can be the person you were made to be."

Rev. Erin walked to the couch where I sat, knelt down beside my knees and took my hands in hers.

"We are all broken, Jules. We all have that feeling that there is a part of us that is missing, a hole that needs filling. Some fill it with addictions or habits, others with possessions or fame. Still others, with hatred and lashing out. As a Christian, I believe the only thing that can fill that void is a relationship with Jesus Christ—everything else is like putting a square peg in a round hole."

I nodded, unable to speak.

"Hatred for oneself is more common than you think, and it is the hardest habit to break. But know this," she lifted my hands to the bodice of her yellow, sleeveless clergy shirt, and pressed them into her chest, "we are loved with an *everlasting love*. We are children of the God Most High, who sent his only son to show us the way and die on the cross for our sins. There is *nothing* we can do that will cause our Creator to hate us or disown us."

My heart was pounding. I could hear the beats in my ears, thumping in my head.

Then, it began to slow and match the rhythm of Rev. Erin's heartbeat, which was thundering up my hand and into my arm.

"Jules ..."

"Yes?"

"You. Are. Loved."

I crumbled into a heap and her arms wrapped around me as I sobbed into her chest, soaking the thin sunshine cotton with tears and snot.

I felt a strip of soft fabric being thrust between my cheek and Rev. Erin's shirt.

I lifted my head and saw Todd's silk scarf, wound in a tight ball, being pushed into my face.

Bubbles of laughter rose in my body and I began to convulse in hiccups.

Todd shook his head in an expression of confused joy and I took his scarf and blew my nose, the fog-horn noise sending the group in an uproar of muffled giggles.

Tension broken, Rev. Erin rose, hovered her hand above my head so that I could feel her heat descend onto my scalp. When Todd had grasped my hand, again, I couldn't remember. All I knew was that it was in his now and I felt his fingers squeeze against mine.

Todd was here.

She was here.

And somehow, I knew, *He* was here, too.

I wasn't alone.

Correction: I was *never* alone.

As Rev. Erin returned to her chair and began to pray, her guttural sounds entered my pores once more, filling my body with their vibrations. I closed my eyes and let the humidity and heat enter my mouth, my lungs. The sweltering breeze from the fans brushed against my skin, peeling off the layers I had grown; dissolving the hurt into the mist. I was left bare, red and raw. I felt as if I had left the basement and the circle around the glowing candle and drifted skyward, beyond the white ceiling with the flaking, dangling stucco balls and exposed oak beams and into the azure cloudless sky outside. I swayed in the darkness behind my eyelids, moving in and out of consciousness, until I drifted back down.

It was hard to breathe.

Todd's voice cut through my own euphoric reality.

It was his turn to tell his story.

I landed back down on the sofa just as his lips began to move.

He discovered his two-spirit form as a young tweenager of ten and through the acceptance of his family and community, he was able to come to terms with his dual gender and embrace it as part of his identity. He spoke of conflicts with his father, Daniel Gladstone, who died in an oilfield accident off reserve. Todd was thirteen at the time, and his mother, Deyelle, became severely depressed. She turned to their Aunties, Irene and Erin, for guidance and comfort. The women helped raise Todd, as did the rest of the family, including his mother's brother, Sam Blackfeather.

While I had come seeking healing, Todd had come to support me in my journey and to find a new path, since his plans to study Blackfoot in the U.S. was now a casualty of the terrorist attacks.

As his words faded into the room of shadow and flame, we were enveloped in silence.

Rev. Erin began praying in Blackfoot and then English for direction and healing, and as she petitioned, I sweated.

My pulse slowed; my mind began to drift.

Rev. Erin hummed.

I swayed, melting back into the overstuffed backrest cushions.

Time passed, the candles burned and pins and needles began to tingle in my legs.

As we sat there, reflecting on the words that had fallen from our lips, and the lips of those around us, Rev. Erin removed a small crystal decanter from a small hide-pouch tied to the belt loop of her white pants.

"This is anointing oil," she turned to each of us, a stream of candlelight streaking up the middle of her face from chin to forehead. Her top lip curled playfully upward on one side. "But it's actually just olive oil that has been blessed by a priest.

"If you were baptized, then you may recall the pastor putting the sign of the cross on your forehead with holy water. This is kind of like that, except with *holy oil* instead of *holy water*—that's if you weren't a baby for your baptism, of course."

A low, rumbling chuckle erupted from Rev. Erin's throat and the sound reminded me of Chief Irene Beaver's throaty laugh. Funny, I never thought they resembled each other until now. Maybe that's what happens the more you spend with a family, the more you see traits and quirks like the way someone laughs being in common with her sister.

I wondered how much of me reminded the priest of my mom and dad, of Jake, even.

Maybe I wasn't as *strange* as I thought.

Was I more like my family than I realized?

What gesture, sound, expression reminded Rev. Erin of Jake?

Was I wrong to think we were two completely different people with no resembling qualities to each other?

Perception, obviously, was in the eye of the beholder.

"The anointing oil is also used as the Oil for Healing, which is what I will be doing now."

The amber liquid shone gold in the flickering candlelight, swirling up against the chiseled glass walls of the small vial with a lid shaped like a leaf.

Gently lifting the lid, a faint smell of olives filled the air—acidic tang mingled with sweet, floral fragrance.

"If you feel so called, you can come to me and I will anoint you with the oil, say a prayer and invite Our Lord and Creator to heal your wounds, whether they are visible or invisible.

"This is an invitation: For us to lift up our pain and for the Lord our God to take control, and because it is an *invitation*, we have a choice. However, I am reminded of a saying Rev. Pete once said at a diocesan retreat: 'All may, some should, none must.'

"The anointing is also a reminder of the bond made between us and the Lord through our baptism; a bond that is tightly woven on one end and on the other, thought to be fraying, torn, knotted and on the verge of breaking. Our Savior doesn't see that broken cord, however. All he sees is the bond, waiting to be grasped—a cord so strong, so long it will withstand the test of time. We just need to reach out and hold it with both hands. Only then can we be pulled up from the pits we find ourselves in."

After she finished speaking, she turned to a small box on the end table beside her, on which white wax was now melting, and pushed a button. Soft instrumental music began to play, filling the room and shadows with strings and keys, and the high melodies of a choir singing about God's grace. Their voices were soft, angelic, comforting and I found myself reeling with emotion. As I listened, my stomach fluttered, my eyes glistened with tears that I fought to hold back.

Where was this emotion coming from?

Where was it going?

The silver-haired man rose from his seat beside me and went to Rev. Erin, knelt down before her rocking chair and placed his head in her lap. The priest put her hand on his head, prayed over his safety, and the safety of his family; prayed for them to find a permanent home and for the Creator to guide the way, and for a renewed faith so he could see his blessings, more than his trials. When she was done, there was silence as the man breathed heavily into her lap, then he raised his tear-stained face and Rev. Erin lifted the oil decanter, tipped it on its end so that it spilled onto her thumb, and she formed a cross on the man's forehead.

"Rakesh, I anoint you with the oil in the name of the Father, and the Son, and the Holy Spirit."

He rose, stumbled, and made his way back to his seat beside me, flopping onto the couch as if he had been drained of all life.

Others followed.

I stayed perched on my pastel cushion, holding Todd's hand.

Then, he too, was kneeling beside Rev. Erin's lap, his silky dark hair being caressed by the wrinkled hand of his aunt.

Should you go, too?
Did you believe enough to go?

I was still debating the voice in my head when my sticky knees pushed into the short-looped rug under Rev. Erin's rocking chair. I could feel the fibers digging into the caps, could imagine the weird swirly patterns already being pressed into my skin.

"What does it mean to be healed?"

Rev. Erin's left hand hovered over my welting auburn spikes as she spoke softly over my hair. I could feel a warming heat escape her palm and seep into my scalp.

"We have this idea in our head that once we are *healed,* we will no longer have any pain or suffering in our lives, but that isn't the case. To be *healed,* means you have put past mistakes and suffering behind you and you are *present* in your today and your future. You are ready and willing to seek help when you need it and you can lift the things you can't control up to a higher power, so that you are not dealing with it on your own. Is the pain still there? Certainly, but you are able to see past it and live your life to the fullest."

She lifted my chin so that she could look into my eyes, which were now shedding a slow stream of hot tears down my flushed cheeks.

"True healing takes time, and it may not look like what we think it will look like."

The priest turned to all the faces searching in the candlelight; faces that were now shedding their own tears, realizing their own shortcomings and struggles and what must be done to move forward.

And they were seeking Rev. Erin's reassuring eyes for the push they needed to move forward.

Nodding at them in turn, she turned back to me. "It may just mean we are able to forgive those who wronged us, even ourselves. That may sound simple, but it is probably the hardest thing we could possibly do—forgive ourselves.

"When you seek true atonement for past mistakes and ask for forgiveness, you don't revisit those aches, those memories because there is no need—you are forgiven. And that, my dear sisters and brothers in Christ, is why forgiveness of oneself is so difficult. We like to revisit past mistakes to punish ourselves but that is not necessary because …

"Through the grace of God and the death and resurrection of our Savior, Jesus Christ, our sins can be forgiven. There is no need for further punishment. It is finished."

Standing, she addressed the group with her hand still on her heart.

I could feel her urgency for us to understand.

"When you are transformed into the child of God you were meant to be, and that pain and hurt you have held so close to you for so long…" she smiled and patted her chest, "… is a memory, a signpost on your path helping you get to where you are going but not holding you back on your journey.

I swallowed the brick that suddenly blocked my throat.

Sitting back down in her chair, she tipped the vile over the thumb of her right hand, lifted her hand toward my forehead and began to paint a cross in the center with the oil.

Up, down, left, right.

"Holy Lord, may this oil be a symbol of our faith in your power to heal and make us whole. Bless this child's life with good health, courage, strength, acceptance, and grace so that they may feel your love and presence every day. Creator God, Lord and Savior, Father of All, deliver us from evil and preserve us in your goodness and mercy. Lord, just as you raised Jesus from the dead with your awesome resurrecting power, resurrect every doubt, every uncertainty, every wound in your child, Jules, so that they are under your domain and they are free of them, so that Jules can follow your will with the confidence of faith at their side. In the precious name of Jesus, Amen."

Then the healing session was over and Rev. Erin was calling on Jesus and the Holy Spirit to bless the group and to be with us on our journeys ahead.

I don't know when my eyes had shut. I only knew I was opening them to a brightened room, now flooded with the recessed ceiling bulbs dispelling every shadow.

Todd was still holding my clammy hand and Rev. Erin was still rocking in front of the fireplace. The other participants had begun to rise, shaking off the relaxation they had experienced and turning to leave the room. I rose, my legs like rippling jelly, and stumbled to the door as the priest rose from her rocker and shuffled over to where I stood and placed a small hand on my arm.

"Whether you believe or not is not the question you should be asking yourself, Jules," she said to my downturned face. "I know the struggle inside you; we've all had it at one time or another, even your father, even me. That is not what breaks you away from the faith; giving up does. When you stop seeking; stop questioning—that's when faith dies.

"Remember, Our Lord is *always* trying to reach you, connect with you, have a relationship with you. He is patient and kind and will not force you in any way. When you start reaching back, that's when you feel his presence the most."

Outside, the blazing orb overhead burst forth light all around the church. The air had cooked as we had grouped, and I inhaled the sweetness of sun-kissed crops and grasses into my lungs. The sweat on my limbs dried in the warm breeze that rustled the leaves of the surrounding trees and fluttered the brown grasses.

Earthy breath moving across the land, and into me.

"How do you feel," Todd asked. His sleek black hair was plastered to his scalp.

"I don't know," I said, truthfully, trying to gauge my thoughts and emotions and put labels on them.

"That's good." Todd scrubbed his scalp with a kerchief he pulled from his skirt pocket. His hair looked electrified.

"How is that good?"

"Well, do you feel sad?"

"No."

"Upset?"

"No."

"Anxious?"

"No."

"Angry?"

Pause.

"No."

Throwing his rescued, snotty scarf into my face, he walked past me and said over his shoulder: "That's healing, Hulk, my man, and you should get used to it!"

Chapter 14

On Canada Day, July 1, the UANN Resettlement Lottery winners were announced.

I was in the Esther House kitchen, washing pots and pans while Jake was unloading the industrial-sized dishwasher under the countertop. As he stacked plates into cupboards and glass goblets into drying racks, I wiped a red ceramic casserole dish and added it to the tower in a cabinet beside the stove. Overlooking the dining hall, the kitchen was twice the size of the one we had left in Calgary. A wall of freezers and coolers rose from floor to near-ceiling, and displayed a depleting store of cuts of game, trays of lasagna, buckets of soups, and various containers of chili, sauces, and leftovers that will be repurposed into yet another meal. In front of the glass doors was a butcher-block topped island that was large enough to have cabinets underneath, a sink embedded into the top and a food-prep area with knife blocks and rolls of aluminum foil and cling wrap mounted to the ends.

Mom stood, pulling at the clear plastic until a strip spread down the wooden surface of the island and over the large ball of recently kneaded bread resting in a turquoise mixing bowl that could have easily doubled as a round hot tub. Before sealing the film, Mom lifted her right hand, placed it atop the dough ball as if she was going to chop it in half, then curled it to form a 'C'. She repeated the two shapes three times. I could hear her mumbling and then the film was placed over the bowl. Dad hoisted it and placed it on a warming rack, covering it with layers of tea towels.

"What was Mom saying?" I asked him, wiping a metal spatula and placing it in a long drawer under the counter by the warming racks.

"Something Nan and her great nan used to say when mixing bread. It's a blessing: 'In the name of the Father, and the Son and the Holy Ghost, Amen.'"

"Does it help the bread rise or something?"

Dad smiled.

"Blessings are not all about us getting something in return, like well-risen bread. It's about declaring that you were not able to make the bread in the first place without God's help."

Dad walked past the island, patting his hand across Mom's backside and gave her a wink, to which Mom replied with a slap across his bicep, giggling.

I turned away from the interaction and looked out into the dining room, where people were already starting to set the tables for dinner in two hours, when we weren't even done cleaning up from lunch.

Each rectangular table was covered with red and white floral tablecloths, with legal-sized sheets of paper at each place setting to act as a placement. The sheets of white were decorated in flowers and trees drawn by the children housed in the retreat center. Todd had gathered them up this morning from the craft room where the children had been occupied and now they sat, with forks and knives on either side, waiting for yet another plate of food.

As I dried my last pot and put it away, Jake closed the dishwasher with a deep sigh and slumped onto the countertop, his head onto his folded arms.

"I'm beat!"

"Well, another family is on clean-up duty for supper," Mom said as she approached us, rubbing Jake's wayward curls. "So, you guys can have a bit of a break."

"What do you want to do?" I hung up my tea towel onto the drying rack beside the sink.

Jake lifted his head from his arms.

"You want to do something *with me*?"

"Why not?"

He stood up, turned to a smiling Mom and Dad, and let his face relax into a slow spreading grin.

"No reason," he replied, opening the kitchen door and waiting for me to walk through.

His blue basketball shorts had a large watermark on them in the front from his escapades with the dishwasher and his orange tank top was spattered with drops of chocolate milk he had had for lunch, and sweat.

Yet, for some reason, I didn't feel the urge to comment.

Walking through the opened doorway, I ruffled his curly mop and said, "I hear they have a broomcorn demo in one of the retreat center buildings. Know which one?"

Jake's face lit up.

He smoothed his frizzy hair into a flattened, curly version of itself, and strode through the door and in front of me.

"It's in the Mary Pentecost Place."

"Well, then, let's get going. Gotta get me some *corny* crafts."

"Aaaah, not again!"

"I ear they are really a-peeling."

"Stoooooppppp!"

His joyful squeal carried over his shoulder.

"Wait up," I shouted back, "Cob back!"

"Aaaaaaahhhh!"

I followed Jake's awkward gallop across the pea gravel.

I had a feeling this broomcorn demo was going to be a lesson in corn punishment and I had to bring my A Game if I was going to get through it in one piece, and without bullying my little bro.

Funny, now that I think of it, Jake had not stuttered since yesterday.

Was I the one who made him so nervous he couldn't talk?

All along, I was thinking it was his lack of confidence in himself, but maybe I had a greater role to play in that than I thought.

He is afraid of you, Jules.
You make him uneasy, uncertain, unsure.

Crap.

Now I felt stupid and awful.

First lesson in healing was already underway.

Dad's joyous laughter could be heard through the industrial kitchen's windows as Jake and I made our way along the path leading to Mary Pentecost Place.

"So, what do *you* want to do?"

Mom's voice cut through the chuckles.

"Nap, of course!"

"Of course."

Once we arrived, the craft room was lined with gray paint-splattered folding tables.

On each, were four-inch-deep rectangular trays covered with metal grid racks. On the table beside the stations were gardening and work gloves and behind them stood about thirty people of various ages, eager to find out how to harvest sorghum.

"The first thing you need to do is put on the gloves," Todd's uncle, Samuel Blackfeather and my Mr. B, was saying from the front of the room, his wife Savannah stood beside him with a long red apron tied around her waist. She held her hands up in front of her face, showing off a thick pair of beige leather work gloves. "Sorghum stalks are quite itchy, so you don't want to try and scrub off the kernels without gloves."

Jake and I hurried over to vacant spots and began putting on gloves. Mine were gardening gloves adorned with tiny roses. Jakes were dark brown leather-topped gloves with a thick twill on the palm coated with some kind of sealant to prevent the fabric from being pierced or frayed.

"Now, grab one of the cut stalks from the bucket beside your table."

Mr. B strode over to one of the tables and fished out a cut stalk from a ten-gallon bucket underneath. Holding up the stock, he showed off its thick, green-brown stem and the bushy head with tiny, yellow-brown kernels embedded into the mangled mess of leaves and stems adorning the top.

"These tiny kernels are what you will be rubbing off. The seeds are inside the kernels. Everything else is just compost."

Savannah walked over to our table, repeated her husband's movements and showed me and Jake the tiny beads whose inner seeds were milled into flour.

"Once you have the top part of the stalk in your hand, you're going to rub it across the wire-grid rack over top of the tray like this …" She scrubbed the bushy top across the grid and underneath, kernels, broken leaves and twigs began to collect.

"Keep turning the stock so you get all sides. When you have it pretty close to being shucked," she held up her stalk, with only a few leaves and twigs remaining, and a scattering of yellow seeds, "you discard them into the compost pail. Those left behind are not ripe enough to fall on their own accord, so they aren't harvestable.

"Now, your turn."

Jake bent down and collected a stalk from the white bucket between our legs and began scrubbing the bushy top against the rack. I mimicked his movements and was amazed when my tray began to fill with golden kernels.

"They look like baby chickpeas," I said.

"That they do," Savannah agreed, picking one of the kernels up and holding it between her gloved thumb and forefinger. "Everyone see this—from here, the kernels will be ground to remove the seed from inside and once it's out, it is milled into flour."

"Don't they have a better way of harvesting the seeds?" Jake wiped his forearm across his forehead to remove the sweat build-up on the surface of his brow. "This is tedious and exhausting."

He lifted his wire to see the small mound of seeds in his tray. Running his hand through the pile, letting the seeds slip through his fingers, he fished out the trigs and leaves that had fallen between the wire grid and threw them into the green knee-high compost pail by the table.

"Is *this* what they eat? Looks … unappetizing."

"No, they have to harvest what's inside the kernels."

The voice came from a plump man in dusty blue jeans, a faded blue flannel shirt over top of an equally faded black T-shirt that looked more charcoal than black. He stood by the door with a group of other men, similarly dressed.

"Everyone, this is Mr. Hurlburt. His family owns a sorghum farm nearby," Mr. B told the class.

There were greetings and waves to the family mulling into the craft room.

"Morning, Mr. Blackfeather. I just thought I'd drop in and see how the demo is going."

Walking over to one of the gray tables, he leaned over the stations, inspecting the collection trays of a couple of girls Jake's age, who had spilled twigs and leaves all over the table while scrubbing their broomcorn heads, and at their parents who were scooping up the debris, muttering about it being a lot of work for very little yield.

"You guys are mighty fortunate we don't harvest sorghum like this because if we did, it would take months to get enough seed to mill into flour," Hurlburt spun on his heel to take in the faces of the people standing by the tables, "especially since there are so many of yous."

"You're not wrong there." Mr. B shook hands with the burly farmer and motioned for him to address the crowd.

Hurlburt walked to the front of the room, while his family went around to the tables assisting the many men, women and children with their harvests. Once he had everyone's attention, Hurlburt rocked on the heels of his cowboy boots, hands deep in his pockets and took a deep breath.

"So, in a large-scale sorghum operation like the one our family has just down the road, after the stalks are cut in the field, they are dried in Quonsets, for sometimes up to a year, before being placed in a grain hammer mill to separate the seeds from the kernel shells."

"How do you cut them in the field?"

The question came from a squeaky voiced teenage boy two tables down. He stood wearing denim overalls over his bare chest with a bushy stalk still in his hand, half void of the seeds and leaves.

"A lot of us have customized old combines to cut the top parts of the stalks off," the farmer explained, motioning for the rest of his family to join him at the front of the room. "That way, we get the least amount of these pesky stalks and leaves as possible. Cause, as you can tell by rubbing them against the wire racks, the unwanted debris falls with the kernels, and we don't really want to start sorting that mess out by hand, that's for sure."

As if to prove his point, one of the young men from his group walked over to our table and plucked a branch from Jake's collection tray and tossed it into the compost pail by his feet. After he did so, he took one of the kernels, placed it on the hard tabletop, and pushed down on it with the blade of his pocket knife. The shell cracked open and a small seed popped out.

"My son, Joey there, is showing you what we want; that is why we do all this work," Mr. Hurlburt said from the front of the room, gesturing to the tiny seed being held by the young man standing by Jake. "From that little seed, we get flour."

"And how do the mills work?" a middle-aged woman from the back of the room, her red-rooster apron sporting fresh twigs and leaves.

"Joey, can you answer that one, son, seeing as you're the operator?"

The stocky young man with broad shoulders and chest turned to his father, nodded his dirty-blond bearded chin and rolled his red Henley-shirt sleeves to his elbows.

"Well, ya see, a *hammer* mill pulverizes the kernels with …"

"Hammers!" A curly-haired brunette boy said beside the middle-aged woman, the top of his head and eyes peaking over the table. The woman, who appeared to be his grandma, lifted him up so he could see Joey Hurlburt. "Hammers, hammers, hammers!"

Everyone laughed and Joey's broad grin made the boy giggle.

"You are correct sir. The kernels go in one end of the mill—the chamber—and get hit on the head a bunch of times by these rotating hammers that are going a mile a minute."

He made a fast-chopping motion with his hands in the air.

"Those hammers are going so fast…"

"How fast is it?" An older man retorted, grinning.

"Up to 100 horsepower."

"Criminy, that's given 'er!"

"You better believe it," Joey nodded, scratching his beard.

"After it's been pulverized to break open the kernels, the seeds are then blown to the cyclone and dust separator by an impeller fan mounted on the drive shaft. Then, they are suctioned through a perforated screen on the other end. The screen looks a lot like the wire racks you have on your trays there, only with a heck of a lot less debris.

"After that, the seeds are shipped by train to processing plants all over the country, which turn them into flour."

"So, if you all use combines and mills to harvest, why are we doing this?" I piped up, already feeling the ache between my shoulder blades from scrubbing several bushy stalks across my rack.

The Hurlburt family snickered in unison, looking slyly at Mr. B for the answer.

"We just wanted to give you all some forced labor work," Mr. B sheepishly said from a table near the back of the room.

Everyone laughed.

"Actually, when you are trying to educate people on where their food comes from, whether it is a trapline or a bison processing plant or a sorghum mill, getting the hands-on experience helps link you to your plate, don't you think? I mean, are you going to appreciate your lunchtime sandwiches tomorrow a little more, knowing this has to happen to make the bread? I think so."

Hurlburt was nodding in agreement.

"Our mill can expel over one hundred pounds of seeds in less than ten seconds, but for every pound of flour, we need to mill about sixteen to twenty thousand seeds—that's a heck of a lot of seeds to feed you lot bread every day, don't you think?"

The mood in the room had changed.

The farmers were staring into the faces of those who had come to learn, and frowning.

"That's a conversation for another day," Mr. B interjected, walking back to the front of the room. "The people here just want to learn about how the grain is harvested. The more people who know, the more people who realize just how valued you and your family's contributions are to this area, the country, and their individual survival."

Hurlburt slowly tilted his head in agreement. His clan relaxed, again, tucking their accusing stares back into the pockets of their jeans.

"We thank you for doing that, Blackfeather, but I just want to stress, it isn't going to last forever, not at this rate." Mr. B's face flushed in embarrassment.

"We all must do our part to help."

"As long as everyone knows there isn't an endless supply, is all I'm sayin'. You can't expect farmers to give up everything for nothin'."

What did that mean?

Were we running out of food?

Tonight's supper of wild turnip and bison soup sounded decadent to me, who never got to eat actual meat when we lived in Poplar Hills but we had other options. Where were soy-based substitutes here? In fact, there hadn't been food shipments delivered at all since our arrival, only departures.

"So, what's so great about this stuff, anyway?"

The young girl asking the question leaned out from behind the table, her brown pigtails dangling down over her shoulders, as she lifted her left leg as if about to do a cartwheel.

"Besides being able to grow in drought-like conditions, sorghum is highly nutritious," Hurlburt responded. "It has about eight per cent protein and about 70-per-cent gluten-free starch, when in raw form, and when processed, it is easy to digest. When cooked, it isn't 100-per-cent gluten free, but it's close."

"It's a *protein*?"

Incredulous, the girl tilted back onto her left leg, swinging her pigtails as she went back to being upright.

"Yes siree," Hurlburt turned to Mr. B "It may not taste like a ribeye but it's a good alternative to meat."

"What's a *ribeye?*" The girl's confusion was mimicked on the faces of others in the group.

Hurlburt sighed and frowned.

"It's a cut of meat from a butchered beef cow. 'Round these parts, there used to be a lot of cattle ranches and even more fields growing feed and hay to feed the cattle that were raised for beef, but that was before your time, young lady. Nowadays, when we talk ribeye, it's a similar cut of bison."

The farmers left us alone with our trays, racks and stalks. Their absence made a vacuum in the room, as if a hole had penetrated the atmosphere and we were all confused about why it meant so much in the first place, and why the remaining void was so noticeable.

Tension.

I knew it well.

Grew up with it; felt it; agonized over it.

And I knew that if it was left to build, the sanctuary that the retreat had offered to hundreds sleeping in the dormitories, nothing good was going to come of it.

The clicking cowboy boots echoing up the stairs leading to the entrance of Mary Pentecost Place was a reminder of that.

It seemed as if only Jake and I had clued in to what the Hurlburt family was cautioning, us and the Blackfeathers, at least, because with their departure, everyone went back to scrubbing their stalks as if nothing had happened; as if there was nothing to worry about.

But there was.

Trying to lighten the mood, I lifted my stalk and pointed it at Mr. B.

"So what we are doing here is not necessary, is that what you're telling me? All this scrubbing is just busy work?"

"It's *necessary* for *your* sanity, as well as *ours*," Mr. B said dryly. "It ain't easy keeping 285 kids entertained, you know."

I tossed my stalk into the compost pail, lifted the grid and emptied my tray of seeds into the aluminum vat in the middle of the table. This *focus activity* was ultra la-hame, but at least it kept my hands busy and away from the elastic around my wrist and I understood why bread was such a luxury. As my tray spilled small pale orange and gold seeds into the awaiting vessel, the alarm on my phone chimed: A Federal Government Alert.

Under the alert was a link for the names, glowing red.

Turning to Jake, I whispered, "We have to go."

I lifted my phone to the table so he could see the alert. Color drained from his face as he slowly nodded. We carried our trays and racks to the front of the room and piled them atop the table in front of the Blackfeathers, turned and left the room, trying not to draw attention to ourselves.

Mr. B noticed, as did his wife.

Their eyes followed us as we walked through the doors and up the stairs. I could feel the heat of their gaze, the understanding.

After all, only my phone had buzzed.

****

The website portal was frozen.

"Too many visitors," Mom said from the stove as she poured hot water into cups of powdered cocoa. "We'll just have to be patient."

That would have been sound advice if not for the fact that I was not known for my patience, quite the opposite.

"What is taking so long?"

Frustrated, I refreshed the website page on Dad's laptop.

After the third attempt, I was finally able to enter our family's last name.

Then, I got the Spinning Wheel of Doom.

Round and around, the multi-colored wheel went, as I tapped my Converse sneakers on the hardwood floor, sending dust mites scattering on the dark-stained surface.

"Hurry up!"

"Telling it to *hurry up* isn't going to change anything, Jules, so just have some hot cocoa and relax."

"Agh!"

Hold breath for five, release for ten; hold for five, release for ten.

Outside, people were already assembling by the church, talking about how unfair the lottery was, how it was leaving millions to die just because they didn't hail from the East Coast.

My heart was keeping time, now, pumping blood at a vicious rate through my veins, causing my head to throb and my chest to vibrate with pulsating rhythms.

Over the past few days, more and more people had come, driving to the borders, asking for food and shelter. The retreat had run out of rooms in the dormitories, and a No Vacancies sign had been erected near the highway turnoff, but many took no heed. Even with the halt of sorghum shipments west, the surrounding farms, ranches and reserves were struggling to feed everyone.

So, maybe the Hurlburts were right to be scared, apprehensive, tense.

"I hear displacement camps are being set up in Saskatchewan," Pastor Erin had said this morning over a bowl of steaming cornmeal, a square of butter melting into the mush with every stir of her stainless-steel spoon. "They are being run by the federal government, and the churches."

She had paused in mid milk pour and looked into Dad's eyes, her brows knit downward in concern. "I do hope history won't repeat itself."

"Me, too," Dad had said, sighing deeply. "Concentration camps and residential schools do not have a great track record in their treatment of displaced peoples in Canadian history."

Pastor Erin nodded and took a sip of her black tea. Swallowing, she sighed and turned to Jake and me: "It's up to this generation to make sure history doesn't repeat itself."

Washing the breakfast dishes later, I couldn't understand how the onus to make sure domestic refugees weren't stripped of their identities, abused or even killed was placed on us teenagers.

Delusional, much?

"There we are," Jake jumped up onto the chair beside me, landing on his knees, and frightening the life out of me.

"Dude! You nearly gave me a heart attack!"

"Sorry, Jules."

Grinning. I had never seen Jake smile so much as he had in the past 24 hours.

It was cool, and disconcerting at the same time.

"I thought there would be more," I leaned over the laptop, squinting at the short list of names accompanied by dates of birth, cities of origin and their Atlantic Canadian family connections.

"More Klassens?"

Mom sounded confused, as if I was telling her ice cream grew on trees. "Yeah."

"Well, hon, not very many Atlantic Canadians married into Mennonite families in the West—I'm somewhat of an oddity."

Dad took his cup of cocoa from Mom's outstretched hand with a lopsided grin, "They don't know what they're missing, eh, my little cod fish?"

"Drink your chocolate, Prairie Boy. It's my heritage that's saving the day here."

While they were still teasing each other, the rambunctious joy normally permeating their interaction barely went beyond their lips: Tight shoulders, straight backs, pursed lips, and red eyes that looked like they hadn't seen a pillow in days. They stood by the rectory's kitchen counter facing Jake and me, and the opened laptop.

"It's just so sad that more people can't go."

Jake's lament echoed in my head. Our fates were now elsewhere, away from the turmoil and terror, yet so many people would remain here, hopeless.

I studied my chipped black nails as they hovered over the keys, and wondered how any of us could stop anything when we were so powerless. We had no control over whose names got drawn, where we would end up, and how we would live wherever they shipped us to.

Yeah, Rev. Erin was Loco Puffs if she thought Jake and I were in any way in control here.

I mean, get real!

If the fate of mankind rested with us, then man, they were screwed royally. Corn Flakes, that's what it was, Ca-orn Fa-lakes.

Absent-mindedly, I flicked the elastic around my wrist, trying to draw me back to the present.

Jake leaned over from his kneeling perch on the kitchen chair and covered my hand with his. He wasn't even looking at me. In fact, he was looking over my shoulder at the flashing screen, trying to see what other Klassens were on the list, and if he knew anyone. The hand that covered mine was bare and I could feel it pressed down over my wrist, the heat and perspiration from his palm soft and warm over mine.

Then, it was gone, and he was settling back onto his butt on the seat.

I couldn't breathe.

Feeling my discomfort, he turned slightly toward me.

Jake knew.

His green-blue eyes were glistening knowingly into mine.

Sad.

I tore my gaze away from his and found Mom's hazel-green pools.

I saw the dark shadows under the eyelashes, the puffy skin. Despite how tired she looked, her eyes drew me in, held my gaze and for the briefest moment, I felt like she was hugging me. I could feel her arms around me; her hair tickling my neck; her spicy, floral perfume in my nostrils.

Her head tilted downward to the spot on my wrist still warm from Jake's touch, and to the thin red line that now rose from the pale ivory skin.

I could barely breathe.

Jake knew.

Now, Mom knew, too.

Butterfly wings flapped in my chest as I searched for a way out; a way to calm my rapidly beating heart and block my brain from the fact that yet another of my secrets was plastered all over my face for the world to see.

For *Mom* to see.

Turning back to the sink, she rinsed her mug and put it in the dishwasher.

Dad followed, then Jake.

No one acknowledged; no one pointed it out.

My chest contracted as I stared after her.

How long had she known?
How long had Jake known?

"Hey, Jules, sauce me a napkin would ya," Jake was nudging me with a hand stained in chocolate, which luckily matched the ring around his mouth.

"Don't steal my slang, Jake-O-Lantern," I said, picking up my mug, which was now full of cold cocoa.

"You don't own *sauce me.*"

"Yeah, I do. It's mine. Come up with your own cool ver-bage."

"Why would I when you do such a good job?"

He was smirking at me.

Jake, the boy who couldn't string two words together, was *ribbing me,* flawlessly.

I nodded at him.

"Respect."

He grinned.

"Respect," he mimicked.

Mom went over to him, placed her small hand on his left shoulder and squeezed.

Jake turned and gave her an awkward twisted hug around the chair back.

"I wish we had some actual corn on the cob. I never thought I'd be sick of hot cocoa, but yup, I'm there."

"I'll NEVER be sick of hot cocoa," Jake shouted.

"Sweet, buttery corn … mmmmm. You do know that most of the sweetness from the cobs of corn we used to eat came from the pot, not the cob, right?"

I looked up at Mom, puzzled.

"Well, years ago when you could still get corn, it was quite bland—the growing season was so short that the cobs didn't mature properly so when you boiled them, you had to give them a little boost with salt and sugar."

"Really?"

Jake was incredulous.

"Yes, really. Because they were harvested before their time, due to droughts mostly, they didn't quite reach their high natural-sugar content, so they needed a bucket-load of sugar in the pot. A little salt and a little sugar can mean the difference between tasty, welcome corn and bland, go-away corn."

"Given how many of them there are out there," I motioned to the window and the growing arguments being had on the pea-gravel path, "I vote for the blandest food possible."

Seeing Mom's stern look, I quickly added, "JK, Mother Dearest. I was just kidding."

"*Sure*," Jake's sarcastic, squeaking voice interjected.

I kicked his shin under the table and he yowled.

Shade emerged from a corner of the kitchen to yowl back. Pouncing, he landed softly on Jake's lap and began to purr. As Jake petted his black hair, the cat settled onto his lap, languishing across both legs, turned onto his back to expose his belly, which Jake promptly rubbed, too, while emitting little toddler-like giggles.

"You're getting awfully ballsy, bro. I think Todd is having a bad influence on you."

I leaned over and scratched behind Shade's ear. Once I stopped, he head-butted me to continue. Cutting through the seriousness in the room with a butter knife, Shade had resorted all the people in the kitchen to coos and caws.

Cats were so awesome, especially ours.

No wonder people used them for therapy.

People like you, you mean?

"I'm serious. Why are we feeding all these people?"

"*You* aren't feeding anyone, Jules. The people on the farms and reserves in these parts are," Dad said, walking to the stove and lifting the lids of four large aluminum pots. Every kitchen in the retreat was making soup this afternoon, since even the industrial-sized one in Esther House couldn't possibly feed the masses that will be sitting around the dining room tables this evening. There were so many people, dinner was being served in three shifts: 4 p.m., 6 p.m. and 8 p.m. As the lids lifted, steam wafted into the air carrying aromas of wild game, onions, garlic, thyme and rosemary.

Bending down to the kitchen floor, he grabbed a large bag of wild turnips and hoisted it over his shoulder and whipped it down onto the surface of the table just as I was removing the laptop. Dirt-coated, dark-skinned turnips the size of my fist spilled onto the oak surface. As he picked one up, Mom handed out paring knives to each of us.

"We *are* these people, remember?" Dad lifted his knife to the purple-blotched skin and began to peel. "We just got here first and Pastor Erin was gracious enough to offer her home to us, while she stayed with her family in Brocket."

"Sorry," I grumbled. "It's just that this is a lot of work and a lot of food."

"Feeding the masses usually does require both," Mom interjected, leaning over to help Jake get started on his turnip. "Then again, anything worth doing is worth doing with grace and love. Otherwise, it's not helping; it's platituding."

Dad was nodding silently, leaving a pale orange misshapen ball on the table beside a coil of thick, dark muddy skin. More wrinkles had creased a path round the corners of his eyes since we had left Calgary.

"And in no time, they'll be shipped off to the refugee camps in Saskatchewan and then, they may not be as lucky."

Mom's soft voice pulled me away from my scrutiny, and I realized both my parents had aged in the short time we were here.

"I hate to think what they'd get fed there. Not meat, that's for sure, or vegetables like this."

She took the peeled turnips over to the sink, washed them in a bowl, turned back to the table, sat down and began dicing them into neat half-inch cubes.

"You have to remember," she said, raising her knife, "hot, filling food may not be on the menu, so this may be their last chance to get that nutrition."

"You mean, the soups we're making are a *hot commodity*?" I grinned at her, and she rolled her eyes.

"Yes, Jules, so we have to *a peel* to everyone's inherent need for grace," Mom grinned back.

"I'm sure something will *turnip*," Jake piped in, holding up a cube of pale orange root vegetable. "Eh, Jules?"

"Stop," Dad groaned.

I rolled a peeled turnip in Mom's direction. She stopped it with her hand, took it to the sink, washed it, and sat back down and resumed her dicing.

Reaching over the table, I ground my knuckles into the top of Jake's curly blond mop, making him cringe and lift his hands up to cover his head. "My protégé."

Mom sighed. "God help us."

Dad chuckled, patting her on the back as she diced. I was busy peeling another turnip when Todd swept into the room with a puff of dust and plopped down on the chair next to mine, nearly causing it to keel over backward and sent Shade screeching out of the room. I grabbed the backrest and righted it before he landed on the floor.

"Now, that's a happy sound I haven't heard in a while. Those people out there," Todd pointed in the general vicinity of the people camped outside, "all they do is complain about the food and the housing, or lack thereof. Jeez Louise, what else are we supposed to do?"

I grinned at Todd's use of my PG curse, which I inherited from my creative-cursing mother.

"We fed them bagged breakfasts of boiled eggs and goat cheese with crackers but they were shouting at us for more by the time we came back with ladles of water," he began, brushing the dust off his denim skirt stitched with a large, bright-yellow peace sign in the middle, and grabbed a mud-caked turnip and paring knife from the table.

"Actually, Todd, I do believe Erin wanted you and Jules to join the other young adults to deliver the food."

Mom's voice was sympathetic with a ring of matter-of-factness.

"It's a *corn*-acopia of food choices," I piped up, and got a kick in the shin by a toe of Todd's red cowboy boots. "Hey!"

Pastor Erin walked in and said, "Any news?"

"Yes, we made the list," Dad said solemnly. "I don't know whether to be relieved or terrified."

"Peace of spirit, Brother Pete; peace of spirit."

Dad sighed as the Holy Creator priest's voice blew out the anxious thoughts with one repeated phrase.

"Thank you, Sister Erin. I needed that."

"We all need that, Pete, me included."

She squeezed Dad's forearm and sat at the kitchen table with the rest of us.

Dad put more turnip cubes into the pots on the stove, as Mom continued on creating piles on the table. As the rest of us peeled, he washed, Mom diced, he scooped them into the pot. Rev. Erin looked pleased with our system.

"It's nice to see you all working together."

It wasn't until the words had escaped her lips that I realized we were, working together that is. When was the last time we did that? I honestly couldn't say. If I tried to remember my interactions with Boy Wonder before coming here, all of them were spiteful, teasing, annoying. There was no *friendly* ribbing, never mind laughter. I glanced into the faces of my parents and brother and it dawned on me that we *were* working together, in harmony.

Huh.

Imagine that.

Dad turned down the burners on the stove and placed the lids back over the pots of soup. Pivoting, he leaned his backside up against the oven handle, grimacing over the heat on his butt, and then stepped forward, adjust his *And That's How I Saved the World* Christian decaled T-shirt with the comic book drawing of Jesus sitting on a brick wall with Iron Man, Superman, Wonder Woman, Black Widow, Captain America, Captain Marvel and Spider-Man.

"This is a time for rejoicing," Rev. Erin began. "Jesus is watching over your family and he will continue to do so on your journey.

"Yes, pray for those who will be left behind—me included," she chuckled, shaking her head of black-silver hair as her round tummy jiggled. "But praise, nonetheless."

Mom let out a deep exhale of breath, got up from the table and grabbed the crook of Dad's arm. She swung him in a circle, while her legs lifted from the floor and the balls of her feet did a rhythmic tap on the wood underneath them, first one foot, then the next—hopping back and forth. Her voice lifted above the table and she sang: "Hi diddly dumpton, Paddy's got the wood and if she don't get nar stick, I think that will be bad. People call us crazy but that will make us mad. Diddly dum dum diddly didley dum dum dum."

"What in the devil's got into Shelly?" Pastor Erin was saying between hearty bouts of laughter.

"Don't look at me: I'm a Prairie Boy. She's the Newf," Dad huffed as he swung around in another turn, nearly knocking Mom into the stove. "Her maiden name is Applin, so I guess the kitchen party starts here."

I was laughing at them when Todd nudged my arm.

"You're leaving us?"

"I guess."

"Well that sucks," he folded his arms over his turquoise shirt with gold stitching around the shoulders and turned his head away from the merriment, and me. "That sucks big time."

Chapter 15

Todd's bright neon-green Ford bounded up and down on the gravel road, the back tires grinding over sun-bleached rocks as dust clouds ballooned behind us. It was the longest time I'd ever seen Todd not crack a smile, and it sent my nerves on edge. Since yesterday's mic drop, he had retreated into himself, and while I struggled to know how to break into the wall he had erected since finding out our family would be leaving Holy Creator.

He was beyond my reach.

His denim-skirt clad thigh brushed up against my cutoffs, yet it was as if he was somewhere else; with someone else.

"This is one way to get a dry sense of humor." My voice cracked in the air-conditioned cab that was quickly filling up with dust being sucked in through the vents.

No response.

Damn.

"How long 'til we get to the donation site?" Giving up trying to lighten the mood, I turned my attention to the object at hand: Picking up food and supplies from the area locals who had erected a donation stand near the highway turnoff to Holy Creator.

"About ten."

There was no ease in Todd's voice, only strain.

We bumped up and down on the black leather seats as we sideswiped, and then hit, deep potholes in the gravel road. Holding onto the door handle above the passenger window, I felt as if I was in a moon rover, except I think little green aliens would be better company than Todd at the moment.

"We don't leave or a couple of days."

"I know."

"Are you angry we are leaving?"

He turned his head to look out his side window, taking in the roaming bison, the swaying fields of sorghum, the flocks of sheep grazing in the distance and beyond, row upon row of wind turbines. Even from a distance, they looked huge.

"Pincher Creek area is one of the country's strongest wind-power regions. The turbines were erected years ago to harness that energy."

Dad's voice echoed between my ears. He and Jake were discussing renewable energy solutions last night over a bowl of the bison soup made for all the people staying at the center.

"Did you know, they are 105 meters tall, and the blades are 136 meters across?" Jake's teen-boy squeaky retort made Dad nod and smile.

"And, did you know there are 236 installed in Southern Alberta?" Dad continued.

Yes, our family has factoid competitions.

Well, to be clear, *Dad, Mom and Jake* have factoid competitions. I just sit there, like a doofus, trying to remember how many feet there were in a meter. After much brain squinting, I landed on three.

Odd ball out, again; always.

Inside the pickup truck, Todd's head turned slowly to me: "No, Jules, I'm not angry. I'm glad you are getting out. I just wish…" he wiped his eyes with the back of his hand and returned to staring out the windshield, "… I just wish you didn't have to go."

He swallowed, coughed at the lack of moisture in his throat, and softly added, "I just got to know you and now you're leaving."

In front of us, the makeshift shelter rose from a turnoff into a field of swaying broomcorn. The roof and side walls were faded barnboard, bleached from the sun and dry air swirling around the frame in dust clouds. Inside, were several long tables on which were wooden crates filled with produce. Behind the tables were sunburnt, sweating farmers and ranchers, handing out baskets of their wares to those in need. The queue was long. It stretched from the highway to the tables, at least a hundred hands waiting for aid. Although the line spread across the asphalt to the gravel driveway into the field, it was the thousands of vehicles behind them that drew bile up my throat.

The barrage of cars blocked the highway and the turnoff to Holy Creator's gravel sideroad, and us.

The tires crunched and spewed dust as Todd pulled off into the ditch by the turnoff.

"Looks like there may not be much left for the retreat center."

Following his gaze to the shelter, the long line of people, and the baskets that were quickly being depleted, I was shocked to see how many needed help; how many were dipping into only one well for that help.

Opening the truck's doors, a man emerged from the food shack, waving a baseball cap to get our attention. He wore a short-sleeved cotton plaid shirt and a white, dust-stained undershirt over a pair of equally dust-stained jeans. As we walked toward him, his flushed, sunburnt face emerged from the shadow of his cap brim.

"Hey, Gladstone, the retreat's supplies are in the pan of the truck."

The Hurlburt patriarch motioned to the white Ford 150 sitting amid the stalks of sorghum. On the driver's side door was a dirt-covered decal, 'Hurlburt Farms'. A bushel of sorghum was stenciled in the center, tied with a red ribbon. The pan of the truck was laden with vegetables and milled sorghum.

Hearing the announcement, the crowd in the line shifted.

While those in front remained waiting for their hampers from the shack, the ones near the back left the queue to follow in our wake toward the awaiting supplies. Turning my head, I saw the desperation in their faces and was instantly scared mushroom-less.

"Let's get a move on." The urgency in Todd's voice cut through the pulse thundering in my ears.

Seeing the mob following us, Hurlburt scampered behind the shack and emerged with a shotgun, and two other men, each holding similar weapons.

"Looks like things are about to get fried." My breathless exclamation was met with a sack being thrown from the pan of the truck. Catching it, I looked up into Todd's similarly worried expression.

"We aren't going to be able to load all this up by ourselves. We need help."

I caught another sack and placed it by the first near my feet, knowing he was right. As strong as we were, we could only manage to carry one sack at a time to Todd's pickup. And there was no way we could load everything before the mob arrived, even if Hurlburt and his family were holding them off with the threat of gunfire.

As Todd was hopping down from the Ford, I picked up the sack by my feet and began a slow-jog back to the lime-green machine. Todd followed. We managed to put both in the truck's pan before the crowd swept past the Hurlburt line.

Pop.

Pop.

Pop.

The rapid gunfire overhead dropped the running mob to the ground but as they realized the shots weren't being fired at them, they soon picked up the pace and were swarming the white truck. Hurlburts rushed forward, too, along with the farmers who were manning the shack. Left unattended, those who remained in the food line rushed in and began grabbing everything off the tables and scampering back to their awaiting vehicles. At the Ford, however, things were even more dire.

Elder Hurlburt was standing in the pan of the truck, rifle raised with the barrel pointed at the faces of the men and women rushing forward to grab the sacks that lay within. Todd and I were trying to push our way through the throng to no avail. Our elbows were met with violent shoves and punches, our faces with shouts and curses. Hurlburt's three sons leaped into the pan to stand side-by-side with their father. The younger models were nearly identically dressed, their taller statures and younger faces only distinguishing them from their patriarch.

"Stand back or I'll shoot."

Daddy Hurlburt's voice was strained, high-pitched, terrified.

I recognized that crazed look, though.

I saw it every time I prepared myself for a wrestling match.

It was a face of rage and terror.

Of what one had to do, could do.

It had stared back at me in the bathroom after I had injured Crystal and it was locking eyes with ravenous, raging evacuees who were grabbing the truck's sides and rocking it, unbalancing the men who held weapons within and causing the sacks of food to fall into the field below. One by one, they disappeared as the truck shook, until only a few remained—behind the legs of the Hurlburt men.

"Todd, go get help."

"I'm not going to leave you, Jules."

"I have to stop this before it gets out of control."

"It's already out of control."

We were trying to catch our breath while leaning against the barnboard structure. In front of us, the mob swarmed the truck; behind us, the food shack was being dismantled and cleared of every scrap of food meant as aid.

I saw it before I heard it.

The barrel pointed at the chest of the man who was reaching for Joey Hurlburt's legs, trying to drag him down into the truck bed. Then, the bang and puff of smoke, followed by silence, then screaming. Then, all hell broke loose, as men clamored into the pan and wrestled the rifle away from Hurlburt's son.

Another shot.

Todd and I watched in horror as the farming men were pulled down into the pan, plaid shirts stained with red.

A child was screaming.

Beside me, Todd began to shake.

Grabbing him by the shoulders, I lifted my hand and slapped him.

"Hey, what was that for?" Shocked, he rubbed his palm across his face.

"You were going cra on me, dude."

"Respect."

His dry response was accompanied by a hand to his now pink cheek and a slow shake of his head. I turned and saw sacks of the food stores meant for the retreat center being carried by the throngs of people to the awaiting cars blocking the highway.

"Crap, crap, crap."

"What?" Todd was still nursing his cheek.

"Let's go! Now is our chance! We've gotta get out of here before they take the stuff in your truck."

"Crap is right! C'mon Hulk McSlap!"

We rushed through the field, passing the Ford 150, trying not to look at the bloodied blue denim and plaid in the truck bed, but as we raced by, I kicked a navy ball cap up from the dirt and onto the gravel sideroad.

"I'll drive." My voice was strong.

"You'll get no argument from me."

He was physically shaking as he opened the passenger door and tossed me the keys. "Let's get out of here."

The engine fired to life just as the mob turned.

I put the truck in reverse and slammed on the gas.

The truck went backward and spun around in a tight half-circle, then lunged forward.

And then we sped away in a cloud of dust.

"Cleo, call 911."

"Who are you talking to?"

"My smartphone."

"You have reached 911. All our lines are currently busy. Please stay on the line for the next available operator."

"Fruit Loops!" I shouted into the cab.

"Cleo, call Holy Creator Retreat Centre."

As Todd's tremoring voice burst from his lips in spurts, his smartphone began dialing the center.

"Holy Creator, Jake Klassen speaking."

"Jake … get help, Jake."

"Jules?"

"Yes, get Dad or Mom or Mr. B or Rev. Erin … anyone, Jake, and hurry."

As I shouted into Todd's phone mounted to the dash, Todd's mouth muttered as he craned his neck to see if there were any approaching vehicles behind us. When he was satisfied no one was, he focused his black-brown eyes at the plumes of dust churning up in front of us; eyes bulging and face a ghastly shade of gray.

I reached across the leather seats and put my hand on his thigh, feeling the electrified muscles underneath, but as the truck swerved along the sun-bleached road, I had to return it to the steering wheel to keep control. Behind us, the tailgate swerved and fishtailed as we sped toward the center.

"What's going on," Dad's voice boomed into the cab as the 150's tires crunched and the axles squealed.

"Gunshots at the donation spot," I breathed. "Some people were shot, Dad, they were shot."

Dad siphoned in air and I could hear the whistle between his teeth as he did so.

"OK, where are you guys? Are you OK?"

Turning to Todd, I wasn't so sure but I replied, "yes," anyway.

"Get back here as fast and as safe as you can. I'll call the Pincher Creek police department," Dad's voice was low, and so very deep.

I rounded a corner in the road and slid into Todd's shoulder, slamming my jaw against the top of his head. Regaining control, I straightened the truck, as Dad spoke to Rev. Erin and Mom, and then Mr. B who was calling the detachment. Then, Dad was talking through Todd's phone again.

"Todd, Jules, you're going to be OK, you got that," his voice was solid again and my heartbeat slowed with his assurance. "You're almost here, right?"

"Yes." Todd's voice was a croak.

Then Dad was gone and all around us, dust churned up from the pickup's speeding tires.

Wind from outside was rushing through the cab, whipping up our hair and adding to the dust already in the vehicle. Chancing a look in the rearview, I saw headlights beaming through the wake of dust and rocks. I pushed my foot further down on the gas and the truck revved, fishtailed, and leaped forward.

Todd turned his head and realized we were being followed.

Tucking his head back into the cab, he coaxed, "C'mon Kermit, you can do it!"

"*Kermit*?"

"My truck."

As rocks flew up around our wheel wells, I turned incredulously to Todd, "You named *your truck?* "

"Of course!"

"After what? Kermit the *Frog.*"

"Duh."

As Holy Creator's steeple came into view, police cruisers sped by us on their way to the donation site, their cherry lights flashing and sirens wailing. Behind us, the truck tailing us tried to do a doughnut on the gravel road and ended up in the ditch. One of the cruisers stopped, while the other six continued their convoy to the altercation from which we had narrowly escaped.

I was putting the truck in park when the driver's side door swung open and Dad was pulling me down from the seat, embracing me in a bear hug. Mom was crying beside him, stroking my sweaty, dust-covered red spikes that were now wilted.

"Thank God, thank God, thank God," she was chanting.

Todd slid from the leather seats, still looking like he was in shock, and was immediately embraced by Rev. Erin.

"Praise be," she said into his chest. "Praise the Lord for his great mercies."

"Amen," I mumbled before it dawned on me that I hadn't said *Amen* in years, and never really meant it when I did.

Until now.

****

The rectory living room was bursting at the seams.

At least fifty people were crammed into the normally large space, making it appear like a clown car. Indigenous leaders, farmers, ranchers, and Holy Creator parish council members stood leaning against walls, sat shoulder-to-shoulder on couches and dining-room chairs, and cross-legged on the rug—all craning their ears to hear Prime Minister LeBlanc on the Rev. Erin's phone speakers.

"This is ridiculous."

Ben Ingreveld's voice was agitated to say the least. The president of the Southern Alberta Ranchers' and Farmers' Association pulled the receiver away from his ear to expose the speakers to the listening crowd.

"We need help here; not your sympathy."

The burly farmer was turning red as his breath heaved in his chest and gut.

I watched as Ingreveld's hand gripping the phone grew white around the knuckles. With his other hand, he took off his baseball cap, wiped the perspiration off his forehead with the sleeve of his red and white plaid cotton shirt and returned the cap to cover his head, with his thin, blond hair plastered to his scalp.

Standing by the bookshelves on the back wall was my family: The odd balls. Jake was flipping through a book titled *Apistoke: The Great Spirit*. Mom and Dad were intently listening to the tidbits of whispers being muttered between the people eagerly awaiting the outcome of the chief's conversation. I sat on a bison rug on the floor, my legs stretched out in front of me; my palms flat behind me. Todd mimicked my pose, his denim skirt covering his shins but not his orange socks with blue triangles.

"Yes … the area is overrun, as are our barricades," the farmer was saying to the receiver. There was a long pause, then, "yes, two seriously injured." Pause. "No, we can't hold them off." Pause. "Well, of course we would, but we don't have enough resources to feed our people and hundreds of others, too."

Pause.

Grunt.

"There are nearly four thousand of us, and even if we did that, it wouldn't be enough."

Pause.

Grunt.

"When? Not soon enough. We need them here now."

Pause.

Jake flipped to the last page, handed his book to Mom and said, "Cool story."

"Shussssch," Mom hissed, pointing to Ingreveld.

Over the past two days, while I was attending group counseling sessions in the church's basement, trying to get a handle on my anger, Jake had been in this room, reading. Over meals, he stammered his way through tales of the Aapátohsipikáni (Northern Piikani) band in Alberta and their northern U.S. Piegan band known as Aamssáápipikani (Southern Piikani). He talked about their hunting grounds, their culture, and the fact that before colonization, the Piikani were a large community of more than five thousand. After colonization, however, the tribe was divided into two bands prior to the arrival of the European traders. Several years ago, their numbers started to grow again, as the Blackfoot app got more young people interested in their culture, and stayed on reserves to raise new generations of families.

"Did you know that each year, their Sun Dance Festival raises enough money to pay for five hundred children to go to school," he asked us over bowls of flavorful chicken soup. "And they still use medicine bundles?"

The more Jake read and talked, the less he stuttered.

At this rate, his stammer will be gone by week's end, as he's powered through nearly all the books lining the prayer room shelves.

Maybe it was the reading, but I think his own trip to Holy Creator's basement was the root cause.

While Todd and I had gone on the donation drop off run this morning, Jake had been in the Prayer Room, sharing.

The receiver slammed into the cradle.

With only landlines servicing the church, Rev. Stillwater had opted for the old rotary-dial phones, liking how they sounded when you stuck your finger in the plastic circular holes covering the numbers. "All part of the old ways," she had explained with a chuckle. "When things feel real, they are real."

Ben Ingreveld stood up, walked to the fireplace, stirred the logs in the fire, turned and took a deep breath. He looked like he hadn't slept in days. The lines around his eyes had become skin canyons and the dark half-moons under his lids, their shadows.

"She has agreed to send reinforcements, as long as we cooperate."

The audience in the room shifted in their seats, rustling cushions.

"What does that mean?" Irene Beaver said from her stance beside Ingreveld's elbow. The Piikani chief brushed her hair behind an ear, tilted her head back so that she could focus her intense stare into Ingreveld's face. "What does she think we've been doing here? Playing whist?"

"Let the man speak," said a woman who reached up on tippy toe to kiss Ingreveld on the cheek. "Go on, hon, tell us what the PM said."

The farmer looked apprehensive and as if to prove yet more sweat could be generated from his forehead, he grabbed a cloth kerchief from his front jean pocket and dabbed the bridge of his nose. Turning to the small brunette beside him, he pulled his wife close to him and then addressed the waiting crowd.

"So, what do they want in return? Our land?" The middle-aged man with closely cropped black hair graying at the temples leaned forward from his seat in a dining room chair, his denim-clad elbows resting on his knees as he pressed down into the joints. When Ingreveld didn't answer him, he stood up and I realized I was nowhere near the tallest person in the room.

This guy was.

His head nearly knocked the antler chandelier off kilter as he rose and he towered over the farmer standing beside Rev. Erin's telephone table beside the couch.

"No, Rob, they don't want our land," Ingreveld said, swallowing. "They want … seventy-per-cent of our food stores and production."

"Hell no," the man spat, whom I would later discover was Kainai Chief Robert Tailfeathers.

"That's the only way we will get help," Ingreveld retorted, emphatically. "The army will arrive in the morning. Until then, we are to set up a camp around the perimeter of our lands to house those fleeing the north."

"What about food for *us*?"

"Well, Todd, the PM figures we have enough to feed ourselves with the thirty-per-cent, obviously, since we have no buyers right now, and she's not wrong," the farmer turned and addressed the boy sitting beside me on the rug.

"This is wrong," Todd argued. "This is all wrong, and you know it."

Everyone was nodding in agreement.

Chief Irene responded, "Yes, but what else can we do? We either give up the percentage or we have it taken from us."

She turned to Tailfeathers, her white hair silver in the light, "You said, yourself, that they are shooting our herd. Whose to stop them if they kill more? We don't have the weapons to stop them or the police manpower, and what about what happened this morning with Nephew, here, trying to pick up donations? They got ambushed, that's what."

"Chief Irene and Ben are right," Mr. B's sober tone caused all of us to stop our grumbling. "If we don't acquiesce, the feds will come in and we won't have anything left. At least this way, it's an agreement they have to adhere to, so get it in writing—every promise, every obligation."

Pastor Erin raised her hands and slowly brought them back down.

The murmurs quieted and everyone turned their heads to hear what the priest had to say.

"Brothers and Sisters, we are called to help, so we must help. It is our way. We cannot let this lead to a war between our peoples and the rest of Canada because if it does, we will not win; we will only lose."

She walked amid the crowd, lightly touching hands and heads, all the while nodding. Angelic in poise, Rev. Erin floated amid the laps and legs until tempers calmed.

"Isn't it good to know our food will be going to starving, homeless people at refugee camps? Doesn't it give you a sense of pride to know we will be feeding these fleeing people from the wrath of terrorism, instead of sitting on our reserves and production, waiting for wholesalers to buy from us, again? Well, who will buy from an association that lets their fellow countrymen starve? Grace is what is needed now; grace and charity. Without them, can we call ourselves Canadian, Christian or otherwise?"

"There is one saving grace to all of this," Chief Tailfeathers said to the bent heads pondering the prime minister's decree, "we keep our lands, we keep our herds and farms."

"But for how long? When will the feds decide if it is in their best interest to control the source, and not just rely on us to supply the quotas?"

The white-haired elderly lady coughed and she lay back against the stallion couch and covered her mouth with a piece of blue and white gingham.

"Chief Sybll, that is my concern as well," Tailfeathers said, turning to the woman. "The Kainai, like the Siksika—like all our indigenous brothers and sisters here—know too well how governments take what they want, when they want it, regardless of rights and liberties. So, who's to say they take over the whole shebang?"

"There is no guarantee," Ingreveld nodded. "You all elected me to represent the association and I'm telling you right here and now, we are in a tight spot—there's really no other way of saying it. If we don't give the feds what they want, they *will* send in the army, not only to end the conflicts but to take control of our ranches and farms, too, whether they are on privately-owned or reserve lands—it won't matter in the least.

"But *you* tell me. Is there anything else we should be doing?"

The room erupted into grumbling and grunts, but no one spoke up with a solution.

There was none.

It was abundantly clear, they were at the mercy of LeBlanc and her cabinet.

Ingreveld said in exchange for the seventy percent of food stores for the resettlement camps in Saskatchewan, the association members would get bundles of canvas, water and medical supplies dropped by helicopter to the area, in addition to the arrival of the military to keep the peace.

Todd rose, grabbed my hand and pulled me upright.

"Sam, can I entrust the encampment to you?"

"Yes, and I'll get some of the youth to help me out with the tipi construction."

I peeked around Todd's frame to see Mr. B talking to Ingreveld.

He turned to Todd and me and added: "They need something to do. Otherwise, they'll get restless and do something stupid."

****

Peacekeepers Come to Southern Alberta Aid

Southern Alberta retreat center gets food supplies and security amid rise in sanctuary seekers

By Doug Faulkner
Calgary Tribune
Special Report

July 2, 2042—Prime Minister Jacqueline LeBlanc has ordered Canadian Armed Forces Peacekeeper squadrons to assist Southern Alberta in a tit-for-tat agreement that would see local farmers and ranchers shipping food to the resettlement camps planned for Saskatchewan later this month.

"It's very simple, really," LeBlanc announced from her new base of operations at Government House in downtown Halifax. "SARFA (Southern Alberta Ranchers' and Farmers' Association) has agreed to ship food stores to designated relocation camps throughout Saskatchewan, instead of selling them to food manufacturers in the country, the majority of which were destroyed in the terrorist attack on June 21, or are in a radiation contamination zone. In return, the Peacekeeping troops will be deployed to the area to keep the peace and help with the citizen relocation plan."

The relocation plan, she explained, will use existing schools within Saskatchewan to create dormitories for those fleeing the affected areas, an initiative modeled after the United Atlantic Nation of North America's resettlement bases in the Atlantic provinces. The retrofitting of these buildings will be done within the next few weeks, with relocation trains arriving by the end of the month.

"We wanted to wait until the UANN Exodus trains returned from their eastern destinations before using them to relocate our citizens, who have now become refugees in their home provinces," the prime minister stated. "This would give us the time we need to remodel the schools and to get our infrastructures in place to best deal with this unheard-of situation."

In Southern Alberta, however, tensions are on the rise. Armed sanctuary seekers have resorted to theft of food stores, bison poaching and erecting barricades to prevent grain and food trucks from leaving the SARFA area.

"We are not equipped to handle this level of unrest," said association president Ben Ingreveld. "We can't pull beds out of thin air. I would hazard to guess every rancher, farmer, reserve member has put a family up in their homes, and that's not counting the hundreds being housed at the Holy Creator Retreat Centre, but we are maxed out. You can't draw blood from a stone, and they just need to realize that.

"Stopping shipments out to other needy Canadians isn't the way to make us help you either."

The sorghum rancher from the Pincher Creek area said the Peacekeeping deployment couldn't have happened at a more opportune time, a sentiment echoed by Rev. Erin Stillwater of the Anglican Church of the Holy Creator and overseer of the retreat center, which is currently housing 548 displaced Albertans.

"We get people showing up every hour of every day," said the priest. "When we ran out of space in our center, we set up tents and when we ran out of tents, our First Nations neighbors erected tipis. That's what we will be doing with the canvas, when we get it, erect tipis for people, in addition to feeding them all. Everyone around here is lending a hand to see that these people get the help they need but I fear for what may come next, and I pray to God Almighty, that whatever it is, we will be equipped to handle it with mercy and grace."

Rev. Stillwater added that with the federal government requesting food stocks for the Saskatchewan domestic refugee camps, the area's surplus food stores will be depleted, which will adversely affect how much locals have to give to those who need help, as well as feeding their own households.

"We have to rely on the fall harvest for the year ahead, which scares the-H-E-double-hockey-sticks out of me," Ingreveld admitted. "With all these angry people around, who knows what they are capable of doing? We've already had one near-death from an altercation just the other day at a *donation* drop-off site. What's next? Murder when we give them water?"

RCMP are combining forces with reserve police departments to monitor the situation in the area but their numbers are a drop in the bucket when it comes to what is needed, the association president explained. "We are in a tinderbox, waiting for a spark."

LeBlanc said the Peacekeeping troop deployed to the Pincher Creek area will remain on site until after the last round of winners in the United Atlantic

Nation of North America Resettlement Lottery depart from its Pincher Creek Station on July 17, which will be overseen by UANNA ambassadors, the names of whom have yet to be announced. Other troops will be sent to other reserves throughout Alberta, Manitoba, Saskatchewan and Northern Ontario in a likewise fashion, as they, too, are experiencing similar onslaughts of violent encounters with those seeking aid after the small-modular reactor terrorism explosions by the extremist environmental group known as Terra Nova.

Much like the UANNA members in Atlantic Canada, the Southern Alberta region's embrace of renewable energy and protection of agricultural lands against commercial and industrial rezoning may have been its saving grace.

When asked if these approaches should have been adopted nationwide, LeBlanc would only say, "hindsight is twenty-twenty. However, Southern Alberta Piikani Chief Irene Beaver had no such qualms.

In fact, according to Chief Beaver, reserves such as the Piikani First Nation implemented cultural camps for their youth more than twenty years ago. These camps, facilitated by elders in the clan, taught everything from hunting, fishing and farming to beadwork, foraging, tipi construction, and collective living.

"This is how we have continued to be relevant, productive, sustainable. If others had done the same, maybe we wouldn't be in this state."

While the troops are waiting to be deployed, the SARFA and First Nations have agreed to give as much aid as possible to those seeking food and shelter.

"We'll do what we can, with what we can," the Beaver said. "But that goes both ways: Peace can only be achieved if we work together—like what SARFA and the Nations are doing right now. All this rage is directed at the wrong people. It should be at the terrorist group that caused all of this but instead, it is directed at us; at the very people who are trying to help. I'm afraid it will come to a breaking point down here because if we can't figure this out—how to work together toward a common solution—then there will be more than just grain being stolen and bison being shot."

Ingreveld and Beaver said they will be holding a brainstorming session at Holy Creator's retreat center July 3, on the eve of the Peacekeeping troop's arrival.

"We need to assess the situation, come up with contingency plans, and utilize the resources we have to the benefit of our members, and the civilians seeking aid," Ingreveld said. "What that looks like, we don't know yet, which is why we are meeting before the Peacekeepers arrive, so that we have something to work with, something that *we* have agreed upon, instead of having it forced upon us."

When asked if that includes weapons to defend themselves, Ingreveld said he wasn't ruling it out.

"If it comes down to it, we will do what is necessary to see that what we have is defended, at whatever the cost. After all, what do we have to lose? Everything."

Unfortunately, the same could be said about the crowds swarming to the area, "which is why the squadron is so essential," acknowledged Beaver. "You can't speak logic to an injured bear; you can only protect yourself from being mauled."

Chapter 16

"What are you so afraid of, Jules?"

I looked down at the ring of elastic around the wrist of my folded hands as Rev. Erin softly spoke in my ear. Sitting beside me on the Prayer Room couch, she tentatively reached over the chasm between us and gently eased one hand's grip on the other.

"There is so much fear in you; so much uncertainty. Why is that?"

Without looking into the priest's eyes, I began to speak—my voice low, rough. I felt like I hadn't spoken in months, years and the croaking noise being emitted from between my lips was the first juvenile attempt at sound formation.

It was raw.

"Of not being in control," I began. "Everything seems to always *happen* to me."

We were in a private counseling session.

Todd wasn't there to support me.

Nail-cleaning dude wasn't there to distract me.

Or Rev. Erin, whose eyes and attention were zeroed in on me, and me alone.

"Jules, I think it's time you let Erin into that brain of yours, especially if you won't let any of us. This may be your last chance to get the help you need, so take it."

Dad's words echoed between my ears.

Yesterday afternoon, Todd and I had found another bison carcass in the field while we were gathering up supplies for Mr. B's tipi crew, which was busy erecting the temporary structures around the perimeter of the Holy Creator property. As we fetched the bundles of canvas that had been parachuted from the sky, the animal's hairy hind legs protruded from the dry, brown-green grass. The fading green blades around the beast were flattened and splattered with spots of blood, which had dried a ruby-black. Beside the exposed chest cavity lay a burlap sack, split at the bottom, spewing vomited kernels of sorghum onto the crushed grazing field. Fuming, Todd and I had delivered the bundles of thick, ivory sheets to his uncle at the construction site.

We were still talking about the find when Ben Ingreveld walked over to us, face beet red, and threw down a pair of metal cutters.

"Blackfeather, we have to do something about these … these … thieves," he puffed. "They cut into the grain bins. The grain bins, do you hear me? I've had it with these ingrates. Enough!"

Mr. B picked up the cutters by the scuffed up red handles and inspected the blades. "How much did you lose?"

"Enough." Ingreveld removed his baseball cap from off his head and ran his large hand through the thin hair, making it stand on end. At this rate, he'd be bald by the time the summer ended, I had thought.

"We found another bison carcass on the Smythe ranch," Todd grunted, and Mr. B gave him the stink eye, but he didn't get the hint and continued talking. "That's the second one this week. Disgusting. Something has to be done."

Ingreveld waited for a response from Todd's uncle and my old social studies teacher but none came. Samuel Blackfeather simply nodded, wordlessly, and Ingreveld shook his head in frustration.

"This isn't just my grain, ya know, or Smyth's bison—everyone who has property and food stores is being raided, including your people."

"My people will consider what action needs to be taken, if it comes to that."

"Well, Sam, look around. We're here."

Ingreveld was wildly gesturing with his arms, taking in the tipis dotting the edge of the fields, and the teens binding poles to erect even more; the retreat center; and the vast fields and ranches that stretched as far as the eye could see.

After he had stormed off, Todd had confronted his uncle, who took his nephew by the shoulders and stared down into his agitated face: "If we fight back, it'll be our people who will be seen as agitators; not the farmers and ranchers—our people. We need to leave this fight alone. You hear me?"

"What do you mean when you say you have no control?" Rev. Erin's voice jolted me back to the prayer room.

"I mean, I don't. Everything that has happened to me … *happened to me*."

I pushed up from the couch and walked over to the basement window and gazed out onto the white-pebbled drive. The hot breeze from outside fluttered the gazey curtains into my face and I brushed them aside, wiping the tears away as I did so.

"From the fight in Calgary to the bus ride from hell to what's going on here—even the Exodus Train—are all things that *happened* and continue to *happen* to me.

"I am just responding, and most of the time, badly."

"And why do you think that is?"

I turned to look at the priest, her white streaks of gray braided with the black on either side of her face. It was a kind face that stared at me, that smiled encouragingly at me to continue, to open up.

"I have no control of my life," I sighed into the room. "Zilch, nada, zip."

"Do you want control?"

"Hell ya."

I paced the room, feeling like a giraffe in a china shop.

"And what would that control look like?"

"I don't know. Deciding something, I guess."

"And then living with the consequences?"

Her head was tilted, waiting for me to respond.

"Well, ya. It's better than having to deal with the consequences of someone else's choices."

"Ah."

Rev. Erin got up from her sitting position and lit the pillar candle in the center of the coffee table, sending a woodsy aroma I later found out was sage, into the room.

"Jules?"

"Yes?"

"Then decide *for yourself.* You have more control than you think. You have control over *how* you respond, *how* you treat others, *how* you view yourself, even *how* you act right now and tomorrow."

"But it is a *response.*"

"So, what? Responding doesn't mean you lack control. Quite the opposite, really. You can choose multiple ways on how to respond. You just need to decide which one will make you proud; which one Jesus has laid for you."

"How do I know?"

"Our Savior was about mercy, grace, love, forgiveness—that is where his strength came from, his control. Can you see yourself using those qualities in your decisions? Can they be part of *who you are?*"

"I don't know."

"It is in your power to choose them, you know, no one else's. Sometimes, the biggest control someone has is to let go and lift up major decisions to Our Lord, so that *he* is the guiding principle, and not all the stuff that distracts us, such as greed, envy, power. So, in the words of our Sunday School teacher, Mrs. Weaselbear, ask yourself, 'What would Jesus do?'"

Her lips widened in a smile.

"That's your control."

****

Ben Ingreveld held what appeared to be a robotic spider in his hands.

The center metal box had two round lights which were now beaming into my chest. Stretching out from the box were metal pipe legs with sprayers at the ends that looked like feet. We were in a storage Quonset on his farm lined with metal shelves containing every kind of automotive part imaginable. Tractor tires were stacked against the corrugated metal walls of the domed outbuilding, and pale light was flooding the dimly lit room from the swinging bulbs overhead.

"What do you want with Attella?"

"Who?" I turned my head to look over at Todd, who was trying to contain a smirk and was doing a piss-poor job of it.

"It's the drone," he whispered.

"She's not just any drone, Todd my boy, she's the cream of the crop."

Ingreveld's hearty laugh made his plaid-coated belly jiggle.

"I've had Attella, here, for nigh on six years, now. What a peach."

Still confused, I leaned into Todd's ear: "Are you sure we're talking about that robot spider thingy he's holding and not Mrs. Ingreveld?"

Todd's suppressed grin split and his mouth burst forth laughter that caused him to hold onto his red-leather-belted hip.

"What's that, now?"

"Nothing, Mr. Ingreveld," Todd said, trying to recover. "Jules has never seen a spraying drone before."

"Ah," the farmer chuckled again, "that explains the look on their face. Attella is a surprise, that's for sure. I mean, get a look of her—beautiful, ain't she?"

Not my chosen choice of words, to say the least.

For starters, the crop-spraying drone looked more than a robotic spider, right down to the bulging orb lights at the head that were currently beaming into my chest.

"She can spray eight thousand square feet in minutes. She's got a camera, a ten-rotor propulsion system and can transport up to fifteen kilograms of chemical solution and can collect data on more than twenty acres in an hour."

The farmer lifted the large drone up with both hands so Todd and I could take a better look.

"A real beaut, she is."

Ingreveld fairly glowed with pride.

"So, what do you want with her?"

"We just want to do some recon …," Todd began, before being interrupted by my elbow to his arm.

"Spraying," I interjected. "Mr. B … I mean, Mr. Blackfeather, is doing a demo on how sorghum is sprayed to protect them from pests and he mentioned you had a spraying drone."

"Well, here she is—the top of the line."

He handed the drone over to Todd, who stretched his arms wide to receive the long pipe limbs protruding from the middle.

"Just be sure she comes back in one piece."

Ingreveld patted the top of the drone as if it was a dog, or his favorite child.

"What kind of pesticide do you spray with it?"

"An all-natural, non-toxic salt solution we mix up ourselves."

"Impressive."

"You're darn tootin' it's impressive," Ingreveld grinned at me. "No harmful chemicals touches our crop; that's why we've lasted this long."

As Todd loaded the drone in the back of his pickup, I climbed into the cab and gazed out the sliding windows behind my head. Attella took up nearly the full footprint of the truck bed, her eight pipe legs stretched to all corners. Built on a grid-like pattern, the drone looked like a giant tic-tac-toe game with a black cube in the center. At the tips of the legs were round elongated balls with sprayer nozzles.

As Todd hopped down from the pan, and brushed his hands down the front of his turquoise ruffled skirt, Ben Ingreveld walked up to him and handed him the remote control.

We drove away in silence.

Todd was staring out the dust and grime covered windshield while I did the same to the passenger window. Seeing only hints of the field, I pushed the button by the armrest and the glass slid down and let a gust of dry, grainy air into the cab.

"What now?"

He turned his head slightly in my direction.

"What's the rest of your plan?"

I sighed deeply and turned to my friend.

My friend who would remain here, while I boarded a train tomorrow.

I swallowed.

The past few weeks had sped by in bursts of activity.

We had helped the teens erect tipis all over the retreat grounds, and then moved onto the farmers' fields and ranches to do likewise. Under Mr. B's direction, there had been enough canvass to set up 612 tipis in all. Todd's friends had helped, and even a few of the local teens who were normally secluded in their ranch houses. Each structure housed two or more families, depending on their numbers. The five-feet-in-diameter canvass homes had a small, rusting half of a drum in the center for a fire and a flap in the side to let in air. Some of the displaced Albertans came prepared with blankets, pillows, and extra clothing, while others dug through the donation bins to find supplies.

Then, yesterday, the Peacekeepers arrived.

In armored jeeps bouncing up and down the gravel sideroads and paved highways, the soldiers set up positions at the barricades, pushing protesters back, removing weapons, and trying to calm the conflict down.

Sometimes they were successful and people moved off, eventually finding themselves in the tipis with their families in tow.

Other times, they remained, pushing back against the soldiers, shouting about rights and freedoms. The soldiers uncoiled cables from the front of the armored vehicles and attached them to the assortment of cars, trucks, and minivans blocking access to the highway, and to Pincher Creek Station. One by one, they were cleared, until the next morning, when they would magically appear again.

Further out in the fields, bison continued to get slaughtered in the dead of night, and grain stores continued to get pilfered.

Then came the chickens, the goats.

In the days leading up to the Peacekeepers' arrival, my days were spent going to counseling sessions with Rev. Erin, preparing and serving meals with Jake, and helping Mr. B.'s crew of teens allocate supplies. Meanwhile, my parents joined Holy Creator parishioners in welcoming the influx of sanctuary seekers, and ensured all their basic needs were met.

Before the Peacekeepers, one day rolled into another. The appearance of military boots on the ground, however, seemed to have lit a charge. Yesterday, ranchers and farmers confronted those residing in Tipi Village, demanding to know where the poachers were hiding.

Getting nowhere, they headed to the highway, where they met up with the Peacekeepers and the protesters.

"I want to use Attella to scare off the poachers," I said.

"How on earth are you going to do that?"

"Jake."

"And what is your little brother going to do that a squadron of Peacekeepers cannot?"

"Use his brain."

Todd turned onto a field road to avoid the highway blockade and we bounced on large rocks and squished mounds of earth until we came to Holy Creator's gravel drive.

Hearing skepticism in his voice, I turned to Todd's angular profile and said the one phrase I never thought would be uttered from my lips: "Jake is a genius. I have every confidence he can pull this off."

"Pull what off, Jules? What are you planning?"

"To catch them all red-handed, so to speak," I said, grinning at my friend who was now shaking his head in disbelief.

"Whatever you're up to, dude, you'd better be smart about it."

"You mean *we'd* better be smart about it, right?"

Chuckling, Todd turned his grinning face to me, "How did I get roped into your diabolical scheme?"

"Because, dude, you're my peep."

Turning back to the windshield and the approaching retreat center, Todd's voice lowered, "Not for long."

"What are you going to do with her, I mean, *it?*" Todd asked from his perch on the revolving stool in the church's workshop.

The outbuilding was adorned in metal shelving, woodworking benches with vices and planes, and a small pot-belly stove that was currently burning a chunk of dried birch. It was evening and the wired light bulbs hooked into the overhead beams swayed, sending shadows against the walls of gardening tools, shovels, spades and scythes.

"Do you know what effervescent paint is?"

"You mean glow-in-the-dark?"

"Yeah."

"Sure. We use it to paint boulders at the entrance to the backroads so we can see them in the night—comes in handy when the roads are blocked."

"Exactly." I turned to Jake, who was busy filling the drone's container with glowing liquid.

"That's what this is," Jake added, pausing in mid-pour. "It is a special formula that won't clog the nozzles. We are going to spray it on the poachers when we find them."

"And then what?"

I turned away from Jake's methodical filling of the drone's canister to take in Todd's concerned expression, adding, "Nothing. We'll know who they are, that's all, and we can arrest them."

"Who exactly is going to arrest them? The police, the army? They are all too busy trying to keep people from killing each other."

Todd was right.

Would knowing who was doing the thieving really solve anything?

"Jake, Todd's right. I think we should go with Plan B."

Todd stopped spinning on his chair to lean forward. "What's Plan B?"

I walked over to one of the shelves lining the wall of the shed and grabbed a mason jar of black rubber pellets. I tossed them into Jake's lap as he crouched beside Attella.

"Are you sure?"

"I'm sure."

"Someone could get hurt."

"They're rubber."

Jake lifted the jar and stared at its contents, his eyes wide and his skin turning a ghostly shade of gray.

"I don't like it, Jules. I … I … don … don … don'T like it."

"I know, but trust me, OK."

"What are you fools talking about? Are you planning to *fire* those things?"

Todd was walking across the wooden floors, clicking his red cowboy boots on the hardwood as he did so, and leaned over to look at the jar.

"What are they anyway?"

"Rubber bullets."

He leaped back.

"Are you two out of your freakin' mind? You're planning to *fire rubber bullets* at people?"

"That's the plan," I said, turning to look at his shocked face. "Just to scare them off."

"Unbelievable."

"Todd, listen, no one will get hurt."

"Are you sure of that? Someone always gets hurt. Look at Hurlburt, for goodness' sake: He didn't think he'd get shot dolling out donations to a bunch of hungry city folks, now did he? Yet, the poor dude's lucky to be alive.

"And *where* did you get them, anyway?"

"Ah…" turning to Jake, I blushed sheepishly and nodded at him to answer.

Jake stood frantically shaking his head from side to side and mouthed, "You tell him!"

"Fine!" I mouthed back.

I pouted my lips at Jake and then turned back to Todd, who looked like he was about to blow his top.

"Jake showed one of the Peacekeepers his collection of First and Second World War eBooks on his smartphone, which is quite extensive by the way, and asked if he could take the soldier's picture and …"

"Let me guess: Get a keepsake."

"Yes! A handful of these!" Jake burst out; an eager grin spread wide. His hand was outstretched and inside the palm, were the black rubber balls the size of grapes. "Bu … bu … bUT it'll be a las … las … laST resort, ri … ri… riGT, Jules?"

"Right," I crooned. "First, the paint, then the sirens, then the bullets."

"Sirens?" Todd was incredulous.

Jake could have lit the room.

"I've hacked into Attella's operating system to emit a high-pitched siren on my command."

"You two are nuts."

"Are you coming with us?"

"When?"

"Tonight."

"You don't give a guy a chance to get his bearings, do you?"

"Jake and I leave tomorrow, so if we are doing this, tonight is the night."

"Jeez Louise, Jules, you'll be the death of me."

Chapter 17

Attella soared high over the six-foot stalks of sorghum, her silent propellers whirring with the wind. Following the range road to the highway, she scaled over Holy Creator's steeple, rows of silver grain tanks and barn roofs from nearby sorghum fields, maneuvered around parked green combines waiting patiently for harvest to begin, and on to the ranchlands where herds of hairy bison grazed. With her bug-lights off, she was stealth.

Ben Ingreveld would have been proud.

Jake adjusted the joystick to turn the drone in a wide arc above the herd. Out of sight, he guided the drone using the infrared camera that was sending video to the small hand-held monitor in Todd's hand.

"Keep it steady," Todd said, as a gust of wind caused Attella to turn on her side before being righted with Jake's gaming hands.

"I'm … trying, but it's so windy out there."

"It always is at this time of year. You're lucky there isn't a dust storm."

We were sitting in the pan of Kermit the Frog—Todd's green Ford F150—with Jake controlling Attella, Todd holding the monitor and scanning the footage, and me twiddling my thumbs.

My whole role in this sting seemed to be done, yet I couldn't sit still.

Instead, I stood behind Jake's back as he lounged on an overturned crate, trying to peer into the monitor in front of him and point to where he should go. Only thing was, I had no idea where to go, so Jake ignored every suggestion and turned to Todd for navigation.

I felt useless, yet this was my mission and I was in charge.

"See anything?"

"No, Jules, just the bison."

Todd's anxious voice trembled, and he glanced back and forth from the monitor to Jake and me to the field surrounding us on all sides.

It was nearly two in the morning, and Jake rubbed his eyes with his free hand to wipe away the cobwebs starting to form in the corners. Yawning, his chin nearly touching his collarbone, he turned his red eyes to me and asked, "Jules, how long are we going to stay out?"

"Only a few hours, dude, I promise."

"Good, I'm beat."

Attella went down a coulee and then up again, spanned across the ranch and moved onto the adjacent property.

"What's that?"

I pointed at the monitor.

Several headlights appeared in a cluster just as Attella rounded a red Quonset.

"Poachers," Todd hissed.

Jake dipped Attella and using the controls, zoomed the camera to get a better view.

"Record, record."

"I am, Jules. I got this."

No doubt.

If there was anyone who could turn a joystick and punch a few buttons in rapid succession, it was my video-gaming brother.

As we watched, transfixed, the camera took in six vehicles parked in a circle. In the center, was a lone male bison. As shots were fired, Jake tapped the orange button on his remote and Attella's lights turned on, flooding the circle with bright, white beams. The burly animal in the center of the ring fell to the earth, sending plumes of dust clouds up around its dead body as it hit the ground. Then came the sirens from Attella's mounted speakers, and the slow swoosh, swoosh of spray flowing from the pipe legs onto those below. The effervescent paint hissed and showered down onto the revving vehicles as the drivers rushed to back up and leave the field. Blinded by Attella's beams, the poachers tried to do doughnuts in the tall grasses, only to bang into the trucks trying to do the same thing beside them.

It was chaos.

Tires squealed, curses were shouted and Attella recorded it all, zooming in to capture the vehicles and horrified faces now glowing a neon green in the black night.

"Chase them, chase them," I hollered, but Jake was already following the fleeing vehicles, until a bullet whizzed by, cracking one of Attella's eyes and cutting off the light.

Jake tilted the drone so it nosedived onto the cabs, and hit the red button on the controller.

Rubber bullets flew from the chamber attached to the drone's underbelly, leaving pocket marks on the roofs of the trucks.

Headlights popped, windows smashed and still Attella pursued.

Pop, pop, pop.

Attella was now blind.

Horns honked and wheels churned up field dust as they neared Pincher Creek Station.

Thinking they were safe, the three drivers parked their trucks beside the grain elevator. Hopping out of their vehicles, the neon green aliens were greeted by others congregating near the station, congratulating themselves on their getaway.

That's when I saw them.

The diggers loomed above the tracks, bucket teeth raised.

"Holy shiitake mushrooms," Jake said as he pointed to the half-dozen pieces of construction equipment poised above the rail line.

"Same," Todd and I said in unison.

Chapter 18

"Nom? Name?" The soldier in green and gray camo asked as he leaned over a desk full of papers, which had a list of names on it—some were crossed off; others were blacked out with a Sharpie. Atop the list was the date: July 4—Exodus 1.

We had arrived at the Pincher Creek Station a little before seven o'clock in the morning, and it had already been surrounded.

Gone were the excavators Attella had captured the night before and in their place, were thousands of protesters forming human chains, lifting placards denouncing the exodus and wanting a ticket to the train east. After showing the footage to Todd's uncle, Mr. B passed it along to the Peacekeeping commander in charge of the blockade.

On either side of the road leading to the station, Canadian Armed Forces Peacekeepers tried to restrain the mob behind coils of barbed wire. Holding military rifles across their sand-colored, bullet-proof uniforms, the soldiers stood their ground against the onslaught of verbal assault and the occasional rock being bounced off their helmets. As the crowd pushed, the wire cut and the anger intensified.

"Don't look into their faces," Dad advised. "They want to engage; don't let them. They want to intimidate; don't let them."

"It just seems so unfair that we get to go and they don't," I turned my head to the picketers and got a squashed up, empty water bottle in the chest. "Arumph!" I said, bending over on the impact. "Serves me right, I guess."

"We are blessed that your mother is from Newfoundland. These people aren't so fortunate."

"So, we just let them die?"

"We are not abandoning them, Jules. They will be housed and fed at camps in Saskatchewan, just not yet. That's why Rev. Erin and I are working with church leaders all over the province to get aid to them in the meantime, but we can only do so much."

Mom turned, grabbed Jake's hand, and pulled him forward.

"We won't be able to help anyone if we don't get out of here. I heard on the news this morning that the contamination zones are spreading," she said.

I thought of the farmers and ranchers, the families living in Lethbridge, Brocket and Pincher Creek, and the First Nations, of Rev. Stillwater and Chief Irene, of Mr. B and Todd.

What will become of them if it does?

We had left them an hour ago, with full bellies and warm hugs.

"Stay safe," I had told Todd, who gave me a lopsided grin and replied, "Hulk, my man, I'm safer here than you will be getting there. So, right back at ya."

How right you were, Todd.

After our reconnaissance mission the night before, Jake and I were on high alert.

Where had the heavy equipment gone?

Was it all a ruse to draw our attention elsewhere?

"Mr. B said thanks to Jake's smarts, tribal police and the Pincher Creek Police Detachment were able to identify the vehicles used by the glow on their trucks," Todd explained. "Your mission was a success, Hulk, my man, so own it."

If it was such a resounding success, though, why was bile rising in my throat? Why did I have this feeling of something more going down; something beyond these placards and thrown water bottles; something bigger?

I turned my head to see the smudged faces of children holding hands with their parents, shouting to be let on the train; to be saved.

****

Before we said our goodbyes, we had one last meal of crispy-fried bison bacon and scrambled, buttery eggs. Outside, the disgruntled crowd grew and became more agitated.

Despite the delectable food on our plates, we had lost our appetites.

We couldn't eat, with the riot outside our doors, so Todd and I escaped to the second floor of the rectory. In the sanctuary of the small guest room decorated with horses galloping along wallpapered walls, Todd blared his music through something called a *boombox*, which looked more like Attella's crazy grandpa than a stereo, to drown out the commotion outside. Then, he began opening twine-tied packages of clothes, courtesy of his Aunt Savannah. Inside were jumpsuits cinched at the waist, baggy tees with built-in chest flatteners, army fatigues embroidered with colorful flowers and vines, skirted shorts, halters and fleece pullovers.

"Auntie knew you didn't leave Calgary with much, because we are tired of seeing you in holey jeans and shorts," Todd nodded at my backpack. "That's sad, Hulk my man, even for you. There are a bunch of accessories, as well, and of course, those dreadful plaid shirts you like so much, but with a bit more flare."

By a *bit more flare*, Todd meant the flannel was tailored to hug my hips and decals stamped into the back of thundering bison and stampeding stallions.

And under each shirt was a built-in chest flattener.

"I know how much you absolutely *loved* that binder," Todd joked, "So, Auntie got you something from her trans line."

I was speechless.

As tears flowed down my hot, flushed cheeks, Todd's arms wrapped around me.

"She threw in a few girly outfits, too, for your fem days."

I squeezed him close.

I was going to miss him most of all.

We thundered down the stairs an hour later, giggling like schoolgirls at a pillow-fighting sleepover.

When we entered the kitchen, we were faced with the reality of what we had fled from: Broken shards of glass scattered across the hardwood floor and paper-covered rocks with, 'Traitor' written in red lodged between fluffy clouds of yellow egg.

Mom was busy sweeping up the pieces of window, tears silently streaming down her face. She swept debris into a dustpan and shook the glistening contents into the trash.

Dad was outside on the step with Rev. Erin, his large, muscular arm wrapped tightly around the priest's slumped shoulders, propping her up as she sobbed.

While we were busy talking about clothes and new identities, my parents and Rev. Erin had been bombarded with violence, and Jake had hid under the dining table overcome with fear. The once sunny kitchen looked haggard, abused.

As the sun streaked in through the broken windows, the light reflected onto the shards atop the dining room table, sticking up from the plates of eggs and bacon; toast slices and jam lids. Under the table, sat Jake, hands over his ears, rocking back and forth.

Dad left Rev. Erin to stride into the rectory.

His brow was furrowed, his lips spread thin.

"Where have you been, Jules?"

"I ..."

"Sorry, Rev. Klassen, I just wanted to set Jules up with some new duds for the trip."

Todd's nervous voice was met with a piercing stare, which relaxed at seeing my friend's concerned and embarrassed expression.

"Thanks, Todd, but it would have been more appropriate for Jules to have helped with this mess instead of running away, don't you think?"

"Yes, sir."

"Dad, we didn't know...."

"And you didn't stay long enough to find out."

Dad closed his eyes and exhaled deeply through his nostrils.

"Jules..." Dad began and then turned to Jake, "*never* forget about your brother, you got that?"

"Yes, sir."

I wanted the floor to swallow me whole.

"Once you get on that train, all you'll have is each other." Dad's Adam's apple bobbed in his throat. "That's it. So, you have to watch out for one another—don't leave him behind. Ever."

His voice cracked and I thought my big, burly father was going to break down in sobs right there in front of me.

I nodded and bent down to peer under the large rectangular table.

"Jake, come on out, Jake, please," I pleaded, my voice a bit too high for my own ears. "Please, Jake, I'm sorry, OK. I will never leave you again."

Blue eyes turned to me.

I could see the fear, the distress.

His lips trembled as he tried to mouth words, reverting to stuttering.

"Pra … pram … promISE?"

"I promise."

He grabbed my extended hand with his soft one and I pulled him out from under the table. Standing beside me, I gave him something both of us needed at that moment: a bear hug.

His head rested under my chin.

Then Mom's arms were around both of us, and Dad's.

"Get in here, Todd," Mom squeaked from under Dad's bicep. "You need one of these, too."

"How do you know?" Todd was cracking up.

His eyes glinted, his hand was held to his mouth, trying to stifle the giggles rising up his chest. To me, he looked like a toddler trying to contain himself.

"You're fam, dude, so get your fab butt over here," I burst out between layers of limbs.

Then he was there, joining my family in a pile-on hug that lasted not even a minute before Jake shimmied down and crawled out between Dad's legs and breathing like he had just run a marathon.

We were all busting a gut laughing when Rev. Erin walked in from outside, smiling.

"Klassens, we sure will miss you."

Dad let go of his grip around us and strode over to the priest standing in the rectory doorway.

"Erin, my beautiful-hearted sister in Christ, the feeling is mutual."

Before the reverend had a chance to respond, all our arms converged around her body, enveloping her sorrow, her distress, her fear until nothing remained but joy.

Chuckling, Rev. Erin pulled herself away from our embrace, looked at the broken windows and said, "He heals the brokenhearted and binds up their wounds. He determines the number of the stars and calls each of them by name. Great is our Lord and mighty in power; his understanding has no limits."

"Psalm 147: One of my favorites," Dad nodded, and then turning to my family and me, he added, "It is time."

"Do we have to go right now? I thought the train wasn't leaving until one?"

"It isn't but I thought we'd get there early."

Dad was checking his watch. It was barely nine, and I wasn't ready to leave.

"Jules, I left a parting gift for you on your bed. Maybe that will pass some time before you have to leave." Todd winked.

I turned to Dad and he smiled at my eager expression.

"Go on, then."

As Todd went outside with Rev. Erin to inspect the damage to the church and rectory, I went back to the bedroom and found Todd's surprise: Two boxes of hair dye, one platinum; the other scarlet red.

"Mom!" I yelled, "I need you!"

The silver and red hair dye had lifted my spirits, when all I wanted to do was shrivel up in a ball and cry. Instead, Mom had led me into the bathroom and opened the boxes. It took an hour to use both dyes, but it kept my mind busy, and Mom's, too. Jake had come in several times to see the progress, took pictures with his smartphone to show me, and then sat on the toilet seat while my hair was rinsed in the white porcelain sink.

"Wicked," he had remarked, grinning ear to ear.

"You're next," I replied.

"No," he squealed and ran out to Dad, who was chatting with Rev. Erin in the sanctuary of the church.

Next came the arduous task of packing up the car and saying our final goodbyes.

Getting our belongings into Mom's station wagon brought up a strange case of Deja vu.

Jake bounced his backpack down the steps leading to the rectory, which had become our home in the eight days since our arrival. My own overstuffed bag was hoisted high on my back, getting dangerously close to toppling me over with every step. Mom and Dad were getting their things loaded into the station wagon that had been parked in the church parking lot and I was trying to find the courage to say goodbye—not to my house or possessions this time, but to my best friend in this world, Todd.

He stood by our car, legs crossed at the ankles and giving me one final glimpse of his red leather cowboy boots under the hem of a purple skirt tied at the waist. His Give Peas a Chance T-shirt made me smile, even though I felt like crumbling in a soggy wet mess.

"You good?"

"I yam what I yam," I replied, smirking.

"Hulk, my man, you better rein in those puns if you want to make friends where you're going, instead of getting the crap beat out of ya," he chuckled.

Pointing to his shirt, I replied, "Nice one to talk."

"Oh, this," he pulled on his black tee decaled with a bunch of large green peas with wide, toothy grins and stick hands making the peace sign, "this, my Black Widow-MacGyver lovechild, is for you."

"Thanks."

I adjusted the shoulder straps of my bag and poked him in one of the peas.

"Until next time," I croaked.

"Until next time."

Dad popped the trunk of the car and we put our bags inside.

Turning to me, his eyes widened as if suddenly realizing my white hair.

"Nice look."

"Thanks," I mumbled.

"I agree," came a voice from the other side of the car.

Chief Irene emerged, arms spread wide.

"It was a pleasure to meet you all," she said bringing each of us in for an embrace. "Take care of yourselves, and each other."

As she pulled me close, her silver hair tickling my chin, a wrinkled hand thrust something into mine.

I looked down in my palm to see a small elongated bison carved into a wooden handle.

"A reminder of those left behind," she said softly. "May it serve you well."

I flipped open the handle and a stainless-steel blade emerged. Closing the pocketknife with trembling fingers, I placed it in the pocket of my jeans and smiled at the Piikani chief.

"I will never forget this place."

"I know," she smiled. "No one does."

Chief Irene moved onto Jake, hugging him and giggling at his flushed cheeks before gently pinching them and whispering something in his ear.

I was walking around the hood of the car when I noticed the Treaty 7 boulders.

Spattered with red paint, and some overturned.

"We'll fix that up, don't you worry," Rev. Erin said, patting my arm. "The only thing that isn't replaceable is our spirit, remember that."

Nodding, I swallowed the rock that had just wedged in my throat.

Todd wrapped his arm around my shoulder as I moved to get into the backseat. "This is a chance to reinvent yourself, Jules—be the you you've been hiding for such a long time."

"What if everyone hates that version of me?"

"Their loss."

Then he reached up and ruffled my spiked hair.

"Best hair a carton of eggs can buy," he snickered.

"You mean *barter*."

He hugged me again and we all piled into the car.

While Dad, Mom and Rev. Erin said another farewell, Jake climbed in beside me.

"You scared, Jules? I'm scared."

"I think you'd be nuts not to be, dude."

Jake nodded and handed me a crate with a puff of black fur inside.

"Maybe Shade will help."

"I'm sure he will. Thanks, bro."

Grinning, he turned to the window just as he began to sniffle.

"We'll be OK, you know that right?" I didn't know whether I was trying to convince him or myself.

"I know."

Then the car was in motion and we were driving down the gravel driveway enroute to the Pincher Creek Station on Highway 3.

Mom and Dad didn't speak.

Neither did me and Jake.

The car was filled with the sound of a contented, purring cat, and somehow, my anxious nerves calmed. We left Holy Creator better than we had arrived, with more clothes in our bags, more food in our bellies, and more friends in our hearts.

To say it was bittersweet was an understatement.

My heart ached.

Would I ever feel so at ease anywhere else?

Would I ever see Todd again?

Would leaving save me or destroy me?

****

290

"Nom? Name?" The soldier repeated angrily. "I do not 'av all day."

"Jules Klassen," I said to the hat bent over the papers atop the pale gray, plastic foldable table.

The name tag above his breast pocket said: "Lafayette."

Lafayette's index finger skimmed down the long list of last names that began with K.

"I have a Julia Klassen of Poplar Hills, Calgary. Is dis you?"

"Yes."

"Please confirm your address."

I recited my home address.

He grunted in response.

"Photo identification, s'il vous plaît."

I handed him my Alberta Driver's License and Lafayette looked at the picture of the girl with long, strawberry blonde hair and disengaged smile, paused, looked up into my face and raised an eyebrow. To be fair, I barely recognized myself, so I could sympathize with the guy. My hair was now bleached platinum blonde and buzzed around my nape and ears. Spiked at the top, the tips dipped in scarlet hair dye, all thanks to Mom's prowess with a pair of scissors and Dad's hair clippers, and Todd's wicked bartering skills.

And now, he was left behind, to battle poachers and protesters, angry mobs and vandalized property.

"Thumbprint," the soldier's voice jolted me from my daydreaming. He was leaning his head to the side and gesturing to the digital pad on the desk. "Se dépêcher," he grumbled. "We do not have all day."

I placed my thumb on the pad and watched a red light underneath my skin scan my print and turn green.

Lafayette looked at the tablet in his hand and the digital ID that appeared on his screen: My Alberta Driver's License.

"Proceed."

I looked around. Proceed *where*?

"Proceed," Lafayette said again, raising his head and arching one black bushy eyebrow.

"Huh? Where?"

Rolling his eyes, he pivoted in his foldable, gray metal chair and pointed to the long line of teenagers under a sign marked Age 15–18, H-M further down the station.

"Your laz name starts with za letter K does it not?"

"Yeah."

"Well, zen, dat is where you line up."

He looked over my shoulder at the person behind me and yelled: "Next!"

Wake up, Jules, and get with the program.

Walking over to the queue, I shifted my backpack so it was better balanced on my shoulders. Mom, Dad and Jake were in the line beside me, talking to another soldier at the table Layfette sat, tapping his pen at my reluctance to move.

Mom and Dad were holding hands in a braced front. Shade's carrier was on the checkerboard linoleum floor beside Mom's feet. His furry black form curled up, sleeping. I wanted to hold him, to feel his whiskers against my face and snuggle into his belly, but he was there and I was here.

Jake was turning red beside them, his round cheeks flushed.

Even though they were a meter away, I could tell Mom was crying.

"He's not old enough," she was saying to the soldier. "He's just a kid."

"He is 15?"

Mom nodded and pleaded, "Just barely. He only turned 15 a month ago."

"Then he needs to join the teenagers in the next line."

Mom began to sob, and Dad held her shaking body. Jake turned to me, his pale blue eyes pleading.

"Come on, doofus," I said, waving to him.

Mom's head lifted from Dad's shoulder and her gaze caught mine.

She smiled.

"Love you," she mouthed. "Be strong. Take care of him."

I nodded as Jake joined me by my side.

"Jules, remember what I told you," Dad shouted. "Never leave him behind."

I nodded, unable to speak for fear of breaking down.

Jake was wiping the snot from his nose with his sleeve as we walked to the teenagers' queue.

"Love you guys," Mom and Dad yelled. "Take care of each other."

"You got this," Dad's low, cracked voice rumbled, "and *he's* got you."

I nodded, too choked up to speak.

My throat had suddenly closed and my eyes were stinging with tears I was refusing to let flow.

Not here, Jules.

Jake didn't have as many qualms.

He was bent over, his shoulders shaking, his whole body wracked in sobs that made him look possessed.

I reached out and held his hand in mine.

It was wet and sticky, and I immediately regretted it.

He lifted his head and tried to smile at me but erupted into more sobs instead.

I squeezed his hand.

"Dude, it's going to be OK. Got me? We're together; Mom and Dad are in the next car down, so not far," I said softly. My voice was shaking and I knew if I didn't shut up, that dam wouldn't hold forever. "We're bros, right?"

Jake nodded and sniffled.

"Then, we got each other's back and I hate to disclose this in public but, dude, I've heard we are actually treated like *adults* where we are going, instead of some dumbass kids."

"Language," Jake hiccupped.

"You're right," I punched him in the shoulder. "Some Corn Flake kids."

We were still snickering when I glanced back at Mom and Dad down the strip of the station floor, where other parents and grandparents were waiting in line, watching their children and grandchildren in the lineups behind the ticket offices, and the barriers separating the queues from the platform on the other side.

Further in front were coral arches leading to steps in front of the train cars.

I say cars.

They were not.

I guess turning a grain train into a passenger one wasn't something that happened overnight, so they had to improvise. Instead of passenger cars, old tour buses sat, tire-less and welded onto metal plates above the train's wheels. Colorful landscapes adorned their sides—images of the Canadian Rockies, with white tops and glaciers; fields of wheat and barley swaying under the orange-magenta glow of a Prairie sunset; whitecap waves crashing into the cliffs of St. Mary's in Newfoundland; the picturesque Cape Breton Highlands along the winding Cabot Trail in Nova Scotia; and the pink sandy beaches with tall wild grasses growing around a cottage titled Green Gables in Prince Edward Island.

When did we stray so far from these images?

I wondered if this was why Terra Nova got such a following—they witnessed the transformation of our once breathtakingly beautiful land into dried up mud fields.

Looking at the landscapes on the tour buses caked in dust and rust, I could see their point.

Further back, the tour buses continued. The one in front of Mom and Dad was decaled in a hockey game being played on an iced over pond. Even from this distance, Dad's eyes were puffy and his unshaven jaw, tight. I wondered if he had slept last night. After our poacher stakeout, Todd, Jake, and I had returned to the rectory, emailed Mr. B the footage and fell, exhausted onto the living room couches. Not wanting to separate, we cuddled on the three-seater, reliving the details of the night. Jake was the first to surrender to the Sandman, followed by Todd. I watched both succumb to sleep, while I was too afraid to let go.

In all, I barely had four hours of shuteye before the alarm clock, aka Dad's Christian Rock Station, woke us up. Today, as he waited in line, he was wearing a red tee with a thick, white cross in the center and 'My Lifeguard Walks on Water' emblazoned in white above and below the cross.

Nice, Dad. Very appropriate.

A guard stepped out and blocked the security barrier in front of their platform. He moved the belt aside, then stepped back to let the parents and grandparents through to the boarding steps.

Mom and Dad looked over at us. Dad gave us two thumbs up, while Mom blew kisses.

And then, they were gone.

Jake shifted his backpack beside me and I helped him pull the straps up so they lodged on his shoulders. He had grown a lot over the summer. The top of curly blond hair rested just below my chin. Looking down, I noticed he was wearing a pair of sapphire blue cowboy boots—a discard from Todd, no doubt.

The line moved and we moved with it.

Jake nearly tripped over his own feet as he stumbled forward.

I guess you won't be the only one with flipper feet in the family, after all.

"Hey, Ju … Jul … Jules," he stuttered, a small smile on his tear-wet lips.

Lightly punching him in the shoulder, I replied: "Hey, shrimp."

He stood facing me, fidgeting with his straps and nearly knocking over the girl in front of us. I pulled his arm to my side to avoid a collision.

"Careful, bro. Watch where your clodhoppers are going."

"My what?"

"Your feet, ya piece of toast."

In front of me, the bushy, brown head of curly and disheveled hair lunged forward, causing a waft of strong, musky flowers to drift from her nape and into my nostrils, causing me to gag.

Crap, girl, easy on the spray.

Yes, this was a load of laughs.

We were all facing a loading platform with a security guard that blocked the steps leading up to the train cars. We were all waiting, shifting our feet; scratching our heads; rejigging our carry-on luggage—all trying to be more comfortable as we just stood there.

Minutes ticked by.

The fluorescent lights above the platform roof flickered and emitted a buzzing sound. The station was one of the few buildings with electricity and after saying as much to Jake, he wordlessly pointed to the large metal piece of equipment near the Exit sign.

"Generator," he whispered.

Beyond the loading platform, crowds stood holding signs: 'Discrimination Kills' and 'Save All or None'.

I wondered if any of them had thrown the rocks that had shattered Holy Creator's stained-glass windows, or those in the rectory where Rev. Erin lived. Hundreds of people stood arm in arm, forming a human chain across the tracks. Then came the Peacekeepers, with wide plexiglass shields to push them aside; and push they did. Several fell to their knees, others lay flat. Yet, still the soldiers pushed, until the track was free of dusty loafers and joggers, slippers and sandals. Parted like the Red Sea, the protesters were divided by the tracks and a contingent of soldiers on either side, keeping them off the metal ties.

A country divided.

The blazing sun shone brightly on the signs, reflected in their glasses and bounced off the swaying fluorescents.

Someone handed me a water bottle and a chocolate-chip granola bar, and I looked down at the plastic-encased liquid and snack and thought how fortunate I was, how blessed, when the people out there had nothing, not even bottled water to ease their thirst.

I knew I should be upset with them for vandalizing the church property, and for poaching the bison and chickens, and stealing grain and supplies, but all I felt at that moment was pity.

I was leaving.

If you ever get on the train.

Blinking away the moisture building behind my own eyelids, I turned and looked at the bushy brown head in front of me. Long hair, curly and disheveled. I could smell perfume wafting from the blue coat the girl wore.

Musky flowers.

Too strong.

I sighed.

Yes, this was a load of laughs.

The ticket office in front of us had two sliding windows. Peeking out from one side was another bobbing head.

I couldn't make out more than dark hair.

There were way too many people in front of me to see if the hair just floated above the opening like some apparition or if it actually was attached to something.

I wondered what was taking so long. The parent cars were all loaded and yet, we stood here, in the heat of the day, watching and being watched. I could feel the sweat trickle down between my shoulder blades and pool at the waist of my jeans. I looked down to see Jake waving a folded granola wrapper as a fan to cool off his flushed face.

"Wha … wha … whAT ti … ti … IME is it, Ju … Ju … JULes?"

"Nearly three."

"Aaaaah, whe … whe … whEN are we le … le … LEaVING?"

"Stop whining, dude, we get there when we get there."

He tilted his red, blotchy face up to look at me and spurted out granola chunks.

"You so … sOUund ju … ju … juST like Mom."

"God help me, then," I replied, rubbing my knuckles over his bushy blond curls. "You need a haircut."

"Now, you really sound like Mom."

"Hey, enough out of you, you whippersnapper."

"That's grandpa!"

"Frig this, I'll shut up now."

He was still giggling when the line shifted and I glanced behind me to see throngs of people filing into the station: Another group of parents and grandparents; another group of teenagers. After they were split up and processed by the awaiting soldiers, the parents and grandparents were walked to the awaiting cars, while the teens remained behind.

I moved so that I could get another glimpse of the cars beyond the archway leading to the platform.

More protesters had arrived, and the soldiers were now on the track.

****

In the station, Peacekeepers went around and pulled down all the blinds to cover the windows. As one shade fell, a rock flew through the glass and the soldier jumped backward and out of the way. She quickly finished the windows and returned to her post by an intake table. The blocked-out windows were making the flickering lights work overtime. We couldn't see the prairie outside, nor the crowds. We were in our own protective bubble that felt like it was going to burst.

"I hope it won't be too long," said a warm breath on my neck. "Or, they'll have to start handing out sticks of deodorant because these people are starting to stink."

I smiled.

I had put on deodorant when we rose this morning at six and upon glancing at my phone, it was nearing 7 p.m. No wonder the station was in the shadows, and no wonder I stank.

I sweat a lot.

Yeah, I knew I stank.

Suck it up, buttercup, you ain't seen nothin' yet!

I straightened my shoulders, arched my back so my backpack hit the guy behind me in the face, raised my arms out in front of me and cracked my knuckles, making sure my pits got aired nice and good.

"Agh!" he groaned.

Yeah, take it in, big guy.

I grinned.

Jake nudged me with his elbow and scowled.

Alright, alright. My bad, bro. I can't be all loosy goosy all the time, now can I?

"You think you're so funny, don't you, beanpole? Where'd they dig you up— Stinksville?"

I turned.

The dude was big.

Wide shoulders.

Muscular.

I smirked and looked down into his eyes.

They were a vibrant sea-green blue with specks of gold.

"No, but I'm figurin' you're from Redneck Central, cause you smell like cow manure. Next time you leave the barn, you may want to scrape off your boots first, or is that your cowpoke mouthwash that's causing that vile stench?"

The line erupted in laughter.

Jake squeezed my hand. He was not impressed.

"Jules," he said between gritted teeth, "not nice."

I ignored him. I reserved my *nice* to non-jerks, and this dude was definitely not in that category.

As expected, my quip response didn't amuse muscle-boy.

He was staring at me and his lips were thinning to a minuscule pink line before my eyes. The squeezing of mouth muscles exposed dimples on either side. Dark blond stubble poked out from his jaw like pins in a cushion.

I stared at the dents, wondering why all the creeps seemed to be blessed with the handsome gene.

If he kept this up, though, his nose was going to stretch down to his chin, I thought.

Now, *THAT* would be attractive.

I snickered at the thought.

Never one to hide how I really felt, I smirked knowing he knew I was snickering at him—making fun of *him*, Mr. Handsome Jerk.

His face was slightly red now.

"Cow caught your tongue?" I asked. "Figures. That's what happens when you're full of bull."

More giggles from the peanut gallery. Amid my bravado, a voice inside my head tried to remind me about choices and control; reactions and grace but I was too tired to listen.

I turned and looked at brown, curly hair again, as her head bobbed up and down in a barely contained laughing fit.

"That was too funny," said a soft husky voice, as she turned her head to look at me, and pinched her nose. "But you do stink."

"Same."

She erupted in giggles and began to snort.

"Think you're funny, do you?"

The warm words tickled the hair on the nape of my neck.

"Don't think. Know. Kinda like I *know* you're an idiot," I said while staring blankly at the floating head of hair by the ticket booth. "Are you sure you're in the right line? H to M stands for the first letters in your last name, you know. They don't mean Hicks and Mouth-breathers."

More laughter.

I was on a roll.

"Jules," Jake whined beside me, but I ignored him.

Without even turning around, I could sense Muscle Boy tensing his shoulders. Hands were probably in fists by now, too, I reckon.

Ah, to piss pissers off.

My life's goal attained yet again.

I snickered.

"If you…" muscle-boy said through clenched teeth.

I whipped around.

"What? A genius compared to your idiot steroid-injected brain? Grow a pair, douchebag, and stop complaining. Everybody in this frigging station is tired, stinking and hungry and your belly-aching isn't helping anyone."

His face contorted in a wrinkled-old-man-prune type of deal where his forehead sloped downward and his square jaw went up, as if to meet it.

Not so handsome, now, are you, Mr. Jerk Face?

"What seems to be the problem here?"

A soldier suddenly appeared beside us.

"Nothing, sir, just a discussion on hygiene, and how most of us lose it when we've traveled hundreds of kilometers in a couple of days without showering and no deodorant," I said.

"Just be grateful you guys are getting out. There are many who aren't as fortunate. So, turn your heads around, face the front of the line and wait your turn, or I'll pull you to the back."

I looked over Muscle Boy's shoulder and saw how in a matter of minutes, the line behind us had more than doubled to what it was in front of me.

"Yes, sir!" I said and spun around.

"Yes, sir," mumbled Muscle Boy.

I smiled.

I yawned and looked at my watch: 4:45 p.m.

Well, that killed some time, at least.

I had already been in this God-forsaken station for nearly six hours!

Hell, at this rate, I could walk to the East Coast.

I shifted my backpack again, knocking it into Muscle Boy—again—and he erupted in a mumble of curse words.

Ah, the simple joys.

Jake and I took turns going to the bathroom and holding our spots in line, then passed the time with games of slap and rock, paper, scissors. It was nearly six when we both found ourselves sitting on our backpacks, while all around us, teens did likewise. The station continued to darken, the crowds outside continued to grow and Muscle Boy behind me continued to breath gusts of hot, exasperated air onto the back of my neck.

At 8:55 p.m., the barrier belt beside the ticket counter was removed and two armed soldiers appeared, each holding a rifle with the barrel pointed down to the concrete floor.

Above the heads of the people in front of me, I could make out a bright light in the black night, and another set of doors. Jake and I stood up, grabbed our bags and swung them around our backs. As per usual, my brother's straps were dangling around his elbows, so I lifted his pack high and set it on his shoulders where it belonged.

It was then that I realized my little bro wasn't so little anymore.

In the weeks we had spent at Holy Creator, the dude had grown probably two inches, and not all were in his feet. Todd had been right about him being in puberty, then.

Todd had been right about a lot of things.

As the line began to shift forward, I glanced down to Jake's blond blob and ruffled his wavy curls. He looked up at me and stuck out his tongue.

I blew a raspberry back.

My false sense of confidence and calm seemed to put him at ease because he hip-checked me, causing my backpack to hit Muscle Boy, again.

"Whatchit, dorks."

"You watch it, Mr. Double Dork Crunch," I said over my shoulder.

Jake giggled and gave me a thumbs up.

Ahead of us, the line moved, and I was suddenly staring at the officers. I took a deep breath and stepped across the threshold and toward the waiting lights.

Walking through the archway to the platform, Jake let go of my hand and moved a few inches away from me.

I let him climb the stairs ahead, then followed up the four steps to the tour bus door.

Turning to look at the crowd behind me, I knew my life would never be the same.

Gone forever were my friends, my school, my home.

And Todd.

I rubbed the back of my neck with my free hand, feeling the peach-fuzz stubble around the nape. By the time we got to where we were going, it will have grown out, I thought, and then all traces of my former life would be gone, too.

"How's she goin' dere?" said a jolly voice in front of me.

"Just peachy," I said and smiled.

"Oh, now, h'aren't you h'a tall drink of water! Who in da blazzes knit you?"

"Mom and Dad, of course, but Dad's a tall Albertan and Mom's a short Newf, so I guess I'd have to think about it."

He chuckled, his chest heaving in hearty laughter.

"G'wan wit ya, ya goof. But what h'odds, eh? Yer 'ere, now. Gotta h'a warn ya though, they'll tink yer from da h'Amazon, where yer goin'."

My grin widened.

In front of me stood a whip of a man, a little taller than Mom, with red cheeks dotted with freckles and the most orange beard I had ever seen. Atop his head was a black, tilted peak cap. He wore a white shirt and black tie under a black single-breasted coat.

He looked like a wax figure in some kid's train set.

His accent lightened the mood in the line and I couldn't help but smile into his gleaming face.

Thank God for Newfies.

If there was any group of people who was going to put these western refugees' fears to rest, it was this light-hearted, funny and charismatic bunch.

"Now, dat's da spirit! Not-ting is h'as bad h'as it seems. Once you gets back 'ome, you'll be h'as right h'as rain, me ducky."

I nodded and looked inside the car.

"G'wan, now. Find h'a seat, h'any seat, h'and take a load off, why don't ya. You fellers must be beat to h'a snot. Der's h'a bite to h'eat h'on yer seats, courtesy h'of da boss h'at TransCanada Railway, cause we h'all knows yer just h'about gutfoundered."

I entered the door and saw my reflection in the nearest compartment window.

Large sapphire blue eyes stared back at me.

The silver ring pierced into my right eyebrow glinted in the glass.

I should remove it before I get, "back home," I thought, but that'll be something to do on the trip. For now, I just wanted to stay *me* for as long as possible.

The scarlet red spikes on the top of my head grazed the doorframe as I inched forward into the tour bus, looking for a place to sit. Further back, I could barely make out Jake's head as he sat near a boy about his age.

Good. I don't have to worry about him for a while.

I spied a seat that only had one occupant and rushed toward it, knocking a few heads with my backpack along the way.

"Ouch!"

"Sorry! Excuse me ... excuse me ..."

I flopped down and realized I was sitting next to Brown and Curly.

"Hi."

She smiled, extending a hand clasping a brown paper bag.

I took it and looked inside: A bottle of water, an apple, a baggie of celery sticks and a dry veggie dog. Better than a kick in the pants, I guess. At least I had dried bison jerky and sausage in my pack. I'll save that for later, like when I have to go to the bathroom. Given the contents of my "small bite to eat," I'd say it wouldn't be that long.

Brown and Curley's lips curled at my disgusted expression, and I could see she was genuinely happy to see me, so I smiled back.

I guess if you got to be cooped up on a train traveling across the country, it'll be good to have an audience who appreciates your wit.

"Name's Jules."

I bit into the apple. At least it was crisp.

"I'm Chelsea Hughes. Those," she pointed at the fruit, "are from us."

"Huh," I said, chewing and spitting apple juice.

"My grandparents have an apple orchard in Nova Scotia's Annapolis Valley. They donated the apples."

"Awesome. You should thank them for giving the best part of this *supper*."

"I will," she grinned, her pink lips spread wide.

"So, Chelsea, eh? Mind if I call you, Chels?" At the side-to-side head shake, I continued, "Nice to meet you."

She leaned forward and whispered: "I sure am glad you saw the seat. I would hate to have that rude A-hole behind you sit with me!"

"You and me both!"

"Besides," she said. "You're funny!"

I am now.

Not sure if that would keep up once we get on the road and my legs started cramping after being tucked up to my chest for days.

"Yeah, but I stink, you know."

"Oh, I know!"

We both laughed.

"You ain't kiddin'!" I replied.

Chels, who will always be known as Brown and Curly in my head, reached into the backpack on her lap and pulled out a stick of Secret and tossed it into my lap.

"That should help!"

I snorted.

Then, lifting up the edge of my shirt, lathered the white stick on my pits.

"I donno, Chels, I think I'll need something stronger," I said and pinched my nose with one hand and waved the deodorant-holding hand with the other. "Pe-e-ew!"

Baby powder scent mingled with my BO and I waved the odors away from my pits.

Brown and Curly laughed and punched me in the shoulder.

"Give me that back so I can disinfect it, you shithead!"

"Oh, that's how it's going to be, is it? Shithead? Well, I may stink but I didn't shiit…ake myself, at least, not like some people," I said, nodding my head toward the jerk sitting across the aisle.

Brown and Curly snickered.

"Shiitake?"

I laughed.

"Yeah, my way of cursing without really cursing."

Brown and Curly giggled.

"I like it! What are some others?"

"Oh, I'm sure you will hear plenty of them on this train," I said dryly, yawning.

"Are they all about food or is food just always on your mind?"

"Well… now that you mention it, food names do make a large part of my PG curse repertoire."

I smiled at her flushed face, thinking how pretty she was when she laughed.

"My folks are from Green Island Cove, which is…" Chels got out before I interrupted her.

"I know where it is—the Great Northern Peninsula! Mom has family in Green Island Brook—the Noseworthys. Know any?"

"Tons!" She smiled.

Chelsea was probably five-foot-three, which meant her head barely brushed my shoulder. She looked about fifteen or sixteen. She had a long face that was, right now, rosy red. Her periwinkle eyes twinkled when she laughed and the dimple in her chin spread wide enough I wanted to touch it with my forefinger and smoosh it in the indent. For someone who had spent hours on the road to get here, she looked fresh: her makeup glowed on her cheekbones and her black-rimmed eyes made the pale blue irises pop, and I was drawn into their forget-me-not pools. Even with the newly applied makeup, she looked young, as if she was a tween trying to be a teen. For many of us, makeup was a layer that separated the *we* that was hidden, and scared, from the *we* that was exposed to the world. And in times like these, I didn't blame her one bit for getting all dolled up to go on a train to the end of the earth.

After all, weren't we all putting on a facade to get through this ordeal? Weren't we all wearing masks to shield us from the cruel nature of others? While I used humor to protect myself from hurt, Chels, like so many other teen girls I knew, hid behind foundation and blush; lipstick and eyeshadow. I wasn't fooled, however. There was no mistaking the little-girl-lost presence she eluded. She had this innocence that reminded me of Jake, in a way, and the expression she wore looking at me was almost identical to the one he had given me in the queue in the station.

Excited.

Scared.

Overwhelmed.

Like the rest of us.

I squeezed her hand.

It was trembling, and cold.

"Everything's going to be OK, Chels," I said, and she looked out the window to the darkening night now awash in the blazing reds and golds of the setting sun. Despite the beauty brushed across the deep blue sky, she saw only her reflection.

"I hope so," her soft husky voice breathed on the glass. She lifted her hand and began drawing a smiley face in the mist, then wiped it away with her palm. "I just wish I wasn't all alone."

Yeah, me too.

I looked away from her sad face and into the aisle still filling up with bodies searching for a seat.

Being *chosen* blowed.

****

We were moving away from the Pincher Creek Station when the tour bus we were sitting in began to rock. I looked out the window, trying to focus on the floodlights erected around the platform's loading area when the building went up in flames. Orange and red fingers flicked up the sides; black smoke and debris billowed from the archways leading to the platform. As my face pressed against the cold glass, I saw people swarming around the sides of the station, throwing flaming bottles into the broken windows, their signs left dead in the tall grass that grew around the building. Shots were fired into the sky, their sparks flying like pitiful fireworks from elongated tubes. From behind grain silos came a forklift, with its tongs lifted high and bright headlights shining onto the train's caboose.

Everyone was on their feet, rushing toward the windows, trying to see what was going on.

Shadows with flashlights, running; burning.

Flaming bottles connected with the side of our bus, crashing into the image of a howling Arctic wolf along the side, causing the passengers to scurry away from one side and cram into the aisle.

The forklift was joined by a backhoe and digger. As they emerged from the grain elevator's green sliding doors, their tongs lowered to the tracks.

The same vehicles that had disappeared overnight from the station.

Now, they were digging into the ground below the tracks in front of the engine, trying to pry up the iron road and our escape.

"What is going on?" Chels was asking, her corkscrew curls flying into my face.

"Looks to me like a riot," I turned my head to see Jake standing in the back, eyes wide.

"H'everyone calm da frig down," the man in the black TCR uniform shouted into the crowd. "Stay h'away from da windows. We're h'all gonna be just fine, mark my words. No need to get yer knickers in a knot. We'll be h'away from da station, lickety-split, so sit yer butts down h'and take a deep bredth."

He walked up and down the aisle, red face getting redder, scratching his beard, mumbling: "Jesus, Mary, Mother of Joseph."

I hurriedly rose from my seat and took long strides to get to Jake.

"C'mon," I said, pulling him up and interrupting a conversation he was trying to have with a curly-haired boy with rectangular glasses.

"Wha … wha … whAT'S going on?"

"Shut up and follow me," I said, then looking down into his hurt face, I added, "sorry, bro, old habits, ya know."

Going up the aisle, I opened the back exit door near the bathrooms.

Behind me, Chelsea was kneeling on her seat, watching our departure with her curly brown hair frazzled and her pink lips mouthing, "Where are you going?"

Ignoring her, I dragged Jake through the emergency door and hopped down the track.

Outside, the now dark night was flooded with lights.

Flickering fluorescent lights above the station platform, mobile flood lights that were rolled to the tracks, and the blinding beams of construction equipment trying desperately to pull up the train tracks.

"Jake, do you know how to hack into an operating system? Tell me you know how to hack into an operating system," I was breathing heavily as we ran to the platform, which was teaming with people throwing Molotov cocktails through the archways and windows. Red, orange and blue flames rose from their impact. Inside the station, soldiers shouted as they scurried to douse the fires and get to safety.

Jake and I watched in horror as they banged on the barricaded doors leading into the building. Protesters had wedged their placards into the handles. Green camouflage uniforms scaled over broken glass windows to escape.

"We … we … we hav … hav … have to … to … to … HELP," Jake huffed as we weaved in and out of the crowd, shoving our way through; being shoved almost off the platform in the process.

"We have to stop the equipment, Jakey."

I looked down into his face.

"YOU have to stop the equipment."

"How?"

I pulled him over to the side of the grain elevator, our backs against the fading pale blue boards peeling from years of dust storms pelting its exterior.

"See that … that's the company logo; hack into the operating system and turn off the vehicles."

"Are you insane?" Jake's stammer had disappeared in his incredulous anger. "That would take hours, not minutes."

My heart sank.

As we stood there against the elevator, breathing in the shouldering station, the gasoline flames and watching a crazed mob try and stop the Exodus Train's departure, my mind went into convulsions.

What can we do?

What can we do?

Think.

Think.

Think.

"Jules …"

"Yes," I said, looking down at my scared little brother's hand in mine.

"You … you … ca … ca … cAN … do … DO … this."

"Do what?"

"Outsmart them."

Jake looked at me, his blue eyes piercing through my brain, trying to drill into a knowledge base I didn't know existed. He was delusional.

Wasn't he?

The shouts continued.

I looked up to see faces pressed against the dirt-stained windows of tour buses.

Chelsea was there, hands on either side of her face, shouting for us to come back.

And do what?

We needed to get out of here.

The backhoe's engine revved and the bucket screeched as the metal lifted and then slowly slammed down on the iron. Beside it, the forklift prongs slid under the ties, but it butted up against a rock under the tracks and it backed up to find a better spot, and that's when I remembered the fuel lines.

"Stay here," I told Jake. "No matter what, wait for me here."

He nodded. "Go."

I pulled up my hood, covering my platinum spikes, and scurried along the back of the grain elevator and approached the equipment. Digging into the pocket of my jeans, I found the pocketknife Chief Irene had given me this morning. The wooden handle with the carved bison flipped open and a sharp blade emerged.

As I approached the rear of the backhoe, the driver got out of the cab, stood on the step and began yelling at the gathering crowd.

Turning, Joey Hurlburt lifted his arm over his head and pumped his fist. A neon-green glow illuminated from the back of the baseball cap on his head.

"Stop the train; stop the train," he shouted to the crowd, and the mob repeated his chant.

In response, the human chain closed ranks in front of the excavator, as the equipment operators continued to try to dislodge the ties from the track.

"What a shiitake head," I seethed while climbing up the rusting bright yellow backend.

The realization that it was the farmer, not the sanctuary-seekers at Holy Creator, who was poaching and stealing food supplies made my blood boil.

I could feel the rage growing inside me.

His father was shot and may never walk again, Jules, and his food stores and livestock were confiscated to feed the evacuees.

As Joey Hurlburt pontificated to the mob while standing on the ladder attached to the cab, I swung around the side to the access panel. My hand shook as I wedged my knife into the lock and turned. Amid the farmer's incitement of the angry mob, I continued my own assault on the panel until it finally swung open.

My hand shook as I grabbed a tube, folded it in half and cut the center. Liquid dripped out and the excavator engine sputtered and went dead. I quickly grabbed a handful of electrical wires and did the same.

I was scurrying down the side when a large hand grabbed me from behind and threw me backwards into the dirt. The wind knocked out of me, I stared up into a face in shadow.

"Get under there," an angry voice yelled, and I stopped to siphon smoky air into my lungs as it dawned on me who this stranger was.

Todd grabbed me by the hood and dragged me under the excavator just as Hurlburt rounded the bucket and the exposed panel, cursing.

"What in blue blazes…?" he growled.

While he lifted up the cut fuel line and electrical wires, Todd and I shimmered under the equipment and emerged scraped and dirty on the other side.

The raging farmer continued his rant, throwing his ball cap to the ground in frustration and raking his hair with his hand. Behind him, Todd and I made our way to the forklift that was digging deep into the dry earth under the tracks.

"I'll distract him," Todd hissed as he moved to the front of the prongs and began waving his hands in the air. His Give Peas a Chance was now caked in dust and dirt; his once beautiful purple skirt was ripped down the side and pink thread dangled by his exposed skin. Beyond the threadbare curtain of dyed suede, blood dripped from scrapes received from our tummy crawl under the excavator moments before.

I stared in wonder as my friend stared down the operator.

"Stop!"

The operator poked his head out of the cab and yelled, "Get out of the way, nutjob."

"Stop or I'll shoot!" Todd yelled back.

The operator laughed.

And then he was pelted with small rubber balls from the sky.

As I jammed my knife into the forklift's access panel, Attella's bulging eyes glared down from newly replaced bulbs, and a rain of rubber bullets crashed through the windshield and fired into the operator's chest.

Crying out in agony, the man sought shelter in the cab as many of the protesters in the human chain dispersed, running for cover near the grain elevator.

I cut the lines and wires, and turned to the pale green building, searching for Jake's hidden form.

A blond head poked out from behind the corner just as the mob reached the elevator's exterior staircase.

I ran.

I ran as if the devil himself was at my heels.

I joined the mob and then passed them, pushing and thrashing my way past their scurrying legs and arms to get to my brother.

As I rounded the corner of the building, soft hands grasped mine and we leaped onto the smoldering platform. The Peacekeepers had escaped and were busy fighting off the agitators with clubs and rifles.

It wasn't until the emergency exit door swung open from our tour-bus car that I looked down into Jake's other hand and saw the remote control.

Hands pulled us up into the bus just as the train's engine roared to life and began to move. The squeal of brakes disengaging was like nails on a chalkboard to our ears and we groaned at the high-pitched sound.

"What the hell, Jake? Where'd you get *that?*"

"Todd," he huffed while bent at the waist, trying to catch his breath. "He threw it to me when he ran after you."

"Crap, dude, you saved my life."

I rubbed my knuckles in his blond curls, sending dust particles into the air.

"What the frig, butthead?" Muscle Boy was saying.

"Shut up, mouth breather, they got us free didn't they?" Chelsea's husky voice piped up as she pulled my arm through the aisle now filled with bobbing heads above backrests, all staring at Jake and me with wide eyes and open mouths. "You should be thanking them."

"For what? Being batshit crazy?"

"If it wasn't for their batshit crazy actions, we wouldn't be moving, now would we," Chelsea fired back and fell into her seat as if it was she who had run out to a raging mob and stopped them from destroying our one means to freedom.

I plopped down beside her for all of five seconds of relaxation until it hit me: Todd was still out there.

I glanced up and Jake was already there, face plastered to the window overlooking the commotion outside.

"I ... I ... don't ... don't see ... see ... him ... Jules. I don't see him."

Fear gripped me and my heart sank to my stomach, making me nauseous.

****

"Show's h'over. Get back ta ya seats," the TCR employee said as he strode up the aisle, his arms pumping as his black legs quickly went from the front to the back of the bus. "Flingin', flangin'—sit yer butts down, h'I said."

The teens moved away from the windows and the station now in full blaze, and sat in the bucket seats. The train worker stopped at the bathroom across from the emergency exit, checked to see that the exit doors were tightly shut, then opened the silver ringed latch on the bathroom door.

Pulling out his flashlight from his belt loop, he shone it inside the small commode. Stepping inside, we heard a commotion and then the train lurched forward and we sped away from the station as the engine picked up speed. As the cars curled around the track, heading east around a bend, we got a glimpse of the burning building, and bright burning lights shining on darkened faces covered in soot and dirt. As their figures shrunk into the night, I relaxed into my seat.

It had been a long day.

And it wasn't yet over.

"Do you think there'll be other trains after this?"

I looked down into my lap to find Chelsea's hand squeezing mine.

It felt warm, and nice.

"I don't know. We may be it."

From behind us, the TCR guard scurried out of the bathroom, holding the scruff of a black-haired boy and pushing him up the aisle.

"Bloody stowaway, dat's what we got 'ere," he said gruffly. "Mark my words, buddy-roe, you won't be h'on 'ere for long, dats for sure."

As they drew closer, a pair of dirt-spattered red cowboy boots swung out in front of the black slacks of the rail worker.

My heart raced.

I looked up into a pair of familiar black eyes.

"Todd," I shouted. "What are you doing here?"

"Dat's what I'd like to know, h'ain't dat da trut?" the worker said, shoving Todd forward. "This bruit snuck h'on board tinking nar h'one would be da wiser, da vagabond."

"Jules," Todd began sheepishly.

"Not h'another word h'out of you," the man said, shaking Todd's dirty green T-shirt collar. "Yer comin' up wit me until we gets dis ting sorted, h'and h'I don't want h'any lip, got dat?"

Todd turned his head around as he shuffled toward the front of the bus and gave me a wide, white-tooth smile, then lifted the corners of his purple skirt and curtseyed.

"You know that guy?"

"Yeah, I do. He's a great friend; a lifesaver, really."

"Must be nice to have a friend on board."

I nodded: "If he can stay. By the looks of things, I wouldn't be so sure."

"Love his skirt, though, even if it has seen better days."

I turned to Chels and chuckled: "Yeah, Todd's got style in spades. Not many can wear a purple suede sarong with pink roses stitched into the hem."

Chels smiled: "I wish I had his confidence."

"Chels, my girl, no one on this planet has Todd's confidence. Trust me."

I leaned back against the faded gray and burgundy swirl fabric of my seat, and let the longest, deepest breath out of my body. The tension I had been holding in my shoulders and neck escaped with the air and I suddenly felt—exhausted.

I turned my head to check on Jake, who was in a very animated conversation with the boy sitting next to him. His long arms moved wildly as he spoke, no doubt telling the tale of Jules vs. The Machines.

Good on ya, dude.

Still smiling, I turned my head and faced the front and wondered how to rescue Todd from certain disembarkment.

That plan was for another day.

Right now, I was too exhausted to think; too sore and scraped up to move. My ripped jeans now had large holes at the knee and thigh, with scraped, raw, dirt-caked skin exposed.

I was spent, as if every cell in my body had decided to give up the fight and power down, and it felt liberating. As sleep overcame me, I realized for the first time since the idea of lotteries and resettlement camps hit the news that once at our destination, we would be on our own. Mom, Dad and my black cat, Shade, would be bussed to Nan and Pop's and Jake and I would be shuttled to the camp to do God knows what—be *pioneers*. The thought of turning back time and learning how to live off the land for the sake of saving the human race and planet did nothing but scare the shiitake mushrooms out of me. I mean, *really?* All that responsibility on the heads of a bunch of *kids* who, when I looked around, were scared out of their wits.

Could we do it?

I glanced in Jake's direction.

Could *he* do it?

Could I?

My brain couldn't handle the stress of being *on* all the time, so it shut down.

I let the darkness take me.

The rumbling bus.

The whistling wind.

The softly snoring teenagers.

And me.

Chapter 19

As the locomotive sped across the tracks heading east, Eric Solberg nervously turned to the sleeping heads leaning against the thread-bare fabric headrests. He saw teens his age, even younger, without a bed, without a home, and he was one of them. He saw terrifying dreams race across their faces, causing creases on soft, youthful skin, and knew they had escaped horrors that his family had caused. So, the question remained: Could he do it? Could he be one of them, act normal, blend in, when inside, he was a plotting, spying nervous wreck?

No, the bigger question was, did he have a choice?

His father's plan; his father's orders—that's what it came down to.

The White Sands explosion had taken far more from him than his mother and his uncle. It had ripped him of any hope that what they were doing was the right thing. Deep down, he knew Terra Nova had taken their environmental message too far. World destruction to prove a point? How could anyone get behind that? All he wanted—all he ever wanted—was to belong. Despite TN's skewed views of righting the wrongs in the war against climate change, Eric knew he could count on them.

They were his people.

His family.

Wiping the dust and dew from the bus window, he glanced out into the dark night. Black evergreens flanked the track as they moved.

The world didn't look so bad, here.

It looked peaceful.

The full moon shone white-yellow light down upon the grass and metal rails, the puffs of indigo clouds moved across the orb as time crawled in rhythmic harmony with the locomotive.

Right or wrong, he was here and his job was clear.

His only escape from that destiny was this train, and knowing it settled his thumping heart and pounding pulse. Knowing it, let the dark night seep into his brain and relax the firing neurons so he could sleep.

He was drifting off when he heard his phone buzz.

It was Dad.

Chapter 20

Exodus I screeched to a halt in a small outport town outside of Argentia, Newfoundland on a cold, foggy July morning, five days after departing from Pincher Creek Station. The locomotive had made record time transporting its passengers from one end of the country to the other—a feat accomplished by round-the-clock crews and fueling stations at every rest-stop. By the time the last of the first contingent of 1,773 passengers aboard began to trickle down the steps and onto the awaiting platform, some 5,000 kilometers had been logged in leg cramps, rumbling stomachs and recycled deodorant sticks.

Since leaving Southern Alberta, it had been rattling across the country, stopping at cities along the way and picking up more people bound for the East Coast.

By Day 2, I was striding up and down the aisle, stretching, lunging, planking.

"I think they are long enough," Chels had joked, pointing at my stride. "You stretch them anymore and you could walk faster than the train will take us to Newfoundland."

By Day 3, others joined me, including Muscle Boy, whose name I learned was Allister MacKenzie, and on Day 4, I recognized a familiar blond bob behind Chels, as she stretched her thirty-one-inch legs behind my thirty-eight-inch tree trunks. Jake and Matt giggled as they tried to keep their balance while kicking their limbs forward. Behind them, a similarly giggly redheaded girl followed in their wake. By the time Exodus had its first disembarkment on Day 5 in Halifax, the car and everyone in it was rank, riled, and removed. The lack of showers, activity and sleep had forced many to suction their stinking bodies to the sides of the cars in the hopes no one would notice.

Everyone did, because everyone was in the same boat.

In Halifax, however, there was hope. As the first stop east, when the train pulled into the station and families and teens began to stumble their way onto the awaiting platform, the protesters we had come to expect were fewer in number and, while they tried to block entrance into the city, their anger wasn't directed at the several hundred families awaiting their loved ones' arrivals, or the police. The Exodus passengers emerged from the tour-bus cars, disheveled and red-eyed, only to hop onto awaiting buses traveling to New Brunswick, Prince Edward Island, and Nova Scotia resettlement camps.

As I watched the reuniting of distant relatives to their East Coast families, Chels gathered up her cosmetic bag that was tucked into the back pouch of the seat in front of her, I prepared to say goodbye to the girl who had quickly become more than a friend to me.

She was crying.

As was I.

Her brown and curly hair seemed to have gained a life of its own in the humidity, springing up over her face and neck as if she had been electrocuted. Smiling through my tears, I hugged her close before she joined the others lining up to get off the train.

"Text me, 'kay?"

"Only if you remember to charge your phone," she had snickered, and then hiccupped when her laughter turned to sobs.

"No promises."

And then she was gone.

Exodus had stopped long enough for baskets of ripe, juicy apples to be brought into the cars by locals, along with buttered raisin tea biscuits, bottled water, and mason jars of pickled carrots, beets and pressure-cooked chunks of moose meat. I was sinking my teeth into a Honeycrisp when I noticed coils of brown, curly hair slowly making their way back onto the train.

"Forgot something?"

"No," she sniffed and sat down beside me, wiping her eyes and leaving a trail of black mascara down her cheeks. "They didn't show."

"Oh, no, Chels."

I rose, looked out the window and down the now nearly empty platform.

"Are you sure. There were a lot of people out there. Maybe you missed them."

"They didn't show," Chels repeated again and blew her nose into a tissue she pulled from her raincoat pocket. "They didn't check in, Jules. I'm worried."

"Don't be," I said, sitting back down beside her and taking her hand in mine. "I'm sure it was something simple, like traffic or … a mix-up in the date or something."

Shaking her head in denial, Chels pulled up her hood and turned to the window. "They told me to join you guys at the Newfoundland base, since I have family connections there, too."

To say I was relieved was an understatement.

As she pushed her bag under the seat in front of us, I couldn't help but notice her trembling hands and flushed pale cheeks.

I leaned over and squeezed her hand, which was ice cold.

"I'm sure they are just fine, Chels."

"I hope so."

Her nearly hoarse voice was barely above a whisper.

Holding her hand, I could feel her quickened pulse.

"I'll look out for you in Newfoundland."

"I know."

I was munching on a pickled carrot, when the engine roared to life. Beside me, Chels avoided her care package of scrumptious delights and stared out the window watching the station flow behind us like a backward river. The sun dipped down over the horizon and was swallowed by the blue-green waves. All around us, vibrant coral, indigo, burnt sienna and canary yellow spread from the sinking orb like paint brush strokes. The ice caps crashed against the cliffs, dissolving into foam on impact. Flocks of seagulls soared, silhouetted in the setting sunlight. Salty sea air oozed into the bus-railcar known as Compartment C, and I inhaled the crisp, sea breeze, which was so much better than the rank stench coming off the teenagers around me.

Me, included.

Over the past few days, the only time we got off this metal behemoth was to empty the chemical toilets on board, and eat at community halls. During that time, I got to see Mom and Dad, steal furry cuddles with Shade, and tease my fifteen-year-old brother, Jake. Todd was still being held somewhere in a car closer to the front and despite my repeated conversations with the Newfoundland rail worker I discovered was Harold Davis, I was no closer to determining how I could stage a prison escape than I was when he was discovered on board.

"Da big wigs got plans fa da bugger so h'it's h'out ov me 'ands."

Harold tilted his head down and winked under his uniform black hat.

What plans?

Thoughts of torture and solitary confinement flitted in and out of my brain until Jake calmed me down with a simple sentence: "Jules, Todd could talk his way out of a paper bag, so give him a bit of credit."

My stammer-less little brother was right, of course.

If anyone could sweet talk an escape, it was Todd.

The rest of the trip was spent listening to East Coast music blasted through the bus's speaker system, playing cards and chatting with our seatmates.

It became quite obvious that the mob mentality we had left behind in Alberta had grown with each passing day on the tracks. In Ontario, people fought through blockades to get onto the train, with many being left behind when the engineer decided it was too dangerous to wait for them to board. Once we arrived in Quebec, we didn't even attempt to slow down, as the locomotive sped by the still smoking embers of deserted stations.

It wasn't until we entered Nova Scotia that things looked a little better. Here, people were getting off rather than getting on. While there was still a small demonstration beyond yellow police tape, they were outnumbered by the family members lining up to welcome their expat-relatives home.

By the time we got to North Sydney, the protesters were replaced with desperate people trying to access the Joey Smallwood Channel Tunnel to Newfoundland. They were met with armed guards and concrete barricades that spanned across the roadway portion of the 500-kilometre transatlantic underground tunnel. The adjacent railway channel tunnel was likewise guarded, and as soldiers signaled the train's advance, the locomotive entered the cavernous space and was immediately consumed by darkness.

Swaying overhead lights made the reflecting lines along the channel walls glow like neon snakes.

While I worried over Todd, at least I had Chels to talk to during the long train ride.

I discovered she was an only child, raised by her godparents in Edmonton after her parents died when she was just a toddler. She liked music, played video games, and visited her grandparents in the summer and fall to help with their apple orchard. I also learned that she was a bit of an introvert, sweet and funny.

Brown and Curly snorted when she laughed, tried to hide her tears by staring out the bus window, and was lonely and scared.

Who wouldn't be, making this trip alone?

My aching muscles were noticeably relieved when on July 9, Exodus 1 stopped at its final destination in Argentia. Once an industrial park and commercial seaport, the outport on the southwest coast of the Avalon Peninsula had an unusual triangular shape that reached northward into Placentia Bay. Emerging from the channel tunnel as if being birthed, Exodus chugged its way around the fishing settlement and screeched to a halt at the Petit Plaisance Station.

As railway worker Harold Davis instructed us to stay seated until the disembarkment announcement, I chanced a glance out the dirty, grime-smeared windows onto the quaint little town with its French and Latin influences prominently displayed in street and business names. Even through the fog, I could make out the colorfully painted houses and the clothes lines stretching from house to shed, with bed sheets and clothes eagerly waiting for the sun.

Rising from our seats, we coaxed our limbs to function and began to move. As I joined the older teens, Jake followed in the rear with the younger ones. He turned his head and scanned my line, finding my face, and smiled. At the sight of me, however, his lips began to quiver. Not wanting the water works to start while he was around his new friends, I pushed my index finger onto the tip of my nose and pushed up, oinking like a pig all the while.

Jake snorted and made his own pig face.

For the next five minutes, we had a weird-face-making contest that drew as many stares as it did giggles, but after it all—and as we inched forward in the line—we were both laughing.

And then he was gone.

There were just three people ahead of me and I closed my eyes tight to block out the emotions playing havoc on the faces—it was one thing to people watch to pass the time but when all the people you were watching were a hair's breadth from collapsing in exhaustion or a fit of tears, you had to block that shit out or it will crumble you to pieces.

"Jules!"

"Jules!"

I turned around to see Mom running toward me, with Dad coming up the rear, swinging a crate with a yowling ball of black fur.

"Have you seen Jake?"

She was out of breath and flushed.

"Yes, Mom, he just boarded that tour bus over there," I said, pointing to my brother's bus. "He's fine. In fact, he's better than fine."

Mom looked doubtful.

"I'm serious! He was laughing with some of his new friends, so don't worry."

"How can I not worry?" she sighed.

I brought her into my chest and gave her a hug. I could feel her tremble and straighten; tremble and straighten. She was trying too hard to stay in control. Her face smashed into my chest and I patted her back.

"We're going to be fine," I said into her ear, while she sobbed. "I'll keep an eye on Jake and you keep an eye on Dad, OK?"

As I finished speaking, Dad came to join in on the hug.

"And who will I keep an eye on?"

"Shade, of course."

I pointed to the swinging cat carrier, "Don't give him whiplash."

Dad looked at me with a cheesy grin.

"No promises."

Shade meowed in response, causing us to laugh.

I leaned down to his crate door and snuggled his nose with mine.

"Don't forget me."

With tears in my eyes, I rose with quivering lips and faced my red-eyed parents.

"We'll keep an eye on each other, Jules," Dad said, nodding. "We'll be with Nan and Pop, so we'll be just dandy. I have every confidence in you and Jake, and what you two can accomplish if you put your minds to it, so just do what you gotta do and we'll be your strongest cheerleaders and prayer warriors."

I smiled at Dad over the top of Mom's head.

"But why do they have to separate *families?*" Mom was on the verge of hysteria.

"Because, hon, they don't want the kids distracted by us overbearing parents while they are learning how to survive this mess."

Dad's arm wrapped around Mom's shoulders and squeezed, releasing Mom's tears.

"I have to say goodbye to Jakey," Mom sobbed. "I have to tell him I love him."

"He knows, Shel, hon."

"But I have to *tell* him."

Mom took one step toward Jake's bus, then pivoted and faced me.

Pulling me close again, she whispered, "I love you so much, Jules, sweetie—more than you'll ever know. I know you will be fine because God brought you, all of us, here for a reason and he won't abandon us, ever."

"Ditto," Dad said, giving me another hug. "Be strong and courageous. Do not be afraid or terrified because of them, for the Lord your God goes with you; he will never leave you, nor forsake you."

He let go and nodded, then they turned and sprinted to the bus in which Jake's face was pressed against one of the windows, crying.

"Don't fuss, me duckies," I yelled in my best Newfie accent, while tapping on the silver cross dangling on my chest, "I've got a lucky charm."

It was only after I said it that I realized I sounded more like the leprechaun from the Lucky Charms' cereal commercials.

"I got me some Newfie spite in me, and so does da wee laddie, so we'll be just dandy!"

Mom's head turned as she pulled herself up onto the bus stairs, and grinned.

"You sound *nothing* like a Newf, you know that, right?" she hollered back. "In fact, I think you've created a whole new accent. I'd keep that under my hat, if I were you, or you'll get the snot beat out of ya!"

"Shel, hon, isn't that basically the Newfoundland accent: A combination of Irish and Scottish?" Dad said, joining her on the stairs.

"Shut yer trap, you," Mom said, poking Dad in the chest. "Don't go gobbing about stuff you don't know nar-ting about."

"Oh, here we go …" Dad grabbed Mom's finger and kissed the tip. "One sniff of seaweed and she's back to Rock Talk."

"You best believe it, buddy-roe!"

As they entered the bus, I saluted an invisible cap on my head and turned my back on their faces, sucking in a mouthful of air to force the whimpers back down into my throat.

"Gawd love 'em," a girl in front of me said.

You love them, too.
More than they'll ever know.

Chels sought out my hand and intertwined her fingers into mine.

Her warmth calmed my nerves.

Was *I really* strong enough?

I didn't have the foggiest idea.

Maybe deep down, I was soft like Jake, and maybe deep down, Jake was stronger than I ever hoped to be.

I closed my eyes and willed myself the power to push down the butterflies fluttering deep inside my chest.

I would be OK.

He would be OK.

We had to be.

Climbing aboard, I found a blue and wine zig-zagged fabric seat with a tall head rest and sat down in a frump. Chels collapsed beside me. While the other teens found their seats, I stared out yet another dirty, steamy window and this time, into the face of my distraught parents coming down the steps of Jake's bus. They thought I wasn't looking. They thought I didn't see them sobbing in an embrace. They were wrong. I saw everything: the ragged appearance, the pale skin, red eyes, Mom's haywire red hair that looked electrocuted and dad's sunburned bald head that was already beginning to peel.

Although in recent years, my faith had been tenuous, I closed my eyes on their image and gripped the silver cross in my hand. I pleaded for their safety, their sanity and that I would see them again; that Jake and I would get through this stage of our lives, that we wouldn't let anyone down and, most of all, that we would all be a family again.

I opened my eyes to Chels's smile.

"Amen," she said, touching my arm in comfort.

Same.

The Viking Tour Co. had filled each freezer bag with treats and had tucked them into the baskets under our seats. The bags had two juice boxes, a chocolate bar, four dried fruit and veg bars, a smaller bag of veggie sticks and an eight-inch hoagie with thick cuts of salami, pepperoni and ham, lettuce, tomato, pickles and a sweet-onion sub dressing. As my mouth slowly circled the sandwich, my eyes closed in ecstasy.

My second favorite meal of the trip, a close second to the Halifax bonanza.

While the train had stopped at cities along the way to Newfoundland, and city volunteers had given us a meal at each stop, it had often ranged from oatmeal and rice to beans and cabbage to pasta and tomato sauce. And through it all, there were slices of something called Klick or Spam sliding all over our plates, with an ice-cream scoop of souring potato salad on top. It was no wonder the car smelled like farts and BO—a winning combination. Like a herd of cattle, we were fed, watered and sent back on the train. A brown paper bag containing an apple, orange, a peeled whole carrot and a bottle of water was handed to us by volunteers lining the tracks. They waved and looked at us with smiling faces. The smiles didn't reach their eyes, though. The red-rimmed pupils all looked the same: dark, squinting, afraid. Or was I seeing myself reflected in them? Hell, even I didn't know half the time. What the hell did it matter, anyway? Riding or dying, we were all one breath away from dust.

Great morbid thought ya got there, Jules!
All the better to eat you with, my dear.

Biting into my sub, all those half-ass meals and snacks were turned to dust as my mouth came alive with the spicy sweet flavors of the hoagie. I actually moaned as I chewed, a habit I blame on Dad.

Chels snickered. "You sure can tuck food away faster than anybody I know."

"I'm a growing teenager—I'm a bottomless pit, don't ya know?"

"That … I can believe."

Chels had already placed half her sandwich back in the plastic bag and was now munching on a carrot stick, pointing one end in my face: "Show some self-control, Jules!"

With squirrel cheeks, I nodded.

Seeing my hesitation, Chels reached over, grabbed the rest of my hoagie and tucked it into my freezer bag. "There," she said. "No more temptation!"

"But I know where you put it!" I said, chewing.

"Yes, but out of sight, out of mind!" she said, laughing.

"OK, then, pass me one of those dried fruit and veg bars for dessert."

"Fine!"

Grabbing the bag again, she dug out one of the bars and a juice box and handed them to me.

"Never say I don't do anything for you!"

I snickered and popped the small plastic bendy straw into the juice box hole and slurped up a mouthful of grape juice, rolling my eyes in delight when the liquid touched my tongue.

"You're hopeless!"

"You better believe it, Brown and Curly!"

"What did you call me?"

I laughed, realizing too late I had said that aloud.

"Brown and Curly! Don't you like your nickname?"

Blushing, I smiled at her, hoping she wouldn't take offence.

"Tsk, tsk, tsk. What am I going to do with you?"

With a face that could have fried an egg, I cleaned my hands on my jeans and watched as the lead bus began to roll out, with the other six following. Ours was second in the queue. For days, our existence consisted in a cramped oven disguised as a train car, being baked in body odor and bad breath. Now, we were in an air-conditioned tour bus inching our way to … who knows where.

A soldier in green-camo army fatigues stood at the entrance of the bus by the driver. He carried a clipboard in the crook of his arm and wore an army cap on his buzz-cut head.

"Attention!" He yelled.

Everyone stopped chewing and talking and stared at his commanding presence.

For a dude a few years older than us, he looked sure of himself and in control. His black eyebrows were furrowed as he stared at each one of our faces. "Take out your electronic devices—smartphones, tablets, laptops, and any other listening and recording devices," he shouted. "As I call your name, you must raise your hand and I will come by and collect your items."

There was a collective groan from the passengers.

He steeled his jaw, squared his shoulders and looked menacingly at the two rows of seats.

"You will be going through a security scanner upon your arrival," he noted, "and those found in noncompliance with this order will be directed to detention to await judgement."

What?
Detention to await judgement?
Were we to be imprisoned?
Tortured?
For keeping our phones?
Unbelievable.

As he began calling names and collecting devices in a large freezer bag, I looked down at my phone. It was new—barely four months old, with the latest apps and gadgets, including the solar-charging panels on the surface.

"What will you do with them?" I said in a raised voice. "Will we get them back?"

He paused taking a tablet from a black-haired girl with a bob cut to turn to me and affix me with a gaze that could curdle cream and replied: "Where we are going, you won't need them."

Oh, crap!

"Don't worry, Jules," Chels whispered into my ear. "I'm sure there'll be a method to connect with our families."

I hadn't even thought about THAT! Now, I felt like a complete douchebag because I had been more focused on my social media accounts and blog sites.

I nodded.

Will anything be the same, again?
What exactly were we getting into?

Apprehension began to build in my stomach and my mind was abuzz with *what ifs*.

At this time of year, I would be shopping with Mom, getting all my gear and clothes for college or university, providing I passed my diplomas, of course. Those dreams were gone, now, and I had no clue what my future held. The idea of summer jobs and wrestling camp and parties and first years at post-secondary were now so far out of reach, they were more than fuzzy; they were nonexistent. Even though I was still undecided about my life's direction, the possibilities were still there, or they were until June 21.

What did your life have in store for you, Jules?

I had no clue.

Maybe that was the point.

A blank slate for someone to write on.

I just hoped it would be me doing the writing.

That was the scary thought: Someone deciding my future; who I was, when they didn't even know me.

Did it really matter?

As we left Argentia, the foggy haze that had gripped the town released its hold. The wisps moved inland, leaving a clear view of the whipped-up waves. Seagulls soared overhead, squawking and dipping down to sit on the rolling blue ripples. Through the receding fog, Christmas lights blinked on the roofs of houses as we drove through town after town, curling around the coastline, high above rocky cliffs that hung over the wide expanse of the Atlantic Ocean. Blue, red, green, and yellow lights lifted my spirits as they flicked on and off, sending hazy colorful halos into the mist. The sight filled me with something I had not felt for a very, very long time: Hope.

"Beautiful, aren't they?" Chels turned her tear-stained face to me and gave me a slow smile that didn't reach her bloodshot eyes.

I nodded, my throat too blocked by an invisible boulder to speak.

"They do that out here, you know."

"Do what?" I croaked.

"Turn on their Christmas lights when people are afraid or worried. They did that during the global pandemic in 2019, too."

"That's a wonderful idea," a voice said from behind me.

I turned around and stared into Todd's black eyes.

"Todd!"

"Hulk!"

"How did you get on this bus?"

"Same as you: Using my two legs and feet."

Chels laughed. "So, this is the infamous Todd Gladstone."

"At your service, and you are …"

"Todd … Chelsea Hughes," I said, gesturing with my hand as I introduced them.

Todd paused, tilted his head to get a good look at Chelsea, nodded and then got up from his seat and came around to shake her hand.

"Nice to meet you, Chelsea Hughes."

Turning to me, he grinned, "I have to warn you, though, any friend of Jules, here, is doomed to a life of chaos and adventure."

"Hey!"

"Just speaking the truth, Hulk my man."

"Well, don't. And, by the way, where have you been all week? I've been worried sick."

Todd laughed and squeezed his skirted butt in between Chels and me.

"Well, after I told them who I was, they were happy for me to join them in ol' St. John."

"You mean, *St. John's*," I corrected. "St. John is in New Brunswick and St. John's is in Newfoundland, but we didn't go to St. John's—we went to Argentia."

"What they said," he tapped my thigh and tilted his head in my direction, "after all, a prairie boy can't be expected to know all these East Coast city names, am I right?"

"Don't get me involved," Chels chuckled.

"Well?"

"Well, what?"

"Where did they take you?"

"Well, *Jules*, they took me to the place where lost toys are stored, of course."

"What?"

Chuckling at my frustration, he added, "I was just ushered into another car with all the supplies, Hulk, nothing devious about it. I was fed the same food you all had; I just couldn't leave the train."

"Why did you leave Pincher Creek?"

I knew how much Todd loved living near Pincher Creek with his family, which is why it was such a shock to see him being escorted through Compartment C upon our departure.

"It was time."

His voice lost all its jovial tone and sunk deep into his chest. It sounded exhausted, worn, with no energy to rise it from his vocal cords to his mouth.

Turning to him, I hugged him tightly.

"I'm so sorry."

He swallowed, his Adam's apple sliding down the length of his throat.

"Nothing was going to be the same after the barricades and fires, least of all my home."

"I hear ya, dude."

After I released him, I noticed that Chels had risen from her seat and had disappeared into the bathroom at the back of the bus.

She must be feeling the same, I thought: Lost, without a home.

As we all did.

Chapter 21

St. Stephen's Royal Academy was incognito.

Nestled on a strip of green lawn overlooking the Atlantic Ocean, the rectangular, red brick building had boreal trees at its back and a sloping hill leading down to the shoreline at its front. Flanking the academy were outbuildings constructed of weathered boards bleached from the sun and salt spray. Isolated, the expansive five-story private school was accessible by a long, winding gravel driveway off an equally long, winding gravel road leading from a small hamlet of 500 fishers and merchants. While formidable in size and design, its serene backdrop softened its institutional exterior, leaving room to notice the soccer field leading to a wildflower meadow at the tree line, the wood-framed glass greenhouse that reflected the evening sun, and the lobster and crab pots stacked in pyramids on the grassy-lawn's edge. Further down the landwash was a mooring dock—a wood-planked walkway that began on the shoreline and stretched out into the lapping waters. As it left the shallows, stilts kept the dock level and above the swirling tide until the planks ended in the deep. Beside it bobbed three white fishing dories, butting up against the dock's legs with every gust of wind. Two were trimmed with red; the other, blue, with painted names of *Joyce's Joy, Maid & Mist,* and *Buddy Row* joining stamped letters and numbers on their prows. Beyond the dock, the blue-black waves rose and fell, spraying foam and salt into the air. The jagged C-shaped shoreline jutted out from the cove in a rocky peninsula. A white and red lighthouse perched on grassless white rocks at the peninsula's tip.

Located in Bessie's Tickle, some 232 kilometers outside of Newfoundland's capital city of St. John's, the Catholic high school had a multitude of elongated windows that reflected the rolling blue and white waves that crashed onto the nearby shore. Built during the great economic boom of the 2030s, when tourism excursion and tech start-up companies joined solar- and wind-power facilities to churn out record taxable profits that made their way to the provincial infrastructure coffers. Cities blossomed with new developments and amenities; small outports thrived with new visitors opening their wallets at off-the-map bakeries, microbreweries and cideries; handicraft and carpentry stores; garden and fish markets.

By the start of 2040, the province was operating in the black, with a rainy-day fund it called The Purse, which grew each year with taxes collected from prosperously employed citizens.

With that growth came new schools, and St. Stephen's Royal Academy was one of them.

"St. Stephen's is a top-notch school with state-of-the-art computer labs, library, fitness facilities, hands-on workshop outbuildings with every gadget and tool imaginable," our tour-guide bus driver explained, pausing as the vehicle bounced along the gravel. "It even has a science and hydroponics lab, an in-house cooking school, and cafeteria that serves up some pretty tasty scoffs—that's what we calls a meal here for you mainlanders who don't rightly know what that is."

The amenities were ideal for the resettlement base.

Class had been out for St. Stephen's since this whole mess started back in June. Now July, the building that once housed 935 students from Grade 9 to 12 was one of many basecamps initiated after the attacks.

Upon our arrival at the school parking lot, a formidable middle-aged man dressed in army fatigues greeted us at the Newfoundland Aurora Resettlement Base. Several buses had already unloaded their passengers and teenagers stood outside the brick building with its elongated windows capturing the golden sun as it rose higher in the azure-blue sky.

Jake stood with his friend Matt, who pulled his navy hoodie close to his chest, lifting the hood over his afro to shield his hair from the road dust being whipped up by large gusts of wind. As he shivered, Jake let his backpack fall off his shoulders, which was an easy task since the straps were dangling at his elbows. Digging inside the large pouch, he pulled out a rain slicker and handed it to Matt, who gave my brother a thumbs up before putting the nylon jacket on over his fleece jumper.

Turning to me, Jake waved and gave me a toothy grin.

I waved back.

The wind whisked up his blond locks and curled them in front of his face, and he tucked the strands behind his ears.

Dude needed a haircut.

Mom had been cutting both our hair for as long as I could remember, and she was good at it. I looked at each shining blond strand clinging to my little brother's nose and lips as he spoke and I suddenly felt homesick.

No. That's not exactly true.

I felt … alone.

Even though I had often longed to leave home, their absence created a void inside me that I never knew was filled.

Until it wasn't.

Chels was beside me, dabbing her cheeks with foundation from a tube and hastily rubbing it into her jaw, cheeks and nose.

It must be awful to have blemishes so bad you felt you had to wear makeup all the time.

Maybe that's something you could help her with—to not care about what people think?

I had a lot of experience with that, at least, even if I never quite got to that point, myself.

Further down the line, Todd was telling jokes to Allister MacKenzie, which made my skin crawl. I stood, looking over the many heads and felt completely and utterly lost.

Without Mom and Dad to ground me, could I cope?

Without Jake to tease, where did I fit in?

"Ready?" Chels asked, pushing into my back as she lost her balance with her oversized pack on her shoulders.

"As ready as I'll ever be."

I tentatively stepped forward, one Size 11 women's runner at a time, butting my toe up against the heel of—you guessed it—Allister MacKenzie, who winced and gave me the stink eye before nudging himself forward, continuing his in-depth conversation with Todd beside him.

"Sorry," I mumbled, but Muscle Boy shook his head doubtfully at me, without even responding.

"Watch it, string bean," a voice hissed beside Allister.

A boy with black crewcut turned his head and scowled in my direction.

"Geeze, I thought they were going to be selective in who got to come here; not just pick the freaks with the biggest feet."

I moved aside, mumbling under my breath and trying not to respond.

It took every ounce of my being, and a little tongue biting.

The boy looked over at Chels and then up at me again and sneered. "Now that's a freakshow and a half."

"Only if you're looking in the mirror, Einstein," I growled.

"Jules …" Chels groaned, "ignore him. He's just being an idiot."

"At least, I'm not a freak of nature."

"Tom, leave them alone. They can't help who they are but you *can help* from being a jackass," Allister said, digging his fist into the boy's shoulder. "It was an accident; no harm done."

Tom sneered again.

I inhaled, held for a count of five, and then exhaled.

I watched as the two boys moved forward, being careful not to stand to close to Tweedle Dee and Tweedle Dum.

Chels nudged my elbow. "Good job not blowing a gasket."

"The day isn't over."

She chuckled.

"Well, then, in that case, good job not blowing a gasket in front of the base commander."

Was I ready?

In the words of my mother, *not bloody likely.*

Chapter 22

Normalcy was a curtain hiding us from the world but the world was awfully hard to hide. After the evening meal of cafeteria food, Commander Douglas Campbell corralled everyone into amphitheater on the main floor of the academy. The uniformed soldier tapped a series of buttons on a panel attached to the side wall and a wall of television screens came to life, broadcasting the news from various countries around the globe.

And just like that, the façade drapery cocooning us was ripped in two.

What we saw was a world in turmoil.

Riots in cities as people left behind to die clambered over rubble, burning window frames and parked cars in search of a road out. We saw craters in highways, destroyed farmland, crying babies and muddied faces streaked with blood and tears. We saw hospitals turning away people and armed police with riot gear pushing crowds away from emergency-room doors. We saw ferry terminals with newly erected electric fencing to keep people away from the ships leaving the harbors. The Atlantic provinces had become a large magnet and it looked like all North America was being drawn to their shores. At the heart of the pull was Newfoundland. Politicians puffed; guards barked; inhabitants cowered in fear. Newfoundland was an *island*, after all.

Before we had even arrived, airports in St. John's, Deer Lake, Stephenville, and St. Anthony had closed. Ferries remained docked in their slips and Royal Newfoundland Constabulary officers were stationed at all major ports up and down the coast, but it wasn't enough. Still people trickled into the coves on fishing boats in the dark of night—so much so that trawlers and long-liners were searched after unloading their catches and the skiffs used in the inshore fishery were hauled onto the tall grasses surrounding the coves, only allowed to go out to fish on designated days with the RNC officers patrolled the waters around the harbors.

The measures were causing chaos among citizens in Newfoundland and abroad, as people felt their rights being trampled on in the wake of the SMR destruction. Our little island wasn't big enough for the world, and the world wasn't going to stand being away from our refuge forever.

"Holy moly," Chels breathed into the room.

"Same," I breathed back.

The Amphitheatre was packed, so much so that many of the late arrivals were lining the wall leading up to the performance stage. As we watched the vivid images flash over the screens, our bodies moved closer, our hands held tighter. Todd appeared beside me, his face as white as a sheet.

"Are we supposed to fix *that?*"

Hearing his question, Campbell turned to face the teenagers crammed into the room, his face grim and his eyes bloodshot.

"This is the reality you all must know," he said loudly over the murmurs and mumbles of his shocked audience. "*This* is your incentive to excel; to swallow any fears you may have about what you'll be doing at this camp because you have to, if you want to survive."

"If you want humankind to survive."

"What a buzzkill," Tom snickered.

Cmd. Campbell strode over to where he and Allister were reclining against a wall. Hands on his hips, he leaned forward so close, Tom could see his nose hairs.

"If you don't want to be here, there's the door."

The soldier pointed to the Exit sign.

"But I warn you, once out, you'll never get back in—now that's what I call a *buzzkill*, don't you."

Tom wordlessly nodded.

"What's that? You want to throw in the towel?"

"No, sir."

Tom's voice was barely above a whisper.

"Again."

"No, SIR," Tom repeated, louder this time.

"Better," Campbell said, pivoting on his heel and addressing the crowd, "I know this is new to you; it is new to all of us but the sooner you realize this is serious business, the sooner you'll fit in and succeed in your objectives."

"And what would those objectives be, sir?" I tentatively asked, raising my arm above my head.

Campbell's eyes met mine and he grimaced. "Well, to survive, of course. The details on how that will be accomplished are on a need-do-know basis. Meaning, I need to know and you don't."

I swallowed.

What was he not telling us?

What did this *survival objective* entail?

We were kids, after all; a bunch of Corn Flakes just waiting to dissolve in the chaos.

And we were the future.

Now that was even scarier than Cmdr. Campbell, or his conjecture.

God help us all.

****

The hallway lockers on the first floor of the school were painted bright yellow. Unlike the feeling of joy I got from Rev. Erin's sunny kitchen, the dorm room's brightness seemed deviously intentional—probably to give pubescent teens a false sense of happiness.

Rise and shine! Look how bright your future is! This yellow-painted locker will put you in a happy mood so you don't see how your life is full of crap! Happy, happy, happy! If you stay happy, all will be well!

Allister's floor was on the top. No sunshine yellow walls for Muscle Boy. No, he was on the pastel blue floor, along with Jake, Todd and the new bane of my existence, Tom Rumbolt.

I adjusted my load so the weight was being carried more with my left shoulder and arm.

The top four floors of the school were dormitories, with each given monikers denoting fish.

Newfoundland. Fish.

Subtlety wasn't St. Stephen's strong suit, I guess.

Yeah, the irony wasn't lost on me either.

I was part of the Halibut group.

"We are yellow, just for the *halibut*," I had joked to my roommates upon entering, none of whom cracked a smile.

Above us was the mint green Cod floor, then the peachy Mackerel floor. The pastel-blue fourth floor was Lump.

Funny name for a fish.

No wonder Allister and Tom were there: They were big lumps of somethin' that's for sure. I didn't want to consider the fact that Todd and Jake were up there with them, becoming friends. I just hoped Tom's and Allister's crabbiness didn't rub off on them.

As I tried to find space for all the clothes Savannah had given me, Riley Hodge and Dillon Maclean played poker on the bottom bunk beside the one I had claimed. Somehow, the prospect of living in a dorm with a bunch of strangers was both exciting and intimidating.

No one knew you, yay.
No one knew you, crap.

Yet, as I unpacked my clothes and placed them in the drawers tucked under the bottom bunk, leaving two for my bunkmate to fill, I couldn't help but think of this as a new opportunity to reinvent myself, to be *me*, and not someone I had been trying to be for the past several years. The thought made my heart beat faster, and I wasn't sure it was out of joy or fear.

Either way, I was here.

While I was lying on the soft pillow of the top bunk, stretching my legs to the end of the twin and letting my feet dangle over the footboard, the door opened with a squeak. I peered down to a bird's nest of brown curls.

"Hey down there," I shouted to Chels, "welcome to the mustard family."

"Huh?"

"Yellow floor … mustard," I hinted, smiling, "just be sure you can cut it."

"Funny."

Only Chels wasn't laughing. She was, in fact, looking manic.

Her brown and curly hair had turned into springs in the humidity and her cheeks were transitioning from a blazing red to a ghostly white.

"You 'kay?"

"I'm fine."

She didn't look fine.

She looked about ready to have a heart attack or a stroke. Her whole body was electrified: Her head bobbed as she moved to the bottom bunk, her hands shook as she tossed her bag onto the yellow quilt stitched in white, and her voice trembled as she spoke.

If this was what being OK looked like, Jules, your elastic-flicking, two-gender personality was just put in the normal category.

"Just worried about my grandparents," she said, sitting down on the bed and causing it to squeak, "and not wanting to be here, that's all."

"You and me both, Brown and Curly."

"Jules ..."

"Yeah?"

"I'm freaking out a bit."

A bit?

More like a bunch.

"How can I help?"

I heard a slow, shaky sigh from below me.

"Just be my friend."

"Done."

Leaning over the railing, I poked my head over my mattress to see Chels lying with her eyes closed and her lips pursed thin.

"Chels?"

"Yah?"

"Want me to show you some breathing techniques to help you calm down?"

Her lips spread and curled upward.

"Sure."

I walked her through the exercises Ali Cameron had taught me in the many counseling sessions I had attended, from the Name Ten Things I Can Smell, Feel, Hear and See to Inhale, Hold for Count of Five; Exhale to a Count of Eight.

As Chels breathed the last puff of breath, she began to yawn.

I flopped back down on my pillow and yawned, too.

"I wish we were on the blue floor," I moaned. "All this yellow is blinding me."

"Well, if it makes you feel any better, the Halibut is hands down the best floor to be on."

I rolled over and hung my head down over the bunk to look at Chels, who already had her eyes closed, and was breathing deeply into the top bunk.

"Because," she continued, stifling another yawn, "we are shooting stars."

"How do you figure?"

"Well," she opened her eyes and smiled up at me, "stars shine brightly and people gravitate toward them."

"They are also balls of gas."

Chels laughed so hard she snorted.

From the adjacent bunk, Riley and Dillon burst out laughing, too.

"And that's why I wanted to be in here with you, Jules. You're a riot."

She was softly snoring when the room was enveloped into darkness.

Outside, the wind howled and the ocean roared in response.

I lay on my bunk, too exhausted to sleep and too tired not to.

Was I really a *star?*

Could I shine in this hell hole?

Could I be *me,* despite my fears and anxieties?

Did I have any choice?

As sleep overcame me, one thought remained. It bounced between my ears, ping-ponging against my brain and causing my eyes to burn.

My home had shattered into a million pieces: Gone were Mom and Dad, Shade, Jake and Todd. I was surrounded by people who thought I was a freak, thought I was weird, thought I was suicidal enough to place me in a sickeningly yellow room on a sickeningly yellow floor. I was judged already from the get go, before I took my first step into a classroom on this base. They thought they knew me; thought they could control my mood and my responses.

Well, this MacGyver-Black-Widow-Hulk was prepared to forge a new way—one they didn't expect.

Chapter 23

The blue-gray waves rolled and crashed against the flat rocks jutting out into the cove, splashing sea foam onto the shiny slate surfaces and drenching the kelp wedged between each plateau. Overhead, dark gray storm clouds moved on gusts of wind toward land, blocking out the sun and dropping the temperature several degrees as they traveled. The 173,000-square-foot Newfoundland Aurora Resettlement Base loomed, its windows reflecting the angry gray plumes. Shadows danced across the red brick exterior in a ghostly rhythm only they could hear.

Further along the coastline were two-story homes with exposed cement basements perched on rocks with tufts of green grass and bushes. Empty clotheslines swung like skipping ropes beside them. The homes were modest in comparison to those in Calgary, yet their brightly rainbow-painted exteriors made them so much more pleasant to look at: Turquoise, teal, yellow, red, navy, cyan, purple, and even orange. Puffs of smoke rose from chimneys and joined the expanding gray ceiling.

Along the roadway leading to the school, telephone lines stretched between tall, white-washed poles secured in framed boxes filled with rocks.

"Pretty much everything is built above ground back home," Mom had said during our visit to see Nan and Pop three years ago. "Too much rock and not enough soil to dig into."

As I stood in the knee-high blades of green and brown grasses, wild irises and daisies, I stared out beyond the white, rocky landwash, the flat rocks and raging Atlantic Ocean. The wind slapped my face with sea salt and spit and I closed my eyes to the cold sting. Beside me, Chels stood, arms wrapped around a pink puffer jacket that the locals had collected as part of an Avalon donation drive for the new arrivals. On her head was a red, wool knitted hat with a white tasseled pompom on the top, which flopped back and forth in the gale.

On my other side was Jake.

Blowing on his gloved hands to try and give them warmth. His blond curls were secured with a gray-and-white-speckled knitted toque with a peaked bill. Wearing a brown parka from the donation bin, he looked like he had not only grown several inches since our departure from Alberta, but had slimmed down and beefed up as well.

A steady diet of beans and apples will do that to ya, I guess.

As we gazed out to sea, Todd sauntered up behind us in a red and black quilted lumberjack coat and wrapped his arms around all three of us.

"You all ready?"

"Ready for what?" Chels sounded nervous again, as if all those anxiety exercises I showed her were as fleeting as her good mood.

"For what comes next, of course."

I watched a white-capped wave rise, roll and crash, sending bubbling foam onto the rocks. "And what would that be?"

"Life, Hulk my man."

Now it was Jake's turn to be confused.

Todd chuckled and then dropped his arms from around our backs and we turned to face him. He was his usual jovial self: smiling mischievously at us with one bushy black eyebrow raised as if he knew a secret that he was dying to disclose.

He tugged at Jake's hat so it fell down over his eyes, causing the dude to giggle.

Well, maybe not so grown up, yet.

Same.

As the fat drops of rain fell onto our heads, we stood there a moment longer to relish in the storm before turning and running back to St. Stephen's Royal Academy.

Maybe Todd was right.

Maybe *life* did begin, here, in this isolated community on the rock in the ocean. What that life would look like, though, was anyone's guess. My mind was plagued with unanswered questions about what we would be learning and, more importantly, where will we be going after we've learned all we needed to learn to breathe new *life* on the planet.

My galoshes splashed in puddles as we raced up the gravel path toward the school, getting my jeans soaked and my legs cold.

Jake reached out for my hand and I let him grab it.

"Puddle jumping!"

Yes, bro, puddle jumping, and we jumped full boar into a deep hole filled with rainwater in the middle of the gravel road leading to the school.

The splash shot muddy water onto my already soaked denim and splattered onto Jake's cold, flushed cheeks, making him spurt and giggle.

It was a contagious sound and all of us joined in as his childlike merriment took hold of our bodies.

Were we ready for what would come next?

Could anyone be?

I slowed my pace to match his and Todd raced forward to open the entrance door.

Crossing the threshold, I pulled down my slicker hood and walked into the shiny, linoleum hallway, past the security desk with the armed soldier gazing at our drenched bodies through plexiglass, the administration office where Commander Campbell was busy talking to his secretary, the adjacent health clinic, the central atrium with its large indoor vegetable garden shaped like an oval, and to the winding staircase that curved above the rows of carrots, turnips, potato, and lettuce leaves.

Above, the skylight tinged with raindrops.

So, this is where I'll find my purpose.

At least, I hoped so.

Although there was much that was still a mystery to me, the one thing that was a certainty was that *here* was a beginning.

As the security guards scanned our ID cards and we sauntered up the stairs to our rooms, all out of breath and dripping, my mind drifted back to a Bible verse that Dad had recited in his prayer over last year's graduates at our church. Jeremiah, Chapter 29, Verse 11 hummed between my ears as I lifted one leg after the other in my climb: *'For I know the plans I have for you,' declares the Lord, 'plans to prosper you and not to harm you; plans to give you hope and a future.'*

"Amen," I breathed into the stairwell, my voice echoing up the vacuous well flanked by black iron handrails, surrounding me in a chorus that was both a plea and a praise.

So, I did the only thing I could do.

I said it again, and again, and again, until the Bible verse vibrated through my whole body and I could feel it in every nerve twitching in anticipation, every heartbeat fearfully drumming against my chest—and I believed it. Remarkably, it didn't take that long.

An echo's breath.

And I was his.

*** The End of Book 1***

Acknowledgements

There are lots of people and resources I wish to acknowledge in the writing of The CurE: Contamination, especially my immediate family: Husband, Rob, and sons, Heath and Ian, without whose support, I could never have hit my first key. They were always my cheerleaders and, in a world where there is so much negativity, they were the positive reinforcement I needed to not give up on this tale of extremism.

Rob, you have been my biggest supporter in being a novelist. As your faith grew, so too did mine, as I watched you walk the road to being ordained, all while helping raise our two LGBTQ+ sons. You are an inspiration. You bring so much joy, laughter, insight, calm and perspective to our little family and I am so blessed to have you as my partner in faith and life. Heath and Ian, since you took your first breath, you captured my heart with your compassion, sensitivity, humor, wit, intelligence, and penchant for all things silly, especially puns and your Newfie Mom. You challenged my views and made me grow along with you, and that is no easy feat. May you always have the courage and strength to choose what is right, what is just, what is gracious, what is merciful, what is loving, and what is kind.

I would also have gotten nowhere in this book if I didn't have the grounding and education of a Newfoundland upbringing. Being raised in a traditional Anglican family, with nine siblings (Dorothy, Gloria, Herman, Sandra, Annette, Allison, Doreen and sister-niece, Tonya), I learned the importance of creative thinking, being in balance with the environment, and above all, that money doesn't buy happiness: It's the relationships we foster, whether they be with God, ourselves, families, friends, culture, traditions, the earth or with the diverse peoples that compile humankind. Newfoundland & Labrador has long been viewed as a province that cares for each other and others, and I wanted to highlight that selflessness in The CurE series, because it is through their actions — and indeed the actions of the have-not provinces, territories, and First Nations — that others can take their cue. Often ignored, I wanted to highlight the importance of these peoples' attitudes toward giving and make them the heroes of this story.

I would not have been able to have had a successful writing career if not for the people and place that inspired me to set out on this path in the first place. Growing up surrounding by crashing waves, beaches, boreal forests, wild meadows, and the wittiest group of people a writer could ever imagine, my parents (Aubrey and Amy King) included, I was given the rare perspective on poverty, faith, community, identity, culture, traditions, and working and living in tandem with the land. That education grounded me and allowed me to tap into that well of identity to approach The CurE with pride in tradition and culture, and all the things that make Newfoundlanders admired around the globe.

I began the journey of writing The CurE series a few years ago and proceeded to spend the first 12 months gathering as much information for the background story as possible, coupled with current and future trends in energy and agricultural production, climate change, cyber terrorism, and indigenous cultural and political considerations. Being a journalist, I wanted The CurE to have authenticity—to push the envelope on extremism in all facets of society, be they industrial, environmental, religious, or communal in nature.

Book 1, Contamination, introduces a transitioning teen growing up in a pre-apocalyptic world, when the extremism needle is pushed even further and engulfs the environmentalist movement. It relies heavily on how the teen, Jules, interacts with their family and friends, based on their mental health and the fear of being in a province when LGBTQ2S+ people are being oppressed. Jules' character is a compilation of traits from my own sons and their friends, as well as a bit of myself thrown in for good measure. Making them come to life took a lot of reflection and self-permission to be raw and honest in the maturity pressure cooker that many teenagers often find themselves in, especially when dealing with gender dysphoria.

A lot of research was conducted to write this book, including on topics such as: Concussions; anxiety and depression; anger management; gender diversity; LGBTQ2S+ and indigenous cultures, especially those in Southern Alberta and in particular, the Blackfoot Nation; and domestic viewpoints to nuclear power, environmental and agricultural impacts of climate change; and the growing trend toward extremism in society, especially in relation to politics, societal interactions and opinions, and biases toward the LGBTQ2S+, Christian, and indigenous communities. It was through this research that I came to realize there is more that connects us than what separates us on this planet, and we must all work together—with love and respect, and using The Seven Sacred Teachings (wisdom, love, respect, bravery, honesty, humility, and truth)—to achieve true reconciliation and change.

In fact, there are many friends who inspired me in the writing of The CurE, especially Rosie Jane Tailfeathers, Erin Black, Raeanne Bad Eagle, and Rowena Gladstone, whose friendships opened my eyes to the culture, language, and history of the Blackfoot Nation in Southern Alberta, especially as practicing Christians who carry on the Sacred Teachings in their daily journeys. I hope I have honored their truths, and opened hearts to the idea that we all play a part in crushing extremism, discrimination, racism, and biases at their root, before they poison future generation and the ground on which they stand.

I would also like to thank Donna Ross of the Calgary Regional Consortium for her insight and encouragement in the writing of a novel series with indigenous elements. As well as being an educator for 31 years, Donna is a Cree Métis from Saskatchewan and member of the One Arrow First Nation, Treaty Six territory. Her passion in teaching First Nations, Métis, and Inuit histories, the impact of residential schools, and the embedding of Indigenous ways of knowing into Alberta curriculum and organizational culture fueled my desire to include some of those histories in The CurE series.

Please forgive any deviations, as all information presented was done so with the utmost sincerity and respect to all cultures, genders, faiths, and points of view.

In addition, the transformation of the The CurE could not have been completed without the direction and insight of several people in the publishing industry.

Special thanks to book coach and bestselling young-adult fantasy author, Suzy Vadori (The Fountain, The West Woods, Wall of Wishes), who helped me focus all that information into a reimagined series though a Wicked Good Fiction Bootcamp.

I also want to thank the many beta readers who volunteered to review Contamination, and in so do, gave insightful feedback and a lot of praise, which encouraged me to keep fighting for its publication: Southern Alberta resident Ven. Dr. Pilar Gateman, Executive Officer and Archdeacon of the Anglican Diocese of Calgary; Calgary educators, teachers and YA enthusiasts, Megan Murayama and Alyssa Clark; Ontario LGBTQ author, C.J. Banks (Dad Jokes and Pine Cones) and the many other LGBTQ2S+ reviewers who gave The CurE: Contamination such high praise — your fight for equality and inclusion is admirable and inspiring.

Glossary

Phishing: A type of cybercrime involving a social engineering attack to steal user data. This malware virus masquerades as communication from a trusted entity through an email, instant message, or text message.

Trojan Phishing: A Trojan horse is a type of malware designed to mislead the user with an action that looks legitimate, but actually allows unauthorized access to the user account to collect credentials through the local machine. The acquired information is then transmitted to cybercriminals.

Zombie: Malware used to take control of a system remotely at a later time.

Worm: Malware that self-replicates and sends itself to other computers in your network.

Cur: A backdoor computer virus that allows hackers to gain control of infected computers remotely. The cur's code enables the virus to hide in the infected computer's files and automatically deletes the original virus file from which it sprang once it is installed on a computer, making it nearly impossible to detect.

CurE: A hybrid zombie/worm/cur malware virus designed to take control of computer operating systems through a Trojan phishing email or direct code injection into the main operating system via a backdoor created by downed security protocols. Zombie script written into the malware code allows the virus to be "switched on" at a later date from a remote location. Once initiated, the cur script in the code then removes all original files of infection and hides the malware program files in the computer's operating system. When engaged, the worm script of the code allows the virus to self-replicate and send itself to other computers on the system.

Milton Keynes UK
Ingram Content Group UK Ltd.
UKHW022157031024
449168UK00005B/169